M000074323

FRESH SQUEEZED

FRESH SQUEEZED

Bonnie Biafore
&
James Ewing

FRESH SQUEEZED

This book is a work of fiction. Names, characters, places, incidents, and dialogue are drawn from the authors' imaginations, or are used fictiously, and are not to be construed as real. Any resemblance to actual events, locales, organizations, persons, living or dead, is entirely coincidental.

Cover Graphics by: Donna Murillo

Icicle Country font by: Ray Larabie - Typodermic Fonts
My Underwood font by: Michael Tension - Tension Type
Typeset using Palatino by: Hermann Zapf

ISBN-13: 978-0-9858195-0-7
ISBN-10: 0-9858195-0-2

Slow Toast Press
P.O. Box 4665, RollingBay, WA 98061
www.slowtoastpress.com
Email: contact@slowtoastpress.com

Printed in U.S.A

BJB

To Pete
For everything from
beginning to end.

JE

To Lauren
For showing me how to
tell a story.

Prologue

March 15, 2007

The once-red paint on the front door of Pacco's Lounge peeled off in finger-shaped pink sheets like sunburned skin baked too long on the Jersey Shore. The east Hackensack eatery's blinking neon sign briefly cast a shadow across Juice Verrone's hard-set face, then flicked off. He opened the door without a sound and stepped inside. The door closed behind him with a soft thud. A dark maroon velvet curtain separating the entrance from the lounge immediately parted, and a short, round guy wearing a red-and-white checked shirt slipped through.

"Juice!" the waiter said in a nervous whisper.

"Yo, Tablecloth." Juice pulled a silenced .40 caliber automatic from beneath the jacket folded over his arm and aimed it at the waiter's nose. "Mikey in back?"

"Uh." The waiter glanced over his shoulder at the curtain.

"Thanks." Juice pointed the gun barrel toward the ceiling and patted the waiter's shoulder with his other hand. "Take a hike."

He pushed the curtain aside with the barrel of his gun and

stepped into the dining room beyond. At the far end of the room, dim overhead lighting illuminated a booth with an unimpaired view of the room. The booth's sole occupant pushed pasta around on his plate. A half-full glass and a straw covered Chianti bottle sat on the table. A white cloth napkin dotted with small red splashes stuck out of the guy's shirt right below his chin. He looked up when Juice came into the room.

"Hey, Juice." The man leaned back against the well-padded upholstery, pulled the napkin from his collar, and pointed at the space next to him. "Have a seat. And put down the fucking gun. You're my brother for Christ's sake."

"Fuck you, Mikey." Juice glanced left and right. "You shot Dad. Any relations ended then."

"Hey, it was just business." Mikey resumed stirring the pasta on the plate. "Dino Faldacci was disappointed with Benny's production. I was trying to help out."

"You were just trying to move up." Juice twitched the barrel of the gun up a few times for emphasis, then clenched his jaw. "Payback's a bitch."

The door to the kitchen swung open, and a man the size of a Fiat squeezed through. His Mac-10 machine pistol pointed in the general direction of Juice's torso.

"Juice," the man-car grunted.

"Angelo." Juice flicked his eyes left, then looked back at Mikey.

To the right, the door to the men's room opened, and another pasta-pounding guido stepped into the room holding a twelve-gauge, sawed-off shotgun, his head wrapped in a grimy, gray-white bandage that looked like it had been there a while.

A small smile flickered across Juice's face. "You look like shit, Stevie."

"Fuck you, Juice."

"I told you not to piss her off."

"Yeah. I don't know who the fuck Gucci is but the bitch makes a fucking tough purse."

"Gucci was a guy, you dope."

Stevie shrugged his shoulders. "Whatever."

"What's with the mummy getup?"

"The fucking logo tore the skin off my forehead." He winced like the memory of it hurt. "They had to take a skin graft off my back to fix it."

"Shit, Stevie. You were ugly to begin with. Why'd you waste the money?"

"Fuck you, Juice." He racked the slide on the twelve-gauge.

"Like I said, I told you not to piss her off."

"Gentlemen." Mikey clinked the wine glass with his fork. "What we've got here is a bunch of wops in a Mexican stand-off."

Angelo stared blankly at Mikey.

"You fucking idiot." Mikey shook his head. "You move to shoot him…" he pointed the fork at Juice, "and he pops me." He put down the fork and made a slow-down motion with his hands. "I don't want to get popped, so put down your pieces."

Stevie and Angelo looked at each other, shrugged, and pointed the guns at the floor.

"Juice, come on. This is business. Look, you always had our backs. You were good at it. But when we needed you out front…Well, you just didn't seem to have it in you." Mikey gave his brother a big fake smile. "This time I'm gonna let you walk outta here. But this thing about Dad…You gotta let it go. If I need you, I'll give you a call. Now, get outta here."

Juice glanced from Angelo to Stevie and finally locked on Mikey. The odds of getting out weren't good, and dying wasn't his idea of revenge.

"Okay, Mikey, okay." He backed up slowly, keeping the pistol trained on his brother. "Remember, payback's a bitch."

Juice Verrone backed through the curtain and just disappeared.

Chapter 1

March 1, 2009

"Ted! It's not underwear!" Rudy Touchous was a chubby, little guy in his mid-thirties, but he squealed like an eight-year-old on Christmas morning. Finding a fish on the end of his line sent Rudy into a happy dance that almost knocked Ted Foteo out of the boat.

Ted pulled up the sleeves of his khaki cargo jacket and grabbed the net from the rack. He dipped the net under the fish and carefully lifted Rudy's prize into the boat. With a practiced hand, he gently removed the hook and laid the fish out along the ruler on top of the cooler.

"It's thirteen inches, Rudy. This one's legal." Ted opened the cooler. On a good day, the catch filled the space in the ice chest left by the drinks Ted and his clients removed. Rudy wasn't much of a drinker, so there was no room for the eighteen-ounce bass. Ted extracted two beers and a Coke, then nestled the expiring fish into the cooler and covered it with ice.

"Time to celebrate." Ted held a beer and the Coke in one hand and offered the cans to his still quivering client.

Rudy took the Coke. "Wasn't that great, Ted? I mean… a *fish*. An actual fish!" Rudy leaned back in the fishing chair looking like the poster child for Orvis catalog addiction: a new fishing hat the color of overcooked green beans sat on his head; he wore a tan shirt and khaki pants stuffed into pristine, knee-high, green-rubber, Le Chameau fishing boots.

Ted popped open his beer, and they toasted Rudy's success. "Beats the hell out of work, huh?"

He had discovered early on that Rudy had an uncanny ability to snag his fish hook on just about anything. The back of his own shirt, Ted's fishing cap, the rag that Ted used to wipe off the seats were all potential targets. The Columbia River offered a bounty of garbage waiting to be recovered, and the trash bag already brimmed with the results of Rudy's unintentional effort to beautify this stretch of the river. Today's take included a five-gallon bucket, a tangled nest of fishing line, and a hot-pink thong.

The two men sat quietly sipping their drinks. The sun dropped into the narrow gap between the sullen gray clouds and the sharp edge of the Cascade Mountains. Light flooded the landscape like somebody had thrown a switch. The sky burst into afternoon red and orange phosphorescence while the technicolor reflections shimmered off the water.

"Hot dog!"

"Yeah, Rudy, you did good today."

"No, Ted! The big hot dog!"

Ted wondered whether his rotund client had forgotten to take some kind of medication. Then, he looked past Rudy's outstretched arm. Above the black basalt rocks, a ray of sun illuminated a frozen ooze of mustard on a giant fiberglass hot dog perched atop the cliff.

"Yeah, that hot dog is right on the edge now," Ted replied. "It's going to fall off one of these days."

"What's a hot dog doing there?" Rudy asked.

"It's Wanderfalls. The old miniature golf course." Ted laughed. "The Boy Scouts were studying plants at the edge of the cliff when the windmill on one of the holes tipped over—knocked their sorry asses clean into the river." He sipped at his beer. "Looks like that hot dog might be next."

"What happened?" Rudy asked.

"The rock underneath was starting to break apart so the town shut Wanderfalls down. That happened right after I moved to town." Ted paused. "Wow, almost two years ago."

Ted admired the sky and drained his beer. He tossed the can into Rudy's recently retrieved bucket.

"Okay, Rudy, looks like you have time for one or two more casts. Let's see if there's another fish out there looking to bite."

Ted reached a small net into the bait well and scooped out a minnow. He grabbed the leader on Rudy's spinner and deftly hooked the little fish through the lower lip. He dropped the line and pointed to the bow. "Right along the cliff, little buddy."

Rudy arced the tip of the rod back over his head and caught Ted under the chin. Ted pushed the tip free. "Careful there, Rudy," Ted said and rubbed at the old scar that nicked the right side of his jaw.

Rudy flicked his wrist again. The short leader swung out over the water, spun back around the rod tip, and slapped him on the side of the face. The minnow started to slide down his cheek.

"Remember," Ted gently reminded his client, "let go of the line when the tip is pointing where you want the cast to go."

"Okay, Ted." Rudy's brow furrowed. He got set to cast again, flicked his wrist, and landed the bait right where he aimed. "Like that?" he whispered smugly.

Before Ted could reply, the line went taut, and Rudy jumped up and down with excitement, rocking the boat again.

"Yo, Two Shoes, watch out." Rudy's nickname slipped out. "The river is like ice-water this time of year. You go in and you wouldn't last fifteen minutes."

"Ted! I caught another one!"

Rudy's shout startled a pair of night herons hiding in the reeds. When their clamor faded, the line was slack. The fish had spit the bait, and quiet returned.

Quiet, but not quite silent.

Low voices drifted down the Wanderfalls cliffs. Another, louder, voice broke in and it didn't sound happy. The hairs on the back of Ted's neck stood up. The boat floated into the darkness gathering at the bottom of the cliff.

"Ted?" Rudy's voice wavered.

"Shh..."

Angry voices bounced off the rocks.

"Ted, what's happening?" Rudy asked, his voice an octave higher than before.

"I don't know. Hang on. We're getting out of here." Ted reached over to start the boat. Small pebbles falling from the cliff chattered on the deck. A truncated scream and two shots echoed off the rocks. Something big splashed a few feet off the bow of the boat. A loud rumbling, almost like thunder, reverberated from the top of the cliff.

"Ted!" Rudy shrieked as the giant hot dog plummeted toward them.

The jumbo frank slammed into the stern and sheared the engine off at the transom. The impact launched Rudy into the air, and he smacked against the cliff. His fishing vest caught on a point of basalt, and he hung like meat on a hook.

"Ted! Help!"

"I can't, Two Shoes. I think my leg's broke." One end of the huge hot dog bun had Ted pinned to the slanted deck. His head was spinning from the pain.

The boat drifted closer to the cliff. Ted grabbed the boat hook and tried to snag something, anything. Nothing. Icy water flowed into the unbalanced boat. The cold water stung like a sandblaster as Ted went under.

He heard a muffled pop as his life vest inflated, and he rose to the surface like a bubble. He screamed when his broken leg changed angles.

Another rumble from above, and a giant smallmouth bass toppled from the cliff. The fiberglass fish hit the bow, counterbalancing the hot dog on the stern. The hulking bass glared at Ted with a look that seemed to ask: "How do you like it, asshole?" He passed out.

He came to hearing Rudy's voice.

"Two Shoes," Ted said through chattering teeth. "It's fucking cold, and my leg's stuck." His body was completely numb.

"I'm gonna get help, Ted." Pebbles splashed into the water.

"Two Shoes!"

"What?"

"Find Dinah. Tell her Juice loves her," Ted mumbled as his field of vision started to shrink. The river was now quiet as a crypt.

"Dinah? Juice?"

"Yeah. Dinah. She's my wife. I'm Juice. Find her. Tell her I love her," Ted said with all the energy he had left. Then everything went black.

Chapter 2

Everything wasn't black anymore. A flickering light came through the doorway from the dining room. Juice floated across the kitchen and looked through the door. At one end of the table, a dozen brightly-colored balloons hovered above a large sheet cake shaped like a truck. The cake was topped with "Happy First Birthday Mikey" written in bakery script.

Juice blinked and found himself sitting next to his little brother Mikey.

"Stuff it, would you kid?" Mikey said in a gravelly grown-up voice. He slammed his fists on the table, and the cake-knife went flying, nicking Juice's jaw. Juice looked down at his pudgy hands and started to cry. Mikey laughed, and Juice's crying got worse. Then suddenly stopped.

Juice looked at his little brother again. Mikey still had his baby head, but his body was fully grown and clothed in an Armani suit.

"You better go get her." Mikey pointed at the door with a yellow plastic fork. "If you don't, I will."

Juice materialized in the living room, his white shirt and pressed jeans streaked with cold tomato soup. He felt his wedding ring slide and pushed it firmly back on his finger. "Dinah, honey, please calm down." He scooted around the living room trying to make sure he kept something solid between him and his wife. "We'll still be together. We'll still have all the money we got hid. We just have to leave our stuff behind."

"You aren't gonna have anything to leave behind." She sailed a plate into the plasma TV screen, which shattered in a shower of sparks. The recessed ceiling lights dimmed and went out.

"Dinah?" Juice asked into the darkness. "You win, honey. I'll figure something else out."

Silence.

"Dinah?" Juice got up and felt his way down the hall to the light switch. The single overhead globe feebly lit the apocalyptic scene.

"Honey, where are you?" Juice groped his way back into the kitchen and found the electrical panel. He flipped on the two breakers that had tripped during the melee and surveyed the damage as a cool evening breeze blew into the room. Sheets of music fluttered across the floor. Balloons drifted, bobbing across the ceiling. The back door stood open.

"Ted…" The soft voice was no louder than a whisper. "Ted, can you hear me?"

Who the fuck is Ted? Juice tried to figure out where the voice was coming from, but everything was blurry and gray. Then everything went black again.

"Ted, are you awake?"

Juice opened his eyes a crack. He didn't remember falling asleep. He was lying on the couch facing the entertainment center, his right leg elevated and resting on the leather cushion against the back of the overstuffed couch. He was wearing navy blue khakis, but his right leg looked like it was wrapped in white cotton. He had on the light blue, short-sleeved shirt that Dinah liked. She said it set off his eyes. It didn't matter that his eyes were Sicilian gray, like his dad's. To her, they were blue.

He turned his head toward the voice. Dinah was standing in the archway between the kitchen and the living room of their house in Passaic, New Jersey. She held a bottle of Mondavi Chardonnay with a corkscrew sticking out of the top, her eyebrows raised, waiting for an answer.

"Well?" she asked.

Juice's eyes started to close. He felt so relaxed.

"C'mon, Ted. You need to wake up." She walked over and tousled his hair.

"Why are you calling me Ted?" Juice ran his fingers through his wavy, black hair and closed his eyes again.

"Mikey and the boys are coming over. C'mon, we have to get stuff ready."

Juice heard the heels of Dinah's shoes clicking on the tile floor as she walked back into the kitchen. Reluctantly, he opened his eyes, swung his legs off the couch, and stood up. His head hit the low ceiling. *What the fuck?* He ducked through the archway into the kitchen. Dinah removed plates from the dishwasher and stacked them carefully in maple cabinets that perfectly matched the color of her hair.

"Look, Dinah, we talked about this," Juice said. "Mikey isn't coming over. I put him away for good for what he did to Dad."

"Juice, honey, this isn't only about Mikey. It's about the whole Family. They gave them a pass for the day to celebrate your dad's birthday."

"What are you talking about? Dad's dead."

A party horn tooted in the dining room. "Ted! Wake up already," came through the kitchen window from outside.

Dinah walked past the brushed stainless steel stove and opened a cabinet door. She took out a crystal wineglass and slammed the cabinet door.

Juice couldn't remember what they had been fighting about, but Dinah glared at him. He still felt relaxed and didn't want to lose that feeling, so he changed the subject. "Smells good. What are you cooking?"

"It's a Bernanke thing I read in the *Wall Street Journal*. I'm making leveraged buyout baked in white wine, tomatoes, and fennel with sautéed derivatives and garlic."

"Is that some kind of a joke?" Juice stepped over to the oven, opened the door, and looked inside. A fish with a cigarette hanging out of the corner of its mouth sat on a bed of hundred dollar bills. It smiled at him.

Juice closed the oven door and turned back to his wife. The doorbell rang.

"Honey, would you get the door? That must be Mikey and the boys."

Juice remembered what they had been talking about. Now, it was too late. He strode into the hallway and opened the door.

Mikey stood in the doorway with a white cloth napkin dappled with red stains tucked into the collar of his shirt. He was flanked by Angelo and Stevie holding their weapons at the ready.

"Aren't you going to invite us in?" Mikey asked, pushing past Juice. The other two men followed.

Juice took a step back. "How the hell did you get out of jail?" He followed the three men into the living room.

Mikey turned and rubbed his thumb against his fingers. "I bought Apple stock in 2006."

Dinah whisked into the living room holding a glass of white wine, smiling at their guests. "Boys! Boys! Put down your guns and have a seat. What can I get you to drink?"

"I'll have some of whatever you're drinking." Mikey winked at Dinah as he sat in a chair next to the fake fireplace. His henchmen grunted.

"OK, white wine coming up." Dinah disappeared into the kitchen and returned with a wine bottle. She raised her right arm and launched the bottle at Mikey. Juice grinned as the wine bottle sailed across the room. Dinah grew up with three brothers. She didn't throw like a girl. The bottom of the bottle embedded four inches into the wallboard next to Mikey's head, the neck pointing down splashing wine onto his shoulder.

"Tough fucking bottle." Mikey dabbed at the wine with his napkin. "That's some purchase momentum."

Juice shook his head and followed Dinah into the kitchen. She stood at the kitchen counter rooting around in her purse.

Mikey came in, sat on a tall stool at the kitchen counter, and smiled. Angelo lowered his massive body onto the next stool, which squeaked under his weight. Stevie shuffled in and headed straight for Dinah.

She picked up her purse, her fingers tightly gripping the leather handle. She swung the purse and caught Stevie on the side of his head. Stevie "Cold Stone" Cremetti crumpled to the floor.

"I told you not to piss her off," Juice said looking down at Mikey's unconscious bodyguard.

Dinah spun. She was holding an oversized six-shooter, like something Yosemite Sam might carry.

Mikey's eyes were as big as saucers. "How did you get Dad's gun?"

Dinah pulled the trigger, and Mikey toppled backward off the stool. A bright red flag popped out of the barrel. "Bang! Back to prison forever," it read. Mikey faded and vanished from the floor. Angelo started to get up, but the barstool shattered. He landed on his ass, and Dinah pulled the trigger again. Another red flag popped out of the gun, and Angelo disappeared. She took aim at Stevie's head.

"Dinah! No! Wait!" Stevie pleaded.

"Asshole!" She pulled the trigger two more times. Two more red flags. She and Juice were alone again. Dinah cocked the hammer and pointed the gun at Juice's heart.

"Ted," she said, "listen to this. It's unbelievable!"

She pulled the trigger, and a yellow flag popped out. It said: "Gone fishing."

Everything went black again.

Chapter 3

"Ted, listen to this! It's unbelievable!" Newspaper pages rustled. "Congress fought tooth and nail over the American Recovery and Reinvestment Act. Almost a trillion dollars of stimulus money. Now, they're patting themselves on the back like they're done!" Another round of newspaper crinkling. "Ted, get this. They say the act is going to create three million jobs over the next two years. But it's only been law for a couple of weeks! I bet these guys can't even balance their checkbooks!" Rudy laughed.

Juice opened his eyes. His right leg looked like a cocoon suspended from a tree branch. The pain felt like the moth was trying to eat its way out. He vaguely remembered seeing his leg bent at an unnatural angle. Something about a giant hot dog. *That makes no sense at all.*

"Rudy, what the hell?" Juice unsteadily turned his head toward the rustling newspaper.

"Ted! You're awake!" Rudy leaped out of the guest chair by the window. The chair skidded back across the speckled linoleum floor and jostled the dusty cream-colored slats of the blinds. The *Wall Street Journal* fluttered to the floor.

"Whoa, little buddy," Juice said, extending his left hand out just in case Rudy couldn't stop. "What the hell were you talking about?"

"Sorry, Ted!" Rudy pulled up short. "I've been reading the *Wall Street Journal* to you. They said reading helps people wake up when they're unconscious."

"Is that some kind of a joke?" Juice muttered. "The *Wall Street Journal*? That's probably why I was asleep for so long."

The smile on Rudy's face faded, and his gaze dropped to the floor.

"Hey, Two Shoes. I'm kidding. But don't you ever calm down?"

"I can't. It's just so exciting to me." Rudy rocked back and forth like he was torn between wanting to get closer and not wanting to bump his friend. "Ted! I'm so glad you're awake! You were out since last night. They were getting worried."

"Hey, buddy." Juice grabbed Rudy's arm to stop him from rocking. "Thanks."

"For what, Ted?"

"You know. For saving my life. I wouldn't have lasted in that water."

"Aw, Ted, I wouldn't let anything happen to you!" Rudy vibrated with pride.

The door to the hallway creaked, and Juice quickly checked to see who it was. The Wanaduck chief of police walked in, a tote bag over his shoulder.

"Chief."

"Ted. How are you feeling?" Chief Gordon asked. His eyes darted around the room but didn't seem to take anything in.

"Better than you look."

"I'm sorry to hear that." Chief Gordon rubbed at the bags under his eyes and slumped down onto the lone guest chair. His rumpled, white uniform shirt had pulled out from his trousers, but he didn't seem to notice.

"Yeah, well, I've felt worse."

"Me too." Gordon leaned forward in the chair and slid the tote off his shoulder. "We have a little business to take care of." He pointed at Juice's cast. "Are you feeling up to it?"

Juice moved his hand to smooth his hair but stopped short when his IV line went taut. He glanced at the tubing, tilted his head at the Chief, and waited for him to get on with it.

"Is this your gun?" Gordon asked, pulling an evidence bag out of the tote. A Glock 19 hung heavily in the bag.

"Could be. Where'd you find it?"

"In your boat, when we pulled it out of the water."

"My prints on it?"

"Yeah."

Juice wasn't supposed to have a gun, so he scanned Gordon's face for any problem. *Maybe he has his poker face on. Maybe he just doesn't give a flying fuck.*

"You shoot it recently?" Gordon asked.

"Nope."

"You sure?"

"Aw, cut the shit, Chief. My leg's broke. I don't need you being a pain in my ass. What the hell do you want?" Juice figured the Chief for somewhere in his mid-forties, but right now he looked like he was pushing sixty. His shoulders drooped and his eyes were dull, like someone who had given up.

"We got a guy, shot dead, near Wanderfalls. And we found your gun in your boat right there."

"Chief, I know I shouldn't have a gun, but, well...you know."

"I never saw Ted with a gun, Chief!" Rudy interjected. "We heard a plop in the water, and then the hot dog fell on him."

"Ted, I don't give a rat's ass about you having a gun,"

Gordon said and shook his head. A straight, dark fringe of hair fell across his forehead. He roughly pushed the hair out of his eyes with his fingers and continued talking, "I haven't since you got here. But I do want you to answer my question."

"I didn't do it, and you know it." The questioning raised unpleasant memories of past interrogations. His brain kicked into gear. "If I'm at the bottom of the cliff, there's no way I could see whoever the hell it was, so I sure as hell couldn't shoot him. He's got cuts from bouncing down the cliff, right?"

"Yeah. No casings up there, and the body got pretty messed up in the fall and submersion, but the entry and exit wounds are about right for your gun."

"Or any nine-millimeter. You checked the gun. You know it hasn't been fired." Juice pinned the Chief with a glare.

"Okay, okay. I checked the gun. I'm only doing my job."

Juice nodded a grudging agreement.

The Chief's phone rang. He answered, listened for a few seconds, and flipped it closed. "They ID'd the stiff." Gordon took a deep breath. "One Eddie Snead. Local real-estate guy and wannabe big shot. Fucking small-town cops. The body was pretty battered from smacking the rocks on the way down, so they didn't recognize him. Nobody bothered to check for a wallet."

"And where were you?" Juice asked.

"My car was in the shop." Gordon shook his head. "It got rear-ended by the recycling truck—totaled it." The Chief dug around in the tote, which had a fish smoking a cigarette embroidered on the side. He extracted another evidence bag. This one held a small plastic fish with a shiny metal tab sticking out of its wide mouth.

"You know anything about this?" Gordon swung the bag back and forth.

"I don't even know what it is."

"It's a flash drive."

"It looks like a fish."

"That too. Walt had the fish flash drives made as give-aways for his store a few years back." The Chief flipped the tote around and pointed to "Walt's" embroidered on the other side. "These bags, too."

Juice grabbed the evidence bag and stretched the plastic on either side of the fish. "Some giveaway. I've never seen it before. Stop yanking my chain."

"So did you hear or see anything?"

"Yeah, we heard voices, and they weren't happy. We heard shots and a splash, and then a big fucking hot dog fell from the sky. Chief, are you just jerking off or do you have any ideas?"

"No, I don't have any ideas. Stuff like this doesn't happen around here." Gordon stopped when the door opened.

A nurse walked in and gave Gordon a stern look. He slipped the evidence bags back in the tote. "Visiting hours were over fifteen minutes ago," she announced. "You can come back later."

Gordon scrunched his eyes closed and squeezed the bridge of his nose. "Okay, fine. I get the hint." He focused on Juice. "I'll catch up with you later." He swung the tote over his shoulder and walked to the door with Rudy close behind him.

"And get some sleep would you? You look like shit." Juice waited a beat. "Sir."

Gordon stopped with his right hand on the door handle. Rudy bumped into his back. Gordon turned back and glared at Juice. "Fuck you, Ted." He pushed Rudy to the side and took a single step toward the bed. His hands balled into fists. "You have no idea," he said, then turned back to the door, yanked the handle, and the two men vanished into the hall.

Chapter 4

Ray Milton loved spring. In eastern Washington, it's the brief period between another winter that never seems to end and another summer too hot and dry to think about. The biologists got cranked up over the first runs of salmon looking to spawn while the rivers are running cold and clear. Ray got all cranked up to get laid.

Every year when the fish people started talking about spawning, salmon stairs, and fish hormones, the early crop of interns would show up—the kids who didn't have the money to party with their friends in Cancun or Cabo for spring break. They'd do their time with grunt work in the field or helping out with administrative tasks in the office. The main intern run began later, in May.

Ray couldn't figure out why these kids were willing to work all summer long for the sole purpose of putting "Indian Meadows Salmon Program" on their pitiful excuses for résumés. But he was as thrilled at their return as the biologists were for the salmon. More than half the interns were female—nubile, sweet, blossoming females. The cute ones fueled his fantasies. Those not so genetically blessed served nicely as target practice.

A rattling noise grew louder in the corridor behind Ray. *Speaking of blossoming.* His gaze went out of focus, and the spreadsheet on his computer screen dissolved into a mirror image of the office behind him.

"Nice shirt, Ray. What is that, dog shit on the beach under the palm trees?" Sara, one of the interns, grabbed a stack of mail off the cart and tossed it onto the desk in the cubicle across the hall. She wore very tight, low-rise jeans and a T-shirt that looked like it belonged to her ten-year-old sister.

"They're coconuts." He smoothed the slick rayon of his neon excuse for a business casual shirt. Ray watched her in the reflection on his computer screen. A small gold ring piercing her navel accentuated the little roll of baby fat below her shirt.

Sara came into his cubicle with his mail. She bent over slowly and gently laid it on his desk. Ray's eyes were locked on his computer screen. He stared at the reflection as her breasts strained against the tight fabric. He hoped they would win in their struggle to be free.

"Bye-bye, Ray. Catch you tomorrow." Sara waved at the screen and grabbed the handle of the cart. The rattling noise resumed.

Ray tried to shake off Sara's image, but failed. The spreadsheet remained a blurred mass of labels, lines, and numbers. *Christ, why do I really care about the budget?* The commissioners didn't—except at re-election time. The directors didn't—except that they wanted to be able to sit down after their meetings with the commissioners. Ellis was probably the only one who gave a shit, because he actually wanted to get something done. But getting something done took money, and there wasn't any more money. The numbers didn't add up. Ray cared about the numbers because, well, it was his job to care. The tidy rows and columns of his spreadsheet left no doubt—the Utility was in bad shape.

Even with financial disaster looming, he couldn't focus. Right now, it was spring, and Ray could think of nothing but Sara and her breasts.

The phone in the next cubicle rang, jerking him back to reality like a hook setting in the mouth of a fish. Over the partition, he heard Ellis' voice.

"They found what? A body?"

Great. Another drunk fisherman fell into the water.

"Where? Wanderfalls?"

Jesus, these jerks are unbelievable.

"A flash drive?" Ellis' voice rose half an octave.

Why would a fisherman have a flash drive?

Ellis dropped into a whisper. "Okay, Dr. Presseley...I'm not sure. Let me check." His tone changed. "Ray? Are you there?"

"Yeah?" Ray's cubicle suddenly felt cold.

"Hang on a sec." Ellis lowered his voice again. "Yeah, he's here...Okay, I'll let him know."

Ray's right foot started jiggling. They found someone in the water with a flash drive and *his* name comes up in the conversation. He navigated over to Ellis' cube and held onto the low partition for support.

"What's up, Ellis?"

Ellis looked distracted, his forehead wrinkled. "I'm not sure. They found some guy belly-up under Wanderfalls. He had a flash drive hanging around his neck. Dr. P. wants to talk to all of us." Ellis finally focused on Ray. "Shit, Ray, how many of those shirts do you own?"

Chapter 5

The hospital door squeaked open. Juice woke instantly. His leg still hung like a ham above him. The walls were still puke green. The pictures on the wall were still butt-ugly jumbles of pink, orange, and brown. "Jeez, Chief, don't you have anything better to do?"

"Yeah, I do. I came back to apologize."

The chief looked better. The circles under his eyes were no longer as dark as his eyebrows, and his uniform was freshly pressed. He looked like he had gotten things under control, but Juice didn't have a clue what those things might be. "Apologize for what?"

"Losing it before. I was out of line," Gordon replied, then looked across the room.

Juice followed his gaze. Rudy sat quietly in the visitor's chair with a stack of papers in his lap. His lips moved slightly as he read.

"Hey, Rudy, whatcha reading?"

"Oh, just something for work." Rudy flashed a small smile and went back to reading.

"Chief, forget about it," Juice said as he turned back to his second visitor. "I was going to call you on it. But right now, I don't think I could catch you to beat the crap out of you."

A crooked smile broke the chief's face. "Thanks."

Juice twitched as a sharp twinge shot through his leg. His thumb hovered over the pain med button on the IV pump, but he didn't push it. He looked over at Rudy and said quietly, "Rudy, you need to know some stuff."

Juice caught the bug-eyed look that Gordon gave him. It wasn't a good look for him. Juice shook his head from side to side. "It's okay, Chief. My buddy here knows half the story anyway." He turned back to Rudy. "Pull up a chair. This could take a while."

The chair legs stuttered as Rudy dragged the chair to Juice's bedside. Dickie walked over to the fake-woodgrain credenza against the wall and sat on it. He leaned back against the wall with his hands laced behind his head.

"Rudy, you know me as Ted Foteo, but my real name's Juice—Juice Verrone."

"I know, Ted. You told me that before you blacked out in the boat!"

"That dead guy…" Juice shot a glance at the Chief. "I don't know what's up with that, but we were right in the middle of it. Anybody finds out we were there…" He left it hang. "You just need to know what's what."

Rudy leaned forward, his eyes wide, waiting for more.

"I'm in witness protection."

"I thought it might be something like that. I wasn't going to say anything, but I have some experience with…" Rudy stopped.

He didn't pick up again, so Juice continued.

"I better start at the beginning." He shifted his butt into a more comfortable position. "Two years ago, I testified against a mob family. I knew some stuff, and a lot of people are spending a lot of time behind bars because of my testimony. It cost me my marriage."

"Dinah," Rudy whispered.

"Yeah, Dinah." Juice shook his head at the memory. "Every once in a while something comes up, and I figure out I'm never going to see her again."

Rudy leaned forward and rested his chubby chin on his hand.

"But those guys I helped put away," Juice went on. "They're not going to forget what I did, and I'm sure they got people out looking for me."

"At the cliff?" Rudy asked.

"Nah, probably not." Juice frowned. "But I gotta keep my eyes open. You know, just in case."

Rudy sat up straight in the chair. "Wow," he said. "This is kind of exciting."

"Not for me," Juice shot back. "It took weeks. Hundreds of pages of depositions. I had to tell them everything. Then the trial, the convictions. The Feds took me back to the office in Newark, showed me a map, and pointed to a little black dot—Wanaduck. The map's blank a half-inch around it in all directions." He nodded his head at the chief. "That map was right, too. That was the day Juice Verrone died."

Rudy's eyes were big and bright. "And you became Ted Foteo." He winked. "Fishing guide to the stars."

Juice and the chief laughed.

A quick knock sounded, and the door to Juice's hospital room opened. A beautiful, red-haired woman walked in wearing a nurse's uniform that could have come from the Frederick's of Hollywood catalog. It clung to every curve of her body. She glided over to the bed as if she intended to climb in, but at the last second, stopped and stuck out her hand.

"Hi, I'm June Presseley. I'm your physical therapist."

Rudy looked at June and did a double take. Chief Gordon hopped off the credenza, stood up straight, and sucked in his gut. He looked like he was trying to stretch his five foot nine to six feet.

June stood with her arms wrapped around Juice's chart, her cleavage framed by the narrow bands of red lace revealed by her low-cut uniform. As if on cue, she took a deep breath, pushing the rounded mounds of breast out even farther. Rudy quickly looked down from her chest, but his eyes boggled at the stretch of leg showing below her form-fitting outfit. He ended up staring at her right foot, which pointed out at an angle and rested on its high heel.

"So, what's the story with my therapy?" Juice asked, giving her a quick once over. "My leg already hurts like hell, and now you want to start pulling on it?"

Gordon stood up to leave. "Well, Rudy and I will get going to let Ms. Presseley here do her job."

Juice shot him a look.

Rudy was hiding behind his *Wall Street Journal*. The upper edges of the paper trembled slightly.

June waved at them to sit down. "Oh, don't leave, fellas. I just stopped by to introduce myself and give Mr. Foteo an overview of my plans for his therapy." June slid her left hand slowly down her hip, smoothing the uniform. Her hand traced the outside of her thigh. She leaned over slightly providing a better view of her cleavage.

Chief Gordon sat down.

"I have to get going." Rudy stood up quickly and folded the *Wall Street Journal* in half. "I have stuff to do." He held the paper in front of his crotch and bolted for the door. He snatched it open and darted into the hall without looking back.

Juice sighed, shaking his head. "Okay, so what kind of torture are you going to dish out?"

"Well, we can't start therapy on your broken leg until this cast is off. But in the meantime, we'll focus on maintaining the flexibility and strength in the rest of your body. When they switch you to a walking cast in a week or so, we'll get you up and moving around." She took a small step closer to the bed and stopped. "Do you mind if I check you out?"

"Nope. Anything that will get me out of here sooner is fine by me."

Gordon waggled his dark eyebrows, like Groucho Marx.

June sidled around the bed. "I'm going to adjust the covers a little. Is that okay?" she asked, her hands poised in the air as she waited for permission. Her fingernails were short and painted Ferrari red.

"Go right ahead."

June half closed her eyes, then smiled at him. She loosened the covers on the bed to expose his left leg and rolled the sheets up to his crotch. Her right hand pushed the covers under his hip while she gently slid the rest between his legs and under his butt with her left hand, her thumb hooked over the top of the fabric.

"Hmmm… I did hear something about a giant hot dog," June said.

"Yeah, the hot dog from the mini-golf course fell on my leg." When June's groping exam went on long enough, Juice nervously tried to edge away. Without success.

"I'm glad it's only your right leg that's broken."

Juice sat up a little straighter, staring with embarrassment at the covers. Gordon had one hand over his face with his other arm around his stomach, stifling his laughter.

"Okay, first I'll help with your range of motion." June continued as if nothing had happened. "We'll begin with some simple movements and stretches. Let me show you what I mean."

She grabbed his ankle with her left hand and rested her right hand on his thigh. She slowly pushed his foot in to bend his knee. The covers under Juice's butt began to loosen.

"I'm starting to feel a draft, Ms. Presseley," Juice joked nervously.

"Oh, I'm so sorry. Let me fix that."

Gordon watched, grinning, as June turned her hand palm up and pushed the covers back under Juice's butt. She gave his cheek a little squeeze before she withdrew her hand.

"There. Is that better?"

"Yeah, thanks."

June pulled his foot back out and slid her right hand along his thigh to lower it back to the bed. She exhaled audibly.

"Even simple moves like this will help your flexibility. We'll start the stretching next time. Your conditioning is *very* good." She switched to a professional tone. "You shouldn't lose too much strength. In future sessions, I'll do massage, some electric stim, and active release therapy."

"What the hell is that?"

Gordon laughed. "Don't you watch any late-night TV?"

"No, not like *that*," June said clinically. "Electric stim is where we run some current through your muscles to activate them. I also get good results with Reiki."

"Reiki?"

"That's where I use my hands to send my energy through your body. Later on, I'll use active release to help strengthen your muscles and release any nerve constriction. And, of course, massage gets the blood flowing."

Gordon stared out the window and muttered in a stage whisper, "Doesn't seem like he needs any help there."

"That sounds like a bunch of mumbo-jumbo to me," Juice said, ignoring Gordon's comment. He screwed up the right side of his mouth in doubt.

"I brought some information for you." June picked up the folder, pulled out a few sheets of paper, and handed them to Juice. "You can read about all of them and ask questions next time."

"Thanks, I'll do that."

Gordon looked up from the paper. "It has to be better than Rudy and his *Wall Street Journal.*"

"Okay, Mr. Foteo. That's it for today, but I'll be back tomorrow at ten. Then we'll get serious."

"Anything that gets me out of here and back on the street."

"Until tomorrow then." June winked at Juice and nodded at Gordon. "Chief." The two men listened to her staccato footsteps fade down the hall.

"That," Juice said as he shook his head, "is one strange piece of work."

Chapter 6

Durk Duffett lowered the passenger-side window of Jesse Blake's S-10 pickup. He laid his arms on the window frame and rested his chin on his hands. While Jesse cruised slowly down River Street, Durk's nose twitched like a dachshund's sniffing the air. They had a couple of hours to kill before they needed to get back to work.

"What do you wanna do?" Jesse looked over at his buddy.

"I don't know. What do you wanna do?"

Jesse chewed his lip. "The Tuck 'er Inn?" he asked.

"Not care-ee-oh-kay again!"

Jesse drove another block then abruptly turned left onto the bridge. The force of the turn sent Durk's head sliding off his hand. His chin banged against the passenger door, landing with a solid thunk.

"Hey!" Durk whined, rubbing his chin.

"We're going to get hot dogs at the Wa-Wa."

"Okay! I like hot dogs!" Durk nodded enthusiastically. "I wonder who the waitress is today."

A few minutes later, Jesse turned into the Wa-Wa's parking lot. The truck crunched through the gravel and angled in next to a police cruiser. Jesse hopped out of the truck, stretched, then pulled the frayed cotton of his shirt back down over his junior beer belly.

Durk jumped out of the passenger side and looked into the window of the cop car. "Hey, I think this is the new girl-cop's car."

"Better not let her catch you calling her a girl again," Jesse said as he turned away. "Last time you dissed her, she charged you with loitering, and you spent the night in the holding cell."

The two stomped across the loose pebbles and stopped at the door. In unison, they hitched up their jeans, pulled down their shirttails, ran their fingers through their hair, and wiped their noses on their shirt sleeves. Jesse waved Durk back and opened the door with a flourish. Both men stepped forward at the same time and got caught in the doorway. They ended up sidestepping through the opening, belly to belly, like synchronized swimmers.

A slender woman with long, silky hair came up to their table. "Food?" she asked.

Jesse rocked from side to side, looking everywhere but at the waitress.

Durk said, "Yes."

Jesse stared at him and wondered why he didn't think of that.

"Follow me," the waitress said. She grabbed two menus and glided off, her blonde hair and gossamer dress trailing in her wake.

Durk nudged Jesse with his elbow and rocked his head in the general direction of the waitress' butt. "Nice ass," he mouthed silently.

The waitress dropped the menus onto an empty table and wandered off to help other customers. The two men sat down, flipped open their menus, and studied them for a few seconds. Durk started drooling, and the menus clattered to the table. The waitress circled back. "A couple of He-Man Hot Dog Specials." Jesse and Durk said in unison. She tucked the menus under her arm and went into the kitchen.

"This place smells," Durk said, then sniffed his armpit to make sure it wasn't him.

"What do you expect? They serve food here," Jesse replied. They eyed the plates in front of other diners, searching for the source of the smell. Seeing nothing suspicious, they both looked over at the restrooms.

"Nah, I mean it. It smells bad." Durk sniffed the air. He squinted his eyes at Jesse and changed the subject. "You think we'll find any more of those gizmos in time for the Guild meeting?"

Jesse reached inside his shirt and shook something, setting off a clatter of plastic rattling. "What?" he asked, making a face. "You don't think we have enough already?"

Durk looked worried. "I dunno, Jesse. Bill and Father O'Donnell seemed really anxious to get their hands on one of those."

"Don't sweat it." Jesse leaned back in his chair and knitted his fingers behind his head. "Bill said it was a favor for Dr. Presseley at the Utility, and if that dickhead doesn't like what he gets, then he can just kiss my ass."

The waitress reappeared and slid a platter in front of each man. Beige hot dogs were nestled in whole grain buns atop healthy mounds of julienned carrots, green pepper, and red cabbage. A hand waving at a nearby table caught the waitress' attention, and she walked off without saying anything.

Jesse inspected his plate, then shrugged and picked up one of his hot dogs.

Durk followed suit and took a giant bite. Self-preservation quickly replaced his initial stunned surprise. He spit out a wad of slightly chewed bun and dog. The tooth-marked bite bounced off his plate and landed on the foot of a woman sitting at the next table. The woman shrieked and kicked the frankfurter fragment from her foot. She turned and glared icy daggers at the two men.

"Jeezus H. Christ!" Durk snatched up his glass and gulped the water down, then wiped his tongue with his shirttail. "Damn, that's hot." He took another drink. "And it tastes kinda like when Bill cooked the salmon that sat out in the sun too long."

Jesse took another bite and peered quizzically at his hot dog, trying to identify the flavor. He chewed thoughtfully, then shrugged. "I don't know. Porcupine, maybe? It ain't the best, that's for sure." He swallowed.

Durk drank Jesse's water, waved at the waitress for more, and froze, staring at the next table. Jesse turned to see what had gotten Durk's attention.

Terry Backster sat with her back to them wearing her police blues. She pushed her hand across the table toward her companion. "Sabrina, you have to watch this. You won't believe it! I had to watch it three times; I was laughing so hard."

Durk whispered, "Isn't that the police chief's girlfriend with Terry?"

Jesse ignored the question and stuffed the rest of his hot dog in his mouth. He wolfed it down as he fished some bills out of his jeans. He dropped the money on the table, nudged Durk to get his attention, and waggled the fingers of his right hand in some hand signal meaningful only to him. Durk scrunched his face up. Jesse flicked his forefinger and middle finger at the other table. Durk still didn't seem to get it. Jesse grabbed his shirt and shook.

Durk grinned. "Yeah, nice tits," he whispered.

Jesse shook his head wildly. He reached under his shirt, pulled out a cluster of flash drives hanging from lanyards, shook them once, then tipped his head at the next table. Jesse could see the light come on in the empty space behind Durk's eyes.

"Gotcha," Durk said.

Jesse mimed a grabbing motion, and flicked his fingers toward the parking lot.

Durk nodded his head knowingly and winked.

"Terry, are you sure it's okay?" Sabrina asked, pulling the flash drive across the table with the lacquered nail of her right forefinger.

"Don't worry, the chief doesn't care about the flash drive," Terry reassured her friend. "Besides, if he wants it later, you can just give it to him at home."

Jesse and Durk sat silently, staring at each other until the waitress disappeared into the kitchen. Then they stood up and moved past the neighboring table. Durk squeezed Sabrina's left boob, leered at her, and ran for the door. Jesse lunged for the flash drive and took off after Durk.

Sabrina yelled, "Hey, what are you doing? Come back with that!" But Jesse and Durk were already gone.

In the restaurant, Sabrina glared at Terry. Sabrina's eyebrows arched so high they were hidden under her bangs. "You're some cop, Terry! Aren't you, like, going to do something?"

Terry leaned her head back at an angle, looked out the window, and watched Jesse waving wildly at Durk to get in the truck. The truck backed up and fishtailed out of the parking lot onto the road back to town. Terry turned her attention back to her friend. "Sabrina, don't get your panties in a twist. Everyone in town has one of Walt's flash drives. He handed them out like candy." She poked at her salad with her fork. "Besides, that idiot Jesse is part of Bill Snead's group. For some reason, I intimidate the shit out of those guys, so don't worry. I'll go over later and get the drive back. After the stuff Bill's guys have pulled lately, he will do anything to keep me out of their hair."

"But that guy grabbed my boob!" Sabrina replied indignantly.

Terry winked at her friend. "Yeah, so the next time we see him, I'll hold him down, and you can kick him in the nuts."

In the office over the Guild's garage Bill Snead sat and watched the Wanaduck Elementary School third grade class perform *The Fishies Do Swim* for the eighteenth time. Father O'Donnell stood behind him and rubbed his eyes. On screen, the cast came to the front of the stage and took a curtain call. Someone dressed as a trout fell off the stage into the front row. A child started crying, and the video ended.

Jesse and Durk stood erect, looking as uncomfortable as nuns at a strip club.

"Goddammit, Jesse," Bill yanked the flash drive out of the computer and tossed it onto the pile of tiny plastic fish sitting on the desk. "Can't you do any better than this?" He swept them off the desk into a shoebox, and then stormed out of the room.

Chapter 7

Juice heard a single tentative knock on the door to his hospital room. "Come on in," Juice called out. After a few seconds, the door opened very slowly and Rudy stuck his head in. His eyes darted around the room. "Don't worry, little buddy," Juice chuckled. "She's gone."

Chief Gordon stood up and offered the single guest chair to Rudy. "Here. Sit down and relax. She's not coming back until tomorrow morning." He glanced over at Juice and winked. "At least I hope so."

Rudy inspected every corner of the room like he was plotting his exit strategy.

"I thought you were going to pop a gasket." Juice tilted his bed up to get a better view. "You okay now?"

"I guess so. I mean, Ted, the way she was touching you didn't seem very professional."

Gordon laughed. "You should have stuck around. She acted more like a pro as she got warmed up."

Juice started laughing too, but Rudy looked even more bewildered. "Where did you end up going to cool off?" Juice asked.

"The Utility!" Rudy nodded an exclamation point.

"Uh, little buddy, that's not your idea of a good time, is it?"

"Sure it is." Rudy nodded again. "When I got outside, I saw this announcement board by the city building. It's got public notices and local items posted there. Do you know there's been a cocker spaniel missing for six weeks?"

"You don't say?" Juice shook his head in disbelief.

"One of the flyers said that the Utility's latest annual report is posted online."

"Man, you do know how to have fun," Gordon said and slapped Rudy on the back.

Rudy winced. "Hey, I spend a lot of time with annual reports. They're interesting." Rudy's voice took on a defensive edge.

"Aw, come on, we're only joking," Juice interrupted. "You going someplace with this, or are you just sharing the details of your exciting life?"

"Gee, Ted, give me a break," Rudy replied with a hint of a whine. "I went over to the Utility's offices, and there's this big information kiosk with the iMUD logo, all these fancy brochures and reports, and a computer. They even have the Indian Meadows Utility District commission meeting videos online!"

"So what?" Gordon asked.

"So, all of the Utility's financial information is right there!"

"And..." Juice rolled his eyes back up into his head and made a gagging sound.

"Guys," Rudy waited until they were looking at him. "The Utility is about to go under. They're broke."

"Rudy, I don't want to rain on your parade, but..." Juice pointed at the window, "that big dam out there is owned by the Utility. Every drop of water goes through that thing, they make money on. How can they be broke?"

"Because they pay more than twice as much for their electricity as they sell it for." Rudy pulled a notepad out of his jacket pocket and flipped through the pages looking for something. "See, the Utility is mandated by law to sell power to its electrical customers for its cost of acquisition plus facilities maintenance and overhead, and a contingency fund for unforeseen circumstances."

"In English?" Gordon asked gently.

"About a year ago, the contingency fund began decreasing. The iMUD bottom line doesn't show them losing money. But each quarterly report shows less and less in the contingency account."

"So they had some unforeseen maintenance issues," Gordon offered.

"That's the thing. The same reports show maintenance expenses dropping to nearly zero. This last quarter, they didn't spend a dime on maintenance. They're hiding the losses by taking money out of the contingency fund and cutting maintenance. In two years the Utility went from solvency to the verge of bankruptcy."

"So what happened, Rudy?" Juice asked.

"I'm not sure. Most of iMUD's business is with other utilities. The management discussion in their annual report says they started selling long-term contracts to buy electricity from other utilities. They'd get a fixed price that was pretty favorable—given the circumstances."

"Selling to buy? Fixed price? Whaddya mean, Rudy?" He looked at Gordon to see if he was the only one not getting it.

"Oil prices were going through the roof. They locked in a long-term price to buy electricity for a lot less than what they'd sell it for in the future."

"Sounds like a good plan to me," Gordon countered.

"Yeah, but then iMUD bought short-term contracts to sell their electricity at current rates."

"So the price went up, and they were making money by buying low and selling high."

"That's right, Chief," Rudy nodded excitedly.

"But what's wrong with that?" Juice couldn't follow Rudy's train of thought.

"At the time, nothing, really. Except that they were charging their customers for the higher-priced power that the Utility bought and then selling the power they produced to other utilities for a massive profit."

"They're ripping off their own customers?" Juice asked.

"But I thought they were a locally owned utility?" Gordon interrupted. "How could they get away with it?"

"I don't think anybody was watching. The Utility's commissioners are also on the town council. It's pretty tight knit around here."

"So, other than a bait and switch scam, where's the problem?"

"2008, Ted. Energy prices dropped by half. iMUD got stuck with long-term contracts to buy power at prices higher than the market."

"But…" Gordon sputtered as he caught on. "They don't have a consumer market for all that electricity, so they have to dump it for whatever the going rate is."

"Right. That's when they started using the contingency fund and maintenance to cover the difference. But now the money is all gone. They're broke."

Juice let out a soft whistle. "Jeez, Rudy, I'd hate to have to listen to you explain something you were really sure of." He shook his head in disbelief. "You came up with all this in what—two, three hours?"

"One and a half. I went to the Tuck 'er Inn for lunch."

Gordon held his hands out and looked at them like he was trying to decide whether he needed a manicure. "How sure are you of this?"

"Uh, these numbers are all in the reports. They could be doing some other things with their internal books."

"And why should I believe you over the public reports of the Utility?" Gordon asked, leaning in.

Rudy looked from Dickie to Juice and back, then his face lit up. "You guys don't know what I do for a living." Rudy chuckled. "I dig through a company's public reports and try to figure out what the real story is."

"Whaddya mean? Like 'CSI: Accounting'?" Juice was stunned. "You some kind of forensic bookkeeper or something?"

"That's exactly right, Ted!" Rudy beamed. "I find out what the numbers really mean."

Juice let out another long, low whistle. "Little buddy, there is a lot more to you than meets the eye."

Gordon pulled out his phone, hit a couple of buttons, and put the phone to his ear. Juice could hear the faint trill of a phone ringing.

"Ellis Spelt, please." Gordon closed his eyes and squeezed the bridge of his nose. His eyes popped open. "Ellis. Hi, it's Dickie Gordon…No, no, Sabrina and Amy are fine. Listen. Did you hear about Eddie Snead?" Gordon picked at a piece of lint on his shirt as he listened. "Yeah, a real shame…You guys knew each other from him being on iMUD's board, right? Could you pull loose for a half-hour or so to come over to the station?" He looked at Juice. "Nothing formal. We're just trying to tie up a few loose ends on the case. Make sure we've covered all the bases." Dickie flexed the fingers of his free hand. "Thanks, Ellis. I don't think it will take long at all… Tomorrow at four-thirty is good. See you." He clicked off.

"What was that all about?" Juice asked.

"We've got a murder. Now, Rudy here thinks there might be something going on with the Utility." Gordon looked at his phone. "And I fucking hate it when weasels like Ellis lie to me."

Chapter 8

Good coffee. One of the things Dickie liked about Washington State. Even a dumpy bar and grill like the Tuck 'er Inn, in a backwater like Wanaduck, brewed great coffee. Dickie sighed, and pushed open the front door of the police station.

"Hey, Bill, good morning," Dickie offered a quick smile to the officer sitting behind the desk.

Bill Branch looked up with surprise, as if he didn't expect Chief Gordon to walk through the door, or anyone else either. Bill meant well.

"Bill, is Cameron in this morning?"

"Yeah, Chief. She is. She came in early to install the new link to the state database."

"Thanks." Dickie walked through the main area to his office on the left. *Yeah, if someone comes in shooting, they'll have to get past Bill and the rest of my staff before they get me.* Dickie thought about recent events and rubbed his face with his left hand. *That isn't that far-fetched.* He put his coffee down, took off his jacket, and sat down behind his desk. He picked up the phone and pressed a button.

"Collins," a no-nonsense voice answered.

"Hi, Cameron."

"Good morning, Chief."

"Do you have a minute? Could you stop by my office?"

"Sure thing, Chief. Be right there." The line clicked. A few seconds later, Cameron came into Dickie's office. She wore a white collared shirt, navy pants, and navy loafers.

"Would you mind closing the door?"

Cameron closed the door and sat down in one of the visitor chairs without being asked.

"What's up, Chief?"

Dickie looked into his cup. "Do you want some coffee or something?"

"I'm good."

"Okay, well, I wanted to talk to you about the Utility videos."

"You mean the board meetings?" Cameron asked.

"Yeah, I hear they're online. On YouTube?"

"I know. It sounds odd, but it's an easy way to get them into the public record."

"So, has anything happened at the meetings recently?"

"Like?" Cameron asked, tucking a short lock of brown hair behind her ear. No earrings or other jewelry. All business.

"You know, anything unusual?"

"Well, there was the fight between Bud Norbert and Chief Shecky."

"That's unusual?" Dickie asked, smiling.

"No, I guess it isn't."

"Anything else at that meeting?" Dickie picked up a pen and gave Cameron an encouraging look, hoping to coax some tidbit out.

"Well, there was..." Cameron stopped talking for a second. "No, nothing really."

"What was it?" Dickie asked, smiling again.

"Well, the video of the last meeting ran extra long."

"Why was that?"

"Well, I don't really know." Cameron stared at her fingernails, which were chewed short.

Dickie's gut kicked in. "Cameron, come on. Something happened, right?" Dickie gave her his best good-cop look.

She folded her hands in her lap, looked down at them, and said quietly, "Well, I wasn't there for the whole meeting."

Dickie closed his eyes and squeezed the bridge of his nose, then looked at her. "Cameron, are you okay?" Cameron starting every sentence with "well" was driving Dickie nuts.

She looked at her thumb then nibbled on the nail, looked again, and put her hands back in her lap.

Dickie didn't say a word.

She shook her head a little and started talking. "Well, after they broke up the fight, Robert Presseley said there was no further business and adjourned the meeting."

"Yeah, and…?" Dickie coaxed her on.

"I had my headphones on, but I heard my Blackberry go off. The A/V booth is sound proof, but I can't help it. I grabbed the phone and answered it." She blushed. "Because, well, my ringtone is Janis Joplin's 'Down On Me'."

"Good tune," Dickie added.

"Yeah, well, I wouldn't want anyone hearing it accidentally. It probably isn't professional, you know?"

"So who called you?"

"Um, June…June Presseley" Cameron stopped talking and her face turned crimson.

"June Presseley called you?"

Cameron looked up. Dickie watched her, waiting patiently.

"Yes. She said that Robert would be talking to Timothy for

an hour." She averted her eyes. "And that we'd have time."

"Look, Cameron." Dickie put down his pen. "I really don't care what you do or who you do it with." He smiled and tried to lighten things up. "At least when you aren't on department time." The smile vanished. "But we've got a dead guy, and there's a possible tie-in with the Utility."

"Well, she wanted to get together. You know, while Dr. Presseley was busy with his stuff."

"Uh-huh," Dickie said as he scribbled on his pad. "So you rushed out and the recording equipment was still running."

"Yeah, I skipped out for a while. I didn't think it would matter." Cameron nervously tucked her hair behind her ear again.

"It's okay, Cameron. If the equipment can run on its own, there's nothing wrong with ducking out for a few minutes."

"Yeah, but," she started and stopped, then nervously chewed at the nail on her pinkie.

"Yeah, but something happened." Dickie gave her an understanding look. "Did you go back?"

"Yeah, I did. That's the weird thing."

"What's that?" Dickie asked.

"Well, I went back in to shut off the equipment and save the files. But the crew was still there."

"The crew?"

"Yeah, the board members and management team," Cameron replied. She took a breath. "And Timothy."

"What were they doing?"

"Well, when I got there, they all stared at me. I actually looked down to see if my shirt was unbuttoned." She dropped her head and checked her nails for rough spots again.

Dickie pretended not to notice. "Then what?"

"Presseley wanted to know what I was doing there, so I told him I came to turn off the equipment. He said, 'What do you mean turn off the equipment?' He was really mad."

"Any idea why?"

"Well, I explained about the high-def camera and the outputs. One goes directly to broadcast. The other goes to a recorder, so we have a copy of each meeting. I thought broadcasting the empty room for a few minutes wouldn't be an issue. Hardly anyone watches the public access channel anyway. But Presseley got all red and looked like he was going to explode. He looked through the window into the booth at the back and saw the red light that means we're recording."

"So what was the problem?" Dickie prompted.

"Well, I don't know. The open access initiative has the board meetings go out on the cable company's public access channel. It's no big deal. Like I said, hardly anyone watches. But Presseley asked me how we know who's watching."

"How do you know?"

"We don't. Like I told him, the cable company has all that stuff. They know what everyone watches—even the dirty stuff," Cameron giggled, stopped, and looked guilty.

"Who at the cable company?" Dickie asked, his pen poised above the notepad.

"Well, that's what Presseley wanted to know. I told him Vernon Nickers would know. You know, the president."

Dickie scribbled the name down.

"At that point, Presseley told Eddie to talk to me about the details. Then he left with everybody else."

"Eddie Snead." Dickie let his breath out slowly.

"Yeah, he stood there for a minute and then said, 'Whew, that was heavy.' He asked about the A/V equipment. I told him Presseley likes his toys, and he winked at me." The crimson blush returned to her cheeks, as if she was confessing something far more scandalous than a wink. "He wanted to see what we had."

"Why?"

"He said he was the first agent in the area to offer virtual house-tours for his real estate business. He wanted to pick up some A/V tips from me."

Dickie tapped his pen against his lips.

"So I took him to the booth and explained everything to him. He flirted with me, but I think he was just pretending. He asked if he could get a copy of the recording. He said it might keep Presseley happy."

"You gave him a copy?"

"Yeah. Actually, I asked him if a flash drive was okay. It's quicker than burning a DVD."

"A flash drive?" Dickie asked.

"Yeah, they're these small devices…"

"Yeah, got it. So then what?"

"Well, I made a copy for him and a copy for NANOOC."

"Who the fuck is Nanuk?"

"N-A-N-O-O-C." She spelled it out. "That's Chief Shecky's group, the North American Native Office of Casinos. They get a copy of every meeting."

"Oh, okay." Dickie crossed out "Nanuk" and wrote the acronym.

"Then Eddie and I headed to the Tuck 'er Inn for a beer." She exhaled loudly and finally relaxed back into the chair. "I needed one after that. Eddie even paid. Boy, was he in a good mood that night."

"You know why?"

"No, I didn't ask. We drank a couple of beers. It was, you know, rooftop casual. Then I went home."

"Okay, Cameron," Dickie said and clicked his pen closed. "I appreciate your honesty. And, really, don't worry about leaving the meeting."

"Thanks, Chief," Cameron said with a smile. "Is that it?"

"Yeah."

Cameron got up, opened the door, and started to walk out. She turned around and stood in the doorway.

"What is it?"

She pinched the skin on her forehead like she was trying to figure something out. "The next day I went back in to post the video, but something was wrong."

"Like what?"

"The video wasn't all there."

Dickie leaned forward in his chair. "What do you mean it wasn't all there?"

"Well, it just cut off. Right after Presseley called for adjournment." She shrugged and left his office.

Dickie closed his eyes and squeezed the bridge of his nose. He let go, picked up his coffee, took a sip, then put the cup down. *Cold.*

Chapter 9

"Whoa, Chief, take it easy, would you?" Juice grimaced as Chief Gordon bounced the wheelchair off the passenger's side of Juice's SUV.

"Sorry, Juice," Gordon said as he opened the door. "Er, I mean Ted."

"Hey, it's okay. The name thing still screws me up. And it's been, like what, two years now?" Juice shifted slowly toward the edge of the seat and braced himself against the door pillar.

"And please," Gordon said as he set the brakes on Juice's rental wheelchair, "outside the office, it's just Dickie."

Juice raised one eyebrow. "I got an orderly named Dickie pushing me around?"

"And the horse you rode in on, Ted." Dickie flipped Juice the bird. "Come on, I want you to have a look at something."

"Then maybe you should put the fucking wheelchair closer."

Dickie skidded the chair right up to the door with the brakes still locked. He put his right hand on the arm of the wheelchair and held his left hand out.

Juice slid carefully off the seat and steadied himself on his good leg. Dickie caught Juice under one arm as Juice gripped his shoulders hard with both hands. Dickie's knees sagged under the weight.

"You ready?" Juice asked.

Dickie spread his feet apart. "Yeah, now I am."

Juice grabbed the armrests of the wheelchair and settled into the leather seat. He winced. "Okay, let's go...Dickie."

Dickie raised the right footrest, flipped the brakes off, and pushed the chair across the deserted parking lot. At the far end of the lot, a sign straddled the entrance with "Wana-Putt Mini-Golf" carved into a single piece of wood, faded silver by the elements.

"You've gotta be kidding me," Juice said, scanning the ramshackle landscape of abandoned fiberglass sculptures. Sagebrush sprouted from the walkways between the holes, spring-green weedy vines climbed signposts and benches. The branches of a few dead trees spread leafless over faded and worn fairways. The only sound came from the wind whipping plastic bags caught on the fence. "What's the deal with this place, Dickie?"

Dickie pushed the wheelchair up to a bronze sign covered by a green skin of verdigris. It read: "Wanderfalls Recreation Area and Mini-Golf, established for the perpetual use of the citizens of Wanaduck, Washington, by the Indian Meadows Utility District, this First Day of June, 2001." Beneath the text an engraved signature and name formalized the gift, "By Robert Presseley, Managing Director."

"Presseley," Dickie muttered under his breath.

"Who's that?" Rudy came up and peered at the plaque from six inches away, then straightened up. "Oh, what kind of bird is that?" He didn't wait for an answer, just turned, and walked away down the path.

"Any relationship to my physical therapist?" Juice tried to look at Dickie, but couldn't turn in the chair.

"Yeah, her husband. June's a handful. Not sure if she's a local, but she married one. She's got a bit of a rep as a run-around." He patted Juice's shoulder. "No surprise there, huh? We've gotten some strange calls from their house."

"Domestic disturbance?"

"Nah. Weird shit. Kinky shit. The kind of stuff most people wouldn't want anybody to know about." His belt radio crackled briefly and went silent. "But everybody does know, and nobody ever says a word. Never. Anyway, don't mess with that. Robert is the one person in town who'd make the effort to find out more about Ted."

"Got it." Juice inspected the ruined attraction. "Uh, don't get me wrong here, Dickie, but how the fuck did you ever end up in a dump like Wanaduck?"

"Presseley hired me."

"You got hired by the Utility?"

"No, Presseley was the acting mayor right before you got here. The elected mayor took early retirement after about eighteen years on the job. Presseley got appointed until they could hold a new election." The muscles in Dickie's jaw clenched.

"Something about him bother you?"

"Well…" The wheelchair shifted in different directions as Dickie tried to decide where to go. "The thing is, he shouldn't have hired me at all."

"Why? Because you're out of your fucking mind, maybe?"

"No. At least, I don't think so." Dickie guided the wheelchair down the path. "It's because they didn't check me out." He stopped and squeezed the bridge of his nose. "No, I take that back. They found out everything about me and hired me anyway."

"Yeah?" Juice prompted.

"Fifteen years ago, I was a beat cop for the LAPD until I figured out it was killing me. I was doing the cop thing. Overtime. Special duty. Day after day—never saw the family."

"You have a family?"

"Had." Dickie sighed. "One day, my wife took my kid and went back home to Mexico City."

"Home?"

"Yeah. She was from Mexico City. So were my parents."

"I figured you for Greek," Juice said.

"No. My family was straight-line Spanish from colonial times."

"But your name's Gordon?"

"They weren't promoting Hispanics back then." Dickie stopped the wheelchair in front of a bench and set the brake. He checked the wood for splinters, then sat down and leaned back. "After my family left, I went back to school and got a degree in law enforcement. I had worked up to detective. Then it all went bad." Dickie brushed a few dry leaves off the bench and said, "My wife's father was a Federal Judge in Mexico."

"Was?"

"Yeah. He and his wife were out driving, and a truck rammed into his car. Some drug guys tore up the car with automatic weapons—killed him, killed his wife."

"Shit, Dickie. I'm sorry."

"That's not the worst of it...my wife and daughter were in the back seat." Dickie grabbed Juice's arm. "The last thing she said before she left me was: 'Better she has no father than one who's never around.' I never saw them again." Dickie put his face in his hands and stopped talking. His eyes stung when he looked back at Juice. "That was five years ago this week. That's when I started drinking. I could still do the job. But they had to keep me away from the drug dealers."

"I knew we had something in common," Juice said with a smile.

Dickie ignored him. "I was a wreck. Drinking myself into a trance every night and barely keeping it together during the day." He stopped and looked up. "Six years. Six freaking years. Then one day I had had it. Like a movie, I went to the chief detective's office and tossed my shield, keys, and gun on his desk, and walked away. Never looked back."

"So you moved up here?"

"No. I kicked around doing investigative shit for a while. Divorces, corporate problems, stuff like that, but I wasn't into it. I wasn't drinking anymore, but the city was wearing me down."

"What do you expect? That would wear anybody out."

"Yeah, maybe. So I thought I needed a small town. Get in some place and take it easy. Write a few tickets, help a few old folks with their groceries. It would be like a vacation compared to L.A. I started looking around on the Internet and found a posting for Wanaduck Chief of Police. I emailed my résumé and got a call back from this Timothy Bentle guy."

"Don't know him."

"He's Presseley's so-called assistant. The fucker gives me the creeps. Anyway, he tells me to hold. A minute later, a guy who sounds like a radio announcer comes on the line."

"Presseley?"

"Yeah. He asks me a few questions. After I babble for ten minutes, he cuts me off, thanks me for my time, and tells me he'll be in touch."

"Ouch. Then tell me why you're here now."

"The next day I get a FedEx." Dickie said as he stood and pushed the wheelchair away from the bench. "It was an offer letter with a contract attached. Ninety days probationary period then—bam—full benefits, full retirement, at the top of the pay range. Ten minutes, Ted, they gave me a ten minute interview on the damn phone."

"You should play the lottery, Dickie…Luck like that."

"So I move up here, do my three months and start changing the way the department operates. It used to be Mayberry, RFD around here. Now we can at least get prints done overnight."

"So I noticed," Juice said.

"Hey guys, check this out!" Rudy waved at them from further down the path.

Dickie got up and wheeled Juice to the next hole and stopped next to Rudy.

"Look." Rudy pointed at a fiberglass structure in front of them. "It's a model of the Wanaduck Dam. You hit your shot in the front." He ran over to a large opening on one side of the dam, then ran around to the other side. "The ball comes out one of these holes here." He pointed and stood at attention. When they didn't say anything, he dashed to the green. "If it comes out of the middle hole, you get a hole-in-one!"

The faded paint on the sign next to the hole read: "Hole 9, Sponsored by Indian Meadows Utility District."

"iMUD, Indian Meadows back then, built this place with the help of local merchants." Dickie pointed at the other course hazards. "Each sponsor got to put their logos or something like this on a hole."

On the opposite side of the path, hole 13 was a straight fairway blocked by four large coat hangers. Juice and Rudy eyed Dickie.

"Tabor's Clothing. The trick was to wait until the hangers lined up, then take your shot." Dickie answered the unasked question. "They went out of business after Walmart opened up in Wenatchee."

The obstacle at hole 16 was gone. "The problems started

when the windmill that was here knocked the Boy Scouts into the river." Dickie pointed at the tattered remnants of Astroturf hanging down the gap in the fairway.

Across from hole 16 stood what appeared to be a small forest of six-foot tall, green dildos. As the three men approached the impressive phallic collection, it resolved into abstract stalks of asparagus. The hole's sponsor was the Wanaduck Asparagus Festival.

Ahead of them, a strand of yellow crime-scene tape stretched across the path.

"That where the guy got whacked?" Juice grabbed the wheels of his chair and pushed. Dickie let go. Rudy took off in the other direction. Juice rolled up and stopped in front of the yellow tape. The sign near the tee said: "Hole 17—Walt's."

"Walt sponsored a hole?" Juice asked nobody in particular. "That must have been the big fish." He wheeled closer.

"You done in here, Dickie?" Juice spun the wheelchair and faced Dickie.

"Yeah." Dickie pointed at the last hole. "We figure the victim was shot over there. A chunk of cliff broke away and took the vic and the hot dog down into the river."

Juice rolled under the tape and peered at the sign. "VeggieTech? What do they have to do with hot dogs?"

"They make them. They're all vegetarian."

"Is that some kind of a joke?" Juice wheeled in a slow circle and shook his head. "Nah, I don't like it. First, if they bring him here, there's too much chance for something to go wrong. The guy could make a break for it. He could jump into the river, anything."

"Okay."

Juice surveyed the area again, then paused and scratched absently at his three-day growth of beard. "No, your stiff came here on his own. He was set up." He aimed his right hand at the end of the path. "The guy he's supposed to meet is standing there. He walks up, has his conversation, and turns to leave." Juice jerked his thumb over his right shoulder. "But he can't leave. Somebody else came up behind him."

"Two?"

"Yeah, the guy he's meeting and the shooter." Juice pointed at Walt's hole. "He panics and runs over there. The cliff starts crumbling so he bolts for the end. He gets shot, falls into the river, and the fucking hot dog crashes into my boat. All the commotion up here drops the fish."

"And ruins your day."

"No shit."

"But where was the shooter hiding? In the parking lot?" Dickie nodded his head toward the scrubby trees. "There's sure no place to hide down here."

"Hey," Rudy's disembodied voice came from the grove of asparagus. "Look what I found." He materialized onto the putting surface.

"There's where the shooter was hiding." Juice said to Dickie. He raised his voice. "Whatcha got there, Rudy?"

"It's a cutlass." Rudy met them on the path holding a tiny red-plastic sword, the kind used for fruit in tropical drinks. He gave a buccaneer-style slash through the air with the little blade pinched between his thumb and forefinger.

"I'll take that." Dickie pulled an evidence bag out of his pocket, and Rudy dropped the sword into it. Dickie zipped the seal.

"I'll see what else I can find." Rudy wandered back into the garden of genitalia.

Dickie's phone played a tune that sounded like the mariachi music at a gringo resort. He checked the screen and answered. "Yeah, what?" A pause. "Got it...Okay...Later."

Dickie stuck the phone back in his pocket and took a deep breath. "The medical examiner."

"What's he got?"

"Eddie Snead's body was pretty battered from smacking the rocks on the way down, but he was dead when he hit the water. Only had two gunshot wounds, though. One in the knee and one in the throat." Dickie shook his head and stared vacantly into the distance. "That's weird."

"What's weird? Dickie?" Juice wheeled the chair and bumped Dickie's leg. "Chief? Come back."

"Huh? Sorry. I just remembered something."

"Like what?"

"The night I met Sabrina at the Asparagus Festival. The local River Girls Club does this fish display and touch tank every year. The girls run around in their uniforms and show other kids how to pet the salmon, and the moms stand by to help."

"A real MILF-fest, huh, Dickie?"

"Not around here. But there's one or two." Dickie smiled. "So I'm walking by the display when some kid grabs a fish, and it goes squirting out into the crowd. I bend over to grab it, and when I stand back up, there's a beautiful woman standing in front of me. She snatches the fish out of my hands and tosses it back into the tank. She looks me over and says, 'Hey, you're like the new police guy, right?' She holds out her hand and says, 'Hi! I'm Sabrina. Sabrina Spelt.' We shake hands, and when I let go, there's these strings of fish slime hanging between our hands. She goes, 'Ewww. Yuck.' She starts to walk away, stops, and asks me to meet her for a drink in a couple of hours. Then runs off."

"You definitely need to be playing the lottery." Juice

laughed. "You are one lucky son of a bitch."

"Yeah, that was almost two years ago. You weren't here yet. We've been an item ever since."

"So what's that got to do with the story?"

"I'm getting there. I stand there grinning like a kid, but I'm covered in fish slime. So, I walk up to the station to get a clean shirt. I open the door, and Bill Branch, the new patrol officer, is looking like he's seen a ghost. 'You have a visitor,' he whispers and looks over at my office. I go in, and there's Timothy Bentle dressed like he's going to somebody's funeral. He says Presseley was wondering what I think of my predecessor's murder. I tell him, 'Nothing.'"

"What?" Juice asked. "The old chief was murdered?"

"Yeah. The old chief died a few months before I got here. I went through the file when I first got the job. The Washington State Police found nothing. They asked the FBI to come in, and they found nothing. No clues. No suspects. Nada. By that time, the case was ice cold. Anyway, the creep tells me to have another look and get back to him inside a week. Then he just walks out the door."

"He say why?"

"Not a word." Dickie started pacing. "I walk back to the records room and go to get the file. On top of the cabinet was a folder marked 'New Chief.' I went through it, and it's all the applications for my job. I knew some of those guys. I found my paperwork and looked at the notes. They knew I had been fucking up my last months at the LAPD." He stabbed at the air with his finger. "They knew I was a drunk." Dickie lowered his voice. "Ted, they were looking to hire somebody they thought couldn't do the job. Somebody like me."

"But you were sober by then."

"Yeah, but they didn't know that. I asked Bill if he knew where the folder had come from, and he said nobody had been in there during his watch. I put the folder back where it belonged and got out the cold case on the old chief. Nothing jumped out. It was completely cold. Until now." Dickie leaned in close to Juice. "Ted, the chief had been shot twice. Once in the knee..."

Juice finished his sentence, "... and once in the throat."

Chapter 10

Ellis Spelt slouched in the last chair on the far side of a long table at the Wanaduck police station. He watched Dickie Gordon carry two cups of coffee into the conference room and kick the door closed with his right foot. Coffee sloshed out of the cups, contributing to an irregular brown stain in the carpet that even the tan and gray pinstripe industrial pattern couldn't hide. Ellis felt like he hadn't slept in a week and was uncomfortable talking to Dickie, who now lived with Sabrina, Ellis' ex-wife, and their daughter, Amy.

This is way too small a town.

The room's decades-old, functional furnishings grated on Ellis' nerves. The cheap veneer paneling was the color of walnut but looked like it was just brown-stained pine. The fourteen-foot, dark wood table surrounded by fifteen brown leather chairs sat like the room had been built around them. Dickie walked past the long wall of oversized windows that provided a view into the main office area. He reached over and set a cup down in front of Ellis, then peered at the inset-framed mirror on the wall to his right.

"Black with sugar, right?" A few drops of coffee dribbled

from Dickie's fingers onto the table.

"Thanks, Dickie."

Dickie took a sip of coffee. "Thanks again for coming in, Ellis. This has got to be tough. Eddie Snead was a friend of yours, right?"

"Not friends, really," Ellis said as he stared at the opposite wall, covered with plaques, citations, training diplomas, and clumsily-posed photographs of Wanaduck's former police chiefs. "Business acquaintances mostly. We'd hack up the golf course a few times a year, but other than that we didn't really socialize."

"But he was with you on the board at the Utility?"

"Uh, I'm not on the board of directors. Eddie is, er, was." Ellis shook his head "Ray and I attend the meetings because we're part of the management team."

"Ray Milton? He's the financial guy at iMUD, right?" Dickie jotted a note on his pad. He looked up and smiled. "Is iMUD the best they could do with Indian Meadows Utility District?"

"I guess. We formally switched to the acronym in '02. The board thought it sounded more twenty-first century."

"So, remind me. Who else is on the board?"

"There's John Parsons, who's been a board member for about forty years, and the chairman…"

"Robert Presseley," Dickie finished for him.

"Yeah. For the management team, Ray handles any financial issues, and I sort of cover new business development and project management."

Dickie scribbled something else in his notes. "And Eddie?"

"Eddie was Community Liaison," Ellis said. "He was the customers' rep on the board."

"Did he work for iMUD?"

"Uh." Ellis stopped and listened for a moment to the

sound of a commotion outside. "He didn't work for the Utility. He was just on the board."

The main office door flew open and slammed against the wall. Two police officers squeezed through the doorway with a struggling prisoner suspended between them. The trio surged up to the counter and stopped. The female cop reached behind the counter and grabbed some forms. The male officer stuck his head in the conference room. "Chief. DWI. Again," he said and vanished.

Ellis watched the prisoner straighten up and shake his head, his gaze fixed miles away. *Travis!* Ellis' eyes grew wide.

Travis opened his mouth to say something, but his eyes rolled back into his head, and he tipped straight over backward, vanishing from sight.

"Shit. Sorry, Ellis." Dickie stood up and headed for the door. "Let me go take care of this. I'll be right back."

"Take your time, Chief." Ellis felt the blood drain from his face.

No, no, no. Not Travis. Ellis watched the struggle to get Travis vertical. *Where did it go wrong?* Ellis' eyes lost their focus and eventually settled on the carpet. *The plan had been perfect.*

Well, it wasn't, but at least it was simple. Back when it started…

Ellis could still see Sabrina walking through the trees scattered along the river. They had just started dating. She turned, grinned, and ran down to the water as she peeled off her tank top, the dam distant in the background. The dam. Back then, he didn't know the league he was now playing in even existed. It turned out he wasn't prepared for it, and now he was in deep shit.

In a fog, Ellis could remember the phone ringing and picking it up. "Ellis! El' ol' buddy, I've got news!" It was Travis Backster, his childhood friend and, now, a director of the

Regional Energy Authority. Travis sounded upbeat. He took the power of positive thinking to heart, and, for all Ellis knew, Travis could be calling to say his wife had died. No, that probably would have made Travis sound even happier.

"T, you sound good. What's up?"

"El', got back from the other Washington yesterday. I heard something I think you're going to like." Travis knew about iMUD's troubles, but didn't know the details.

"Yeah, so tell me." A Travis story was always good.

"I sat through some homeland security briefings. You know, new measures to make sure no one blows something up or dumps anthrax in the water. Employee background checks. Terrorist profiling for dummies. I was practically asleep so I almost missed it—the 2003 Homeland Environmental Liability Legislation. Heard of it?" Travis sounded smug.

"What the hell is that?"

"You got that right," Travis chuckled. "It is hell, H-E-L-L. But get this—the federal government will support these security measures with funding. That's a first. Here's what you'll really like. If a terrorist attack destroys property and disrupts operations for a state or local agency, the feds will pick up the tab for repairs or replacement."

For a second Ellis didn't say anything. "And this helps me how?"

"There's more." Travis sounded like a late-night TV commercial announcer. "The legislation basically gives you a do-over."

"What do you mean?"

"If the terrorist attack destroys infrastructure and interrupts operations, say at a power plant, how are you going to fulfill your power contracts? The legislation says the local agency can renegotiate contracts based on the post-attack operations. Kind of like bankruptcy."

"Shit, Travis, you may have just saved my life."

"What did you say, Ellis?" Dickie stood in front of him, looking pissed.

"Sorry, I must have zoned out. I was thinking about that time Travis... when he saved me down at the river."

"Yeah, that's nice, but your pal is a pain in my ass. This is the second time this month he's been hauled in here for operating stoned." Dickie let out a heavy sigh. "Next time he's going to get more than a slap on the wrist."

"Want me to talk with him?"

"No, I want you to get him cleaned up before he kills somebody."

"I'll see what I can do."

"Thanks." Dickie sat down "Okay. Back to Eddie Snead." Dickie picked up his pen and seemed to collect his thoughts. "Did Eddie have access to anything—you know, information, financial stuff, personal dirt, that sort of thing—at iMUD? Anything that might make somebody want him dead?"

"Not that I can think of," Ellis replied. "He didn't work there so he didn't even have a key to the building. The only time he was involved was at the board meetings."

"Okay," Dickie said as he scribbled. "The board meetings. Anything happen at a meeting recently?"

"Happen?"

"Yeah, confrontation, argument, somebody sitting in the back of the room staring at Eddie and not saying anything; anything at all that seemed suspicious?"

"No, nothing."

"You guys have videos of the meetings over at the iMUD information booth, right?"

"Yeah. We broadcast live on the local public service cable channel. Afterward, our video tech..."

"Cameron, right? She's a part-timer here at the station,

too," Dickie interrupted.

"Uh, yeah, she posts the videos on YouTube."

"YouTube?"

"Yeah, that puts them in the public record, and then we put in a link from the iMUD website."

"iMUD dot com?"

"No, that was taken. IndianMeadowsUtilityDistrict—all one word—dot com."

Dickie scribbled furiously. "How very convenient." He stopped and looked at Ellis. "Okay, thanks. I really appreciate your coming in. Sorry about that," he said and tipped his head at the window into the reception area where Travis' upper body lay draped over the counter.

"I'll have a talk with him, Chief." Ellis shook his head. "When he wakes up."

"I hope you have better luck than his sister." Dickie looked into the main office. Terry Backster sat in a chair crying.

"Terry's your new patrol officer?" Ellis asked. "I didn't recognize her in her uniform."

"Yeah, tough luck. Her first two arrests were her own brother." Dickie stood up, and Ellis quickly followed his lead. They shook hands and said their goodbyes. Ellis made for the door.

"Oh, one more thing, Ellis," Dickie said casually.

Fuck. Ellis stopped cold in the doorway. "What's that?"

"We received an anonymous tip about…" He pretended to look at his notes. "…uh, irregularities in the Utility's financial reports. You know anything about that?"

"Like what?" Ellis grabbed the doorframe. His knuckles were white.

"Not sure. That's all the tipster said. Maybe, accounts not balancing? Something like that?"

"No, all the accounts balance. They have to. I think you

might have a prankster instead of a tipster." Ellis offered a grim smile. "But Ray's the guy who knows the numbers inside and out. He'd be the one to talk to."

Dickie watched Ellis walk through the main office and out the front door. He sat for a moment rubbing his chin, then stood up, looked at himself in the mirror, and brushed his hair away from his forehead. He left the conference room, turned left down a short hallway, and opened an unmarked door.

The small room had a single window looking into the now empty conference room. Rudy jumped up and down repeatedly like a jack-in-the-box, and Juice sat in his wheelchair with his leg elevated. They were both laughing uncontrollably.

"Just what the fuck's so funny?" Dickie snapped.

"Hey, Chief." Juice said. "We were just picturing Rudy here as a prankster. You know, with the joker hat and collar with the little bells." They both dissolved into laughter again.

"Pop goes the weasel." Rudy finished the song, and then jumped as high as he could. Dickie couldn't help but smile.

"*Your* weasel's dirty, Dickie," Juice said, no longer laughing. "He's not a killer, but I think he has a pretty good idea of the who and why Eddie got killed."

"What makes you think that?"

"Me. I'm thinking I'm in that iMUD group and somebody else gets whacked, I'd be shitting bricks. But he wasn't nervous until you got to the financial stuff. That means he knows why your stiff got it, and he knows he doesn't have to worry about the same thing." Juice stopped to take a breath. "It's the financial stuff. I thought he was going to pull that door frame clean out of the wall. Yeah, he's dirty."

Dickie and Juice looked over at Rudy who finally started to settle down. Rudy coughed once, stifling a laugh, and smiled. "I really like YouTube."

Chapter 11

"Travis, it used to be women." Ellis dragged his buddy down the street. He was pissed off.

"El', old buddy. I know. Don't you think I know?" Travis looked down at the death grip Ellis had on his arm to keep him upright. "But, shit man, the stuff is everywhere now. It's so easy." He stopped suddenly almost tipping both of them into the street. "And you know how weak I am."

"Yeah, poor me, poor me."

"Hey, I'm sorry. But thanks for bailing me out."

"Fuck you, Trav. Let's get something to eat."

"Oh, yeah! Wa-Wa here we come." He pumped his fist like he had thrown a strike. "I like the candy at the spa."

"No, Travis." He felt like he was talking with a toddler. "Those girls are what got you into this mess to begin with."

"Oh, but Ellis—she was so cute. And those little lozenges are so tasty. C'mon. We should go." Travis started tugging toward where the cops had parked his car.

"Sorry, Trav. Right now we're going to get some food into you." They turned left on River Street. "We're going to the Tuck 'er."

Travis stared down the street at the wobbly neon sign marking the bar's entrance. As the sign swung in the wind, the red tube that spelled "'er" flashed on and off. When they reached the door, Ellis grabbed the worn, brass handle and pulled the door open. He stepped through first and yanked Travis in after him. Ellis blinked away the daylight as his eyes adjusted to the dim interior.

Travis pulled away and clasped his hands as if in prayer. "God, Ellis…I love this place." He ran over to the bar. "A couple of drafts, Joe." Travis rubbed his hands together in anticipation.

"And a bowl of nuts," Ellis added, walking up behind him.

Joe peered intently at his hands, or something in them, then raised his head and scanned the room as if trying to figure out where he was. Ellis could never tell with Joe; he could be napping on his feet, tying a bass fly, or contemplating the lint in his navel. Joe stood up, pulled two mugs from the chiller, and filled them from arbitrary taps on the bar. One glass was probably ale, the other half full with chocolaty brown liquid topped with three inches of foam. Joe pushed the mugs across the bar. He grabbed a bowl, held it up to the light, blew into it to remove some crumbs, and set it on the bar. He wiped his hands on his jeans, reached into a giant plastic container, and tossed a couple handfuls of nuts into the bowl.

"Thanks, Joe." Travis grabbed the beers. Ellis took the nuts and followed Travis over to an open booth in the back. Travis slid in opposite Ellis and pushed the dark beer over to him. The foam had vanished. Ellis gazed at his half-empty glass with apprehension.

Travis took a long swig and belched. "Ellis, my friend, you have saved my life." He grabbed a handful of nuts and began tossing them one by one into the air. He caught a couple then pulled a piece of fluff out of his mouth. He offered the nuts to Ellis.

"No thanks." He shook his head. "Travis, you have to clean yourself up. You don't need that stuff."

"Nope, you're right." Travis leered at Ellis. "But it sure is fun."

"Shit." Ellis shook his head. "I can't even remember what fun feels like."

"Still bad at the Utility?" Travis tilted his face to the ceiling and caught another nut on the fly.

Ellis simply nodded. "Worse. Worse than the last time we were here." Ellis drained his flat beer and tried to get Joe's attention.

The Tuck 'er Inn was a great place to talk because nobody paid any attention to anyone else. This included the bartender. Ellis got up and walked over to the bar. Joe twirled a fishing lure in his right hand, the hook hidden by a white feather.

"Joe, another round. Both ales this time."

Joe put the fly down and poured the beers, pushed the mugs over to Ellis, and returned his attention to his lure. Ellis carried the beers back to the booth and sat down.

"I'm here for ya, buddy," Travis said. "So, what gives?"

"It's that legislation you told me about. I can't stop thinking about it. This... this is going to sound crazy. I was thinking about someone blowing up the dam."

"What are you worried about? We talked about this. Terrorists aren't going to target your dam. They'd want something that'd make more of a statement." Travis tipped his head back and caught another Beer Nut. He smiled as he chewed.

"No. What if something goes wrong? What if our plan ends up wrecking the dam?" Ellis regarded his friend and waited for it to sink in.

The airborne nut bounced off Travis' nose. For a moment,

he looked confused, then his smile returned. "El', you got to think positive." He shook his head. "We went over all this at the last board meeting. It's not going to destroy the dam…just mess things up a little."

"But T, it's worse than we thought. The dam needs a lot of work—work it should have had already. There's no money to pay for repairs and won't be for a long time. And the energy contracts only make it worse. That dam is a disaster," Ellis lowered his voice. "Maybe another disaster—a bigger disaster—is exactly what we need."

"Hold on there, El'. I know those energy contracts have cost iMUD a load of dough. But what's the deal with the repairs?"

"Jimmy D got these incredibly low bids for maintenance work, which couldn't have come at a better time. The savings helped offset the losses on the energy contracts. It made the numbers look better, so I gave him the go ahead."

"Sounds like a good deal." Travis flipped another nut.

"It did at the time." Ellis drained his mug. "But then, we got this call that the wife of one of the contractors went into labor. So one of our guys went into the turbine area to tell him and saw that they weren't actually replacing the corroded pipes, just wrapping them in new insulation."

"It's a scam?"

"Yeah, I knew Jimmy was up to something, but my name's on the contracts. If this gets out, I'm done."

Travis pensively chewed some more Beer Nuts. "Hmmm, yeah, I can see how that might not look good on your résumé. So, what you're saying is we need to get the boys to put in a little extra effort. Something that will make the maintenance problems just disappear." Ellis nodded, and Travis continued. "Stupid people will do anything for a little money. And it's even better when they're *our* stupid people."

He stared past Ellis at Joe's regulars.

"How do we make that happen?" Ellis asked as Travis reached for his cell phone.

"I'm on it, El'." Travis pushed a couple of buttons and switched the phone to speaker mode. He laid it on the table between them. Two rings sounded, and a man answered.

"Robert Presseley's office," the voice said in a smooth, icy tone. Travis and Ellis both winced.

"Timothy, good afternoon. This is Travis Baxter and Ellis Spelt."

"Yes?"

"Hey, Timothy, we're in a meeting here and need to talk to Dr. P. Is he around?"

"May I ask what this is concerning?" They heard papers rustling in the background.

"Sure." Travis nodded at Ellis. "Just tell him it's about the cash-flow enhancement issues we discussed last month."

A soft click came through, and the line went quiet. A few seconds later, an impatient baritone picked up the call.

"Boys, how can I help you?" Presseley said, all business.

"Dr. P." Travis winked at Ellis. "I'm in a meeting with Ellis, and we're talking about some new developments at the Utility. I think we might want to ramp up the level of effort in that contract we discussed."

"Well, that sounds interesting." Presseley's voice switched to smooth politician. "This isn't the place or time, and we don't have all the interested parties either."

Ellis and Travis both nodded their heads in agreement.

Presseley went on. "Let's discuss the changes tomorrow. Then we can finalize the deal with our consultants."

"Ahhhh," Travis and Ellis whispered together.

"Good work staying on top of this. You two will work with Timothy tomorrow to add the proper language to the contract." The line went dead.

Beads of sweat dotted Ellis' forehead. Travis grinned from ear to ear. He tossed two Beer Nuts in the air and snagged them both.

Chapter 12

Three weeks after his accident, Juice Verrone was sitting alone in a booth at the Tuck 'er Inn. June Presseley walked through the door like she was on a mission from God. Juice struggled to his feet. She put her hand on his shoulder and pushed him back down into his chair.

"No need to stand up for me, Ted." June shook his hand and held on for a little too long. She inspected his light-weight plastic walking cast and shook her head. "You have to keep that elevated for another week."

"Yeah, it's kind of tough in here though." Juice pointed at the battered furniture with his cane. "These chairs don't lend themselves to elevation."

"Shall we eat?" June waved to get Joe's attention. Not getting a response she shouted, "Joe! How about a little service over here?" She looked at Juice demurely. "So, how are you progressing with your stretches?" She slowly closed her eyes, then opened them, like a cat contemplating a small bird.

Juice couldn't keep up with these rapid-fire transformations. "Uh, pretty good." He tapped the cast with his cane. "Glad to get this thing on. Those crutches were killing me."

"Hi, Joe." June looked up at the barely attentive bartender. "I'll have the burger—rare, no toppings, no bread—and a double order of fries."

Juice raised his eyebrows in disbelief. "The usual, Joe," he ordered when Joe's attention shifted to him.

Joe wrote on his pad and retreated into the kitchen.

"You have a usual?" June smirked.

"Yeah, pastrami on rye, dark mustard." He could taste it already. "Since I have to walk so much, lunch here has become my therapy destination. I got Joe to order some in." He paused while June stared vacantly past his head at the TV at the end of the bar. He pulled his leg off the seat next to him and turned to look.

On the screen, a pair of bathtubs sat in the back of a pickup truck parked on a cliff overlooking a flaming-red Pacific sunset. A man relaxed in one of the tubs. In the other, a woman. They held hands across the gap between the tubs. The Cialis logo faded in over the sunset, and the emblem for Lilly Pharmaceuticals appeared in the lower corner of the screen. Juice could barely make out the voice-over: "Remember, seek medical help immediately if you suffer a priapism, an erection lasting more than four hours." The screen faded. He turned back to June as she delicately blotted a drop of saliva from the corner of her mouth.

"You okay, June?"

"That sounds painful."

"What?"

"That priapism thing. Imagine…four hours." Her eyes misted over. She took a deep breath and exhaled. "Anyway, back to business. Today, I want to evaluate your progress. We'll take a turn up to the park and see how you're doing." She squirmed in her chair. "Mechanically, that is."

Joe showed up with their order and put the burger in

front of Juice. He picked it up and passed it across to June. Joe didn't notice and put the sandwich down in front of June next to the burger.

"Medical marijuana," June whispered as he walked away. She passed the sandwich across the table. "He just hasn't been the same since that law went into effect." She smiled coyly, then dug into her burger like she hadn't eaten in a week.

After lunch, they headed up River Street to the park. "You're doing much better, Ted." June grabbed his arm and squeezed. She put her other hand on his back and rubbed gently. "Now let's try stepping on and off the curb as you walk." She leaned into him and whispered, "I'll keep you steady."

They bumped along, and June held him against her chest as he stepped from the curb down to street level and then back up. "Oh, yes, Ted. Very good." They turned the corner onto the two-lane road known as the Wanaduck Highway. "Okay, that's enough for now. You're *so* big and strong, I don't know if I could keep you from falling over if you lost your balance." She gave him another cat look.

They crossed the highway and entered the Wanaduck Memorial Park. A black basalt obelisk sat at the center of a small grass square. A circular asphalt walkway looped through the park connecting the four gated entrances.

"Let's do a quick circuit around the monument for today." She pointed at the plinth about 150 feet away. "And then I'll let you go until our next appointment." They climbed the slight hill and circled the polished pillar.

"Oh, look at the time." June glanced at her phone. "You're making a lot of progress, Mr. Foteo." She poked him playfully on the chest. "In another couple of weeks, I won't be able to keep up." She turned away and waved back over her head. "Bye-bye for now."

You have gotta be kidding me. Juice shook his head and sat down on one of the benches symmetrically spaced around the monument.

"So, I'm sitting at the house and it hits me—I forgot my jacket," Juice said.

Dickie leaned his chair back against the railing of Juice's front porch. Rudy sat upright with his chair planted firmly on the ground. Each of them held a can of Rainier lager. "So I start hobbling back to the Tuck 'er to get it."

Rudy perched on the edge of his chair, listening in rapt attention.

"It's nice out, so I decide to backtrack through the park. I'm coming up on the monument from the north and I hear these voices," Juice said as he leaned in. "It was that guy with the Hawaiian shirts talking with June."

"Yeah, Ray Milton. He's the finance guy at the Utility," Dickie said.

"Right. That's the guy. Well, they look like they're not too happy to see each other. Talking kind of, you know, stiff. But I didn't want to interrupt, so I'm hanging back out of sight." Juice held his hand out and pointed to his thumb to show his location in the park. "I'm like here."

"Then what, Ted?" Rudy leaned forward.

"So, she tells him she's going to be running the iMUD Picnic Committee this year. This Ray guy looks like he wants to be any place else but there. But she keeps talking. She asks if anybody in his department could help out. Then he goes, 'Yeah, maybe Ellis or Sabrina.' Ray's looking at the cracks in the tiles, but he keeps yakking. Like, 'Oh wait. They're not together anymore. Maybe Ellis, then. I'll get you his number.' He pulls out his phone. Still hasn't looked at her."

Rudy rocked back and forth. "This is going to be good."

"Then Ray's phone rings, and I thought he was going to jump out of his skin." Juice smacked his cane on the porch. Rudy jumped. "Then our boy says, 'June, I have to take this,' and he turns away. June stares at his back for a few seconds and walks off. But Ray doesn't leave." Juice gave his audience a crooked smile. "Ray sits down on a bench and answers his phone. He says, 'This is Mischievous Milton.' You're going to love this." He paused for effect. "'Your wireless sex therapist.'"

The punch line caught Dickie mid-sip, and beer sprayed out of his mouth. He pitched the chair forward onto all fours and tried to stop laughing and coughing. Juice waited. Dickie wiped the beer from his face.

"Ray goes on talking loud, like he forgot that the mike was on his head and not in another county. He says, 'How can I help you today?' I look across and see June looking back over her shoulder." Juice took a sip of beer. "She's hearing all this shit too, so she sits down on another bench. Kind of behind him."

Dickie drained his beer as a precaution.

"Ray's talking like he's on stage. 'Why, Miss Bunny! You *are* a naughty, naughty girl. Do you need a *spanking*?' I'm about ready to bust a gut. I see June lean in like she's trying to hear better. Ray doesn't know we're both listening. He just keeps talking. 'No spanking, eh?' Then he switches into this kind of voice. 'Then perhaps "The Dark Closet"?' I tell you, I almost pissed my pants at that."

Dickie popped another beer. "Pretty good Dracula there, Ted. That is too funny."

"Wait, wait," Juice put his can on the floor. "It gets better. Ray goes on. 'Oh, yeah, sorry. I forgot you were afraid of the dark.'" The three men erupted in laughter. "But Ray's getting a little pissed off. Next he tries sounding like some surfer-boy. You know, like Dickie here when he's imitating his girlfriend." Dickie flipped him off, but Rudy nodded in agreement. "He keeps going. 'How about "The Pool Boy?" You really liked that last summer.'"

Juice reached down for his beer, took a long drink, then looked from Rudy to Dickie and back, giving them a conspiratorial smirk. "So, I check on June and she's leaning back on her bench. She's got one arm wrapped around her chest and the other pinned between her legs. She's rocking back and forth, getting off on this shit. And Ray still hasn't shut up. 'No, you're right. It is still a little cold to be thinking about water.' Ray's sounding angry now. He shuts up and thinks for a second. Then he shouts, 'I've got it.' Mischievous Milton drops it down a notch and gets this lounge-lizard voice going on. June is quivering but she tilts her head to hear better. 'Are you ready for it?' June starts nodding her head yes. 'Are you sure?' She's nodding faster and faster." Juice stopped and took another sip of his beer. "Then Ray yells, 'Waterfowl Bondage!'"

Rudy fell off his chair onto the floor. Juice and Dickie broke out laughing.

"Careful, Rudy. You don't want to get hurt before the end of the story." Dickie helped Rudy back up.

"Now June looks like she's going to pop. Ray says. 'They open their bills and start caressing you with their soft tongues.' I'm like 'Huh?' but I can hear June moaning from across the park. And Ray's still talking, 'Yes…They are *very* soft…and pointy.'"

Dickie collapsed in a fit of laughter.

Juice went on. "June screams, 'Oh my God, yesssss!' and Ray jumps to his feet. His cell goes spinning through the air and busts open on the ground. He's staring at June like he had been condemned to die. June scrambles over the armrest of the bench, like she can't get to him fast enough. She wraps her arms around his waist and pulls him up against her. Then reaches down, grabs his butt with both hands and pulls. Hard. She's whispering in his ear. Our boy Ray can't even get any words out. He's going like 'What? Where?' over and over. June starts dragging him toward the statue. Ray says, 'I've got a little camp right outside town.' He's shaking like a leaf. 'It's only a trailer and…' They walk right by me like I wasn't even there. She says to him, 'Take me there. Now! You'll be glad you did.'"

Juice waited for the laughter to subside. "Anyway, I thought you might want this." He reached into his jacket pocket and handed the fragments of Ray's cell phone to Dickie. "Might be something useful there."

Juice reached into his other pocket. "I also found this next to Ray's bench." He opened his hand revealing a small plastic fish with a silver tab sticking out of its mouth.

Dickie looked at the fish, then up at Juice. "Not another one."

Chapter 13

Juice came back out onto the porch with another six-pack and handed out beers to his two friends. Rudy put the fresh, unopened can on the floor next to his other unopened can. He was still working on his first.

Dickie studied the can. "Uh, Ted, you know Washington is famous for its micro-brews. Why do you buy this shit?"

"Reminds me of Schlitz." Juice looked at his Rainier. "So, Rudy," Juice patted him on the leg, "you got any interest in meeting June?"

Rudy's face went beet red. "I don't think I'd like that. She seems so…" He thought for a moment. "Direct." He shook his head. "No, I don't think I'd like to meet her."

"It's weird," Juice said to Dickie. "From about ten feet away she's a total dish. When you get up close, there's all these little lines like she rear-ended a semi carrying a load of Ginsu knives."

"They're scars," Dickie said. "Everybody always said she was the best-looking woman in town, but when she hit forty she decided she didn't look young enough. Since I've been here, she's gone to Costa Rica twice. She'll probably keep it up until her ears meet at the top of her head."

Juice choked on his beer. Rudy just looked confused.

"But this Cialis stuff..." Dickie rested his elbows on his knees and held onto his beer with both hands. "This is some strange shit. A few weeks ago we got a call from the Presseleys' neighbor. She heard screaming from inside their house."

"That's the big white house on River Street?" Juice asked.

"Yeah. Bill went over with Terry, and it sounded like somebody was hurt really bad inside the house. So, they were pounding on the door, but nobody answered. Bill kicked it in right when the paramedics got there. They found Presseley in a big room with twelve-foot ceilings, wearing some kind of fuzzy jump suit."

"June?"

"No, Robert. And it gets better...he was stuck about three feet up a Velcro wall, screaming, 'It hurts!' over and over with a hard-on sticking out of the front of his suit."

Rudy's beer can fell out of his hand and rolled under the porch rail into the shrubs. He turned and looked through the railing to see where it landed.

Dickie said, "June was naked in a leather swing. Unconscious."

Rudy jerked up like he'd been shocked. He smacked his head against the top rail and spun back around.

"Careful there, little buddy." Juice said.

"Anyway..." Dickie took a long pull on his beer. "That's when I showed up."

"The paramedics start trying to get him off the wall. One of them is up there on a ladder with a pair of scissors trying to cut the Velcro. Bill's holding Robert's legs to keep him from falling. The medic slips and nicks Robert's back with the shears. He jerks, and his woody hits Bill in the side of his head. Bill yelps and lets go. The Velcro starts ripping, the suit tears away, and Robert lands face down on the floor. Luckily, the fall knocked him out."

"Luckily?" Rudy asked.

"Yeah." Dickie glanced sidelong at Juice. "He stopped screaming."

"Hah!" Juice slapped his leg. "So *that's* why she was so interested in the Cialis ad today."

"June was talking to you about Cialis?"

"Yeah. There was an ad on TV when we were at the Tuck 'er. I thought she was going to cry."

Dickie laughed. "Maybe she got the idea from the commercial?"

The sun had dropped low, and only the tops of the trees were still lit. Juice got up and switched on the porch light.

Dickie continued the story. "Terry found a blanket and wrapped June in it. She starts waking up and she's mumbling about Cialis and a mojito. Terry gives her a little shake and she snaps out of it. She's looking around at everybody like *what the fuck?* She says, 'Robert?' I tell her he's at the hospital. She blinks her eyes like a cat and goes, 'Mmmmmm…it worked.' I ask her what worked. She says, 'The Cialis, silly.'"

"She mention the bathtubs?" Juice chuckled.

"Yeah, she did." Dickie put his empty can on the floor. "Apparently, she browbeat the pharmacist to fill a prescription for Robert that she claimed was a refill. He sold her four pills just to get her out of the store. So when Robert gets home she has a mojito waiting."

"She told you this?"

"Yeah, no hesitation at all." Dickie reached out his hand, and Juice passed him the next to last beer. "She said she dressed him in the fuzzy suit and made him climb up a ladder and stick himself to the wall."

"This sounds like some kind of joke."

"All the time she's feeding him the mojito."

"What's that?" Rudy asked. Dickie and Juice looked at him.

"It's a kind of cocktail, little buddy."

"Oh, okay."

"He finishes the drink, but—"

"It's got Cialis in it!" Rudy brightened like a light had come on.

"That's right, Rudy. All four pills. Our girl gets naked and straps herself into the swing. When the Cialis kicks in, June ends up fucking herself unconscious and Robert into the hospital." Dickie stretched.

"Excuse me." Rudy said quietly and walked into the house.

"What's your friend's story?" Dickie nodded at the door.

"Don't really know. He's got some dough and he sure is good with financial stuff."

"I noticed."

"I just don't think he gets out much."

The door opened, and Rudy peered out at them. "Is four hours a long time?"

Chapter 14

It took a second after Juice and Dickie stopped laughing before they realized that Rudy had returned with his computer bag. "You guys are going to like this." Rudy pulled his MacBook Pro out of the bag and set it up on Juice's small porch table. "I've been looking at the iMUD commission meetings on YouTube." He opened the lid, and the glow from the screen bathed their faces in blue light.

Juice patted Rudy on the shoulder. "Jeez, little buddy, we do need to introduce you to June."

"Very funny, Ted." He stared up at Juice fearlessly. "And this is coming from some tough guy hiding out in B.F., Washington."

Juice grinned. "You got a point there, Rudy. I'm sorry."

Rudy looked back at the screen with a gleam in his eyes. "First off, I want to show you a typical meeting." His hands whipped across the keyboard. "Here's the last meeting of last year."

"Do we have to watch the whole thing?" Dickie moaned.

"No, only the ending." Rudy clicked to the end of the progress bar. "Okay, here's the last, uh, twelve seconds." He pressed Play. The threesome watched a few people milling around the dais, like fish waiting for their turn up a salmon ladder, with a soundtrack of scraping chairs and muffled voices. The screen faded to black and the playback stopped.

"See how it ended?"

Juice and Dickie looked at each other skeptically. "Uh, yeah. But?" Dickie asked.

"It ended cleanly. Nice fade out. Professionally done." Rudy popped up another video. "Now, *this* is the recording of a different meeting. It's the one from when your tech person left the equipment running."

"Cameron."

"Yeah, and there's a problem with it." Rudy dragged the play slider to near the end of the video. "Now, watch the time."

Rudy pressed Play. The screen showed two men pushed unceremoniously out of the room with, what appeared to be, a full Indian war bonnet tossed out after them. The door slammed behind them. "Look at the timer—one hour, three minutes, six seconds."

The video continued with Robert Presseley's deep baritone straining the computer's tinny speakers. "Any further business?" The gavel banged down before anyone had a chance to speak. "Meeting adjourned." The men on the dais stood and stretched as the audience started filing out. The video cut to a few seconds of on-screen static then suddenly stopped.

"See, now it's fifty-two seconds." Rudy pointed at the timer. "It was forty-six seconds from when the door closed to the end. This video didn't fade out like the first one. The picture cut to snow and finished. No editing at all."

"You going somewhere with this?" Juice shook his head.

"That man in the Indian war bonnet?"

"Yeah," Dickie and Juice said at the same time.

"That's Chief Shecky of NANOOC." Rudy clicked a couple of buttons.

Another video window appeared. It showed a close-up of Chief Shecky with the title "The Quest for Rightful Compensation" superimposed. The title faded, and the Chief started to speak. "Recently there were developments that concern us all at the Indian Meadows site. You'll see how badly your delegation was treated in the following excerpt." Chief Shecky faded from view, and the iMUD commission chambers faded in.

"You have gotta be kidding me," Juice said over the video.

"Shhhh," Rudy shushed him. "Just watch."

In the center of the video, four people sat in a group. The two at each end were dressed as salmon. In the middle a woman with straight, blond hair wore a headband with a feather tucked into it. Standing next to her was an Asian woman with short, black hair wearing what looked like black pajamas. One of the salmon-people shouted, "Down with the dam!" The group stood up and held a banner over their heads. It said, "Fish are people too!" On each end of the banner, they had drawn a cartoon looking like a set of stairs in profile with tiny fish jumping from step to step.

Rudy hit Pause.

"Rudy?" Dickie looked down at him. No response.

"Ruuuuudy?" Juice gave a try. Nothing.

"Jesus," Juice whispered and pointed at the screen. "He's looking at the girl."

Dickie laughed. "Those are the vegetarian wackos that live in the commune on the other side of the river."

"Yes," Rudy whispered. "Vegetarians. Isn't she beautiful?"

"Rudy," Juice gave him a shake. "C'mon back. You were

trying to show us something other than your new girlfriend here."

"Uh, right. Yes." Rudy pressed Play.

Presseley banged the gavel and called for order. The protesters sat down obediently. "Thank you for your input," Presseley said. "Perhaps next time you could be a bit less dramatic?" He pointed his gavel at a man who sat at the end of the second row. "Now, Mr. Norbert, I believe you asked to comment."

The man got up slowly and stood in the aisle. He cleared his throat and nervously addressed the board. "I'm interested in finding out if you intend to do the right thing is all." He stuffed his hands into the pockets of his jeans. "All of us here could be ay-ffected if you decide to build another dam or put up some kind of new-fangled energy dee-vices."

Presseley began, "Mr. Norbert— "

Chief Shecky stood up and cut Presseley off. "I'm interested in the rightful owners being compensated!" he announced with an energetic twist of his head, which shook his feathered headdress. A grizzled braid of hair hung halfway down his back.

Presseley frowned at the second speaker and rubbed his temples. "And you are?"

"Chief Shecky Schmulker." The man stood with his moccasined feet set apart and glared at Presseley. "The Yakima tribe is the rightful owner of that land, and they got bupkis!"

"Uh, Mr. Schmulker..."

"Chief Shecky."

"Yeah, okay, Chief Shecky, are you a member of the Yakima tribe?"

"No, Mr. Presseley, I am not." Shecky hooked his forefingers into the front loops of his overalls and rocked back on his heels. "My name is Ira Schmulker. I am a retired attorney from Piscataway, New Jersey. Mr. Presseley, I moved out here five years ago to help Native Americans reacquire rights that were taken from them unjustly. The honorific title, Chief, is for helping the Yakima tribe open three casinos."

Presseley rubbed his eyes.

"Now, wait just a second," Norbert interrupted. He narrowed his eyes and scowled at Chief Shecky. "You mean to say that those Yakimas are raking in hundreds of thousands of dollars—hell, most likely, millions—at their casinos, and they want money for the land along the Columbia?"

Chief Shecky flipped the tethered feathers behind his back. "What do the casinos have to do with compensation for their land? You said yourself that the utility just took the land."

"Well, yeah, but the government lets the Indians build casinos in return for the land they gave up. If they took my land, I wouldn't get to build a casino!" Norbert took a step toward the Chief.

"The noble Yakima gave up their forefathers' hunting grounds, their birthright! Casinos are an inconsequential gesture compared to what the tribe has lost." Chief Shecky pushed his palms toward the sky, as if worshipping the natural gods of the land.

Norbert took another step closer to Chief Shecky, and the muscles in his jaw began clenching. The camera followed him.

"Mr. Norbert. Mr. Schmulker." Presseley tried to regain control of the meeting. "Perhaps we should take this discussion—"

"You lousy revisionist dickhead," Norbert growled and kicked a chair out of the way.

"Paleface asshole!" Chief Shecky shouted. He tossed off his war bonnet and dropped into a crouch holding his wrinkled, white arms out in front of him. With one hand, he beckoned at Norbert to bring it on.

Norbert lunged for the Chief, who sidestepped deftly. Norbert flew past him, putting his hands out to break his fall. Chief Shecky leaped onto his back and grabbed a handful of Norbert's greasy hair.

Somebody shouted from the gallery, "Careful Bud, he might scalp you."

The camera zoomed in on the fight as several men in the audience jumped up and pulled the two apart. Norbert and Chief Shecky glowered at each other and muttered, but they were quickly losing steam. Timothy Bentle snatched open the fire exit, and the two got tossed out into the street. Somebody threw the Chief's headdress through the open door and slammed it closed, muffling the sounds of the argument outside.

Rudy paused the video. "Okay, this whole video's shorter than the official version, but look at the time." He pointed at the screen. "That's at the same place when the door closed behind the Chief in the official video."

He clicked Play to start the video up again. The image quickly focused on the chairman. The ruckus in the room quieted, and Presseley spoke. "Okay, let's move on here! Any further business?" The gavel banged down. "Meeting adjourned." The hall emptied fairly quickly.

Rudy let the video play. The camera continued to record the vacant room. Slowly the image faded out.

"Shit." Dickie did the arithmetic in his head. "That's a minute and twenty seconds. This video runs over half a minute past the end of the official one."

"So?" Juice didn't get it.

"That means the meeting was still being recorded after it was officially over." Dickie looked at him. "Cameron was right. Somebody tampered with the original version."

Rudy nodded, then added, "But somebody *else* has the whole thing."

Chapter 15

Ralphie Hinz's aging desktop computer squeaked like the warm-up wheel at the Run for the Rodents hamster race. A vibration coming from somewhere inside the computer had buzzed a lamp, glass bong, and coffee cup filled with ashes dangerously close to the edge of the case.

Ralphie barely heard the loud ding from the computer over the din of his neighbor's wife and girlfriend screaming at each other from the trailer next door. He took a swig of beer every time he heard, "Stupid whore." This had gotten him through his first six-pack of Natural Ice, and now it was time for another. He snatched another Natty from the fridge, climbed over the stained futon that doubled as his sofa, and went to look at the monitor. The new message was a bite on his "Pest removal specialist" posting on craigslist.

The message read: "I have two large pests to exterminate. My neighbors are PETA members, so the extermination has to be discreet. What do you charge?" Vague. Indirect. Always a good sign that the work was illegal and paid well. Ralphie rubbed his hands together in anticipation.

Ralphie liked this so much better than his old job at

Orkin. A stupid uniform and a lousy paycheck for wearing it. Then they fired him just because he thought that the lady's tiny dog was a rat and gave it a shot of pesticide. The nasty little poodle just flopped over on its back with its legs curled up. Like the spiders.

Ralphie took a slug from his Natty and fired off a reply. "Cool. I can handle big pests. Whatever discreet is, I can be it. Setup is ten-grand plus one large a day until the job is done. Figure ten days."

Soldier of Fortune classified ads used to be the standard. But now, the Internet made finding clients so much easier and safer. No more "I know a guy who knows a guy." No names, no faces. Temporary email addresses. Even payments were more convenient with PayPal.

Twenty minutes and three straight losing games of Spider Solitaire later, a loud bleep burped from the computer. Ralphie jumped, spilling beer from a fresh can onto the keyboard. He blotted the keys with his shirt. Cards moved around like an invisible hand played the game. He hoped he had gotten all the beer. His last keyboard stopped working after he ran it through the dishwasher.

He opened the email. *Yes!* They wanted his PayPal information. No question about the charges. The message said to go to Wanaduck, Washington, and get a room at Whitey's Fishin' Inn under the name "Hugo Drax." Funds would be sent to his PayPal account.

He pulled out the road atlas. A dark brown coffee ring circled Coeur D'Alene, Idaho, his hometown. It looked like the interstate would take him almost all the way to Wanaduck. Only one right turn before he got to the Columbia River.

This called for a celebration. Ralphie dug out the French's French Fried Onions container in the cabinet next to the fridge and opened it. The smell of the can reminded him of his grandmother's Thanksgiving green bean casserole. Ralphie peered inside like he had just opened a treasure chest. He picked out one pink and one blue pill. *I wonder what these are?* He popped them in his mouth, washed them down with beer, and left the container open on the counter.

The pills were the one thing he missed about the Orkin job—finding those poorly hidden personal stashes. In the houses he serviced, he helped himself to the kids' pot, old prescription bottles under the beds, whatever he found. No one ever complained. What were they going to say? "Hey, honey, I think the Orkin guy stole some of my Viagra."

After several more losing games of solitaire, his palms were sweating, and he noticed the brightly-colored astronauts on the backs of the cards. *Why are they waving at me?* Astronauts made him think of adventure, and that made him think of his new job.

He shoved a Black Sabbath CD into his boom box. *Wait, I'm heading to Washington.* He shuffled through his piles of disks and pulled out *Bleach*. He pushed the play button, and Kurt Cobain started mumbling "Blew." *Yeah, a little Nirvana is much better.* Ralphie bopped along with the music as he went into his bedroom to pack.

He pulled his well-worn duffel out of the closet and tossed it on the bed, then went back to the closet and grabbed two plaid cotton shirts on hangers. He held them by the shoulders and shook them until the hangers fell onto the floor. He could feel small nubs in the cotton. *Ooh! Like little nipples.* Ralphie could have stood there for hours, playing with the fabric, but shook off the feelings, rubbed his fingertips over the cloth one more time, and stuffed the shirts into the bottom of the duffel.

He found a pair of jeans on the floor. He picked them up, sniffed them, then rubbed his fingertips in small circles on the denim. *So soft.* He reached into the duffel and stroked the already packed shirts. *Wow!* Reluctantly, he wadded up the jeans and crammed them in the duffel on top of the shirts.

He had to pee, which made him think about underwear. The laundry basket sat right in front of him. He pulled out two pairs of thick wool socks and two pairs of brightly-colored briefs, and then threw them all against the wall. They fell to the floor. They were fine. He picked them up and tossed them into the duffel.

Turning back to his closet, he stumbled into the bathroom door. A bottle of baby oil on the sink caught his eye. *I almost forgot.*

He still had to pee.

He marched to the bathroom and lifted the lid. *Yuck.* He dropped his jeans and his underwear and grabbed his dick. The skin was so soft. The stream gave a soothing burble as it hit the water. The sound bounced around in his now nearly vacant skull. It sounded like sunshine. He shook off the last few drops and stared at his dick. It started to rotate up and to the left, his hand still holding on. The skin felt really soft. He reached over and grabbed the bottle of baby oil off the sink.

Ralphie shuffled into the bedroom with his pants around his ankles. He kicked off his pants and underwear and squeezed a pool of oil into his right palm. His dick was staring right at him now.

"That's right, Buster." He carefully smeared the cool, silky oil all over. His hand stroked the shaft once, then again, and again. That felt *really* good. "Hooo, yeah!" Ralphie began hopping, timing his jumps so his feet landed as his hand started on the upstroke. *Good!* He hopped higher. *Really good!* Sweat began to break out on his forehead. Ralphie tilted his head back. He saw Phyllis floating on the ceiling.

"Phyllis! Do you want to play?" Ralphie giggled, and grabbed one of Phyllis' helium-inflated feet as he hopped in the air. He snatched at her thigh with his left hand. Because of the oil, it took three tries before he got his left arm around her back. He stuck his right hand into one of the several orifices thoughtfully provided by the designer. *I wonder what this is supposed to be?*

He hopped over to the bed. One more big jump and he was on the mattress. Working the springs, he could get some real height. "You like that, baby?" Ralphie hooted. He pulled his fingers out and thrust her onto his dick.

He hopped faster, thrusting himself harder into Phyllis with each leap. "That is really…" Hop. "Really…" Hop. "Really…" Hop. "Really…" Ralphie bent his knees and leaped high into the air. He screamed, "GOOOOOOOOD!" as he came. Phyllis hit the wall and burst with the impact. Ralphie's head slammed into the ceiling. He was unconscious before he hit the bed.

Chapter 16

The Tuck 'er Inn was only a few blocks from Juice's house. The cloudy weather typical of mid-March had broken, and the sun shone brightly for a change. A good day to take his bum leg out for a spin. Juice got a good rhythm going with his cane and left leg for the two and a half blocks down to Bridge Street. He was sweaty and sore by the time he made it over to River Street, but he felt good. A sandwich board in front of the Tuck 'er Inn beckoned with a buck fifty happy hour beers. Rainbow-hued tape secured a neatly printed flyer to the sandwich board's top edge. When Juice got close, he read:

TONIGHT
Wanaduck's NEWEST
Karaoke Star!
Mustafa "CousCous" Farouk

This has to be some kind of a joke. He opened the door and went inside. He needed a beer—or two.

The Master of Ceremonies, a very good-looking—very gay-looking—guy worked at setting up the karaoke machine. Juice placed good odds that the Middle Eastern-looking guy at the front table was Mustafa "CousCous" Farouk. The familiar instrumental strains of "My Way" began burbling from the speakers and ignited uncontrolled twitching in CousCous. Wanaduck's newest star appeared to be warmed up.

Joe, the bartender, leaned against the wall behind the bar rolling his shirttails between his fingers, lost to his surroundings. A meticulously-dressed guy sat at the bar as far away from Joe as possible. Juice had seen him around town from time to time.

He hobbled over to a stool a polite distance away from the one other customer at the bar. He sat down and rested his cast on the adjoining seat.

"Beer," Juice said, watching to make sure Joe grabbed Juice's personal mug from its hook on the wall and rinsed it before pouring a draft. Satisfied, he glanced at the other guy who held a sweating martini glass. Juice had never talked to him, but he needed a distraction today. "What's that you're drinking?" Juice asked casually.

"Vodka martini, shaken not stirred."

"You have gotta be kidding me," Juice said. "Like that Roger Moore guy in the James Bond movies?"

"Exactly. I'm his biggest fan. My name's Timothy, Timothy Bentle."

"I'm Ted Foteo." Juice took the carefully manicured hand Timothy extended. His grip was surprisingly firm. Timothy smiled, but the look in his eyes made it feel like the room temperature had dropped ten degrees.

Timothy smoothly released his hand from the grasp and took another sip of his drink. He gazed at Juice's cast and the cut-off jeans neatly hemmed half an inch above the fiberglass.

"Boating accident." Juice anticipated the question.

"Oh, no, that isn't it," Timothy chuckled. "I thought I was the only guy in this town who ironed his Levi's." He pointed at Joe's frayed red, green, and yellow plaid shirt. "That's more like the local couture."

"Old habit," Juice said and sighed. "My wife used to iron them for me."

He held up his glass in salute. "To old habits then." Juice tapped his mug against Timothy's martini glass and nodded. Timothy drained his drink. "Another one, Joe," he said.

The front door of the Tuck 'er opened, and both men automatically looked over.

Two guys stopped right inside the door. They wore plaid shirts and denims that looked like they could have been new sometime in the last five years. One wore work boots; the other had on a pair of old Nike walking shoes, the sewn-on logo dangling from a few stitches. Their faces appeared haggard, like they had a date with the hangman. They noticed Timothy, straightened up, and came over. One carried a thick folder with papers sticking out both ends. Two large rubber bands secured the bundle.

"Hey, Timothy, we're here for the meeting."

"Hello, Bill. Fred." Timothy's expression darkened. "Bill, I'm sorry to hear about your brother."

"Yeah, thanks." Bill gave Timothy a weak smile.

"Ted, this is Bill Snead and Fred Antzberg." Timothy indicated the two men in turn.

"Ted Foteo. Nice to meet you." Juice stuck out his hand and traded handshakes with the two men. Bill glanced at the door in the back wall of the room. Fred hitched the folder higher on his left arm, as if cradling a baby.

"Okay, guys, go on back. They're waiting for you," Timothy said, dismissing the two with a wave of his hand.

Bill and Fred shuffled to the back and disappeared through the dark wood door.

"I'm sorry, Ted. Got to go. My boss has a meeting back

there. If I don't keep an eye on things, it all goes to hell." Timothy knocked back the rest of his martini and replaced the glass exactly on the ring of condensation it had left on the bar.

"Yeah, no problem. I know how bosses are."

When Timothy swiveled around to get off his stool, his jacket swung against the bar and gave a resounding clunk. He walked to the back of the room, the left side of his jacket drooping from the weight of whatever was in the pocket. When Timothy opened the door to the back room, Juice caught a glimpse of several men sitting around a table. Bill and Fred were hunched over, writing. It looked like they were signing papers. Ellis, the guy Dickie had questioned at the station, leaned into view holding a folder. The door closed.

A squawk shot out of the speaker by the stage. Juice turned to see CousCous standing in the spotlight, a white linen jacket hooked on his left forefinger and hanging casually over his left shoulder. His right knee flexed to a disco beat. He lifted his face to the spotlight, his eyes closed. He opened his mouth and sang to the tune of *I Will Survive*. CousCous belted out what sounded like, "Thirst, I love air raid. I was batter fried. Kept tinkling I good ever give you-ooh a mother slide." He rotated his hips twice around then thrust his pelvis toward the closest table. Two women screamed.

Juice sipped his beer and smiled. *Now, that's entertainment.*

After fifteen minutes of heartfelt singing and mangled lyrics, the door to the back room swung open and hit the wall with a thud. A middle-aged man in a charcoal gray tailored suit marched through the doorway. He stopped and turned back toward the room. "I want copies ASAP," he snapped at no one in particular. The man spun back around and headed out the door. He smoothed the gray hair at his temple with his right hand. Juice checked out the dark circles under his eyes and a thickness around his waist. *The boss.*

Bill and Fred came out next, looking like they'd just seen a dead guy. They kept their heads down and followed the honcho outside. Ellis came out next, his eyes nervously skimming the length of the bar as he tightened his grip on the folder that Fred had brought. With his right hand he steered a stumbling Travis more-or-less toward the exit. At the end of the line, a Hawaiian shirt spattered with palm trees and martini glasses grabbed Juice's attention. The guy wearing it didn't seem nervous at all. They all bee-lined out the door. No beers. No good-byes.

Timothy came out last and closed the door behind him. He ambled back over to the bar and sat down next to Juice.

"Tough meeting?" Juice asked.

"No, everything went as planned. We were finalizing a maintenance contract," Timothy replied distractedly. "Joe, another round, please." He pointed his finger at his empty glass and Juice's half-filled mug.

"I'm okay, thanks." Juice put his hand over the top of the mug. He turned to face Timothy and inclined his head at the door. "But who's the guy on vacation?"

Timothy seemed confused for a second, then smiled. "Ah, Ray Milton. The guy is a piece of work. Ever since the Utility…"

"iMUD?"

"Yes." Timothy drank half of the fresh cocktail in one swig, then picked up the tiny sword and sucked off the olives. "Anyway, ever since the Utility went to a business casual dress code, Ray has been wearing those absolutely horrid shirts." He downed the rest of his martini and waved at Joe.

Juice stared at the little sabre slashing the air. "Careful with that, you could hurt yourself," he said and raised his eyebrows at Timothy.

"It's okay. I'm walking." A quiet snort resonated in

Timothy's nose. His new drink arrived, and he let it sit. "Excuse me for a minute." He stood up and wove his way back to the single bathroom that served both genders. As he returned, Timothy stumbled over an uneven floorboard. He glared at the offending plank, then walked to the bar and climbed back on his stool.

"I don't know where Ray gets those. Mail order from the Internet? Walmart?" He made a noise that almost sounded like a giggle. He leaned forward to pick up the cocktail glass, and there was another solid clunk on the bar. He took small sips of his fourth martini but didn't stop until he emptied the glass. He waved Joe over. "One more, Joe. Oh, wait." He shook his head. "Sorry, juice." Timothy said loudly and reached into his pocket. Juice flinched. "Joe, I meant juice, give me some grapefruit juice. I think I've had enough vodka. God, this thing is a pain in the ass." Timothy tossed a metal notary stamp onto the bar. "I think I'd rather carry a gun. Where was I?" Timothy peered intently at Juice for a moment. "That's right. Walmart. Jeez, I can't believe that place." Timothy slurred his words a little. "All those spandex-swaddled behemoths lumbering up and down the aisles."

"They are something to see," Juice murmured.

"Oh, oh." This time he definitely giggled. "You'll love this. I was coming back through Wenatchee after doing a job out of town." Timothy looked like he was having a hard time focusing. He took a long drink from a bottle of pink-tinted Snapple. "It was my turn to cook, but I was in a rush, so I figured I'd go the junk food route and pick up a frozen pizza for Simpson and me."

"Simpson?"

"My partner," Timothy said, tilting his head toward the well-groomed guy running the karaoke machine. "He owns the flower shop in town."

"Oh, okay." Juice shifted uncomfortably on his stool.

"Anyway, I run into Walmart and all of a sudden, I get this feeling. Do you know what I mean? You kind of sense danger before you see it?"

Juice regarded the slightly-built, well-dressed, and totally shit-faced guy sitting next to him and wondered what kind of danger he could sense.

"Two Walmart shoppers were oozing down the frozen food aisle. One of them was dressed in a housedress with foot-thick green, yellow, and red horizontal stripes. She looked like she stole the flag from some Caribbean island embassy. You could see the stains from the far end of the aisle. Disgusting." He shivered. "The other one was wearing a sweatshirt the size of a hot air balloon with silver lamé kittens pawing at balls of yarn. Oh. My. God."

"That does sound dangerous," Juice joked.

"I looked at the freezer case. There was only one pizza left. They were both going for it." Timothy snorted and blew juice on the bar. "Sorry." He extracted a white handkerchief from his pocket and wiped his face.

During the pause, Juice caught a few bars of CousCous crooning up a storm. He was now trying to sing "Bridge Over Troubled Water," but the lyrics came out: "Then sure cheery, peeling Paul, when beers are in your eyes, I will buy them all." CousCous reached his hand up to the light dramatically, his eyes still closed, his palms outstretched, as if beckoning to Allah.

"Anyway," Timothy continued, "at the last minute, they both pushed their carts to the side, grabbed the handles on the two adjacent freezer doors, and snatched them open. They dove in, but they just stopped dead. They tried to move forward, but they were stuck fast, their legs scrabbling on the linoleum, like a dog looking for traction on a hardwood floor.

They were grunting and trying to squeeze in one more inch to snap up that last pie."

"I'm not sure I'd want the pizza after seeing that," Juice said and waved his hand at Joe for his check.

"It gets better." Timothy sniggered. "I pushed my cart off to the side, leaned into the case, said 'Sorry, ladies,' and plucked that last pizza out of there."

Juice laughed, pushed himself off the stool, and clapped Timothy on the shoulder. "Timothy, good story, but I've got to go." He slapped seven dollars on the bar. "My leg's killing me, and I'm walking too."

"Of course. Take care of that leg," Timothy said.

Juice carefully put his weight on his walking cast and angled away from the bar. He crossed the room and pushed the front door open as CousCous hit his finale: "Like a bitch blowing bubbled water, I will wear your gown." The Karaoke King dropped his voice to a whisper and repeated the words. The music stopped, and the spotlight dimmed.

Chapter 17

Ralphie woke up to light shining through the tattered curtains of his trailer. Vinyl bits of Phyllis were glued all over his body. He peeled sticky pieces off his stomach and carefully unwrapped the plastic film from his dick. He looked at his dick and smiled. Buster smiled back. Ralphie picked the clock up from the floor: 9:32.

When he sat up, he picked Phyllis' face off the duffel bag on the floor. He pulled his clothes back on, hit the bathroom for a pee, and snatched up his bag. He had a trip to take. Ralphie slammed the flimsy aluminum door closed, shaking the trailer as he bounced down the steps. When he reached the ground, he heard a fierce scrabbling behind him. He turned, leaped up the stairs, and unlocked the door.

"C'mon, Mr. Willie. Road trip!" A grey and white ferret porpoised through the doorway and boarded the bag. He chuckled at Ralphie all the way to the car.

Ralphie's battered, pink Pontiac Vibe sat waiting in the weed-choked, gravel driveway next to his trailer. Its back end sagged like the trunk was full of dirt. Ralphie dropped the duffel, pulled up his drooping jeans, and opened the car door.

Mr. Willie jumped into the car, onto the dash, and wrapped his hind legs around the faded Madonna glued to the dashboard. Ralphie slid in the driver's side and struggled to pull the over-stuffed duffel past the steering wheel. He gave the duffel a shove and it flipped into the passenger seat. Mr. Willie scurried onto Ralphie's lap, sniffed his crotch, rolled onto his back, and fell asleep.

Ralphie drove to the bank and pulled up to the ATM. He reached into his back pocket for his wallet as the car began to roll forward. He jammed on the brake and sent the still sleeping Mr. Willie flying onto the floor. Ralphie checked his bank balance and blew a big sigh of relief. His checking account had been running on fumes, and his credit card was ten bucks short of its max. This gig would keep him afloat for months.

He took out 500 bucks. His wallet had never seen that much cash and wouldn't fold, so he peeled half off the stack, crumpled the bills into his front pocket, and tossed the wallet onto the passenger seat. He stomped on the gas. Mr. Willie woke up squealing with his tail pinned under the pedal. Ralphie let up on the gas, and the ferret ran up his body and took refuge on the top of his head. He curled up and immediately fell back asleep.

Ralphie drove the half-mile south on Ramset Road and pulled into the parking area at the Greyhound Bus station. He weaved carefully through the twenty or so homeless people who had spent the night camped in the lot and pulled up to the window at Café Ta-Tas drive-through. The barista leaned out the window to get his order. She wore a red lace push-up bra and matching panties. In lieu of a nametag, she had "Tiffany" tattooed in fancy letters across the top of her left breast.

Ralphie leered at her. "Hi girls, Tiffany. Cold this morning, huh? Large coffee and a breakfast special."

"Sure thing, Ralphie." She glanced at his head. "Nice hat.

Wait 'til the PETA people get a hold of you." Tiffany gave him a fake smile and turned away to make his order. Ralphie knocked Mr. Willie onto the passenger seat and pushed himself up off the seat to check out the barista's thong. She turned around and caught Ralphie licking his lips. Mr. Willie jumped onto Ralphie's lap and stood on its hind legs tracking the scent of sausage.

"Keep that thing in your pants." She eyed Mr. Willie warily. Ralphie glanced down at his crotch. He wasn't sure what she was talking about. Tiffany leaned out the window with the coffee in one hand, the breakfast burrito in the other. Ralphie reached for his breakfast. He grabbed her wrist and slid his fingers down her hand to his burrito.

Mr. Willie scampered up Ralphie's arms and launched himself through the window. Tiffany shrieked and stepped backward. Mr. Willie landed on her chest, his front paws grasping the red lace of her bra.

Mr. Willie's hind legs and tail swayed side to side as Tiffany backed away from the window, screaming. The ferret finally caught its hind paws on her lace panties and stood there, momentarily resting his snout between the barista's boobs.

Lucky fucker. Ralphie put the coffee and burrito down on the console. He pulled the car forward so he could open the door, jumped out, dashed around the coffee hut, and ran inside.

"Mr. Willie!" he yelled. "Hold on! I'll get him off you." She kept screaming. Ralphie scooped his hands under Mr. Willie's belly, getting the fingers of his right hand inside Tiffany's bra. She cocked her left arm and knocked Ralphie back with an uppercut that left him seeing stars. Mr. Willie went flying through the air and landed inside the open microwave. She slammed the door of the oven. Tiffany was pushing her breasts back into her bra when Ralphie stumbled into her.

She sent him to the floor with a knee to the balls.

"Get the fuck out of here—now!" She opened the microwave, snatched out the ferret, and tossed him through the window. "Now!" she screamed. "Else I'm calling the cops."

Ralphie dragged himself through the narrow door and struggled to his feet.

"Wait a minute, you pervert. You still owe me ten bucks."

Ralphie pulled out a twenty and tossed it through the open door. He shuffled around the shack and got into the car. Mr. Willie hopped through the driver's door and snuggled around the clothing sticking out of the top of the duffel. Ralphie dropped the car into drive and eased out into traffic.

"Woo-woo-mama." He adjusted his jeans to take the pressure off his nuts and glanced at his furry friend. "Wasn't that fun?"

Mr. Willie stood on his hind legs and looked back and forth between the burrito and Ralphie, chittering expectantly.

Once he got up to speed on I-90, Ralphie couldn't resist the smell of breakfast. He picked up the foil-wrapped burrito with his left hand. Mr. Willie jumped onto the console and waited to be served. Ralphie took his right hand off the wheel and peeled back the edge of the wrapper. He tore the foil away with his teeth, spitting the pieces out over his right shoulder.

The end of the tortilla exposed, he took a big bite. In an instant, his mouth was on fire and he spewed chunks of tortilla, sausage, and egg across the dash. The blazing burrito fell onto Mr. Willie. The ferret jumped onto the dash and happily chowed down on blown bits of scrambled egg.

Ralphie pushed his knees against the bottom of the steering wheel to keep the car straight and opened the console with his right hand. He pulled out a small bottle. Mr. Willie stopped eating, hopped off the dash, and nuzzled Ralphie's hand.

"Here's a little treat to go with your breakfast," Ralphie said as he spun the cap off the half-pint of Cuervo Gold. He poured some tequila into the cap. Mr. Willie lapped it up and clucked contentedly. A few minutes later Mr. Willie lay unconscious on top of the duffel, his soft belly exposed, legs twitching above him in the air.

Two hours and thirty empty minutes of scraggly trees and sagebrush later, Ralphie was pressing the seek button on the car radio in a futile attempt to find a station. He glanced up at the road just in time to see the sign for the Wenatchee exit. He hauled the steering wheel over to the right and jammed his foot on the brakes. The car skidded through the gravel in front of the big green exit sign. The chassis rocked back and forth until it settled into the curve of the exit ramp.

On one side of the road, a scrappy looking orchard spread along the hillside, the gnarled trees still bare. After about twenty miles, Ralphie saw the sign for Road 3.5 NW. He turned left. Wanaduck was only a couple of miles now. The road curved to the south. Three giant wind turbines perched on the hill in front of him. The ground dropped away behind them. On his right, a sign read "Wa-Wa Day Spa" in bright red letters. Ralphie grinned and looked at Mr. Willie. "This place is happening, my furry friend," he said. "Yeah, happening."

Finally, the road took him over the bridge into Wanaduck. A right on River Street and he could see Whitey's Fishin' Inn directly in front of him. He rolled into the parking lot and pulled up to the office. The front desk was deserted. He dinged the bell on the counter and waited.

A door squeaked. An old black woman, about four foot ten, shuffled up to the desk. Her eyes, magnified by her glasses to the size of dinner plates, examined Ralphie intently from head to foot.

"You want a room?" she finally asked.

"Yes, ma'am, I have a reservation," Ralphie replied quietly. Old ladies scared him.

"Name?"

"Uh." Ralphie suddenly panicked. *What was that name I'm supposed to use?* "Uh..."

"Name?" she repeated sharply.

Suddenly, it came to him. "Hugo Drax," he blurted out.

"Eh?"

"Hugo Drax!" Ralphie shouted like she was in the next room.

"Drax? What the hell kind of name is that? Canadian?" she asked, her hands on her hips and her bosom bulging out at waist height like a feather pillow.

"No, I'm from Idaho."

She glared at him with her giant eyes. She muttered something under her breath as she wrote in the book. "Fifty-five twenty a night," she said. "Breakfast from five to eight. Room five. Card."

Ralphie stood there, staring at her.

"Card!" she barked.

"Huh?" Ralphie was still trying to figure out who Hugo Drax was.

"Credit card!" Another withering glare.

"I'm paying cash," Ralphie replied. He whipped out his wallet and placed six twenty-dollar bills on the counter.

She pawed the bills back with her left hand and pushed the key to room five out with her right. Then, without another word, change, or a receipt, she turned away and disappeared behind the squeaky door.

Ralphie went to find his room. After jiggling the key in the lock, he opened the door. The interior had been decorated with a nauseating mixture of burnt orange, yellow, red, and dinge. He dropped onto the bed, which sagged under his weight. He turned on the TV, pushed the buttons on the remote, and settled on a rerun of *Lethal Weapon 2*.

Ralphie's stomach growled. He hadn't eaten since breakfast and—Mr. Willie!" Ralphie jumped to his feet and ran out to the car. The ferret's beady eyes stared desperately out the driver's side window, his panting mouth painting patches of fog on the glass. Ralphie yanked the door open. Mr. Willie dashed out of the car and made a beeline for the woods.

"You better go have yourself some fun," he shouted. "Just watch out for the squirrels. I'm not paying your damn vet bills this time."

Ralphie took his duffel inside and tossed it on the bed. He freed the wedged zipper and pulled out a crushed bag of Cheetos and a warm Natty Ice. He settled in the rust red side chair and stared at the TV. *Man, that Joe Pesci is great.*

It took several rings before Ralphie realized that it was the phone. It took a few more to find it. "Hullo?" he cleared his throat and tried to sound awake.

"Hugo Drax?" a voice asked.

"Huh? What? Oh yeah. That's me." Ralphie remembered his cover story.

"I trust you had a good nap?" Without waiting for a reply, the smooth voice continued, "I left a package of information at the front desk for you. I'm sure you will need some time to familiarize yourself with it. If you have any questions, email me at the address you used before."

A twinge of panic surged through Ralphie. *How did he know I was taking a nap?* "I don't have a computer with me. Is there some place I can go online in town?" he stammered.

"The Wanaduck Professional Center has an information

kiosk you can use at no charge. The center is just south of the Tuck 'er Inn on River Street."

"Yeah, yeah, I know where the Tuck 'er Inn is. I'll let you know if I have questions." Ralphie didn't think he wanted to have any questions.

"Fine." The caller hung up.

He dreaded seeing the woman at the front desk, but he got dressed and walked over to the office to pick up the package. A young guy was sitting behind the counter. Ralphie blew a sigh of relief.

"Someone left a package for me. Room five?" Ralphie waved his room key. The guy turned around, retrieved a bulging envelope addressed to Hugo Drax, and handed it to Ralphie.

Back in the room, Ralphie opened the envelope and looked inside. It contained a small plastic fish with a metal tab in its mouth and a slim stack of printed pages. He tossed the fish in the trash, pulled out the papers and placed them on the table. The first page listed three names. He leafed through the rest. It looked like a couple of pages for each person on the list. Addresses. Hobbies. Habits. Typical schedules.

Jeez, this guy is thorough. This job wasn't going to be like Ralphie's usual gig: middle-aged guys wanting to ice their wives to avoid paying alimony. Ralphie would just take the up-front money and skip out on the actual work. *What were they going to do? Call the cops?*

So far, his business plan had allowed him to make a living without ever having killed anybody, but this new guy… Ralphie shivered at the memory of the voice on the phone. That guy won't call the cops either. And he sure wouldn't let it slide.

Chapter 18

"Hey, Rudy, get a load of that shirt!" Juice pointed through the one-way glass at the guy walking into the police station conference room.

The fluorescent lights of the station lit up the shirt's faux-Hawaiian scene: distant islands silhouetted by an improbable sunset of electric blue and violet; bright red cocktail glasses, topped with orange slices and little green umbrellas tilted drunkenly along the hem. The pattern repeated two and a half times around the shirt. His pants were a muted pink.

"Where did they find this wacko?" Juice whispered. "Rudy, turn up the volume."

Rudy reached to the recorder and turned the knob. Dickie's voice came clearly through the speaker.

"Ray, thanks for coming in. Please have a seat." Dickie reached into a box labeled "SNEAD, EDDIE" and pulled out a pair of evidence bags. "Here's your phone." He handed the bag containing the shattered remnants of Ray's phone across the table. "Cameron was able to trace you from the SIM card. Lucky, huh?"

"Thanks, Chief." Ray looked worried. "Glad you found it,

but…" He pulled an iPhone out of his pocket. "I already got a new one."

"That's good, Ray." Dickie picked up the other bag. "The concerned citizen who found your phone also picked this up nearby." He held up the bag containing one of Walt's flash drives. "I wondered if it might be yours?"

"No. I've got mine right here." Ray fumbled a fish dangling from a lanyard from around his neck. "See?"

"Okay. Well we've got dozens of these things in lost and found." Dickie plucked the fish out of the bag and tossed it on the table. "This one's yours if you want it."

Ray's eyes bugged out momentarily, and he snatched up the micro-bass faster than a trout snapping up a mayfly. "Thanks."

"Hey, did you see that?" Rudy pointed at Ray.

"Yeah," Juice said. "He really wanted that thing bad."

"Ray, I've got to be honest with you." Dickie rubbed the back of his neck as he sat down. "This thing with Eddie has got us stumped."

A few seconds of static came out of the speaker. "How so?"

"We've got no leads. Zip." Dickie pulled a folder from the box. "So, right now we're grasping at straws." Dickie slid his finger down the page in his file. "You're at the board meetings as part of the management team, right?"

"Yeah. In case there are any financial issues to talk about."

"But Eddie was on the board."

Ray nodded his head in response.

"We're trying to find out if anybody noticed anything, uh, out of the ordinary at any of the recent meetings."

"Like?"

"Not sure. Maybe something that would make you think that Eddie was in trouble." Dickie checked his notes again.

"A couple of weeks ago we got a tip that there was a problem at the Utility."

"Problem?" Ray tried to look puzzled. "Oh, yeah. Ellis mentioned that you said something about that."

"The problem?"

"Yeah," Ray went on. "It's really not much of a problem, though." He smoothed the front of his shirt. "The dam is in a maintenance phase right now. We've had to draw down the contingency fund to cover some unexpected issues."

"Like?"

"You'd have to ask the engineers, but I seem to remember it had to do with the piping and pressure stress in the concrete." He brightened. "We've recently hired some consultants to do a study on the dam. It sounds interesting. They use sound waves to measure the structure of the dam or something. It's all beyond me. I just pay the bills."

"Bullshit," Juice commented to Rudy and leaned in closer to the speaker.

"In any event, the engineers have dropped the power output of the dam as a precaution until the study is complete. We've had to buy some electricity from other utilities to make up the difference." Ray smiled smugly and leaned forward in his chair. "It was all discussed at the last board meeting."

Dickie's eyebrows shot up. "It was?"

"Yeah. A last minute addition to the agenda. We took a break, then reconvened."

In the observation room, Rudy tapped Juice on the arm. "He's lying. Nobody said anything about taking a break."

Dickie pinned Ray with a stare. "You sure? That part of the meeting didn't show up on the video."

Ray's face flushed. "I don't know why. Maybe something went wrong with the equipment?"

"Maybe. Do you guys make a transcript?"

"Yeah, yeah. We do." Ray took the fish-drive from around his neck. "I've got a copy right here. It's called transcript February oh nine." As he offered the drive to Dickie, his hand shook like a bartender's on two-for-one martini night.

Dickie took the fish. "Hang on a minute. I'll get someone to copy the file." He stood up and left the room.

Rudy already had his hand out when Dickie came into the observation room.

"Get as much as you can off of this thing in the next sixty seconds." Dickie handed him the fish and spun out of the room.

Rudy plugged the flash drive into his MacBook Pro and highlighted all the files that appeared on the screen. He dragged them onto the desktop. When the progress bar read "20 seconds remaining," the door flew open, and Dickie stood there holding two cups of coffee in his left hand. "Give it to me now." Rudy pulled it from his computer. Dickie grabbed it and vanished.

"Sorry for the delay, Ray. Thought you might like a coffee." Dickie put the cups down on the table. "Here's your drive. Terry's printing the transcript out right now." Both men picked up their cups. "Now back to Eddie."

Ray paused with the cup to his lips, then set it down, and folded his hands on the table.

"Maybe Eddie got mixed up in something he wasn't expecting." Dickie shrugged and blew on his coffee. "The thing with the Utility is just a loose end we're trying to tie up. You're sure there's nothing with this maintenance thing, or the contract, or even the meeting that could have gotten Eddie in a jam?" Dickie asked, and set his cup down.

"Nothing that really jumps into my head, Chief. But..." Ray took a sip of coffee. "Eddie was something of a player. He wanted a lot and was always trying to find an angle that would let him come out on top."

"Like?"

"Like he really wanted to be rich. He was the first guy doing a real estate website in the area. He was first with video walk-throughs on his listings. He loved that tech stuff. He was always scrambling for an edge. Probably stepped on some toes along the way." Ray put down the coffee and looped his flash drive back over his head. The little fish seemed to be jumping out of the neon sea on his shirt. His eye's locked onto Dickie's. "Maybe he just pissed off the wrong people."

Chapter 19

Ralphie wanted a paycheck bad, but before he could start killing people, he had a couple of questions for the voice on the phone. His stomach churned at the thought of talking to him again. At least he could send an email.

He walked down River Street to the Wanaduck Professional Center. It was 3:30 on Friday afternoon, and the lobby was already deserted. Ralphie plopped into the chair at the free Internet station and logged into his Hotmail account.

Three people keeling over one after another in a small place like Wanaduck would attract some attention. He needed more than ten days. Ralphie's hands hovered over the keyboard for a few seconds, then he began to type. "Three hits in ten days in a dump like this is stupid. It'll take longer so I'll need more money." *Cha-ching!*

Frank Hollowell, one of the names on the list, liked to fish. *A boating accident was a no-brainer, but how?* He leaned back and gazed at the photographs on the wall above the kiosk—the dam under construction, the last girder of the bridge being lowered into place, and a cluster of people at the top of the

Wanderfalls Scenic Overlook. *Ha! Looks like they're all taking a leak.* The last picture in the set captured a huge explosion blowing out an enormous section of cliff. He grinned, leaned forward, and ended the message, "Where can I buy some farm supplies?"

Ralphie sent the email, logged out of his account, and headed next door to the Tuck 'er Inn for a quick beer to help settle his stomach. The tavern was a lot more popular than the professional center. Several telephone repair guys sat at the bar, their plug-in phone sets dangling from their tool belts. He briefly fantasized about walking up to Tiffany's trailer and knocking on the door. "Ma'am, I'm here to fix your phone." She would welcome him in and close the door. Then a light went on in his head, killing the illusion.

According to the background info, John Parsons, the second name on the list, was eighty-six years old, forgetful, and most importantly, heavily medicated. He had been hospitalized twice in the past month. Ralphie could pretend to be a phone repairman, get inside, and help the old fart take a few extra doses of his medicine. *Maybe there'll be some left for me!*

After two beers, Ralphie returned to the public computer to check his email. One new message. His stomach flipped despite the beers. His lips moved as he read: "Good point. Yes, please wait between assignments. I will send another $500 for expenses on Monday. I will also send you a progress payment the day after you complete the first assignment." *Yes!*

Ralphie exhaled and realized he had been holding his breath. The last line of the message read, "Big R, Moses Lake." Scratching his forehead with his pen, he wondered what that meant. He logged out and went back to Whitey's to collect his car. He wanted to scope out his targets.

John Parsons lived out in the sticks. Parsons' house was a small, green box with a few tired shrubs in the front. A beat-up, brown '79 Dodge Polaris sat in the driveway, its dented rear bumper held on with wire, its rear window plastered with American flag stickers and a large Semper Fi decal. The nearest neighbor lived a few hundred yards further down the road. *Piece of cake.*

Ralphie cruised past the house. The road dead-ended a half mile farther, near the river. He turned around and headed back to town. A small, ugly car drove by in the opposite direction. Ralphie jabbed his left hand in the air, pointing toward town, to tell the driver there was nothing back there, but the other person didn't even look over.

His information said that Marion Shill, the third name on the list, pushed her walker to the medical center at the south end of town every weekday to visit her internist, Dr. Tabouley. She was eighty-eight.

Ralphie drove back to Wanaduck and parked across the street from the center. Sunshine reflected from the three-story glass wall on the front of the building as he walked up to the door. Inside, sunlight glinted off the polished rectangular steel railings that guarded each level's balcony. He gazed up at the third floor, trying to see where Dr. Tabouley's office was. He took the stairs to get a closer look. His sneakers caught on the sharp metal treads of the steps as he climbed. He got to the top and caught his breath on the landing. Dr. Tabouley's office was to his left, the elevator to his right. The edge of the balcony was right in front of him, overlooking the lobby.

Ralphie took the stairs back down to the first floor and looked back up. There was something here he could use, but he just couldn't put his finger on it.

He got in his car. Thirty minutes later, he was whipping through the Walmart in Wenatchee. A blue-gray work shirt and pants. A blue baseball cap. A pair of cheap work boots. His new cotton twill pretend-uniform shouted Maytag repairman, but the old geezer probably didn't see that well anyway. He added some fried chicken, crunchy Cheetos, and a six-pack of beer to his cart. He got antsy waiting in the check-out line and turned around scoping out the magazines and displays. He jerked back in surprise when he found himself face-to-face with a well-dressed guy holding a flock of helium balloons. *Poor Phyllis.* The guy looked through Ralphie like he wasn't even there. Ralphie turned around, paid, and took off.

The guy in the checkout line looked familiar. Ralphie couldn't figure out where he'd seen him before. It bugged him all the way back to Whitey's.

Back in the room, he opened a beer, poured some into a shot glass, and put the glass on the floor. Then he placed a chunk of chicken and a small pile of Cheetos on the floor next to the beer. Mr. Willie hopped over to eat his dinner. Ralphie drank beer, tried on his uniform, and practiced saying "Good morning! Are you John Parsons?" until he got it right three times in a row.

He lay on the bed, ate two pieces of cold chicken, drank the rest of the beer, and watched *Walker, Texas Ranger* reruns. Mr. Willie slept curled up on Ralphie's chest, snoring softly. Right before Ralphie dosed off, the details of the medical center pushed back into his consciousness. *That's it! Push Marion Shill down the stairs!* He smiled drunkenly and drifted off to sleep.

At 8 a.m. Monday morning, Alan Jackson singing "Country Boy" blasted from the clock radio, spewing Ralphie out of bed and onto his feet. He looked around in a panic, then remembered that today he would earn another paycheck.

Showered and dressed in his new outfit, he took one last practice pose in front of the mirror. "Good morning! Are you John Parsons?" *Yes! Right on the first try!* Thirty minutes later, Ralphie was in his Vibe heading east over the bridge.

Ralphie walked up to John Parsons' front door. *Remember, look official. You can do this.* He stood up straight, forced a friendly smile, and rang the doorbell. Muffled TV sounds, grumbles, and thumps came from behind the closed door. Minutes went by and the only sound he could hear was the TV, so Ralphie rang the bell again. The grumbles and thumps started back up and, this time, grew louder. Ralphie heard feet scuffing on the floor.

When the door opened, Ralphie touched the bill of his cap. "Good morning! Are you John Paycheck?"

"Nope," the old guy said and started to close the door.

"Wait! I mean John Parsons!" Ralphie shouted. "Are you John Parsons?" The door stopped moving.

"Who's askin'?" Mr. Parsons demanded. He stuck his head out the door and looked up and down the street.

"Telephone repair. We got a trouble report. I have to check your phone."

"Where's your truck?" Parsons snapped, his tongue snaking out to wet his flaky lips.

Ralphie squirmed. He hadn't planned on questions. "Uh, broke down. I had to drive my own car."

"How can you fix the problem if you don't have any tools?"

Ralphie struggled to keep himself under control. *Come on. You can do this.* He took a deep breath. "Sir, if I find a problem, I'll get my tools out of my car. Do you want me to fix your phone or not?"

"I don't know. You look like you work for Sears. Does Sears fix phones now?"

"Sir, I'm from the phone company," Ralphie said through clenched teeth. "May…I…come….in?"

Parsons scowled at him. Ralphie waited with a fake smile pasted on his face. When he couldn't wait any longer, he pushed Parsons back into the house. The old guy's slippers caught on the runner in the hall, and he started to fall backward. Ralphie caught Parson's frail shoulders, pulled him upright, and dragged him past the La-Z-Boy recliner into the kitchen. He dropped him onto one of the chairs at the dinette table.

"Oops. Sorry about that," Ralphie said.

Parsons glared for a moment, but then seemed to forget what he was glaring about. He picked up the newspaper with gnarled fingers, shook the pages once, and began reading.

Ralphie made a big show of lifting the phone receiver, pressing the hook several times, and unplugging then replugging the cord.

Within a minute, Parsons' head drooped onto his chest, and the newspaper fluttered to the floor. Ralphie quickly moved over to the kitchen table, grabbed a giant pill container, and dumped the contents of the pillbox into his left hand. He opened the cupboard next to the phone, got out a drinking glass, and filled it with water. Parsons started snoring. *Piece of cake.* Ralphie came up behind the old guy's chair. With each wet snore Parsons' head lifted briefly, his mouth wide open. Ralphie's left hand moved up and down under Parsons' chin, following his head through its circuit.

At the top of the third snore, Ralphie clapped his left hand with the pills over Parsons' mouth, tossing them way back into his throat. He wedged his fingers between Parsons' teeth and grabbed the glass of water. Ralphie tipped the glass up and started to pour. Parsons woke up wide-eyed and choking. He bit down, taking a chunk out of Ralphie's thumb.

"Damn it!" Ralphie yelled and dropped the water glass. It shattered on the gray linoleum. With one hand, he pushed Parsons' chin up to keep his mouth closed, and with the other, he pinched Parsons' nostrils. The old man's hands clutched madly at his chest as if he might have been having a heart attack. His right hand got stuck underneath his cardigan.

Beads of sweat broke out on Ralphie's forehead and trickled into his eyes. Ralphie blinked them away. When his eyes opened, he was staring at the .38 caliber opening of a short-barrel Smith and Wesson revolver.

Ralphie's head snapped back in panic, and he stumbled backward as Parsons pulled the trigger. Ralphie's feet tripped over the edge of the rug, and his back slammed into a glass-doored hutch. He went down under a pile of broken glass and World War II memorabilia. He pushed a German helmet off his face to see Parsons aiming again. Ralphie rolled to his left. The shot missed him by five feet. *I am outta here!* He leaped to his feet and bolted through the door as another shot rang out.

Ralphie jumped into his Pontiac, turned the key, slammed it into drive, and stomped on the gas. The world passed by his windows in panic-fueled slow motion: a boulder, a bush, a mailbox, a clown. *A clown?* Yes, a clown driving a flower van filled with balloons cruised by in the other direction. His hands followed his head, which was tracking the clown, and his car swerved off the road to the left. He spun the steering wheel back to the right and skidded wildly through the sagebrush. The car went airborne when it hit a small berm and slammed back down on the road.

With his thumb bleeding, his heart pounding, and his head hurt, he sped back to town determined to accomplish something today. He checked the dashboard clock. Still time to catch Mrs. Shill. He got to the medical center at 10:30. He took the stairs to the third floor, wincing every time his thumb hit the railing. His breath was ragged when he got to the top. He leaned against the wall next to the elevator, pressed his thumb into his pants to slow the bleeding, and tried to catch his breath.

The front door of the medical center opened. Ralphie peeked over the railing and caught a glimpse of curly, orange hair before it disappeared under the balcony.

He stepped back against the wall as the door to Dr. Tabouley's office clattered open. The front legs of a walker lurched into view. The tennis balls on the bottoms of the legs pushed along the carpet in the hallway. Marion Shill stopped halfway through the doorway, followed by a tiny dog that looked up at her with eyes bulging from being choked by the leash tangled around one leg of the walker. Marion held onto the walker with a steel grip and turned around to smile back into the office. "Toodle-oo, Doctor." She set the tennis balls tunneling through the carpet to the elevator.

Ralphie rocked off his heels and quickly approached her. "Ma'am, the elevator seems to be stuck." He realized that he hadn't pulled the elevator's stop button and hoped no one called it to another floor. "I'm checking to see what's wrong with it. Let me help you down the stairs, so you don't have to wait."

Her eyes were a watery, deep-sea blue. "Why, thank you. What a nice young man." She started to turn toward the stairs, then stopped suddenly. She squinted at him and said accusingly, "I know what you're up to!"

Ralphie frantically tried to figure out how she knew.

The dog growled.

"No, really, ma'am. The elevator is stuck. Let me help you." He put his hands on the right side of her walker and tried to guide it down the hall to the stairs. The dog sank its teeth into the cuff of his left pant leg and tugged, tearing the fabric. Ralphie shook his leg, but the dog held fast. He kept walking, dragging Mrs. Shill and the dog to the top of the stairs.

"You pervert!" Marion shrieked. "I know what you want. Well, you aren't going to rape me!" With that, she wheeled suddenly, the leash falling off the leg of the walker. Ralphie watched, paralyzed, as the walker came around and slammed into his knees. He crumpled at the top of the stairs. The dog lunged for Ralphie and bit his ear. Ralphie held his arms in front of his face. Mrs. Shill lifted the walker and brought it down. Hard. "Take that, you monster!" One tennis ball hit his shoulder, the other hit his ribs. The cross-bar caught him cleanly across the throat. He started gagging. She struck again. One of the back legs landed squarely on Ralphie's nuts. He hacked, grabbed his crotch, and blacked out.

A nurse regarded him with concern. "How do you feel?" she asked.

"Awful. What happened?" Ralphie peered around an exam room.

"Mrs. Shill thought you were attacking her. She hit you with her walker."

"I was just trying to help!" Ralphie whimpered.

"Oh, I know. This isn't the first time we've had to deal with Mrs. Shill's, um…outbursts. She's pretty spry for her age."

Ralphie's head felt like it was filled with wasps. He gingerly felt along the side of his face. A large bandage covered his left ear. "What's this?"

"Uh, dog bite. Nasty one, too. We stitched you up and have some medication for you. Do you want me to call the police?"

"No!" Ralphie shouted.

"Well, okay," the nurse said, her eyes wide with surprise. "That's up to you. I thought you might want to file a complaint."

"Oh. No. No, thanks. It's okay."

He heard the front door of the office open. Women's voices and giggles drifted into the exam room. The nurse opened the door to see what was going on. A clown with bright orange hair stood at the reception desk, balloons jiggling behind his head.

"Shelly, balloons from a secret admirer!" the clown teased. Someone behind the counter was giggling uncontrollably.

A dog growled. The clown turned around and said in a saccharin-sweet voice, "Oh, hello, Mrs. Shill. How are you today?" The hair on Ralphie's neck went up. *I know that voice.*

"Get lost, buster, I'm not interested," she snarled.

Chapter 20

The iMUD offices buzzed with the random resonance of fluorescent lights, air handlers, and the erratic clicks and pops of a building cooling down. The whoosh of blood rushing through Ray's head drowned it all out. It was late at night, and Ray frantically worked through the numbers in a financial spreadsheet. His pulse rate and blood pressure climbed into the stratosphere. Presseley was looking ahead now and wanted to know how much the utility could claim as lost revenue after the boys finished with their work on the dam. There was the cost of repair. And the money they would save when the Feds stepped in and canceled their existing power contracts courtesy of the HELL legislation. It really was brilliant. If it worked.

How did that stoner Travis ever come up with the damn idea in the first place?

The numbers got bigger with each run. Ray thought his boss might be losing it. It was clear that Presseley was going all in, and he hadn't gotten as far as he had by playing by the book. Still, this was out there, even for him. But if he pulled it off…then iMUD would be back in business with money to spare.

He had to get through the numbers, but another window on the screen kept dragging his attention away. A freeze frame of a naked June Presseley holding the tattered shreds of a Hawaiian print shirt over her head beckoned to him. *How did that get started?* He couldn't remember, but he couldn't forget how he felt when they got together. Beneath the uppermost image, several other shots of June fanned out. Ray shivered and reached inside his shirt. He drew out a flash drive and unclipped it from its lanyard. He could feel the heat of its contents searing his fingertips.

Something groaned. Ray froze. *What was that?* He stood up quickly, like a prairie dog worrying about a hawk. *Like a tomb. Just nerves.* Ray sat back down in his chair and jammed the tiny fish-form flash drive into his computer. A window opened on the screen. He typed in the six characters he used to keep prying eyes away.

The thumbnails from the flash drive popped into the window one by one. A shot of June bending over the bed, looking back at him, posing for his cell phone camera. An out-of-focus shot of her breasts that he took with his left hand while she straddled him. A close-up of a stuffed duck. *That was fun.* Then, one of his favorites—June and Cameron nipple to nipple, locked in a passionate embrace.

He quickly dragged the stack of new images to the flash drive's icon. He popped the fish out of the USB port and clipped it back on the lanyard. He dropped it behind the technicolor rayon of his shirt and patted it once.

He felt, more than heard, a door close somewhere in the building. A slight change of pressure in the room. A soft click. Panic rushed through his body in a wave. He spun up out of his chair, grabbed his jacket, and ran.

Timothy slipped out of Presseley's darkened office. He pocketed the flash drive with the new information he'd just bagged from Presseley's computer. Something didn't sit well with him, something he couldn't quite put his finger on.

In all the time he'd worked for Dr. P., he had never seen him like this. Nervous, irritable. At the merest hint of difficulty, his whole persona became arctic-cold. That spelled trouble. Timothy could handle it, but it required effort, without waiting for a reply and it was becoming annoying.

He weaved through the halls on his way to the back exit. He glanced left and right into the cubicles he passed. Movement caught his eye when he reached the opening to Ray's cube. The screensaver still cycled through a series of typical tropical scenes. *Ray must have just left.*

Ray was in on all the meetings about the plan, so Timothy had as much dirt on Ray as he needed. But curiosity got the better of him. He sat down in Ray's still-warm chair and wiggled the mouse. The screensaver evaporated. Ray's floral-print login icon came up. *A password.* Timothy frowned at the screen. Passwords were usually easy to guess. All it took was some knowledge of the person and a spark of intuition. He pictured Ray and saw him dressed in a dazzling, emerald green shirt, flamboyantly patterned with flame-red and lemon-yellow birds of paradise. He leaned over and typed in six characters. He pressed Enter and Ray's desktop reappeared. *Hawaii. Come on, Ray, that wasn't hard at all.*

As the thumbnails filed into neat little rows, Timothy did a double-take. He opened one picture, another, and then another. June Presseley. More June Presseley. June Presseley fully clothed. June Presseley with nothing left to the imagination. Timothy smiled, quickly pulled the small fish out of his breast pocket, and slid it into an open port. The fish's eyes flashed blue for several seconds. Timothy extracted the flash drive and replaced it in his pocket. He backed out of Ray's cube and left the building.

"Yes, Dr. P.," Timothy said as he tried to get comfortable on the unpadded, straight-back chair. "They were on Ray's computer."

Robert Presseley leaned back in his black leather chair and pressed his fingers to his temples. "This puts things in a whole new light."

"Yes, sir. If these ever got out..." He left the implications to his boss' imagination.

"What, I don't understand—don't even have a clue about..." Presseley said flatly.

"Yes, sir?"

"When did June get so damn interested in ducks?"

Chapter 21

"Could that be what this is all about?" Dickie asked of no one in particular. Rudy and Juice waited for him to finish his thought as they walked from the police station to the Tuck 'er for lunch.

"We got this image off of Ray's flash drive." He shook his head. "June Presseley basically naked buried in a pile of toy ducks. So Ray's taking pictures of June." His companions nodded their assent. "We've got you…" Dickie pointed at Juice, "overhearing that 'Mischievous Milton' crap at the park. But then you…" he indicated Rudy, "come up with this financial shit at the Utility." Rudy's chest puffed out. "So what is this about? A jealous lover goes off on a rival? Or is it about a financial scam at the Utility?"

"Nah, the June thing doesn't hold together." Juice held up his fist and extended his index finger. "First, your boy Eddie gets whacked before June and Ray meet up." His middle finger. "Next, you don't have an Eddie and June link." Then his ring finger. "And *you've* got a dead predecessor with the same cause of death as this Eddie character." He stopped, and poked the three fingers into Dickie's chest. "What you need is the thing that both Eddie and the dead Wanaduck Chief of Police had in common."

A silver Cadillac passed them and turned onto the bridge.

Crossing the Columbia River, Robert Presseley caught a glimpse of the dam out of the driver's side window of his new Cadillac STS. He flipped on the seat heaters and rolled down all the windows, trying to clear his mind. A warning buzzer sounded, and a small puff of smoke came from the seat heater switch. *Youch!* He raised his butt off the seat to let it cool down and stared incredulously as the windows rolled back up as if by magic. He banged his fist against the recalcitrant windows, blew out a breath, and started thinking about his situation.

The outcome of his plan to rescue the Utility wasn't certain yet. He mentally ticked through the checklist, but thoughts of June rushed into his head like rising flood waters. *I love that bitch, but what a pain in my ass.* June embodied every man's sexual fantasy. Unfortunately, for Robert, every man seemed to be hers. For the twenty-six years they had been together, she never let him forget why he had fallen in love with her. Her passionate imagination was still just as exciting and adventurous as in the beginning.

Then there was Ray. His unique skills with public utility accounting procedures had bailed Presseley out more than once. Ray had even managed to keep him out of jail. But loyalty had its limits. *Fucking pictures.* Robert could put up with some embarrassment from his wife's escapades, but June was getting sloppy. Rumors and innuendo? Fine. Hard-copy proof with her photographed or videoed? Not so good. Lately, she seemed to be going a bit over the top, and he didn't want to hear about his wife showing up on RedTube. Her pursuit of satisfaction was now hovering between extreme and desperate. *How do I get this back under control?* The car windows rolled back down. *One more annoyance to deal with.*

Two weeks had passed since the Cialis incident. Physically, at least, Robert felt better so he could resume his usual Friday lunch appointment. The Utility thing will work out, he was sure. But Ray and June...*I'm going to have to deal with that.* Presseley rolled up the Caddy's windows and punched the accelerator. He sped up around the curve on the far side of the bridge and shot out of sight behind the first hill.

Ray Milton and June Presseley were on Timothy's mind as well. They were bothersome beyond their illicit images. Their actions, particularly Ray's, could jeopardize the plan to rescue iMUD. Timothy sighed. *Something else I need to deal with—and soon.*

Timothy drove past the turnoff to the Wanaduck Dam Recreational Area access. The small air-cooled engine on his 1962 Citroën Deux Chevaux rattled as he urged the zeppelin-shaped vehicle up the slight incline. He smiled. *Still sounds like it did when I bought it.* He glanced down at the Spartan instrument console. *Wow! Forty-five kilometers per hour! Love those French!*

He could see his destination near the top of the hill. A small, discreet sign marked the entrance to the parking lot. Another sign, permanent and electrified, peeked out from behind the branches of a tree. Large, illuminated red letters proclaimed "Wa-Wa Day Spa." Below that "An Epicurean Paradise" glowed in neon italics. "Executive Retreat and All-U-Can-Eat Oriental Buffet" flashed in blue script at the bottom of the sign.

Timothy slowed for the turn, and his mint-condition 2CV rolled into the gravel parking lot next to Presseley's car. He shut down the clattering engine and climbed out. Presseley leaned against the driver's side door of his Caddy.

"Good morning, Dr. P." He sniffed the air. "Is something burning?"

"Good morning to you, Timothy," Presseley said. "Just the damn switch again." He pointed through the car window. "Come on." Presseley pushed off the car and started walking. "Let's get some lunch." He took the stairs two at a time and held the door for Timothy.

Timothy wondered at the sea change in Presseley's mood. They entered the Wa-Wa's dining room, looked around, and approached the cashier/reception counter. A hand-written flyer taped to the wood-grained linoleum announced, "Today's Special!!! Curried *Vegetarian* Hot Dog Spring Rolls!"

"Sit anywhere you like," a youngish hippie-type with flame-orange hair said, "and help yourself." His outstretched arm indicated the buffet. An embossed name-tag pinned crookedly to his blue vest identified him as "Karat."

"Umm." Presseley squinted at the tag. "Karat is it? I've got a 12:30 appointment with Melissa. Please let her know that I'm here." He turned and headed straight for the buffet.

Karat turned and opened a frosted glass door with "Spa Entrance" painted on its far side. "Rissa, your 12:30 is here!" he screamed down the hall.

"Okay," came the faint response. "Tell him it'll be rocks today." A man's maniacal laughter drowned out the rest of her reply. Karat turned and started to speak, but shut his mouth when he saw Timothy's glare.

"I think he heard," Timothy said. He chose the table furthest from the entrance and hung his coat over the back of a chair. Then, he weaved his way through the other tables back toward the food. On the wall behind the buffet, black velvet art depicted gaudily colored Chinese landscapes of dubious authenticity.

Presseley, already at the buffet, leaned in to inspect the array of steaming oriental dishes and smacked his forehead against the clear Plexiglas snot shield. He picked up a dinner plate and a side plate as if nothing had happened. Timothy followed his lead. They moved down the line filling their plates. Each took a pair of shiny, golden-brown spring rolls.

Presseley and Timothy returned to their table. The places were set with paper mats showing the Chinese Zodiac, stainless utensils, and snap-apart bamboo chopsticks. Timothy could see his and Presseley's cars through the window. At the far end of the lot sat a sad-looking, pink Pontiac Vibe. *What is that idiot doing here?*

Timothy split his chopsticks and rubbed them together to get rid of the splinters. He deftly lifted a spring roll, took a bite, then quickly raised his napkin to his mouth and spit out the food. He took a gulp of water to wash away the foul taste.

"You okay, Timothy?"

"Yeah." He tossed his balled-up napkin onto a nearby buscart. "I don't know. It just tastes kind of gamey." He tentatively sampled a steamed dumpling. "Yes. This is much better."

Presseley picked up his fork, speared a spring roll, and sniffed it. He took a bite. "Hmm. Not bad, but I see what you mean." He took a larger bite. "How is the project going, Timothy?" he asked as he chewed.

"I'm not feeling too good about it, Dr. P." Timothy shook his head. "The outside vendor we hired has made the rounds but, so far, no positive results." He moved the chunk of partially-eaten spring roll off to the side of his plate and snatched up another steamed dumpling with his chopsticks. "The list is still intact."

"This is not good. Not good at all." Presseley took another large bite of spring roll and chewed thoughtfully. "Perhaps we need to discuss alternative options."

The entrance door to the spa opened. A short Japanese woman stood in the doorway with her hands on her hips. Small silver bells on the recurved toes of her slippers tinkled gaily as she tapped her feet. Timothy took in the see-through, lime-green, chiffon Bedouin pants she wore over a dark green bikini bottom. A belt of gold coins held the pants up around her narrow waist. A sequined vest and a conical green hat with a wisp of chiffon flowing from its pointed tip completed the outfit. She reminded him of an Asian-heritage version of Barbara Eden in *I Dream of Jeannie*.

I wonder where she shops.

"Ah, Melissa." Robert Presseley stood up and looked down at his dining partner. "Timothy, please enjoy your lunch and, if you would, wait for me here. We've got a lot to talk about."

Presseley strode to where Melissa stood and said, "What a vision you are."

"Dr. Presseley, you are a bad, bad boy," Melissa chastised. "You didn't finish your lunch." They walked down the hall, and the door closed behind them.

"And how many times do I have to tell you? Say it like Marissa, not Melissa." Melissa spanked him playfully as they headed for the massage room.

"Yes, my dear, I remember. You're from California."

"But my parents were originally from Japan."

"Yes. They moved here before you were born. For Toyota?"

Melissa laughed. "You do pay attention."

"They named you Melissa but could never pronounce it correctly."

"They said it just fine," she said in mock reproach. "Just not the way it's spelled."

"I stand corrected." He bowed slightly.

Melissa opened the first door on the left and held it for him to enter. Inside, they squeezed past the massage table that dominated the small room. She removed a large, white Turkish towel from a cabinet and placed it on the padded table. On a small table in the corner, a blue bottle with a cork stopper sat next to a circular stand that held a shallow dish over a candle. She pirouetted over, picked up the bottle, and held it to her lips. Melissa winked at him and, with a single breath, sucked the cork out of the bottle. As she dribbled oil into the dish, the scent of lemongrass filled the room. Puffing up her cheeks, she shot the cork back into the bottle and returned the bottle to the stand. Melissa's sparkly vest fell open as she bent over backward and placed her palms on the floor. Her muscles tensed as she inverted into a brief handstand, continuing over to come up standing by the door.

"Now you make yourself comfortable, Dr. P." She indicated the towel and the table. "And I'll be right back." She winked at him again and opened the door. He heard a fit of insane laughter from the hallway. "Will you want hot or cold today?" she asked as the laughter faded.

"I think cold will be best." He leered at her. "After seeing you all dressed up, I could use a little cooling off."

"Okee-dokee." She bounced away in a perfectly executed handspring.

He took off his suit coat, tie, and shirt, carefully placing them over the back of the only chair. He sat and took off his shoes, storing them and his socks squarely beneath the chair. He stood, stepped out of his pants, grabbed them by the cuffs, shook them once, and laid them on top of his jacket. Clad only in his red silk boxers, he stretched, reached down, and touched his toes. The pattern on the shorts—small upright hockey sticks, each flanked by two pucks—reminded him that his Cialis setback was in the past. He removed the boxers and tossed them onto the chair. He picked up the towel, lay face down on the table, and awkwardly pulled the towel over his butt.

Soft music filled the air, and he started to relax. His face stuck through the padded hole in the massage table, his arms rested on the soft support below. Each small sound anticipated her return—the tinkling of tiny bells, the annoying squeak of a wheel that needed oil. The door opened, and Melissa rolled a small, blue plastic fishing cooler up to the table and into his field of vision. The squeaking stopped. The cooler had an extending handle like a drag-a-bag suitcase. He raised his head but Melissa pushed it back down into the hole in the table. Her feet vanished from sight. He heard a cabinet door open followed by the sound of a bottle being shaken. The little bells came closer. He felt her tug the towel straight, then the warmth of her body as she got closer.

"How are we feeling today?" Melissa's lips were close to his ear.

"Uh, Marissa." He took a deep breath. "I've been under a lot of stress lately."

"Mmmm....We can take care of that. Now can't we?"

Fabric rustled. Something tickled his back. Melissa flipped off her shoes. His pulse quickened. He heard the clink of metal coins as her chiffon pants deflated onto the floor. She kicked them out of the way.

He raised his head to look. Melissa wore only her vest and bikini bottom. She stood on her left foot, poised like a Balinese dancer: her right leg bent, and her right foot pressed flat against her left knee. She extended her leg, brought it over his head, and pressed his face back into the hole.

"Naughty, naughty boy," she said. "Relax now. Watch later."

His pulse maxed out.

Mad laughter momentarily broke through the heavily insulated walls. As the laughter faded, the soft music reasserted itself. The nimble toes of Melissa's right foot grabbed the lid of the cooler, and it opened with a plastic squeal. A soft mist flowed out of the cooler. Her apparently prehensile toes grasped a smooth, black, oval river stone about three inches long.

"Brr," Melissa said. "Ready?"

He mumbled, "Mm-hmm."

Melissa's foot vanished from view. The chill spilling off the rock as it hovered over his skin sent a shiver up his spine. His muscles tensed as she placed the frosty stone on his lower back. The iciness receded, and he relaxed again. Her foot reappeared and rummaged through the stones in the cooler. She picked up another rock, slightly larger, and placed it higher on his back than the first. Then another. And another.

Melissa put both hands on the table next to his head, bent her knees, and kicked into a handstand. The table quivered. Her soft voice whispered into his ear. "Relaxed now, you naughty, naughty boy?"

"Mmmm. Not quite."

"Good! More rocks!" She pushed off the table and landed on the floor.

A sudden boom shook the room as something pounded against wall. Presseley raised his head as the small table tipped over spilling the scented oil. A loud, cackling laugh came from the next room. A woman screamed.

Suddenly, the wall disintegrated in an eruption of wall-board and yellow fiberglass insulation. Melissa was knocked away and the massage table collapsed, dumping Presseley onto the floor. He jumped up, slipped on an oil covered, icy rock, and fell back to the floor. He clambered to his feet as the cloud of dust started to settle. Stunned and exposed, he stood face to face with a laughing, naked man. Presseley snatched up his towel to cover himself.

Bright yellow insulation stuck to the veneer of massage oil coating the maniac's body. His bloodshot eyes flashed left and right with a freakish gleam. A small, gray-pelted mammal leapt from his shoulder to the top of his head and back, chattering like a Chihuahua on meth. The madman shot a quick glance over his shoulder through the hole in the wall, let out a coyote howl, and ran straight through the next wall.

In the dining room, the Day-Glo dragons flying out of woven silk clouds on the overhead lights began to shake. A naked man burst though the wall across from Timothy, stopped, and howled. Timothy didn't think. In a single smooth motion, he shoved the table and chair clear of his body, whipped out his gun, and leveled it at what looked like a caveman covered in yellow fur, tinged with pink. The neon Neanderthal stood there and cackled at the sight of the gun.

Ralphie!

Shouts coming through the hole in the wall distracted Timothy momentarily. Ralphie bolted for the door with his ferret clinging precariously to his hair and ear. Timothy spun and aimed the pistol, but checked his fire when he saw Karat's red hair sticking out from behind the cash register. The other diners huddled on the floor, peeking over the table tops at the naked man running across the parking lot. Timothy holstered the gun and slowly approached the hole in the wall. His boss, half-dressed, yanked at the wisp of green chiffon sticking out of the fly of his suit pants.

Thirty minutes later, Officer Bill Branch had arrived on scene to take statements.

"No. It's MARISSA!"

Branch looked confused, so Melissa spelled it out with a huff, "M-E-L-I-S-S-A. My last name is Parmer. P-A-L-M-E-R."

Presseley, now dressed, sat at a table with Timothy and an agitated Travis Baxter. Timothy had called Travis, whose five one-hundred dollar bills had already made sure that nobody in the room had seen a gun. Travis was completely wound up and alternated between feverishly eating a tomato salad with ranch dressing and trying to find his birth year on the placemat's horoscope.

"Cool!" Travis looked from Presseley to Timothy. "I'm a Rabbit!"

"Focus, Travis, focus." Presseley squirmed as the itchy glass fibers worked their way into his skin. "Timothy, do you have the list?" He absentmindedly reached down and scratched his crotch.

Timothy extracted a folded sheet of paper from his coat pocket. He opened it and smoothed it out on the table. The sheet contained a list of three names and addresses. He removed a Mont Blanc fountain pen from his shirt pocket and pulled the top. He waited.

Presseley's face was like stone. "Time to clean up

some recent mistakes," Presseley said decisively. "First, Ray Milton."

Timothy wrote.

"June." Presseley shook his head in disappointment.

Timothy looked up, saw his boss was serious, and inscribed her name on the list.

"And let's take care of our latest problem."

Timothy added Ralphie Hinz's name.

Chapter 22

Timothy winced at the anxious staccato that Presseley tapped out on his leather desk pad with his pen. Presseley's own Mont Blanc, a gift from Timothy, was a beautiful writing instrument, and Timothy hated to see it abused. But he waited in silence while Presseley collected his thoughts. Talking out of turn would just make it worse.

Finally, Presseley spoke with a forced calm. "Ten thousand dollars and the idiot hasn't killed anyone?"

"Dr. P., I know you don't like this." Timothy cast his eyes down to convey remorse. Then, he looked Presseley in the eye. "But Ralphie is completely incompetent. Marion Shill and John Parsons both got the best of him. It was my screw-up. I should have checked him out more thoroughly." Timothy knew from experience that Presseley didn't like when people asked for forgiveness. He simply wanted somebody who would take the blame.

"Don't worry about it." Presseley stopped tapping the pen. "You couldn't have known that this guy was a total fuck-up." His voice came out cold and robotic, but his shoulders relaxed.

Timothy couldn't have cared less but didn't let it show. He wanted Presseley to feel powerful and in control.

Presseley peered across the desk. "You know, we were lucky to find out about those viewers. I had to pull some strings to make that bastard, Vernon, hand over the names. My own brother-in-law." The pattering of his pen resumed.

"Yes, Dr. P. We caught some lucky breaks."

"I want to see this list cleaned up." He pointed his pen at the sheet of paper. "Hire someone else. Make it fast and make sure they're competent."

Timothy stood up, squared his shoulders, and buttoned his sport coat. "I will take care of it," he said dutifully. Timothy left the office and closed the door quietly behind him. *What an asshole.*

Timothy stopped in front of the mirror outside of Presseley's office to adjust his tie. He squinted his eyes as he thought, creasing his delicate crow's feet. He wasn't worried about his relationship with Presseley. He knew he could keep a lid on that situation, but his boss was anxious and anxiety led to mistakes. Not good in a small town like this.

Outside, the cool evening air helped clear his head. He walked quickly up the alley, eager to spend some quality time with Simpson. He bounded up the stairs to their apartment above Simpson's shop, unlocked the door, and went inside. Although it was still a few minutes before closing time at the flower shop, the apartment had that occupied feeling. "Simpson? Are you home?"

No reply.

Timothy took off his suit coat and hung it on a wooden hanger in the closet. He dragged his fingers across the fine wool as he started down the hall. "Simpson?"

Still no reply.

Timothy rounded the corner and found Simpson sitting

at the desk, silhouetted by the glow from the computer, his back to the door. "Simpson? Hi, baby. Why didn't you answer me?"

Not a word.

This was not like Simpson. Normally, he would start chattering away about his day and the customers whose bizarre requests simply *drove…him…mad.*

Timothy came up behind Simpson who sat silent and motionless. He was about to put his hands on Simpson's shoulders when he saw the computer screen. *Oh, shit!* Timothy's fish flash drive stuck out of the side of the computer, and one of the more prurient pictures of June Presseley filled the display.

Without turning around, Simpson whispered so softly it was barely audible, "Why do you have these pictures?"

He did not need this. Not now. But, there it was. Timothy took a deep, but totally silent, breath. "Simpson. This sounds trite, but it is not what it looks like. That is not my flash drive. And those are not my pictures."

"You're right," Simpson replied. "That is total bullshit. I would have thought you could come up with something better than that." He turned and glared at Timothy, his mouth pursed into a pout. "What? Aren't you interested in me anymore?" He turned back and stabbed at the screen with his finger. "My God! If you're going to experiment, couldn't you pick someone classier than that…that…hussy?"

Timothy held out his hands with his palms up. "It's not a lame excuse, baby. I don't do that." Timothy's mental battery pack was running low from hard use. "Think about it. Do I act like I've lost interest in you?" Timothy took Simpson's hands and lifted him out of the chair. He stroked his partner's damp cheek then slid his hands lower onto Simpson's chest.

"Well, no," Simpson conceded. "But you have been

staying late at the office more often. Or at least, that's what you told me," he said accusingly, but the indignation had vanished from his voice.

"Presseley has had a lot for me to do." Timothy stopped as soon as he said those words. *Not the right name to say.*

"Yeah, I bet, Presseley. Except it's June Presseley that has a lot for you to do." Simpson slumped in the chair, the pout back on his face.

Before Timothy could answer, a loud knock rattled the door to the apartment. They both turned toward the sound in surprise. No one ever knocked on their door.

Perfect time for an interruption. Timothy left the room and opened the door. Robert Presseley pushed past him into the apartment, not saying a word and not waiting to be invited in.

"Dr. P." Timothy followed him down the hall. "What do you need?" he asked Presseley's back.

Presseley spun around and stared straight at Timothy, all business.

"I called Arthur Caley, down in Grant County. Christ, he's an asshole, but he has a lot of useful information. He knows a guy in Chicago who knows a guy we can use. I want you to hire him. Here's his number."

It was almost the last straw, but Timothy fought the urge to tell Presseley what he really thought. "Yes, sir," was all he said.

Presseley held out a torn piece of yellow lined paper. *Not his personal stationery. At least Presseley is being careful.* Timothy took it. A phone number scrawled across the page in a legible but hurried hand, but no name. Short crossbars through the sevens like in Europe. *The jerk's never been east of the Rockies.*

The purpose of his visit satisfied, Presseley finally noticed his surroundings. "Oh, hello, Simpson. I'm sorry to barge in like this. Urgent business, I'm afraid."

"No problem, Dr. Presseley. Not at all." Simpson was always gracious, no matter who he spoke to or how rude they were.

The chair squeaked as Simpson pushed it back. Presseley went rigid, his eyes narrow slits. He glared at Simpson like a hawk about to launch on its prey.

"What are you doing with pictures of my wife?" Presseley asked in a chillingly measured voice. "I thought you were a fucking faggot, for God's sake!"

Presseley burned an unhealthy shade of red. Simpson sat with a smile frozen on his face. Timothy rushed to regain control of the situation. He quickly glided over to Presseley's side, careful not to touch him. "Dr. P., these are Ray's pictures."

"What are you talking about?" Presseley wheeled around with a murderous look on his face.

"Look at that chair in the picture." Timothy pointed to the atomic explosion of color on the right edge of the photo. Presseley and Simpson both leaned forward to look. "That's a Hawaiian shirt."

Simpson pulled the fish-shaped flash drive out of the computer, and the picture vanished. "I needed something to store the new ad for the flower shop on. I found this hidden in the drawer." He gave the flash drive a little wave.

Presseley stabbed his finger in the air in front of Timothy's face. "Make the call. Now. No more delays and no more excuses." He snatched the flash drive out of Simpson's hand, marched across the room, stopped, and pivoted to face Timothy. In a cold monotone, he added, "And move Ray and June to the top of the goddamned list." Then he stormed out.

Simpson stood up, trying to keep up the huff. Finally, he broke the silence. "If they're Ray's pictures, why do you have them? It's all June doing stuff with other people!"

"You saw how Presseley acted. Something's up and I need

some leverage to protect myself." His voice softened. "To protect *us*. It's getting too hot here."

"So, you really aren't interested in June Presseley?"

Timothy smiled and shook his head. "Simpson, we've been together for how long?"

"Ten years."

"That's right. Ten years. And your cute little ass is still as firm as the first day I pinched it."

"Really?" Simpson cast a glance backward over his shoulder.

"Really, Simpson. I am dead serious."

"Well, you're right about one thing. It is getting a little warm in here." Simpson coyly lowered his eyes and began to unbutton his shirt.

Two hours later, Simpson snored softly with a contented smile on his face. Timothy threw on his plush white bathrobe and tiptoed into the living room. *Time to take care of Presseley's business.* He picked up the piece of yellow paper and reached for the phone. He punched in the numbers. On the third ring, a sleepy voice answered, "Hullo?"

"Hello. Someone recommended you." Timothy kept it short.

"Really?" The voice sounded amazed.

"Yes, really," Timothy replied. The response didn't instill confidence, but Presseley had been clear. "My employer has some work. How soon can you get here? We're in central Washington State."

"Uh, well, I'm busy for a couple of weeks. I can be there the beginning of May. Will that work?" the voice asked hopefully.

"I would prefer earlier, but that will be fine." Timothy relaxed. *The guy's working, so maybe he'll be okay after all.* "What's your email address?"

"Hitman3 at Hotmail dot com."

"Really?" It was Timothy's turn to sound amazed.

"Yes, why?"

"No reason. I will email you instructions. What's your name, by the way?"

"Hiram. Hiram Gund."

"Okay, Hiram." Timothy smirked at the obviously false moniker. *Yeah, this guy might just work out.*

"Thanks," Hiram replied. "See you in two weeks."

Timothy hung up the phone and made his way back to bed.

Chapter 23

Marion Shill's magnified blue eyes blinked once. "He seemed like such a nice young man." She smiled primly, then a scowl spread across her face. "But I know what he was after. Men are all the same. Only after one thing." She looked down at her little dog. "If The Colonel here didn't save me, I don't know what would have happened." Hearing his name, the pint-sized pooch wagged his pitiful excuse for a tail. "Probably would have ended up in a shallow grave down by the dam…" Her voice trailed away and she navigated her walker toward the door. "Yes, my little poopsie, you rescued me again." The dog's eyes bugged out further as the leash tightened.

After she left, Dickie Gordon leaned back in the chair in the reception area and closed his eyes. *Why the fuck did she wait two weeks?* He heard the outer door to the police station open and close. *Thank God, she's gone!* He opened his eyes.

John Parsons stood in the space vacated by Mrs. Shill. His right arm dangled by his side, a snub-nose revolver in his hand. Instinctively, Dickie rocked forward, stood up, and snatched his pistol from his belt. When his brain caught up with his reflexes, he lowered his gun and said sternly, "John! Put down the gun!"

"Goddamned hippie! That's what he was," Parsons groused as he shoved the revolver into the waistband of his pants.

Dickie clipped his pistol back on his belt. "That's what *who* was, John?"

"The guy who attacked me, that's who." He started shaking his finger at Dickie. "Prob'ly a drug attic. Trashed my kitchen."

"Slow down, slow down." Dickie sat back down. "When did this all happen?"

"Coupla weeks ago."

"Two weeks and you're just reporting it now?"

"Yup." Parsons leaned forward and put his hands on the reception counter. "Got off three shots." He winked at Dickie and smiled. "Mighta nicked the bastard, too. Last shot blew the goddamned phone clean off the wall."

"And you waited two weeks?"

"Didn't need to come to town." He stood up and squared his shoulders. "Been carrying my piece with me just in case he shows up again."

Un-fucking believable. Dickie squeezed the bridge of his nose. "Did you know the guy?"

"Nope. Just some goddamned drug attic hippie trying to steal my medicine. Claimed he worked for the phone company." He made little quote marks in the air. "Dressed in gray and blue."

"Branch! In here—now!" Dickie shouted at the door.

Bill Branch rushed into the room, saw the gun in Parsons' pants, and drew his weapon.

"Whoa, Bill, it's okay." Dickie held up both hands in front of him. "I need you to take a report from Mr. Parsons here.

He was attacked a couple of weeks ago by somebody who matches the description Marion Shill gave us a couple of minutes ago." Bill looked disappointed but holstered his gun.

Dickie grabbed his jacket and moved to leave. "I have to go check some things." He pointed at Parsons' gun. "Make sure that thing's unloaded before you let him go."

Dickie opened the door on his lime-green Ford Fiesta. Since the recycling truck had flattened his last car into scrap metal, he was forced to drive the vehicle usually used by the neighborhood watch patrol. It smelled like old cigarettes and wet dogs. Clumps of hair kept floating up out of the back seat. He pulled his cellphone from his belt as he climbed in, speed-dialed, and pressed the phone to his ear.

"Yo, Dickie," Juice answered.

"Hey, Ted. Can you and Rudy meet me at Eddie Snead's house?"

"Sure thing. What's up?"

"I'll explain when you get there."

"See you." The line went silent.

Dickie drove up Broad Street, turned right, and parked facing the wrong way in front of a large white house. Juice and Rudy were two blocks away, walking toward him. He shut off the car and walked around the house to the back door. One end of the police tape guarding the door had detached and fluttered aimlessly in the light breeze. Dickie reached for the knob. The door leading into the small kitchen swung open without resistance. Dickie unclipped his gun and cautiously went inside. He moved past the counter, stood against the wall, and glanced into the dining room. Empty. He stepped into the room. Eddie Snead's faux-rancher's jacket lay on the dining table. A stack of files had slid off the table and spilled their contents onto the floor. Dickie ignored the mess and walked directly to Eddie's desktop computer. *It's powered up. Somebody's been using it.*

A sound like a slide racking on an automatic pistol came from the kitchen. Dickie spun and flattened himself against the wall, holding his gun at his shoulder. A small voice in the kitchen said, "Help me." He slid along the wall and paused by the door. The slide racked again. *That's weird.* The voice repeated its appeal for help. Dickie went back into the kitchen.

A light flashed on Eddie's Italian coffee maker. The grinder hopper made another racking sound. A small voice buried in the machine pleaded for help. The display screen on the front flashed, "I need beans." Dickie exhaled and relaxed.

"You gonna shoot that thing or make us some coffee?"

Dickie jumped at the sound of Juice's voice.

Rudy pushed past Juice and headed straight for the dining room. "I'll take a hot chocolate, Dickie."

"Careful in there," Dickie called after him. "We're looking for something." He waved Juice to follow him.

Juice hobbled into the dining room, his lightweight walking-cast squeaking all the way.

Dickie stood by the dining room table. "We had a couple of seniors come to the station today and complain about being assaulted two weeks ago. Their description of the assailant was almost identical."

"So?"

"When Eddie got killed, we searched this place and didn't find anything that seemed relevant. But I do remember seeing a piece of paper with 'John Parsons' printed on it. John was one of the people who came in."

Rudy shuffled through some papers by the computer. He bumped the mouse, and the screen lit up. "Hey, was the other report filed by Frank Hollowell?"

"No. It was…"

"Marion Shill?" Rudy finished for him.

Dickie replaced the stack of papers he was holding and went over to see what Rudy had found. A document titled,"WACCOF Customer Profile: Company Confidential" was open on the computer. Only three names appeared on the list: Frank Hollowell, Marion Shill, and John Parsons; the names followed by addresses, account numbers, and contact information.

Juice came up behind Dickie and read over his shoulder. "WACCOF? Is that some kind of a joke?"

"Wanaduck Area Cable Co-op Facility." Dickie looked over his shoulder. "It's the local TV Company."

"What are these?" Rudy pointed at the four-digit numbers lined up on the far left margin.

"I'm guessing channel numbers." Dickie tapped on a line. "That could be channel 20, the Community Access Channel."

"That's where your tech said the commission meetings get broadcast." Rudy looked up at Dickie and back at the screen. "I'll print it out for you." The laser printer on a small table next to the computer whirred to life.

"Okay. Rudy, look through this stuff." Dickie indicated the piles of paper. "See if anything else pops out at you. But be careful," he said, putting his hand on Rudy's shoulder. "Somebody has been snooping in here. Eddie got interested in something, and he turned up dead."

Dickie turned to Juice. "Come with me."

"Sure. What's up?"

"I might need 'Juice' to help me ask some questions."

"C'mon Vern, help me out here." Dickie stood in the cable company president's office and that familiar good-cop tone, soothing and calm, oozed out. "I'm taking some heat from the new mayor. He's got two old folks whining about being attacked, and both of them show up on this list we pulled off a dead guy's computer." Dickie slid the list across the desk. "I'm kind of in a bind here."

Vernon Nickers didn't even blink. "I'd like to help you, but I don't know how anybody could have gotten this information. See." He tapped the paper that Dickie had brought. "It's marked confidential."

"You know, you look kinda familiar," Juice interrupted.

"And you are?" Vernon Nickers looked at him.

"Ted Foteo. I'm a fishing guide."

"I see you've got a problem with your leg."

"Yeah, broke it in a boating accident. Snapped just like that." Juice clapped his hands together for effect, and Vernon jumped.

"Maybe you've met my sister, June," Vernon said as he settled back into his seat. "She works as a physical therapist. People say there's a family resemblance."

"Maybe that's it."

"And why is he here?" Vernon asked Dickie.

Juice broke in. "Because Mrs. Shill is my grandmother's cousin." He leaned forward and looked Vernon in the eye. "And I was raised to look after family."

"How nice." Vernon returned his attention to Dickie. "So how can I help you, Dickie?"

"We're trying to find out who got this list from you."

"Me?" Vernon tried to look hurt.

"Not you specifically." Dickie shook his head. "From WACCOF." He pointed at the report's header. "Who has access to this information?"

"Pretty much everybody who works here has access. That's all stored on our main system."

"What are these numbers?" Dickie pointed at one of the lines.

"Oh, that's the channel, when it was tuned in, stuff like that."

"What's the 'D' mean at the end?"

"That says there's a DVR on the set-top box."

"DVR?"

"Yeah, digital video recorder." Vernon sounded superior. "Some folks like to watch stuff later."

"Okay, Vern. Thanks." Dickie stood up to leave. "If you think of how this list might have gotten out of your system, give me a call." Dickie picked up the report and left Nicker's office.

Juice stood up, as if to follow, but waited until the door closed behind Dickie. He turned and moved behind Vernon's desk as quickly as he could with his cast. Vernon swiveled his chair to face him. "Get out of my office, Mr. Foteo."

"Or?"

"Or I'll call the police."

"Hey, Chief!" Juice shouted and waited for a response. He lowered his voice. "I don't think they're coming."

Juice grabbed Vernon's shirt, lifted him out of the chair, and held him about two inches from his face.

Vernon started to sweat.

"Look, Vern. This can go two ways."

Vernon nodded repeatedly.

"First, I know you know all about that list. And now, you

know I know. So why don't you tell me the story about the list?"

"Or?" Vernon's starched white shirt had pulled out of his pants, and the blood had drained from his face.

"Well, it's gonna be tough seeing how I got this broken leg." He bent his knee to make the cast squeak. "But I'll reach over, pick up that Mr. Big Deal name plate from your desk, and shove it sideways up your ass."

Vernon's knees buckled.

"Stay with me, Vern." Juice gave him a little shake. "I'm not particularly concerned about the guy who whacked Eddie. But I'm betting that you are." Juice let go of Vernon's shirt, and he collapsed back into his chair. "What do you think might happen if I wandered over to the Tuck 'er and blabbed about how old Vern told me the whole story complete with names, dates, and times?"

Vernon could barely speak. "I had to." He buried his face in his hands.

"Speak up there, Vern. My hearing's not what it should be."

"I had to." Vernon looked up. His eyes pleaded. "They had pictures. A video."

"Jeez, you too?"

"Let me show you something." Vernon straightened his chair and pulled it up to the desk. He skidded the laptop near enough to type, opened a browser window, and keyed "www.blackmail-r-us.com" into the address bar. A plain web page appeared. The heading "Welcome to www.Blackmail-R-Us.com" was followed by the tagline "No Secret Is Safe With US!"

Vernon quickly typed in a username and password. He angled the computer so Juice could see the screen. It flashed once and displayed a high-resolution picture of a car parked behind Walt's fishing shop. Leaning against the car, a very happy Vernon Nickers gazed down at the head of a girl kneeling on a jacket. She was dressed in a Washington State Cougars Cheerleader's outfit.

"That's my niece, Monica."

Underneath the photo, a caption said, "The account balance has been paid. Thank you for your patronage." Vernon stared blankly at the screen.

"I had to," Vernon whispered. "He was going to tell my wife."

"You know, Vern, you're right."

Vernon seemed puzzled.

"There is a family resemblance."

Juice lowered himself clumsily onto the passenger seat and closed the door of the Fiesta.

Dickie looked at him. "Well?"

"It's Robert Presseley." Juice smiled and winked. "Sometimes, it's not what you ask, but how you ask it."

Chapter 24

Bill Snead lay on his back under the trailer. He pushed with his heels, and the shop creeper wheeled forward another few inches. He reached his hand out from under the frame, and Jesse deposited another fist-sized wad of crumpled blue crepe paper into it. A plastic cable tie held the ball in shape. Bill glued the paper ball onto the trailer and held out his hand for another. As he waited, a drop of molten goo from the hot-glue gun fell onto his shirt.

"Goddammit, Jesse! Can't you move any faster?"

"Sorry, Bill, sorry, Bill," Jesse stammered. "I didn't want to drop another one of these on the floor."

Bill turned his head to the side and looked at the dozens of oil-stained blue balls scattered around Jesse's feet.

"Shit, I must have dropped thirty of them already. Thirty already." Jesse sounded ashamed.

Bill raised the glue gun once again, squeezed a dollop onto the trailer frame, and stuck the paper wad onto the glue. He counted out five seconds while the glue cooled. The lead trailer for the Guild's entry in this year's Wanaduck Asparagus Festival Parade was almost finished.

Over the past ten years their entries had grown larger and more elaborate. This year would take the cake. Above the simulated blue water he glued to the frame, the chicken-wire form of a twenty-foot long papier-mâché bass was taking shape.

"Woohoo!" A loud cry went up from the twenty-odd other Guild members in the garage. Startled, Bill jerked up and smacked his head on the trailer frame. He fell back onto the creeper, a lump growing on his forehead.

"Jesse, you little dipshit, get me out of here."

Jesse's hands grabbed Bill's boots and dragged him out from beneath the trailer. "Sorry, Bill. But Dale just now took the lead."

Bill stood up and peered at the twenty-five inch tube-TV sitting on a steel shelving unit at the far end of the garage. The cable TV box was duct-taped to the wall next to the set. Open fishing coolers, each packed with ice and Budweiser, splayed out in a rough semi-circle in front of the shelves. Crowded behind the coolers with open Buds and mouths to match, the entire membership of the Guild stood fixated on the drama unfolding on the television. An aerial shot showed what looked like jellybeans hurtling around a gray D-oval track inside a stadium. Fred Antzberg stood holding the remote in one hand and a Bud in the other.

"Hey, Fred, turn that goddamned thing up." Bill Snead yelled across the room.

Fred pointed the beer at the TV, realized his mistake when beer poured from the can, then raised the remote. Nothing happened. Suddenly the TV switched to QVC where two attractive women hawked something called "Bidet-in-a-Box." Then the screen went blank. Fred went over and smacked the cable box. The TV resumed its coverage of the race. Fred pressed the remote again, and the volume finally increased.

"In an amazing development, Dale Jarrett, substituting for the injured primary driver, David Ragan, has once again taken the lead here at the Richmond Motor Speedway," an announcer's voice babbled excitedly.

"Yeah, Bubba. Too bad about old David. In what could have been a tragedy, he sat down on the battery for his electric trolling motor. The terminals shorted, and he almost fried his..."

"VWOOOOM, VWOOOOM, VWOOOOM, VWOOOOM, VWOOOOM, VWOOOOM..." The TV cut to a series of racing cars flashing along the rail next to the safety fence.

"I guess that'll teach him to not wear his rain pants when he's out fishing," the second announcer chuckled.

The TV cut to the view through the lead car's windshield. The scene looked like a movie starship going into hyper-drive. Fence posts flashed by in front of the colorful blur of the fans in the stands. A hundred feet ahead, a cluster of cars jockeyed for position. Dale hit the back straight.

A small sliver of the driver's right shoulder appeared in the view; his hands gripped the wheel making subtle course corrections to prevent the car from turning into a tumbling ball of wreckage. Advertising plastered the cockpit, the UPS logo featured prominently. Dale set up for turn three.

The view forward through the massive roll cage showed two cars running side by side. The bright yellow car on the left had "Cialis" painted between the silhouettes of two bathtubs on its upright rear spoiler. The sky blue car to its right sported a prominent Viagra logo.

The announcer cut in. "Can we get a close-up on that?" The view zoomed to the back of the Cialis racer. "Looks like an alarming bulge on the right rear tire of John Thomas' car!" No sooner were the words spoken than the tire erupted into a cloud of burning debris. The Cialis speedster jerked to the right and slammed into the blue Viagra car. Their fenders locked together on impact.

The TV cut to the overhead view and focused in on the spinning cars. They came to rest at the bottom of turn three. Both drivers scrambled out of the windows and ran into the infield. The entwined cars burst into flames just as the emergency trucks pulled up.

"Looks like the race will finish under a yellow flag, Bucky."

"You bet, Bubba. And look—the wreck knocked old Dale out of first. Kyle Busch is going to take this year's 400." The camera switched to the finish line where the cars passed at a stately fifty-five miles per hour.

Bill turned away from the TV, took two steps toward the garage door, then spun back. "Hey, Fred, rewind that back to the crash."

Fred pushed the remote, and the DVR stepped backward through the last few minutes. He pressed Pause. The on-track fireball was at its peak.

Bill whistled. He walked out of the garage, peeled a glob of fused glue off his shirt, rolled it between his fingertips, and tossed it into the bushes. He turned in a thoughtful circle while the rest of the Guild members gathered around him. He pulled a soft pack of Marlboro Reds from his pocket and, still looking down, tapped a cigarette out. He put it between his lips and looked back at the assembled Guild members who waited in anticipation. He shook his head, and then fired up the coffin nail.

"Boys, y'know this dam project we're working on for the Utility?"

As one, the Guild members nodded their assent. "Yeah, seismic-tectonic-something-or-other, right?" Fred answered for everyone.

Bill couldn't believe these idiots. He toed at a paint spot

on the concrete and shook his head in disappointment, like his dog had just eaten the sofa. He stuffed his free hand into his pocket to keep from slapping Fred. "That little fender-bender at the race gave me a thought." His eyes traversed the group to make sure he had their attention. "Any idea how much concrete that thing holds?" Bill inclined his head toward the bright blue concrete truck sitting out in the yard.

"That baby carries nine yards full-up," Fred announced.

"What's that in gallons?"

"Jeez, Bill, I dunno. Twelve, fifteen hundred? Something like that." Fred, confused, looked at Bill for an explanation.

"Remember that day at lunch?" Bill asked. "Somebody said something about thermal stress."

Fred nodded. "Yeah, if you get concrete too hot it expands and cracks. Some of the calcium carbonate dehydrates, and the bond between the concrete and reinforcing rods weakens. The whole structure becomes unstable."

Bill's eyes widened in wonder, like his dog had just recited the Gettysburg Address. "Fred, sometimes you amaze me. So, that truck…" As one, the Guild members turned to look at the mixer. "What if we filled it with gasoline?"

Fred nodded his head in approval. "That'd be some serious thermal stress."

"C'mon Fred." Bill tossed his lit cigarette into the bushes. "Let's go work up the numbers."

Chapter 25

Fog from a cold Cascadian breeze lifted off the Columbia River and slipped stealthily into town. Timothy Bentle materialized out of the mist like an apparition. His dark felt fedora took shape first, followed by his grey trench coat, the collar pulled up around his neck to ward off the chill. He walked south on River Street, but his steps made no sound. The stores had closed hours ago. A few pickup trucks and cars were parked on the street near the Tuck 'er Inn. Otherwise, the street was deserted. *Perfect.*

Timothy stopped at the lamppost at the corner of River and Broad streets. He looked both ways, pulled out a fat stick of light-blue chalk—the kind kids use for hopscotch—and quickly scrawled a single vertical line followed by three diagonal slashes on the base of the post. He pocketed the chalk and dissolved back into the gloom.

Hiram Gund hit the brakes on his ancient Corolla hatchback and skidded to a stop on the gravel shoulder alongside the Wanaduck Highway. The clock on the dash said 12:12 a.m. He hadn't changed the clock to Pacific Time yet. It was still set for Muncie, Indiana, and now read fast by three hours and twenty-three minutes. *At least I won't be late.*

Hiram shifted into park and pushed the button next to the overhead light. Both bulbs in the dome light flared briefly then flickered out. He tapped the fixture twice to bring the uncooperative bulbs back to life. A large-print road atlas sat open on the passenger side floor underneath a tipped-over Starbucks cup. Two hours earlier Hiram had placed the half-full, venti, double-shot, cinnamon Frappuccino down on the atlas where it had immediately fallen over. The Frappuccino floodwaters had receded, but the map was now permanently streaked with shades of brown. The remains of the whipped-cream topping traced the Cascade Mountains from the Oregon border north into Canada.

Hiram opened the glove compartment, stuffed a pile of napkins inside, and slammed the door shut. He reached under the empty Dunkin' Donuts box on the passenger seat and pulled out six sheets of paper, each containing the same online map and driving directions. He picked up the uppermost map, held it up to the light, and rotated it to get it right side up. "Okay, this is the right way," he said out loud and dropped the map. The sheet of paper fluttered to the passenger side floor and settled into the caffeine-rich swamp. Hiram shoved the shift lever to drive and made the turn for Wanaduck.

Ten minutes later, Hiram slid into a parking space near the Tuck 'er Inn. He got out and scoped out the entire street. The sidewalk was deserted except for the sandwich-board sign, which advertised "Karaoke Tonight!!!" in front of the bar. He headed south, the ending stanzas of Sinatra's "That's Why the Lady is a Tramp" following him down the street. He stopped under the first streetlight past the bar and pulled a crumpled piece of paper from his left back pocket. A drawing on it detailed a large *L* with a small dot inside the corner of the *L*. An arrow labeled with a tiny *N* ran parallel to the short leg of the *L*.

Hiram looked up and down the street, scratched his head, and kept walking the way he started out. At the corner, he checked the base of the lamppost and breathed a sigh of relief when he spotted light-blue, diagonal lines. *Okay. The lines on the map are streets, and these slanty ones are light poles, so I have to go one street over. But which way?* He looked left and saw nothing but black. *The river?* He turned right onto Broad Street, walked the block over to Main Street, and turned right again, heading north.

Hiram repeated the word "one" in his head until he got to the second streetlight. When he got to "three," he was standing in front of a small store. "Simpson's Shoppe" was painted on the darkened window with "Flowers, Distinctive Gifts and Accessories" in smaller letters underneath. The glass door was covered with stickers for credit cards, FTD, and 1800FLOWERS.COM. At the upper right corner of the glass was a discreet rainbow decal.

Hiram knelt in front of the lamppost. The base of the metal pole had a small access panel with one screw missing. He glanced around again, then pulled out his Swiss Army Knife and used the largest blade to pry off the cover. He quickly snatched out the envelope jammed inside and stuffed it into his back pocket. He replaced the cover, stood up, looked around—saw no one—and continued north up Main Street.

Timothy emerged from behind a cluster of trees next to the Wanaduck Professional Center. He watched Hiram disappear around the corner. When Timothy flipped his phone open, the fog around him glowed a surreal blue-green. He pressed Speed-1 and held the phone to his ear.

"Dr. Presseley," Timothy whispered in a fake British accent. "This is James, James down at Merrill Lynch. The new broker you requested has been assigned to your account. He has a copy of your portfolio." He flipped the phone closed and oozed back into the shadows.

Hiram awoke in room 15, the furthest from the office at Whitey's Fishin' Inn. He got out of bed and caught a glimpse of himself in the mirror. *Not bad.* He turned from side to side wearing nothing but his gray briefs with a white elastic waistband. He sucked in the soft gut that came from forty-one years of not working out. He stood up straight and reached just shy of five foot eight. He smiled, revealing his newly whitened teeth. All 152 pounds of Hiram was pleased. Even the light gray streaks at his temples gave his wavy, orangey-red hair a hint of maturity. *At least I don't look like Opie anymore.*

Hiram opened his zippered black carry-bag and reached in. He retrieved a nearly-empty, but unopened, Coca-Cola can. He shook the can, and a single drop of soda leaked from a small hole on the side. His clothes were a sodden mess of high-fructose corn syrup and natural flavorings. He pulled out a wad of cloth and watched it disintegrate in his hand.

"Shit."

He threw the clothes into the small, white wastebasket in the bathroom. He extracted his .40-caliber Beretta from the bag and returned to the sink. He filled the basin with hot water, disassembled the gun, and soaked the tacky, syrupy coating off the finely machined parts. He used the hair dryer to dry the components, oiled them, and reassembled the weapon. He slapped home a clip and checked the action by chambering a round. He put the gun down on the counter.

Hiram emptied, and then refilled, the sink to clean his black nylon shoulder holster. He hung it on a hanger to dry. He rinsed his carry-bag and hung it next to the holster.

He sighed as he picked up his pants from the floor and pulled on the black SansaBelt slacks. "Well, they were good enough for the drive out from Indiana," Hiram said out loud. He hadn't unbuttoned his gray polyester shirt before he took it off, so he pulled it over his head, did up the second from the top button, and tucked the tails into his pants. The shirt had a large, brown stain from when the lid popped off his Daylight Donuts coffee a couple of miles outside Rock Springs, Wyoming. Now, two days later, his chest was still tender from the burn.

Hiram knelt down beside the bed and reached underneath. He came up with two shiny-white tennis shoes and three socks. He tossed the sock that didn't match back under the bed and sat down to put on his shoes. Finally dressed, he opened the door to face the day, squinting as he stepped into the bright light of the Wanaduck morning. He jogged over to his Toyota, opened the passenger side door, and grabbed his wrap-around sunglasses. *Much better.* Hiram felt like a million bucks. He set off south on River Street. Other than a few cars already parked in front of the Tuck 'er Inn, at nine in the morning the town was almost as deserted as it had been the night before. Three vehicles passed him and turned left to rumble across the aging steel bridge.

Further south, the only building that showed any sign of life was the Wanaduck Professional Center. The directory near the street listed the Indian Meadows Utility District and Dr. Sarah Gant, DMD. "Terri's Kittens," the last entry, was partially obscured by a crisscross of masking tape.

Hiram took a right on Broad Street and crossed over to the other side. He walked up to the police station, opened the door, and stepped inside. *These guys will know.*

"May I help you?" the woman behind the desk asked.

"Oh, hello." Hiram peered over the high counter at the cute, diminutive officer on the far side. Her patrol blues bulged from the Homeland Security-issue Kevlar vest underneath. It gave the impression of a sausage on a grill right before the skin burst.

"Detective, er... Backster," Hiram said after spotting her nametag. "I just got into town last night. I had sort of a clothing disaster." In the office behind the desk, a tall chubby cop leaned back in an old-style, wooden, swivel chair. He took a look at Hiram, and almost lost his balance. He quickly straightened the chair and rolled forward, disappearing from view.

Officer Backster stood up and gave Hiram the once over. "It's just officer. I'm not a detective...yet." She looked at the stain on Hiram's shirt. "You do have a problem, don't you? The Laundromat is a block and a half up on Main," she said cheerily.

"Uh, no," Hiram stammered as he looked down at his shirt. "It's a bigger disaster than this. I need to buy some new clothes."

Officer Backster giggled and said, "Been there. Done that. Up until two years ago, you could have gone over to Tabor's. But then Walmart came to Wenatchee, so now that's your only choice."

"Too bad," Hiram sympathized. He wondered if she'd say yes if he asked her out to dinner. "Where's Walmart from here?"

"You come in on the Wanaduck Highway?" When Hiram

nodded, she said, "Okay, take the road back out of town a mile or so. You'll see the 'Leaving Wanaduck, WHY?' sign at the town limit. When you hit Highway 23, take a right." Hiram nodded and tried hard to remember. "After about ten miles, you'll go past the Rock Island dam." He kept nodding. Two miles further on is Walmart. You can't miss it."

"Thanks." Hiram smiled. "And, Officer Backster…" Hiram hesitated when the other cop appeared at the door. "Uh, where can I get some food around here?"

"The Tuck 'er Inn is about it." She pointed over the desk in the general direction of River Street.

"Okay. Thanks again." Hiram waved. "See you."

At five that afternoon, Hiram emerged from his room looking like the cook at a logging camp. He wore a new, red-plaid shirt over stiff denim dungarees, shiny, black work boots, and a green and yellow John Deere tractor cap. He carried a flannel-lined, denim jacket in his left hand and a manila envelope in his right. He pulled a list of names from the envelope and studied the first entry: "Ray Milton. Wanaduck Prof. Ctr. Leaves work at 5:30. Look for the shirt." The rest of the entry listed Ray's contact information. The list contained six names. *I'm going to make a fortune on this job.*

Hiram strolled along the river promenade until he reached the south end of town. He checked his watch. 5:26 p.m. He leaned against the railing by the water and pretended to soak up the rays of sunlight beaming down from the west. Hiding behind his Oakleys, he waited for Ray to leave work.

The front door of the Wanaduck Professional Center opened at 5:32 and a radiant canary stepped out—a man wearing a yellow, Hawaiian-print shirt with a turquoise and red striped tie. As he strutted across the parking lot, his pants glowed a deep pink in the afternoon sun.

I guess that's him.

Hiram settled his sunglasses and started across the street after Ray.

Hiram followed him through the parking lot but lost sight of him by the time he reached the next street. Hiram scurried to the center of the Main Street, looked around, and hurried north when he caught a glimpse of brilliant yellow. After several blocks, Ray crossed the Wanaduck Highway and walked into a park. He stopped in front of a monument. Hiram slipped to the left and entered the park from the other side of the memorial. He sneaked a peek around the large block of stone as a stunning, middle-aged woman walked up to Ray.

"Ray!" she exclaimed.

Bingo!

"Oh God, June, I've missed you so much," Ray took her into his arms.

June? Hiram pulled out his list and read the second entry: "June Presseley. Stunning middle-aged woman. A loose cannon." Hiram returned the list to his back pocket and peered around the monument with elation. *Two-fer!*

"Ray, oh Ray." June hugged him tight. Then she grabbed his crotch and held on. "Sundays and Thursdays are not enough. I need more." She bit his ear.

"Yes! I want you every day."

Ray and June pulled out their cell phones, split up, and sat down on separate benches. June took off her jacket and spread it on her lap. She flipped open her phone and dialed. Ray's phone barked like a dog. He answered, but Hiram couldn't hear the conversation. June had her other hand under her jacket. She began twitching, her motion speeding up as time passed. Her head hung down and began swaying back and forth. Suddenly, she shouted, "Oh, God, yes!" She and Ray jumped to their feet, rushed to each other in the middle of the path, embraced quickly, and ran back toward the street.

That was weird.

Hiram pulled out his cell phone and dialed. After one ring, a deep voice said, "Yes".

Hiram used the code he was given. "Uh, this is, uh, Tom. Uh...Tom down at Merrill Lynch. I've completed research on two of the stocks and should be able to make the purchase by the end of next week."

"Good." A click followed the one-word reply and the call ended.

Chapter 26

Ralphie Hinz pulled his pink Pontiac into the gravel lot at Walt's Master Bait and Tackle Shoppe. The back end of the car bottomed out as it dipped off the pavement. Walt's sign displayed a large, smiling fish with a cigarette hanging from the corner of its mouth. The name was lame, but it was a damn fine fishing store. Ralphie shut down the Vibe, got out, and walked up to the wood-framed, screen door. He pulled it open, and the door spring squeaked in protest. He stepped into the cool darkness of the shop. The door slammed behind him and bounced once before it settled back into the frame. Ralphie headed straight for the counter in the back.

The grizzled, aromatic individual behind the counter looked up from his breakfast. The donut he was eating was almost gone, and a generous sprinkling of crumbs now decorated his shirt.

"Walt?" Ralphie asked.

"Depends." Walt's eyebrows arched, bringing the bristly forest of hairs to attention like so many tiny fishing poles.

"Hey Walt—Ralphie Hinz." He didn't bother extending his hand. "Friend of mine said this was the place for bait."

Walt didn't move and said nothing. Other than the still quivering eyebrows, he might have been dead.

"Frank Hollowell?" Ralphie smiled. "I met him out fishing yesterday. Told him I didn't want to run all the way back to Moses Lake for more supplies. He said to talk to you."

Walt took a bite out of his donut and smiled, his grin revealing about half of the evolutionarily-determined allotment of teeth.

"Why didn' ya say so?" Walt looked excited. "'Nother friend of his was in yesterday. Whatcha looking for?"

"I'm fishing deep."

Walt checked for other customers, then walked to the front, bolted the door, and flipped the sign to "Closed."

Walt returned and pushed aside a curtain that looked like it had spent more than half of its life on the floor of a garage. He motioned for Ralphie to enter the back room. At the far end of the room a piece of canvas covered a small pile. Walt pulled the blanket back to expose two small cardboard cases. The labels on the cases read, "Dyno Nobel" and "DANGER HIGH EXPLOSIVE HANDLE GENTLY" in six different languages. A small image of a stylized human blown in half provided emphasis.

"Exactly," said Ralphie.

Walt grinned even more, but his dental prognosis did not improve. He opened the top crate and casually tossed eight sticks into a steel bucket.

"Great stuff. You can hit it with a hammer and nothing happens. But get a little bit rougher with one of these..." He counted out eight small, tapered, plastic cylinders and rattled them into the bucket, "and it's ker-fucking-BOOM!"

He pulled a guesstimated length of fuse from a spool on the wall and bit through it with his two remaining teeth that lined up. "Jus' stuff the fuse into the little hole at the square end of the detonator an' you're all set." He headed back to the front. "Let's go, sonny."

About thirty seconds later the calculator read, "22.75."

"That'll be twenty-two seventy-five," echoed Walt.

Ralphie handed over two tens and a five. "Keep the change."

"Well, thanks," Walt said, pocketing the bills.

He handed Ralphie a plastic bag with his new fishing gear and turned his attention back to breakfast.

Ralphie went to the front, unlocked the door, and flipped the sign back to "Open."

He got in his car and tossed the bag into the back seat, then cranked the engine, and pulled out of the lot. He poked at the small, furry bundle asleep on the passenger seat. "Hey, Mr. Willie." The ferret looked up at him. "Time for a boat ride!" Mr. Willie reacted like a cocker spaniel hearing the "W" word. He spun a couple of three-sixties in place, hopped up on Ralphie's shoulder, and stared out the front window.

A beam of sunlight blasted off the Vibe's window as it slowed to turn off the highway. A brown sign showed a boat stopped on an improbably steep ramp with its stern to the water, a directional arrow pointing left.

Hiram Gund accelerated and passed Ralphie's car as it turned toward the ramp. He had been following the pink piece of shit since it left Whitey's Fishin' Inn at 6 a.m. He went another half-mile down the highway and turned his beater Corolla onto the old Wanderfalls access road.

"Aaiiee!" Hiram shouted involuntarily as his car slammed into a pothole. He slowed to a crawl and gingerly maneuvered around the pits in the road, like he was driving around craters on the moon. Every few seconds, he'd check the box on the passenger side floor. Thick bubble wrap, layered with orthopedic foam, a nest of Styrofoam peanuts, and a wadded up towel protected a single stick of dynamite. It scared him to death.

Hiram pulled into the outer parking lot, close to the path that ran along the shore and up to the scenic overlook. The lot was empty. He had followed Ralphie out here yesterday and hoped he was going to fish the same spot today. He guessed it would take about twenty minutes for Ralphie to rent a boat and get to the bottom of the cliff.

The sparse willows rustled soothingly in the breeze. Hiram slipped along the path to the edge of the cliff. Small ripples of water lapped at the rocks beneath. Further along the shore, where the cliffs grew taller, he thought he saw a submerged, giant hot dog pursued by an equally large fish. Hiram shook his head. *Gotta stop smoking those Tiparillos.* His gaze shifted onto the river as Ralphie motored toward him about thirty yards from shore. The engine cut off, and the boat drifted to a stop. Hiram gently fingered his stick of dynamite and watched Ralphie root around in a plastic bag. What looked like a squirrel perched on the bow of the boat. Hiram shook his head again. *Definitely.*

"Tofu....Tofu...TOFU! Goddamn it, Tofu, drop that!" A female voice roared out of the woods nearby. Hiram turned toward the sound. A yellow Labrador retriever dragged a fairly good-sized tree onto the beach. Seconds later, a blonde wearing a tie-dyed T-shirt and a floral-print peasant skirt ran barefoot along the water, chasing the dog.

Hiram stood transfixed.

"Tofu, drop that goddamn branch and come here!"

The dog ignored the woman and trotted down the beach still holding the sapling.

Mad, cackling laughter from the boat drew Hiram's attention away from the girl. The boat rocked slightly as Ralphie stood up holding a stick of dynamite with a sparking fuse. He jerked his arm, and the stick flipped end over end into the water. A tiny splash and then—FAWHOOMP! A column of water rose from the river. Shortly after the explosion, dead fish floated to the surface. Ralphie flung open the cooler, laughing as he scooped fish into his net and slapped them on ice. He tossed partial fish back into the river.

Hiram felt a slight change in the wind. "Woof!" echoed down the beach. The dog sniffed the air, dropped the tree, and headed back the way it had come.

Hiram settled his stick of dynamite in his fist. His nerves tingled. He focused on breathing slowly and deeply. He lit the fuse and started his windup. Mid-throw, his cell phone vibrated in his front pocket. Surprise and a mildly pleasurable sensation made his arm twitch. The stick of dynamite sailed off and landed in the water a few feet in front of Ralphie's boat. Hiram hunched over the phone.

"Hullo?" he whispered.

"Beep," said the phone.

Hiram looked at the screen. An X displayed where the signal bars normally were. The screen read, "Signal Faded." He stuffed the phone back in his pocket.

Hiram spotted the dog swimming for the boat, paddling madly. It grabbed a floating thirty-inch sockeye salmon, and turned for shore. The squirrel-thing on the boat jumped onto Ralphie's head, chittering in alarm. When the dog reached the beach, it dashed up the path, stopped next to Hiram, and shook itself dry, the fish clamped tightly between its teeth while its brain rattled around inside its head. It spit the fish onto Hiram's feet and wagged its tail, panting. Hiram looked down. Alongside the fish, the fuse he thought he had carefully secured in the now-sinking dynamite sputtered out.

"SHIT!" came across the water from the boat.

Hiram looked up to see what was going on. Ralphie kept reaching at something behind his cooler. The squirrel scampered back and forth along the gunwales. Ralphie grabbed frantically, but his hand kept coming up empty.

Must be a slippery fish.

Then everything went white and wet. The shockwave from the explosion knocked Hiram off his feet.

"Oh, yeah, that feels good," Hiram moaned. The cheerleader straddled him, nuzzling his crotch and swishing her blond hair up and down his thighs. He put his hands on her flanks and slid his tongue down her stomach. Her slippery thighs pressed against his cheeks. Her breathing sped up as she licked his leg vigorously and pressed harder against his face.

"Oh God, this is great!" He liked enthusiasm in a partner.

Hiram started to make sounds like a squeaky toy, which grabbed the cheerleader's attention like a magnet. "Don't stop! Please, don't stop," he begged.

His body wriggled against the cheerleader's, and he felt damp hair all…*over?* Hiram's eyes opened to find that the blond hair in his face was short and wet, and belonged to the yellow Lab. The dog joyfully licked Hiram's leg through a gaping tear in his jeans. Hiram looked around in a panic. He was lying in the sagebrush with the fish wedged between his face and the dog's butt. He pushed the dog off and sat up, wiping his mouth vigorously with his sleeve.

Hiram heard sirens, distant but getting closer. The sound

snapped him fully awake. He staggered to his feet and gaped out at the lake. Fishy bits, splintered scraps of wood, and tattered cloth floated over a huge area of the water. Shards of shattered fiberglass and pieces of the cooler littered the ground around him. Hanging from the branches of a nearby bush was a small tuft of gray fur.

The sirens got louder and he could see flashing lights near the ramp turn-off. *Time to go.*

He picked up the fish and tossed it to the patiently waiting Tofu.

"Good, er…boy, Tofu. Go find your mom."

Chapter 27

"Why do I do this?" Timothy asked his reflection in the mirror. His mirror-image had no thoughts on the matter. It stood silently, wearing a flouncy, oversized, polka-dot jumpsuit; a curly, orange wig; white-face makeup; and a red nose. He sighed, sat down on the bed, and pulled on a pair of red plastic shoes, size forty-six. He stood up, shook his costume, and gave himself a final once-over in the mirror.

I look great.

Timothy knew the answer to his question. He did it because he loved it. Everything about it. When he lived in Vegas, he spent some time performing as a dancer in the chorus line of an all-male cabaret review called "Bruce is Loose," a show about an ex-con trying to readjust to modern society. During the comedy sketch, he was a clown. He was hooked. Now, even though he spent most of his time cleaning up other people's messes, he still kept his sideline as a clown.

Timothy's reflection smiled like Bozo when he remembered the night he told Presseley about his love of performing. Since then, Presseley insisted that Timothy don his clown outfit to entertain his niece, Jessica, and all her friends at their respective birthday parties. Timothy was happy to oblige because "Timmy the Clown" loved the children's squeals of delight as he danced and sang, and tied strange animals out of tubular balloons.

The clock showed that it was time to go, so he gathered up the flotilla of helium balloons resting against the ceiling. He slapped down the back stairs, twirled around the post at the bottom, and opened the rear door into Simpson's flower shop. He wound his way carefully through sprays of freesia and tubs filled with daffodils and tulips in the darkened store. He settled into the shadows about four feet from the front window and waited. He had to make sure somebody died.

Outside, Hiram Gund leaned against a street lamp in the light of an early May evening.

Hiram took a long drag on his Tiparillo and checked his gun. He had the silencer on his Beretta. The inside of the barrel was polished smooth so no one could trace the bullets. A special low-velocity load would keep the noise down even more. He had the gun set up for working close to the target. He bought the whole package from a guy on craigslist.

Twenty minutes passed, and Hiram had smoked his Tiparillo down to the last bit of tobacco. He inhaled a noxious mixture of nicotine, tar, and the toxic by-products from the now-smoldering mouthpiece. It made his head swim.

He heard footsteps behind him and glanced back. Ray Milton hurried up Main Street toward the park to meet June for one of their bizarre, public phone-sex sessions. June Presseley was next on his list, so he'd do the hit on Ray, go to the park, and take care of June.

The untucked hem of Ray's red and orange hibiscus-patterned Hawaiian shirt flapped in the breeze. Ray rushed past Simpson's Shoppe, wheezing. Hiram stepped from behind the lamppost, raised his gun, then stumbled, faint from the hydrocarbon stew circulating in his bloodstream. "Shit," Hiram said as he dropped his arms to break his fall.

Ray spun around and saw the pistol aimed directly at his crotch. His eyes flashed with panic, then he clutched at his chest twice, and dropped like a stone. Hiram and Ray hit the pavement at the same instant.

Hiram staggered back to his feet with a nasty gash on his forehead. He stood in a small red puddle, turning in confused circles and wiping the blood from his eyes. Ray lay face down on the pavement. It didn't look like he was breathing.

The door to Simpson's shop opened, and the "you've got a customer" bells attached to the doorframe tinkled brightly. When he heard the jingling, Hiram turned as a six-foot tall clown, surrounded by a halo of colorful clouds, stepped through the door.

"What the fuck?" Hiram stammered, pointed the Beretta at the clown, and pulled the trigger. Nothing happened. Hiram fumbled with the gun and wiped his eyes with his other sleeve. He took aim. One of the clown's balloons found a nail head projecting from the doorframe and exploded. Hiram's arm twitched, and the wild shot took out a small piece of brick out of the wall a few feet from the clown. The flying mortar grazed Hiram's face, and he pulled the trigger—another brick-chipper.

The clown looked at Hiram, then at the gun, and took off running, the oversized red shoes slap-slap-slapping on the brick sidewalk as he ran away.

Hiram started to follow, but slipped in the pool of his own blood and slammed face first into the lamppost. He pushed off, aimed, and fired. The toe of one of the clown's shoes shattered into a shower of red plastic as he turned the corner. Hiram fired again.

Hiram dashed up the street and rounded the corner to follow the clown. The street was empty. Hiram jogged another block up Main, crossed the street, and stumbled into an alley. The adrenaline had worn off, and he could feel the throbbing in his head. He sat down on a crate with his gun in his lap. *Time for Plan B.*

The wail of sirens broke through the wall of his fuzzy thoughts. He struggled to his feet and tried to remember where he had parked.

Timothy Bentle ran up Oak Street as the last bullet ricocheted off the concrete behind him. A half-block up he hung another right and galloped up to the service alley between the Wanaduck Professional Center and the shops on Main Street. Looking over the fence, he watched a battered Toyota Corolla hauling ass up Main Street. Timothy walked down the alley behind his apartment.

"Jesus Fucking H. Christ!" Timmy the Clown kicked open the gate to his yard with his shot-up shoe. "What the goddamned motherfuck was that all about?" The gate recoiled and shut itself. He pushed the gate open again and stepped through. Timothy took a deep breath. He looked down at his blasted shoe, then pulled the limp string and popped balloon out of the gay armada, and tossed it into the trash. He peered over the fence again and listened. The sirens were very close.

Better not be seen outside. He opened the door to Simpson's shop and parked the balloon flotilla in the back hall. He ran, as best he could given his footwear, to the front of the store and bolted the door as the first police cruiser turned onto Main Street. He retreated up the stairs to the apartment, put a kettle on for some tea, dropped into an overstuffed armchair, and checked his pulse.

A few minutes later, he picked up his cell phone and hit Presseley's speed dial. "Dr. Presseley," Timothy said after the voicemail greeting finished, "this is James down at Merrill-Lynch. Just wanted to let you know that the first trade went through after hours. There was a bit of a snag, but you should have your confirmation by e-mail tomorrow." Timothy stuffed the handset into his pocket and went to the kitchen to get his tea. He looked at the clock. He had to get moving to make the party on time.

He kicked off the shot-up left shoe and hobbled—SLAP, step, SLAP, step—down the hall to the bedroom. He knew he had another shoe back there somewhere. He did. Another right shoe. *Shit. Timmy the Clown with two right feet.* He jammed the shoe on anyway and grabbed an un-silenced Walther PPK from the top drawer of his dresser. He dropped it in the bag with his juggling balls. On his way out, he grabbed the balloons and left the door unlocked behind him.

Timothy went through the back gate and turned left, walking up the slight incline toward Oak Street. As he reached the intersection, a police cruiser sped around the corner and screeched to a stop next to him.

"Hey, Timothy." Officer Bill Branch got out of the car and blocked Timothy's progress.

"Good evening, Billy." Timothy made "Billy" sound as gay as he could. "What's up?"

Bill Branch took a step back. "An individual just keeled over outside of Simpson's shop." Branch paused to listen to some static on his radio. "It looks like a heart attack or something. But there's blood on the bricks, and somebody heard a commotion. We knocked on Simpson's door but no answer. Where were you?"

"I was upstairs getting the idiot-suit on." Timothy hoped a little self-deprecation might calm the homophobic asshole down a bit. "I had the soundtrack to *Oklahoma!* turned up loud, singing along with Gordon MacRae." Timothy stepped forward to close the distance Branch had put between them, trapping the cop against his cruiser. Timothy looked him in the eyes and winked. "Anything else I can help you with, Bill?" he asked. He had pressed the insecure cop enough, so he took a size-forty-six step back.

Branch's shoulders relaxed. "We'll probably need to talk with you and maybe have a look around the shop," Branch said. "It's not very clean out front, and the guy was..." he hesitated, "somebody known in the community."

"Jesus, no." Timothy feigned shock. "I know you'll be discreet. You guys know how to handle things like this." Timothy pulled back the sleeve of his clown-suit and checked his Seiko. "Bill, I've got to get going, if it's okay. This birthday party is a favor for Presseley, and I've got to go play the clown for a bunch of kids." He pointed at his red, rubber nose. "Listen, I should be home about nine or so, if you need to slap the cuffs on me and drag me 'downtown.'" He paused and held his arms out with his wrists together. "Or anything...Just give me a call later."

Timothy stepped away from the petrified officer. "Oh yeah, the back door to the shop's open if you need to have a look around. Don't worry about a warrant or anything. Simpson's out of town for a few days, and I'm looking after things for him."

"Thanks, Timothy." Officer Branch shook himself back to life. "We'll be in touch if we need you. And the chief's probably going to want to take a quick look inside."

Branch went back to intently listening to static on his radio.

Timothy halted at the sound of squealing tires, a crash, and the tinny rattle of a wheel cover making its escape. A Toyota tore up Main Street in the same direction as before. Branch jumped into his cruiser, hit the lights and siren, and took off.

Chapter 28

Hiram careened south on Middle Street. A block and a half down the street, he hit the brakes and swung into an alley. He noticed an open garage under an abandoned building, skidded to a stop, and backed the car in. He hopped out and slid the garage door closed. Returning to the car, he rummaged through the glove compartment for something to stop the bleeding on his forehead. He found a pile of Dunkin' Donuts napkins glued together with hardened frosting. *I hope it's frosting.* He pressed the wad against the cut. *Five minutes and no peeking.* Hiram remembered the advice but not who had given it to him.

Five minutes later, Hiram tentatively peeled off the napkins and looked in the rearview mirror. The bleeding had stopped, but a severe bruise bloomed around the gash. The ink from the napkins had tattooed a faint pink "Dunki Donu" on his forehead. He tried to rub it off, but the cut reopened, so he left it alone. His head throbbed. He needed ice and aspirin.

Hiram got out of the car and opened the trunk. He grabbed a bottle of club soda that had been rolling around back there since Christmas, unscrewed the cap, and was rewarded with an effervescent shower. *Ooh! It tingles!* He washed off the dried blood and gently patted his face dry with his shirt-tail. He pulled on an old sweater to hide the stains on his shirt, and took a look around the garage. It was empty. He slammed the trunk, stepped over to the garage door, and pulled it open a crack. A spring breeze blew a few dry leaves up the deserted alley. He rigged the latch so he could get back in and eased out into the high-desert twilight. A number of pickups lined the far side of Middle Street. He crossed over in search of ice.

A small folding sign stood on the sidewalk outside of a nondescript gray building. The professionally-lettered sandwich-board said:

"The Dale Earnhardt Memorial Literary Guild
Meets the 3rd Monday of Every Month
Downstairs Room A
FREE Coffee and Cold Drinks
Everyone Welcome!"

The 3 in "3rd" was drawn in a zoomy-looking, race-car style. In a metal frame on top of the main sign was a race-car-shaped cutout with "Dale look-alike contest TONIGHT!" printed on it in the same font.

Hiram hoped that the "cold drinks" included ice. He climbed the outside steps and entered the building. Inside, another set of stairs led down to a long, poorly lit hallway. Hiram gagged at the smell of old cigarettes and moldy carpeting. Music, like the soundtrack to a Muppet movie, and children's laughter came from an open door halfway down the hall. An ethereal, blue glow bathed the passage. Hiram stepped into the light.

When he reached the doorway, he saw preadolescent girls scurrying about the room, playing and dancing. *It is the soundtrack from a Muppet movie.* On a table in the center of the room a large sheet cake decorated with flowers and unicorns announced, "Happy Birthday #9 Amy!!!!!!!!!!" A handful of the sexiest women Hiram had ever seen chaperoned the boisterous herd. *Several handfuls.* Uniformly young, curvy, and fit, the women could have stepped from the pages of *Playboy* magazine. His eyes darted from one bared midriff to another. His senses were overwhelmed as a young woman in a CFM-red tank top and hot pink short-shorts approached him and stopped inches away.

"Are you the clown?" She gave him the once over.

The cacophony of screaming children, the nearness of the young woman, and Kermit the Frog singing "Love Led Us Here" to Miss Piggy made Hiram's throbbing head feel like it would burst. "Uh, no," he said, and fled the room for the relative quiet of the hallway.

The door slammed behind him, and the noise level dropped instantly. The wobbly metal *B* taped to the door fell off and bounced across the damp carpet. Another unlabeled door down the hall had cranberry-colored light radiating through the gap beneath the door The light changed slowly to purple and then to blue. Hiram pushed the door open and took one step into the room.

Eleven orderly rows of metal-frame, vinyl-padded chairs faced a large pulpit, which looked as if it had been snatched from the gospel-side of a church. A framework of welded, L-shaped, steel supports held the lectern upright. Several strings of LED rope-lights were wire-tied to the frame. Hiram watched the lights slowly change colors.

About twenty-five men, culled from a broad cross-section of society and with every physique imaginable, mingled behind the seating area. Half were dressed in painter's coveralls plastered with the logos of numerous products and corporations. All the outfits were some combination of black, red, and white, and all bore the numeral *3*. The men wearing costumes all had mustaches—some real, some stick-on. *They look familiar.*

At one end of the room, a brilliant spotlight illuminated a larger-than-life cardboard cutout of "The Intimidator," old Number 3—Dale Earnhardt. A black, silk ribbon was draped across the standup statue. *That's who they look like.*

Costumed or not, they all had one thing in common: each grasped a copy of the current month's *Penthouse* magazine, featuring a provocative image of Veronica Split on the cover.

After the reality disruption of the birthday party, Hiram was prepared for weird, but he hadn't counted on this much weird. A small laugh escaped his lips.

As one, they turned and looked at him. Most of the men went back to what they had been doing, but one middle-aged guy with a long, scraggly ponytail limped over, his right leg swinging out to the side, like his knee didn't bend. He wore a blue plaid shirt, jeans, and a cowboy hat with a feather fan above the hatband. He extended his hand and introduced himself.

"Hey, I'm Bill Snead. Don't believe I've seen you at one of these before." Bill's eyes drifted up to Hiram's forehead.

"Hiram Gund." He shook Bill's hand. "I'm in town for a few days and was out for a walk when I saw the sign on the street."

"Pleased, Hiram." Bill's eyes crossed trying to make out the pink smudge on Hiram's forehead. "Nasty gash you got there." Bill appeared concerned. "Doc Gant is here tonight. Want him to have a look?" He pointed to a small man in a gray tweed sport coat.

Hiram shook his head. "Thanks, no. I tripped on the curb and cracked my head against a lamppost. I'd appreciate some ice and a cool drink, though." He reached up and touched the expanding knot on his brow.

Bill pointed to a pair of folding tables across the room and said, "Help yourself. And be sure to grab your copy." He tapped his own issue of *Penthouse*. "Meeting's about to get started." He hobbled away.

One table held a couple of cases of Sam's Choice soda, a bowl of ice, and small bags of cookies. On the other, *Penthouse* magazines fanned out in a semi-circle. All those beckoning Veronica Splits reminded him of the party across the hall. Hiram smiled for the first time since the shootout with the clown. He grabbed a magazine, a wannabe-Coke, and a plastic cup of ice, and sat down in the far seat in the back row. He popped open the can, slumped back in his chair, and pressed the cup of ice against his forehead. He closed his eyes as the cold settled in.

"Okay, gentlemen, we can begin now." A deep, clear voice startled Hiram from his reverie.

A brief interlude of sliding chairs, clearing throats, and opening magazines followed. At the podium stood a tall, gray-haired man wearing black trousers, a black shirt, and the unmistakable starched white collar of an ordained priest. As one, the assembly, magazines in hand, rose to their feet. Hiram jumped out of his chair for, what he thought was, the meeting's invocation.

Bill Snead held his right hand out toward the man at the lectern and addressed the assembly. "Father O'Donnell will be guiding the meeting tonight."

Hiram studied the congregation tightly clutching their *Penthouse* magazines. *What kind of fucked up twelve-step program did I stumble into?* His head was clearing. He drained the can.

"Anybody published this month?" Father O'Donnell asked and raised his hand. Three other hands joined his. "Great," his warm baritone filled the room. "I guess I'll start, and then we'll hear from Fred next."

Almost everyone sat down. A small, wiry man with thin glasses and a three-day growth of beard slinked to the back of the room, opened a door, and slipped inside a darkened closet.

"It doesn't take much to get some of us going, does it?" O'Donnell quipped. The rustling of men squirming in their chairs was followed by a smattering of uncomfortable laughter. "Please turn to page twenty-one. I'm the second letter on the page."

Hiram opened his *Penthouse*, turned to page twenty-one, and stared back at the podium in alarm.

The priest started reading.

"Dear Penthouse Forum: I know most of the letters you publish, like the one just before mine, are bullshit. But this, honest to God, happened to me last Friday, and I thought your readers would get a kick out of it." He paused and surveyed the room over his reading glasses.

"My girlfriend Cheviot and I…" Father O'Donnell paused for emphasis and the room snickered, "were hanging out with a flock of her friends at a local watering hole. She and her girlfriend, Barbado, had been knocking back tequila shooters and were acting very friendly. I abided my time, waiting for the inevitable." Father O'Donnell stopped and took a sip of water. He grabbed his belt and twisted his pants right then left to adjust the packaging.

"Chevi was on one side of me and Barbie on the other. Barbie, one hand on my thigh, reached across me, grabbed Chevi's blonde ringlets, and pulled her across my lap. She planted a deep, wet kiss on her full, red lips that was immediately returned in kind. Barbie's hand was still tangled in Chevi's hair as she pushed her head down onto the growing bulge in my way-too-tight jeans."

A small yelp came from inside the closet at the back.

"At the same time, she slammed a kiss on me that sent my head spinning. I was stunned but opened my eyes just in time to see this absolute angel walk into the bar and stare right at me. This was going to be my lucky night..."

In the hallway, Timmy the Clown could hear party noise and a droning male voice. Because of the acoustics, he couldn't tell which room had the party or hear what was being said. Both doors were unnumbered. He opened the door on the left.

"...I was taped to the kitchen floor and tangled in a web of blonde, brunette, and auburn hair when—" Father O'Donnell stopped short at the sound of the door opening. As one, the assembly turned to follow O'Donnell's gaze.

Oh shit! Wrong party. Timothy and Hiram locked eyes. Hiram reached into his jacket and snatched out his gun. He fired but missed high. Timothy released the balloons as he pulled his Walther out of his juggler's bag. The balloons sailed up to the ceiling. He fired once, but Hiram was moving into the aisle. The round slammed into the back of Hiram's metal chair, knocking it over.

The sound of the two shots and the acrid smell of gunpowder snapped the crowd out of its stunned disbelief. As one, they shouted, "Return fire!" Eighteen of the attendees, including seven ersatz Dale Earnhardts, pulled out a diverse selection of handguns and aimed at Timmy the Clown.

I'm gone. Timothy spun and bolted down the hall as the

fusillade erupted. He heard plaster blast repeatedly from the wall right behind him as someone blindly sought his target. Timothy made it unscathed to the stairs, then up and out.

Hiram emptied his clip into the wall between the room and the hall where Timothy had fled.

Sitting calmly next to Hiram, Bill Snead removed his jeans and unstrapped his hollow prosthetic leg. He extracted a sawed-off, 12-gauge shotgun from his fake limb, pumped it once, and fired an unsteady shot at the bullet-riddled wall. The force of the blast ripped a hole through the wall and tore the door across the hall off its hinges. The flying door took out the birthday cake, the table the cake sat on, and the few remaining chairs from a game of musical chairs that had been in progress when the melee erupted.

Through the gaping hole in the wall, Hiram could see all the little girls, scared but safe, huddled together on the floor at the far side of the party room. "I'm Your Baby Tonight" scratched out into the smoke-filled rooms from the CD player's mangled speaker. The CD player gave one last squeak and stopped. In the back of the room, a girl started to cry.

Chapter 29

Sulfurous smoke swirled in the dank basement. Hiram shouted, "Get him!"

As one, the trigger-happy members of the Dale Earnhardt Memorial Literary Guild took off after the clown.

With the room cleared of heavily armed men, Hiram grabbed his chance and crept through a back exit onto a small lawn. The clown stood not a hundred feet from him, facing the other way and talking on his cell phone. *I have to get the hell out of town.* Staying low, Hiram slinked around the corner and scooted across the street to the abandoned building where he had stashed his car.

Hiram reached the garage, lifted the latch, and ducked inside. The driver-side door gave a loud groan as he opened it. He levered himself into the driver's seat, started the wheezing four-banger, and pulled out. He turned right and eased onto Middle Street, hoping not to attract any attention.

* * *

By the time Timmy the Clown got to the front of St. Theresa's Community Center, two police cruisers were roaring up the street with lights flashing. Officer Terry Backster pulled her patrol car onto the sidewalk to block the steps to the building. The second cruiser overshot the community center, screeched to a stop, made a U-turn, and pulled up facing the other cop car. Officers Backster and Branch stood with pistols drawn when the Guild burst through the doors, guns in one hand, and *Penthouse* magazines in the other.

"Drop your weapons and put your hands over your heads," Officer Backster shouted with authority. The Guild members were, by-and-large, pussies, and did what a woman with a gun told them to do. They dropped their weapons and put their hands in the air.

Officer Branch glanced over. "Everything alright, Timothy?"

"Jesus, Bill," Timothy said breathily and tried to appear shaken through his clown makeup. "I don't know what happened. I was on my way to the birthday party." He nodded at the covey of small, crying girls. "I opened the wrong door downstairs. Everybody just jumped up and started shooting."

"Stick around." Bill's head ratcheted side to side as he scanned the area, his forehead scrunched into a delta of worry. "Chief Gordon wants to talk to you."

Timothy watched as Dickie's Ford Fiesta pulled up, the blue light on its roof flashing. The sound of a metal rim scraping the curb made everyone else turn and gawk. The driver's door opened, yanking the blue light off the roof by its cord. It shattered on the ground. Police Chief Dickie Gordon crunched through the fragments as he got out of his car.

"Officer Branch! Please get some tape up and keep those onlookers back. I want everybody who knows anything inside the tape."

"Right, Chief."

"Officer Backster!" Dickie shouted, stepping onto the sidewalk. Behind him, the Fiesta started slowly rolling away.

"Uh, Chief?" Officer Backster said.

"Start taking statements from those guys." Dickie pointed at the Guild.

"Uh, Chief?" the Guild said as one. The car picked up speed.

"What are you waiting for?"

"Uh, Chief, your car," Officer Branch said.

"Chief!" everyone screamed simultaneously as the car glided through the Oak Street intersection.

"What?" he screamed back.

"Your car!" The crowd pointed down Middle Street.

He turned in time to see his unmarked car careen into the hospital parking lot. It clipped the fender of an ambulance and crashed into a dumpster filled with medical waste. Dickie whispered, "Fuck, not another one."

"I'll call the wrecker, Chief," Officer Branch said quietly, then pulled out his phone.

"Okay. Then go start taking statements from the ladies."

Branch lit up like a kid finding an extra present under the Christmas tree. He dialed as he hurried over to talk with the chaperones.

Dickie turned away from the crowd and bumped into Timothy. Startled, he jumped back. "Jesus Christ, you shouldn't sneak up on people like that, Timothy."

"Sorry, Dickie, I didn't mean to. Normally, these shoes make a racket."

Dickie grimaced but launched into cop mode. "What's going on here, Timothy? We get reports of shots outside of Simpson's." He reached into his pocket and pulled out a plastic bag containing shards of red plastic. "You told Bill that you didn't hear anything, but we found these at the corner of Oak and Main." He gave Timothy's clown shoes a glance and shook the bag.

Timothy sank down and sat on the step. "Look, Chief, I'm sorry I blew Branch off. I had to get over here for this gig for Presseley. I was running late and getting ready to leave. I looked out the window and saw Ray drop like a rock. I went out the front door to see if I could help, and—bam—some guy starts shooting at me. I took off and ran down to Oak. That's when he shot my shoe." He pointed at his foot. "My only left shoe."

Dickie glanced down at Timothy's two right feet and chuckled.

"I ran up to the apartment, called 9-1-1, then left for the party."

"You called?"

"Yeah, check your records," Timothy said, pulled out his cell phone and showed the screen to Dickie. "See, it's still in emergency mode."

Officer Branch's raised voice interrupted their conversation. "How's that spelled?"

"Not Sabrina Spelled. Sabrina Spelt." A soft feminine voice responded.

"Look, Ma'am, I'm not here to argue tenses with you. I just need your last name."

"Whatever," she said. "It's Spelt." She angled out her hip and put her right fist against it.

"Just say it, please," Branch pleaded.

"It's Spelt!" She repeatedly jabbed her finger into Bill Branch's chest. "S-P-E-L-T."

A dark Toyota Corolla pulled slowly onto Middle Street.

"Bill, what kind of car are we looking for?" Dickie asked, but didn't wait for an answer. He pointed at the Corolla creeping toward the Wanaduck Highway. "Bill, Terry, go!"

The Toyota turned the corner onto the Wanaduck Highway, heading down to the river. The two officers bolted to their cars, jumped in, hit their lights, and peeled out, leaving the stink of burning rubber behind. Officer Backster shot north on Middle Street and turned right onto the Wanaduck Highway after the Corolla. Officer Branch followed but turned left at the highway. His car immediately reappeared, going backward, tires squealing. The rear end dipped as he slammed on the brakes and spun the car. The crowd at the community center cheered his move.

The sound of over-revving engines faded in and out as the cars passed cross streets on their race around town. The people in front of the community center rotated slowly, following the cars' progress like sunflowers tracking the sun.

The two police cruisers came into view racing west on Wanaduck Highway past the Middle Street intersection. No Corolla in sight.

Dickie sighed and turned around. He jumped again when he saw Timothy still standing there, staring at him through his clown makeup.

"Are we done, Dickie?" Timothy asked.

"Yeah. Get out of here."

Slap, slap, slap went the clown shoes as Timothy headed off.

The women and girls from the birthday party huddled in a group at the bottom of the stairs. "Okay, you can all go. We might have some more questions later."

They scattered except for a short blonde holding a young girl's hand.

"Rina? Are you okay?"

"Oh my God, Dickie. It was awful." Sabrina Spelt stood on her toes and threw her arms around him. "Thank God nobody got hurt." She shot a glare in Timothy's direction.

"How about you, *Chiquita*? Okay?" Dickie kneeled down in front of the red-eyed, little girl standing next to her mom.

"Yeah, I guess." She gave him several exaggerated nods. "It was kinda exciting."

"Rina, did you see anything in there?" Dickie asked gently.

"The girls were playing musical chairs, and we were waiting for the clown. He was late." She cut her eyes at Timothy. "All of a sudden all these…there were—like—really loud bangs, yelling, and more bangs. Then—like, you know—the whole door blew off its hinges and wrecked, like totally, everything."

Dickie gave his girlfriend a big hug and stroked her hair. "Listen, Rina. Take Amy home. I'll see you when I get there."

"I, like totally, can't wait." She winked and gave him a little kiss on the cheek. She took Amy's hand and walked away up Middle Street.

Dickie watched them go.

My girls. Wow, it really has been almost two years since the Asparagus Festival.

"You're that cop guy?" She had introduced herself.

Dickie shook her fish-slimed hand without hesitation. "Yeah, Richard Gordon. Call me Dickie." A silly grin spread across his face. "Your accent? Southern California, right? Mission Hills?"

"That is so—like totally—cool. How did you know? Are you, like, telegenic?"

"Nah, fifteen years LAPD. You get to know stuff."

"Mom!" Dickie and Sabrina looked at the tiny blond girl next to the tank. She stood with her hip kicked out to one side and pointed at an invisible wrist watch.

"Oh, yeah. Hey, I've got to take Amy to her Dad's."

Sabrina looked back at Dickie. "Listen, don't take this wrong but would you like to get together for a drink later?" Her face scrunched up with anticipated rejection.

"Sure."

"Well, cool! I've got to come back and pack up the tank. I'll meet you at the beer tent in a couple of hours." She waved back over her shoulder as she skipped down the street.

Over beers, she told him about moving to Wanaduck with Ellis. "I mean like, sure, he's a big guy with the Utility and everything. But it's a little pond." She blushed.

"I like this little pond," Dickie said.

"But then Ellis changed overnight." The festival lights glinted off the tears welling in her eyes "All of a sudden, he and his pal, Travis, were always gone, always meeting with somebody, always thick as thieves." She started to cry. "He told me, 'You don't like it here just go on. Go back to the city.' I couldn't because, I mean, Amy needs to know him. She needs to know she has a father. Right?"

Dickie's heart cramped up, but he replied, "Yeah, she does." Then he smiled. "But if you had left I wouldn't be here having a drink with you."

She smiled back at him, and the melancholy in her eyes evaporated. "Exactly, it's like so totally karmic, or…" she thought for a second, "tantric, or whatever!" She glanced at her watch. "Listen, have to run. Let's get together again, okay?" She stood up and started walking away.

"Wait, I don't have your number," he said

"Yeah, you do. You're a cop."

Dickie's cell phone twittered, snapping him back to the present.

"Yes?" he said into his phone.

"Chief, we're at the Portland Highway T. No sign of the Corolla," Officer Branch reported.

"Okay. Did either of you think to check out the other road out of town?"

The call dropped. In the distance, he heard wailing sirens and roaring engines. Minutes later, the two cars flashed by, now heading east.

Dickie headed down the hill to meet the wrecker that was trying to pull his car out of the dumpster.

Chapter 30

At the Wanaduck Highway intersection, Hiram turned right and then right again onto River Street. Almost to the bridge, he glanced in the rearview mirror right as a police cruiser skidded around the corner behind him. He killed the headlights, turned the wheel hard, and floored the gas. The tires laid rubber through an arc, and the car flew onto Bridge Street back into the middle of town. Midway down the block he stomped on the brakes, threw the car into reverse, and backed into an alley. With the rough start and stop, his head snapped back and forth, and the painful throbbing resumed.

The police cruisers zoomed south on River Street past the bridge. *They didn't follow me.* He leaned his head back, closed his eyes, and took a deep breath. A moment later he heard squealing tires and howling engines. The cop cars whizzed past, now heading north. *Let's try this again.* He pulled slowly up to the intersection of Bridge and Main to see what the cops were going to do. The two cruisers turned west onto the highway, lights flashing, sirens wailing. He waited until they were out of sight, then turned his headlights back on and retraced his route to the river. He accelerated through the turn onto

River Street. The engine whined as he picked up speed. His hands clenched the wheel, shoulders hunched over, his chin jutting out. His eyes focused on the bridge out of town.

At the intersection, he heaved the steering wheel to the left. The car skittered into the turn. Cups on the passenger side floor rolled to the right. An explosion of color burst into his tunnel vision: an old lady wearing lemon-yellow Capri pants topped off with an orange, green, and purple striped blouse glowed in his high beams. She dragged a tiny bug-eyed dog, its leash tied to her walker. The old lady stepped off the curb. A shot of adrenaline hit Hiram's system. He yanked the wheel hard left to avoid them and slammed into the guardrail for the oncoming lane. His car ricocheted off the steel beam, bounced across both lanes, rebounded off the opposite rail and caromed back into the right lane. He pushed the pedal to the floor and rocketed out of town.

On the other side of the bridge, the road curved north. The Toyota howled in protest as Hiram pushed it hard up the hill past the Wa-Wa Day Spa. The car lifted slightly as it topped the hill, flying through the broad right turn. Hiram closed his eyes momentarily at the sensation of weightlessness. The suspension compressed, and the car sank back onto the road. His phone vibrated. He twitched, and the car fishtailed. He wrangled the car back under control, dug the phone out of his pocket, and checked the caller ID. The guy who hired him. He'd just have to wait.

Hiram raised his eyes back to the road. A large, yellow dog ran toward him, its head held high, carrying something furry in its mouth. Hiram's eyes tracked the dog to, what he thought would be, an inevitable collision. He jerked the wheel to the right. The front suspension hit the stops as the car slid across the gravel shoulder and bounced up the hillside next to the road.

In the beams of the headlights, Hiram could see only sagebrush, but the overgrowth hid a minefield of rocks. The right front tire blew out when it connected with a boulder. The Corolla launched through the air in a spiral that an NFL quarterback would have been proud of. Hiram stared out the windshield watching the dark sky slowly transition through improbable angles, yielding to greenish gray where the headlights lit up the field. When the sky was on the bottom, and the ground on top, Hiram saw a beautiful angel with long, blond hair, wearing a flowing, white dress. She was flying toward him from heaven.

BAM! A spider web of fractures flashed across the windshield. Branches cracked and scraped against the sides of the car. The seat belt held Hiram fast, but the air bag didn't deploy, so his head hit the steering wheel as the car came to rest upside down on three enormous branches about ten feet off the ground. His wound reopened, and blood dripped from his forehead onto the upholstery of the car roof. His angel was running the other way. He mouthed the words "Help me, angel! Come back for me!"

Timothy sat at his desk with his head in his hands and his first chai latte of the morning growing cold by his elbow. "Timothy, would you come in my office, please?" Presseley's voice squawked through the intercom. Timothy turned the volume down. "We need to discuss some particulars."

He pushed himself up out of his chair, took a deep breath, and exhaled slowly. He plucked the fronts of his pant legs to release the wrinkles in his light gray, wool slacks, then smoothed his tie, a classy, dark blue, textured silk with a pattern that resembled tiny starfish rendered in muted maroon and yellow.

"Yes, Dr. P.," Timothy said flatly as he stood in Presseley's doorway.

"Come in, Timothy. Close the door."

This is getting old. Really old. Presseley had started to micromanage. This, especially, by someone who thought of himself as a big-picture guy, was the first step on the road to disaster. Timothy took two steps into the office. Without turning around, he placed his left hand on the edge of the door. He backed up with his hands behind him to close it. He stood very straight pressing against the door, as far from Presseley as he could get.

Presseley's fleshy face was haggard. Dark bags hung under his eyes. His thinning hair was combed back, but one clump above his right ear stuck out like a broken bird's wing. The Mont Blanc pen was tapping again.

"Timothy, what's the news on our friend's progress?" Presseley asked impatiently.

Ralphie had disappeared into the dynamite-fishing-hole in the sky on Sunday. Ray had been scratched off the list yesterday. "Dr. P., no more news since Ray's death." *How many deaths does he expect each day?*

"Why not?" Presseley said peevishly. The corners of his mouth folded into unattractive crevasses.

"I think he bolted after the shootout with the Guild." Timothy failed to mention that everyone had been shooting at him. "The word from the cops is that they found skid marks off the road past the Wa-Wa Day Spa and broken branches in that big old tree out in the field. There was broken glass at the base of the tree and a little blood." Timothy shrugged. "But no car."

"Yeah, so? Why hasn't he given you a progress report?" Presseley asked.

Timothy took a deep breath. "I've left him several messages since last night, but he hasn't returned my calls. With the glass and blood at the tree, he may have gotten into an accident. Maybe he can't return my calls."

"Where's his fucking car, then?" Presseley spat out. "Have you checked the hospital?"

"Dr. P., I don't know where his car is. Neither do the police." Timothy paused to breathe from his diaphragm. "And yes, of course, I checked the hospital. No one treated for injuries like that last night. He seems to have just disappeared."

Presseley distractedly picked at the corner of his desk mat. He wasn't looking at Timothy. Very quietly he said, "Find him."

"Yes, Dr. P. I'm working on it," Timothy said with a hint of exasperation.

Presseley stared at him without saying anything, his face growing redder as seconds passed.

"I'm going out to the Wa-Wa to ask around. Maybe somebody there heard something."

"Okay. Just be discreet. We don't want anybody tying us in with this." Presseley's hue lightened, and his head bobbed a little.

You're telling me? Timothy spun on the balls of his feet and stepped back as he opened the door to Presseley's office. He quickly left and closed the door behind him. Presseley's growing disquiet was a problem. Timothy had to be especially careful. He had no interest in being the fall guy if the plan went south. Getting the work done, while distancing himself from the players, would have to be his top priority from now on.

Chapter 31

The sun hung low over the headlands west of the Veggie-Tech compound. Nearly horizontal sunbeams streaked a white, cotton blanket with gold. Dr. Denise Murphy leaned across and kissed her lover.

"Happy sunset, darling," she whispered as she gazed into eyes as blue as a tropical sea.

Denise basked in the waning rays of the sun. She slipped off her sandals and rested her toes on the tops of Louise DeLuis's large feet. A heady combination of lust and contentment settled over her. She smiled and entwined Louise's powerful fingers with her own.

Louise reached out to the simple meal spread on the blanket and speared a tiny cocktail frank with a toothpick, lifted it from the plate, and waited for the sauce to drip away. Louise held the teeny-weeny wiener out and Denise nibbled at the bait. A small drop of marinade remained on her lower lip. Louise licked off the come-on condiment, then kissed her deeply.

Suddenly, Louise jumped up. "Denise, my dear, would you mind sharing this moment with me?"

"Of course not, Louise," Denise whispered. Her partner's eyes sparkled with the light of the setting sun. She reached up and took Louise's offered hand.

"Good, good, good." Louise smiled down at her.

Louise towered over Denise in so many ways. She always felt small in her lover's presence. In her view, Louise's vast intellect dimmed her own not-inconsequential mind. They made a perfect pair.

Until she met Louise, she had not dared to hope for feelings like these. Her early years had been a series of cruel emotional twists. She had adored her father, who called her "Daddy's little girl." He had been tall, blond, and strong, like Louise. But, unlike Louise, her father lacked power and direction. He made up for his missing strength with cruelty, sorrow, and, eventually, abuse. Denise's mind shut that door and locked it. Again.

Then, Louise entered her life. The power that Louise radiated was a gift as welcome as the sun breaking through a long, sodden, Northwest winter. Louise led Denise to this place. The strange attraction she felt for Louise grew into lust. Eventually, their time together turned to love. Standing on the hill in the gathering twilight, the pair stood hand in hand, gazing out at what they had built together.

There was the main house, where they lived. To the north, a circle of seven yurts provided living space for VeggieTech's associates. The greenhouses and a barn sat on a low hill nearby. To the east of the main house, a line of neatly-parked vehicles stretched down the grassy slope. Denise's black convertible, the roof down revealing bright-red, Hawaiian-print seat covers. Aubergine's late model European station wagon, parked next to Karat's showroom condition, red over beige, 1968 Volkswagen Bus that he and the other spoiled-brat hippies drove around in. Next, Louise's Hummer—an original, not some candy-ass H2 or H3 like the yuppies drive—squatted alongside an antique Bluebird school bus painted in a camouflage pattern of fluorescent green and orange. Barely visible beyond the bus, they could see the front end of Mustafa's antique, rust-pocked, shag-wagon, which looked like it might still move if the cliff you pushed it off were tall enough.

Louise and Denise soaked up the scene of tranquility, of peace, and of completion. They had worked hard to build it all, and their effort was about to pay off.

Across the compound, near the greenhouses, a dog barked.

"Goddamn it, Tofu! Put. That. Down!" Aubergine yelled at her recalcitrant retriever. The dog vanished behind the other greenhouse. She sighed and refocused on her work. She opened the door to the greenhouse quietly, as if trying to sneak up on someone.

The door squeaked. "Shhhh!" she whispered, glancing around to make sure she hadn't disturbed the residents. A garden cart sat right inside the door. She grabbed the handle and started down the first row.

She hunched over the plants, her long neck craned at an almost unnatural angle. The rows of beads braided into her hair ran past her shoulders and clicked as she moved her head from side to side. "Shh!" she said again.

She searched for the patch of red she had seen when she was leaving the day before. It was somewhere nearby.

"Ah! There you are!" she said. "I thought I'd find you here. Ooh! You are ready now."

Aubergine swung the pack off her shoulder and pulled out a small plastic box. She extracted a small vial and a hypodermic syringe. Thomas said the painkiller was like Tramadol, but better. She hoped he was right. The vet had given Tramadol to Tofu after he bit that nasty clown. *Why did the clown kick poor Tofu?* Aubergine had tried it first, as she did with everything she gave to Tofu, but she wasn't impressed.

She extracted the hypodermic from its protective cover, wiped the needle on her tunic, and inserted it into the top of the vial. "Only a few more minutes now," she whispered soothingly.

After filling the syringe with twenty milliliters of clear fluid, she solemnly withdrew the needle from the bottle and deftly flicked it with her finger to dislodge any air bubbles. "They always do that on TV," she said and smiled reassuringly. "I don't know why that's so important, but I want to get it right, now don't I?"

She carefully inserted the needle. "That didn't hurt, did it?" She pulled back on the plunger, and a plume of red swirled into the clear liquid. Slowly, she pushed the plunger all the way in.

Aubergine extracted the needle and pressed a small oval label over the puncture mark. A green V dominated the label with the number *81666* printed below.

"There now, let's just give that a little time to take effect. One hundred, ninety-nine, ninety-eight, ninety-seven. Okay. Here we go!" Aubergine quickly pulled the pruning shears out of her pack, cut clean through the stem of the tomato, and caught the heavy, red fruit in her left hand. She nestled the tomato into a box in the garden cart.

Thirty more minutes of anesthetizing and harvesting had filled the boxes with tomatoes, cucumbers, peppers, radishes, and carrots. Time was crucial now.

Aubergine wiped a few drops of sweat off her forehead, setting her hair beads clattering again. The vegetables were all asleep now, so it didn't matter. She wheeled the cart out of the greenhouse and rushed down the hill.

Behind the yurts, a dog barked.

"Goddamn it, Tofu! Leave those chickens alone!" Aubergine shouted as she hurried into the space encircled by the felt tents. A central cook-fire burned, and the primitive dwellings reflected the amber light. "They're ready!" Aubergine panted.

Stu rushed out of the closest dwelling. "Come on! Let's eat before they come to!"

"Wait! I have to take some of this to the packing house." Aubergine picked up a box of vegetables from the cart. "You take these. I'll be right back." She handed the box to Stu and took off with the garden cart and tomatoes.

As Aubergine passed the main house, she admired the VeggieTech logo emblazoned on the east-facing wall. A large green *V* symbolized farming with respect for the earth and the crops it produced. A yellow circle representing the sun hovered above the right arm of the *V*. A series of blue, diagonal dashes over the left arm signified rain. And brown lines, for the earth, stretched out beneath. Aubergine smiled. *That says it all.* She passed by the parking lot and loading docks on the east side of the packing house. She waved to her blue Volvo station wagon. *Henry is so cute.*

As usual, the shipping area was a flurry of late-day activity with crates of prize fruit and vegetables stacked and waiting for overnight shipment via FedEx to anxious clients. Aubergine dropped off the box of tomatoes and raised her arm to get Hammill's attention. He waved back and returned to what he was doing. A FedEx driver was closing the rear door on a truck packed to the ceiling with boxes labeled, "Crockett and Tubbs Best Vegetables," VeggieTech's green logo prominently displayed under the arched text. Aubergine waved to the driver and hurried back to the yurts.

Even with the time she took delivering her harvest, the others were only now emerging from their fabric houses. They slowly took their places at the round, stone table next to the fire and placed their plates and knives in front of them.

Aubergine joined them. Each person took a different vegetable and, with grave concentration, began to slice the nutritious gifts from the earth into six pieces. Pepper very gently poked her tomato with the knife to make sure the painkiller had really taken effect. Aubergine prodded her cucumber. She certainly didn't want to hear that green screaming like last week.

After they sliced their produce, everyone paused, lowering their heads. Karat said grace. "We thank you plants for willingly sacrificing your children and, in some cases, your very bodies, so we might nourish ourselves. We hope that you felt no pain from this and promise to help your families around this world suffering from the indignity and torture of current farming practices!" The group mumbled in agreement.

Aubergine looked at the empty place across the table. "Where's Thomas?"

"Oh well," Karat said as he chomped into a slice of fresh red pepper. "You snooze, you lose."

Thomas stood in a circle of light. The central room on the second floor of the main house was a cone-roofed construction with a decahedral skylight. Intense spotlights around the skylight illuminated the hapless figure standing below.

"Thomas, Thomas, Thomas," Louise said, rocking the chair forward and back. "You showed such promise. Why did you have to betray me like this?"

"I know what you're doing. I know what's going on here." Thomas quavered in the presence of VeggieTech's leader. "I know about the drugs. I know about the shipping. I know about all of it."

Louise stood up from behind the desk and strode into the middle of the room.

Thomas suffered a withering stare.

"All of it? I think, maybe, not quite all of it."

"Maybe not, but a lot. You know, one word from me and this whole operation goes down." Thomas seemed to draw strength from his defiance.

"I know, Thomas, I know." Louise's voice grew gentler, calmer. "That's why you showed such promise. You've got a lot on the ball." Louise walked across the room and sank into an overstuffed, calf-skin-leather sofa. "And that's exactly why we had such hopes for you." Louise smiled. "You're not like all the others. You've got a mind of your own. You could have gone places with us. Not like the rest of those idiots." Louise nodded at the window. "Not like that Aubergine, or whatever she's calling herself this week. I tell you what Thomas, when she had *her* flowers delivered it was definitely a couple buds short of a dozen." Louise chuckled.

Thomas smiled weakly.

"But she does look great. Doesn't she, Thomas?"

Thomas hunched over, like a man beaten.

"Jesus. Thomas, you look like shit." Louise tried to sound truly concerned. "Let me have the doctor take a look at you. Okay?"

"Uh, sure." Thomas didn't seem sure at all.

Louise had already punched a button on the telephone set and a chirp responded.

"Dr. Murphy, could you come into my office please. I don't think Thomas is well."

The door opened almost immediately, and Denise came in. She wore a lab coat over her Levi's and carried a black soft-side valise. A stethoscope hung around her neck.

"Dr. Murphy! That was fast."

"I was on my way out of the house when you called." She smiled like the Mona Lisa. "Glad I was still around."

"Yes, yes, yes. Well, Thomas and I were just discussing his future with us. I told him we thought he held such promise. I was hoping we could put him on the production line, maybe inside packaging." Louise winked at her. "But he still wants to leave us."

Denise nodded.

"Anyway, I think Thomas looks a little peaked. Would you mind checking him out?"

"Not at all." She glanced over at Thomas. "Thomas, come sit over here in the light." She pointed to a vinyl-covered chair sitting in the center of an area of white tile, illuminated by the spotlights.

"Gee, you do look a little under the weather." She pulled down his eyelids and examined him closely. "Have you been sleeping?"

"No, not very well," Thomas sniffled. "I think I might be allergic to the straw beds or whatever the yurts are made from."

"Well, I should be able to help you with your sleeping problem. Maybe even clear up your allergies." She smiled broadly at him and moved behind the chair.

Denise bent down and opened her bag. She got out a tongue depressor and a number 11 surgical scalpel. She opened the sterile package on the scalpel and threw the wrapper into her bag. Standing upright, she kicked a throw rug off of the tile, revealing a drain.

"Let me just have a look at your throat." She returned to

the front of the chair. "Open up and say 'ah,'" she commanded.

He complied. She took the tongue depressor in her left hand and peered into his mouth. "Hmmmm."

"Hglunh?" Thomas tried to speak.

With her right hand, Denise quickly stabbed the scalpel into the left side of Thomas' neck. She pulled the scalpel through his carotid artery. Blood spurted onto the white tile. She backed away from the red shower. The air filled with a metallic, organic scent as Thomas collapsed, twitching, onto the floor. Denise went over to Louise's desk and pulled out a tissue. She licked it and dabbed at a red spot on her lab coat.

"Thank you, Denise." Louise exhaled loudly. "Your skill in such matters is undeniable."

The stain proved stubborn, so she licked the tissue again. "Well, somebody's got to do the dirty work." She smiled coyly.

Louise leaned over and pressed another button on the phone. The electronic chirp was followed by "Yes?"

"Hammill, good evening. I believe there's something in the office that you might find useful." Louise clicked off and stood up. "God, I'm hungry. Let's go get some dinner."

Chapter 32

Daylight lit up the eastern horizon as Juice pulled his white Explorer up to the front door of Whitey's Fishin' Inn. A short, plump figure stood attentively out front. In his left hand, Rudy held a tackle box. His right grasped a rod and reel, the information tag fluttered from the tip of the rod like a tiny pennant.

The fishing competition was less than two weeks away, and Rudy's adrenaline level had reached new heights. His beach-ball physique bounced over to the SUV, his eyes and nose straining to see over the top of the door panel. "Ted! Look what I got!" Rudy showed off his new G. Loomis Shaky Head rod equipped with a Quantum Pro baitcast reel.

"So, you finally figured out that you couldn't catch fish with that fugazzi rod and reel you had."

Rudy's forehead furrowed. "But it wasn't a fugazzi. It was a Zebco."

Juice eyed the new gear and gave Rudy an approving nod. "Those fish won't stand a chance, little buddy."

The passenger door opened. The tackle box and rod jiggled back and forth in Rudy's hands as he gauged the distance up onto the Explorer's passenger seat.

"Whoa, there. Let me help you with those." Juice quickly exited the driver's side and limped around the front of the car. He grabbed the gear, opened the rear passenger door, and laid the equipment across the cargo area. Each item had Rudy's name and phone number embossed on plastic tape. "What's with all the labels?" Juice asked.

"I like things organized," Rudy said as he opened the top of his tackle box, revealing twenty or so individually marked compartments.

"Two Shoes, you are one piece of work," Juice said smiling.

"Thanks, Ted," Rudy said distractedly as he closed the tackle box then walked to the passenger door. He put his hands, palm down, on the Explorer's passenger seat, his elbows up as high as they would go. He pushed off the car seat with both hands and launched himself off the ground. Turning in midair, he landed his left butt cheek on the seat, then wriggled the rest of the way onto the cushion. He snapped the seat belt into place, closed the door, and stared ahead with the eager expectation of a dog waiting for a trip to the park.

"Aren't you getting tired of staying in the motel?" Juice asked as he started the car. "You could have rented a place and saved some money."

"I'm so used to living in hotels, I don't even notice." Rudy said. "Where are we fishing today?"

"We're going to Walt's first. Gotta pick up a few things."

"Okay, Ted! I'm ready."

As soon as they drove onto the road, Rudy began the tale of his Internet search for his new fishing gear. He kept talking until Juice pulled into the parking lot at Walt's. When the car came to a stop, Rudy opened the passenger door, turned to the side, and pushed himself out as if he were making a parachute jump.

Juice looked up at Walt's trademark giant bass mounted above the entrance and shook his head. A miasma of blue smoke wafted through the screen door. Walt was in. Juice took a deep breath and opened the door for Rudy. Two steps into the shop, Rudy came to a full halt, his mouth open, little coughs catching in his throat. Breathing at Walt's took practice.

Juice didn't see Walt but he heard voices in the back room. Wanting to minimize his exposure to the thick plume of cigarette smoke that hung a few feet below the ceiling, he went straight for the bait section.

Walt came out of the back room with an almost-toothless grin plastered on his face. He waved to acknowledge Juice and Rudy. Frank Hollowell followed him out and rushed down the aisle.

"Morning, Frank," Juice said and looked at the box cradled in his arms. "Fishing today?"

Frank clutched the box tighter to his chest. "Not today, Ted." He cast a furtive glance at Rudy. "Gotta blow a stump in the yard." He hurried to the door.

Juice turned back to the bait to pick out the day's menu. Since his last visit, the feathered lures had been rearranged by color into the bands of a rainbow. Juice glanced over at Walt. He carried his selection over to the counter, then turned around looking for Rudy.

Rudy was standing in front of a close-out bin filled with fish-scented rubber worms, supposedly irresistible to fish but definitely irresistible to him. Before Juice could say anything, Rudy stuck his right hand in a bucket of very sticky rubber cylinders. When he jerked his hand back out, a mass of squiggly fake worms coated his hand like a glove. He dropped his hand to his side and shook it tentatively to get rid of the gummy wigglers. When that failed, he pursed his lips in concentration, scraped his left hand over his right in a more aggressive attempt, and ended up with worms dangling from both. Rudy raised his arms over his head as if he were invoking the Lord for assistance. With a forceful snap of both hands, Rudy sent the worms flying. Several stuck to the inside of the screen door. Some hit the ceiling and immediately began a slow peel from the smoke-varnished surface. One landed on the counter, draped over Walt's half-eaten donut.

Walt plucked the worm off and dropped it in with Juice's lures. He picked up the donut, gave it a sniff, and took a bite.

Juice sighed, pulled a couple of paper towels off a roll on the counter, and delivered them to Rudy to wipe the worms and worm goo from his hands. He then prodded his friend in the direction of the cash register. He tipped his head at the wastebasket. Rudy deposited the used towels and worms. After another nudge, Rudy paid with his credit card, and they headed toward the door. Juice carried the bag in his left hand and pushed the beaming Rudy outside to the Explorer with his right.

A few minutes after they left Walt's, Juice turned off the road to the boat launch area. He backed the trailer down to the water, set the parking brake, and got out.

Rudy hovered right behind Juice and tapped him on the shoulder. "What can I do to help, Ted? What can I do?"

"Just stand back for now." Juice turned the winch and the boat slid smoothly into the water. Catching movement out of the corner of his eye, he saw Rudy run down the dock, take two long strides toward the boat, then launch himself over the gunwale. Nailing a perfect landing in the boat, Rudy's face crinkled with a huge smile. He sat in the left seat, staring intently out at the river.

"Yo, Two Shoes, stay put. I have to stow the car," Juice said as he tied the boat to the dock.

Juice climbed in the SUV, started the engine, and pulled the trailer up the ramp. Water poured off the metal framework as he drove across the parking area and pulled into a double-long space. He got out and tossed the keys onto the floor.

He checked the trailer as he headed back across the parking lot and caught a glimpse of the lone bumper sticker on his truck: "Work Is For People Who Can't Fish—Fresh Squeezed Fishing 509-555-5545." *Yeah, right. And fishing is for people who can't get laid.* Juice thought about Dinah, the woman who kept him from fishing all those years. *Damn, I still miss her.*

To the east near the highway, a siren wound up from a low growl into a high-pitched warble. Juice stopped in the middle of the parking lot and faced the entrance, his fists planted on his hips. A few seconds later, Dickie's Ford Fiesta came around the turn, the squealing tires harmonizing with the wail of the megaphone siren alarm that was strapped to the passenger window frame with plastic wire ties. Dickie did a hand-over-hand to pilot the Fiesta into the spot next to Juice's Explorer. As the battered car jerked to a stop, the rope tied to the front of the car gave way and the front fender fell to the ground. The siren cut off abruptly. Dickie opened the door and got out with a twelve-pack of Rainier beer in his right hand.

"This is the swill you drink, right?" He smiled at Juice and kicked the door closed behind him. The hood of the car popped open two inches.

"No new wheels?" Juice asked with a smirk.

"Fuck me. We don't have budget for another car, so this is it until October." Dickie passed Juice and walked downhill to the boat. He stopped and turned around. "You coming?"

Juice shook his head, smiled, and followed Dickie.

Dickie clambered on board and handed the twelve-pack to Rudy. "Here you go, Rudy. Toss this in the cooler. No soda for you today. It's beer-thirty."

Juice stepped lightly into the boat. He pulled a chamois from a storage locker, wiped Dickie's footprint off the white gunwale, and stowed the cloth back in the locker. He stepped behind the steering console and twisted the key. The Honda four-stroke cranked over once, caught, and idled with a quiet thrum. Juice flipped the rocker switches, and the GPS and gauges came to life. He gave the panel a practiced scan. Satisfied, he stepped around the console to the bow and untied the boat from the dock.

"Dickie, did you bring your bait?" Rudy asked.

"I brought the only bait I'll need." Dickie reached over and patted the cooler. Then he leaned back and rested his heels on the edge of the boat.

Juice leaned over and tapped him on the shoulder. When Dickie looked around, Juice handed him a small towel and cut his eyes at Dickie's feet.

"Yeah, yeah. Okay. New boat. Sorry." Dickie wiped the gleaming white surface with his sleeve, laid the towel down, then put his feet up again.

Juice eased the boat away from the dock, arced out into deeper water, and accelerated up river. The three men watched the cliffs and said nothing as they sped past Wanderfalls. Up ahead, the vanes on three wind generators rotated lazily on top of the bluff. When the boat pulled even with the first turbine, Juice pulled back on the throttle and let the boat drift to a stop.

"Rudy, this is going to be your lucky day. Go ahead and lower the anchor." Juice shut off the engine, stepped around the console, and sat next to Dickie. "You go for it, little buddy, we've got your back."

Rudy cast his line and sat motionless, watching the spot where the line broke the surface of the water.

"So, Dickie, where are you at with this case?" Juice nodded down river in the general direction of Wanderfalls. He popped a beer, slid it into a "Fresh Squeezed Fishing" coozie, and rested it on his right thigh.

Dickie exhaled and took a pull on his beer. "I gotta say, it's damn frustrating. I know *who* is up to something, but I don't know *what*." He raised his left fist and extended his forefinger. "I know Presseley is behind all this." His middle finger popped out. "I know the Utility is broke." He straightened his ring finger. "Then Eddie's shot and killed after their videotaped meeting." He held out his little finger. "And Ray, their financial guy, is dead—a heart attack with shots fired." Finally, he stuck out his thumb. "Now, we've got a shooter who vanished into thin air right over that hill." He pointed at the wind generators.

Rudy spun his head around and said, "Remember, that video had been tampered with."

"Right." Dickie folded his fingers. "Something happened after the official meeting ended, and whatever happened was recorded. John Parsons and Marion Shill were on the list of viewers, and they both reported assaults. Somebody's trying to cover their tracks."

"What about that Indian group?" Juice asked.

Dickie shook his head. "We checked with Shecky and he didn't keep the complete video. He edited the file he got from Cameron."

Rudy reeled in his line and cast it toward shore. The line went taut. He sat up and whisked his right hand in quick circles to haul in his catch. The lure came out of the water dragging a tangled nest of fishing line from some other fisherman's bad day. He pulled the snarled wad off the end and stuffed it in a trash bag. Without saying a word, he turned and cast his line away from land.

"But it isn't even circumstantial evidence. I need something hard."

"What about June Presseley?" Juice asked.

"Nah, that's just noise." Dickie shook his head, then took a swig of beer. "Presseley isn't happy about his wife's behavior, but Christ, he should be used to it by now. It's only something else to raise his blood pressure."

"Or whatever," Juice added.

"Yeah, that too." Dickie winked, leaned in, and poked Juice's knee with his finger. "But I'm betting that the part of the meeting that was recorded by mistake was about what they're going to do to clean up their financial mess."

"Makes sense." Juice tilted his head back and gazed at a wisp of cloud drifting by. "You know, Dickie…"

"What?"

"All the iMUD players were in the back room at the Tuck 'er Inn that one day. And then those other guys came in. Something Snead."

"Bill Snead. Yeah, Eddie's brother." Dickie sat up. "Eddie's brother! Huh. I wonder how he fits in?"

"Maybe that Guild is the muscle they hired to cover their tracks."

"Nah, those guys don't have it in them. They couldn't actually hurt anyone."

Juice raised an eyebrow. "What about the shootout at the community center?"

"Yeah, okay, they are armed, but that's just their trailer-park interpretation of the Second Amendment. They wouldn't kill Eddie. Besides, Parsons and Shill only reported one guy, and the Guild members never work alone."

"It's all wrapped up in that video. You find the missing part, and you find your answer." Juice tipped his head back and drained his beer.

"Now there's an idea, Mr. Obvious." Dickie laughed. "But what? Where?"

A low rumble drifted over the water from the south. Another boat appeared to rise out of the river as it approached. Dickie squinted.

Juice grabbed his binoculars. "Now there's a guy I could see covering up tracks."

"Who's that?" Dickie shielded his eyes from the glare.

"Timothy." Juice lowered the binoculars and said, "That guy sets off my radar every time."

Dickie nodded. "You know, I can see that. He's Presseley's boy. He does have something about him. And he keeps showing up in odd places at odd times." Dickie stroked his chin.

"You have gotta be kidding me." Juice snickered as he looked through the glasses.

"What now?" Dickie reached for the binoculars. "He's dressed like a clown?"

"Kind of," Juice said as he handed over his binoculars.

Dickie raised the glasses to his eyes and snickered.

Rudy hauled in a sneaker, put it in the trash bag, and rested his tackle on his lap. He reached into the cooler and pulled out a can. The three men sipped their beers as Timothy motored up and drifted to a stop about ten feet away. His boat had the same finish as Juice's—white, metal-flake gelcoat, with unstained white, all-weather carpeting.

"Ted, we have the same boat!" Timothy called out. "Don't you just love it?"

"Got it a week ago, Timothy. Still on the honeymoon." He glanced at the large decal on the side of Timothy's boat.

"Glad I got the CDC model upgrade though. Feels bigger."

Timothy's shoulders drooped.

"Hey!" Rudy shouted from the bow. "I've got that hat!"

Rudy and Timothy gaped at each other across the water. They wore identical fishing hats, tan shirts, and khaki pants stuffed into rubber boots. They looked like the reflection in a funhouse mirror.

"Hey," Juice said to get their attention. "What's with the boots?"

"They're French!" Timothy and Rudy replied in unison.

Louise and Denise stood below the wind generator closest to the cliff, holding hands.

"I love you, Louise."

"Yes, yes, yes. I love you, too, Denise." Louise's absent gaze drifted down to the river. Two white boats rocked from side to side near the base of the cliff. The boats floated no more than ten feet apart. "Why won't they leave us alone?"

"Soon, Louise, soon," Denise said soothingly and stroked Louise's hairy arm. "Not long now, and they won't bother us anymore."

Louise stared at the boats: one man in one boat, three in the other. "No, no, no! Denise, that man in the green and tan fishing clothes! Timothy Bentle is back, and now he has reinforcements."

Denise put her arm around Louise's waist and squeezed. "Louise, please be patient."

"No, no, no! This will not do. The time has come. We must advance our plans." Louise turned abruptly and marched away from the cliff.

Chapter 33

Hiram Gund thought he might be dreaming. The angel stood next to his bed, then flew away. A door closed. He fought his way back to consciousness, but he was alone. *I feel like I've been drugged.* When he sat up, aches and pains blossomed throughout his body, like dandelions in an un-mowed lawn. He settled into the most comfortable position he could find. Soft light filtered through sheer curtains fluttering in the breeze from the open window. Hiram couldn't tell if it was early morning or dusk.

As his head cleared he took in his surroundings. The furnishings were simple. The double bed he sat in, and a set of rough-hewn shelves against the wall. A few well-hung paintings, amateurish landscapes mostly, encased in heavy wooden frames, dangled from metal hooks. A mirror on the back of the door. A sturdy, hand-made table with two chairs, right next to the door. Blue and yellow floral-print cushions on the chairs matched the tablecloth, which was angled forty-five degrees to appear diamond-shaped. The table held a plate of muffins and a steaming pot of coffee.

Hiram checked his pulse. He had not died and gone to

heaven. His legs shook when he stood up so he waited until his knees steadied, then shuffled over to the table. He sat down and winced as a bruise met the chair seat. He snatched a muffin from the plate and scarfed it down. *Cranberry raisin oatmeal. Still warm.* He was very hungry. He jammed another muffin into his mouth and chewed as he poured coffee into a hand-thrown, earthenware mug and stirred in four heaping spoons of sugar. He took a sip and swallowed.

After he finished the coffee and two more muffins, he made the trek to the window, feeling stronger with each step. As he passed the door, he caught his reflection in the mirror and nearly dropped the mug. He wore a knee-length nightshirt made of natural-colored, coarse-spun cotton that looked like it had been hand woven. *What the fuck?* Hiram's pale, skinny legs extended beneath the gown like support poles for a circus tent. A large bandage hid most of his forehead. Livid purple bruises mottled the rest. He leaned closer for a better look. He couldn't remember what happened.

The hand-forged, steel door handle rotated clockwise with a metallic grating sound. Startled, Hiram started to back away from the door. Never catlike, his dulled reflexes managed to save him from another night of unconsciousness. A glancing blow caught the right side of his forehead, but it felt like he'd been hit with a brick. As he fell butt first to the ground, a blur snatched the coffee mug cleanly from his hand.

The afternoon sun shining down the hall blinded Hiram. A surreal figure stood silhouetted by a dazzling light, a hand holding the coffee mug out from the ethereal radiance.

What the fuck? still topped Hiram's list of available thoughts.

"Hiram Gund!" The androgynous giant entered the room and tossed a metal rectangle across the rough terra cotta tiles. An Indiana tag embossed with "HITMAN3" clattered to a stop at Hiram's feet.

Whoa! took over first place.

"Good afternoon!" the glowing form said and placed Hiram's coffee mug on the table. The door closed, and the shining silhouette resolved into a slender person standing over six feet tall. The visitor's shirt matched Hiram's. Rough cotton pants and a pair of *zapatas*, like the ones worn by the Anglo-Mexican bad guy in a 1950s black and white cowboy movie, completed the outfit.

"Hiram, welcome to our home." A firm grip on Hiram's shoulder and another on his arm lifted him to his feet as if he were a child. Hiram staggered, but the hands held him steady.

"Who are you? Where am I? What happened to me?" Words spewed from Hiram like water out of a broken pipe.

"First things first, Hiram." His visitor smiled.

The smile made Hiram feel like he had finally come home.

"I'm Louise DeLuis," the person said as a pair of strong hands closed around Hiram's with a vise-like grip.

"Louise?"

"Yes."

Hiram took a step back and stared in confusion.

"You are in my home. We found you hanging in a tree about two miles from here and brought you here. Your car was trashed."

Memories rushed back. Everything was clear, up to the point where it all wasn't. "Why here? Why not a hospital?"

"You are safer here from the people who are looking for you. And honestly, we are better equipped than the local hospital—much better." Louise gave Hiram a concerned look. "How's your head?"

Hiram risked a gentle touch. "Actually, much better."

"Have a look."

Hiram warily approached the mirror and gingerly pulled back the tape securing his bandage.

"Holy shit." Hiram turned back to Louise. "Those are the best stitches I've ever seen. Who did them? You?"

"No, no, no. They are courtesy of Dr. Denise Murphy,

formerly a board-certified plastic surgeon before joining us. Now, as my spouse she handles the—shall we say—'medical issues,' for us." Louise fingered quote marks in the air.

"Spouse? As in husband or wife?" Hiram went fishing.

"'Or' is so limiting, don't you think?" Louise arched one eyebrow. "But come, let me show you what I've built."

An unyielding grip took Hiram's shoulder and steered him over to the window. Louise pulled back the curtain revealing as pastoral a scene as Hiram had ever seen. The sun lay just over the hill to their right and suffused the rolling fields with a green-gold light.

"But why me? Why did you take my license plate? And, how the fuck do you know my name?" Hiram searched Louise's face for answers.

Another smile graced Hiram.

"One of our associates notified us of your plight. We beat the police to the scene of the crash. Your plates struck us as—shall we say—unusual, so we took your car as a precaution."

"But my name? How?"

"Hiram, Hiram, Hiram." Louise's tone sounded at once condescending and reassuring. "Haven't you ever heard of the Internet?"

Hiram silently admitted to himself that yes, in fact, he had, but for some reason he didn't feel the need to speak.

Louise's long, delicate fingers turned him around, and Hiram gazed up into intense blue eyes. "Hiram, have you ever heard the Buddhist saying 'When the student is ready, the teacher arrives'?"

Hiram nodded yes while silently admitting that no, in fact, he had not.

"It works the other way, too."

"But Louise..." A hand in front of his face stopped him short.

"Please, Hiram, call me what everybody else in my home does." Louise smiled like a saint.

"Sure, what's that?"

"Father."

The sun winked through the wind turbines' white blades as they spun slowly in the afternoon breeze. Hiram felt a little fuzzy but could not remember ever feeling more at peace. And he had finally met his angel. Her name was Aubergine. For the past two days, each morning, afternoon, and evening, Aubergine floated into his room with a tray of food and her devoted attention. That fateful day, when he followed Ralphie to the river, Aubergine was the vision in earth-tones dancing along the shore. Her dog, Tofu, had saved his life in the ensuing explosion. Now, after his accident, she brought him food, cleaned and re-bandaged the wound on his forehead, and tidied his room. But mostly she talked. And talked. And talked. Hiram would eat, listen, and grow sleepy. Afterward he always felt great.

The door opened, and Aubergine came in with his dinner. Once again, his world spun about the new center of his universe. She brought the freshest produce he had ever eaten. The vegetables were sometimes raw, but today they had been lightly cooked with a delicate sauce. The plate also contained a hot dog on a whole-grain bun. "It's all vegetarian," Aubergine assured him as she danced around the room cleaning up.

Aubergine told him a story while she worked. It always began with how her privileged upbringing left her feeling unfulfilled and longing for a freedom she knew existed somewhere. She told Hiram about how she met Louise and how Father shared the plans for making dreams like hers come true Louise showed her how people could live in true harmony with nature, taking from the Earth only what they needed to survive, and thriving by putting back more than they took out. Father invited her to see for herself that this wasn't a dream. She found what she was looking for at the compound, over the hill from the river a few miles outside of Wanaduck, Washington.

Aubergine talked of the others, about Dr. Murphy and Hammill. She went on at length about Karat and Stu and Pepper. She told him about Mustafa—happy Mustafa, always singing—and how he was working on a secret project. She worried about Rute and Thomas, the only members who, so far, thought it necessary to leave. Her eyes filled with tears as she told how a weeping Father relayed the story of Thomas' leaving, how Father had begged him to stay and how, in the end, Father had let Thomas go to find his own peace and sanctuary.

"It was only fair." She paused with a pillow half-stuffed into a handspun cotton case. "Father wants each of us to find our dreams. If not here, then by following our own path." Just like every other time she got to this point in the story, tears streamed down her cheeks. She grabbed Hiram's used napkin from his plate and blew her nose, sounding something like a cross between an elephant and a train wreck. Out in the hall, a dog barked.

"Tofu! Goddammit! Shut up!" Aubergine yelled over her shoulder at the closed door. This, too, had become part of the story.

Hiram gazed at Aubergine from under heavy eyelids. "Aubergine, I think I found my dream. I love…" he trailed off, nearly asleep. His heart skipped as she bent over and kissed his forehead. She put everything on the tray and padded across the room. She hit the latch with her elbow and silently pushed the door open. The door closed with a quiet click.

"Goddammit Tofu! Get out of that!" was always the last thing Hiram heard.

Louise DeLuis and Denise Murphy stopped outside Hiram's door.

"Are you sure he's ready?" Louise asked.

"Yeah," Denise answered. "It's a new formulation, but all the preliminary tests went perfectly. We've ramped his dosages aggressively, but the lab results show values within the expected range.

"The new formulation makes him feel very well, but also makes him especially pliable and compliant. It's a custom mixture of Xanax, Versed, and MDMA. The MDMA brings on feelings of happiness and connection. The heavy dose of Xanax kills the stimulant effect of the MDMA, lowers his anxiety level, and, more importantly, prevents him from realizing he's been drugged. The Versed ensures that he won't remember anything if anybody asks him questions later. He's ready alright."

"Good, good, good. See you at breakfast." Louise kissed her and reached for the door handle.

"Good morning, Hiram!" Louise pushed into the room. "Dr. Murphy tells me you're doing better. How's your head feeling? Good. Good. Good." Louise hurried to the east window, peered out, turned, then rushed to the west window and surveyed the compound.

"Good morning, Father. I didn't expect to see you this morning." Hiram pulled the covers up to his chin.

"I know, I know, Hiram. But big things are afoot. Big things! I think you might be a gift from heaven for our little group." Louise paused. "Do you remember when I said you might be the exact person we were looking for? That you may have shown up at the exact moment we needed you?"

"Uh—yes?" Hiram replied and sat up in bed.

"Good, good, good. Because now I am sure of it." Louise grasped Hiram's shoulders and looked into his eyes. "Please, Hiram, Dr. Murphy and I would be honored if you would join us for breakfast this morning."

"No, Father. It would be my honor." Hiram recited the conditioned response like a robot. Louise smiled. Hiram was responding exactly as Denise had predicted.

Hiram slipped into his clothes, and Louise led him out the door. They walked down the stairs and into the eating area adjoining Louise's office. Two people sat waiting.

"Hiram, this is Dr. Denise Murphy. She's the doctor who stitched you up when you first got here." Louise's hand rotated toward the woman seated at the table. "She's been closely following your progress since then."

Hiram shook Denise's hand. "Thanks for everything. I'm feeling so much better. I almost can't believe it." Hiram smiled but appeared puzzled. "I don't know why, but you seem really familiar."

Denise and Louise exchanged a quick glance. "And this is Mustafa Farouk." Louise pointed to the small man standing by the table. "Mustafa joined us from Syria. He sought to escape the persecution he suffered as an artist, and we were more than happy to help him follow his dream."

Hiram took a few steps forward and extended his hand, but Mustafa only bowed slightly. "Yes, Aubergine told me about you. I'm very glad to meet you," Hiram said. Mustafa's expression didn't change as he made another small bow.

"Thank you, Mustafa. That will be all for now," Denise said. Mustafa bowed once more and left the room through the kitchen door.

"Good, good, good. Ah yes. Aubergine. Hiram, you two have been spending a lot of time together, eh? I think she has taken quite a liking to you." Louise winked.

Hiram blushed.

"But let's eat. Hiram you sit there, next to Dr. Murphy. Doesn't this look good?" Louise surveyed the breakfast feast on the table: plates of scrambled eggs, a pot of coffee, cream, sugar, freshly baked breads and muffins, butter, juice, and a huge pile of bacon.

"Huh?" Hiram pointed at the meat.

"Looks can be deceiving, Hiram." Louise smiled at him and patted his arm. "We are all vegetarians. Some of us eat eggs and dairy products, but we all gave up meat a long time ago. You tried one of the hot dogs, I believe?" Hiram nodded. "This bacon is a new product our food operations manager, Hammill, is working on. All vegetarian, but tastes just like the real thing."

Denise picked up the plate and held it out to Hiram. "Father and I find it not to our taste, but please give it a try."

Hiram tonged a few pieces onto his plate. He picked up a strip and took a bite. "Not bad," he said and munched away. "It's a little, I don't know, gamier, than real bacon, but not bad."

Louise and Denise shared another glance.

"Good, good, good, Hiram. Please help yourself to whatever you like."

Platters clattered, but otherwise, the threesome ate in silence. Louise finished first, pushed back from the table, stood up, and poured more coffee for everyone. "Now Hiram." Louise remained standing. "We know Aubergine has given you the inside perspective of our little group. We asked her to do that so you could get a general idea of how things work around here and who all the players are."

Hiram sipped his coffee and nodded absently.

"But, as I told you, we need you." Louise flashed a brilliant smile at Hiram. "Not as one of the workers. We need you at the top level of our organization."

Hiram looked surprised.

"You'll work closely with me and Dr. Murphy, of course. Mostly though, you and Hammill will manage the, uh, business end of things." Louise paused. "Hiram."

"Yes, Father?"

"We know who you are."

Hiram broke into a sweat. The coffee cup slipped from his hand and shattered on the floor.

Denise reached over and patted his arm again. "It's okay, Hiram. It's okay. Calm down."

"Your skills, your—shall we say—calling? Exactly what we need right now."

Hiram looked like he might bolt.

"You see, Hiram, we are the collective that Aubergine told you about, but we are also much more than that." Louise strode over and placed both hands on Hiram's shoulders. "And Hiram. We are all in extreme danger—you, me, Mustafa, Dr. Murphy, Hammill, and even—no, particularly—poor Aubergine."

Hiram jumped to his feet, knocking the chair over. "What do you mean Aubergine's in danger?"

Louise frowned. "Bad people are after us. They haven't found us yet, but they're getting close." Louise suddenly brightened and flashed a broad smile. "However, your skills, your particular skills, are exactly what we need to save us all."

Hiram's forehead furrowed, but he leaned in to listen.

"The dynamite work near the dam? Excellent."

"How'd you find out about that?"

"The removal of that corrupt accountant downtown? Brilliant."

"Or that?"

"Those are precisely the skills we need to protect us. But as you have shared some of your secrets with us..." Louise paused.

"I have?"

"We need to trust you with some of our own."

Louise glanced from Hiram to Denise and back.

"Hiram," Louise said with a serious tone that sounded like the start of a facts-of-life talk. "Hiram, can we trust you with our secrets?"

"Father," Hiram responded mechanically, "I would be honored to serve you however I can."

Denise released an audible sigh. Louise grinned at the pre-programmed answer. Hiram was theirs.

"Good, good, good," Louise began. "What do you know about biology?"

Hiram blushed again and shrugged. "Only the basics, I guess."

"That was me as well before I met Dr. Murphy." Louise reached out and petted Denise's shoulder. "She, however, knew more—much more—and, with her knowledge, we have been able to generate the funds we need to keep our dream alive. But to keep growing, we need more room. Room for facilities, fields, and housing. And room to shield our operations from unwanted attention."

Louise stared vacantly into space. Denise softly cleared her throat, and Louise snapped back to the present. "Excuse me. I'm getting ahead of myself. Aubergine gave you an initial perspective of the organization. Other than her and

Mustafa, have you met any of the others?"

"No, Father."

"Well, they are all pretty much of a piece—idealistic young fools who have not found the whatever-the-hell-it-is they are searching for. We recruit people who come from means because we bring them into the fold as partners rather than mere followers. They invest in the organization and feel they have an ownership stake. That partnership is real. By—shall we say—sharing the risk, both their productivity and our group's security are greatly improved."

"But Father, Mustafa and Aubergine don't seem anything alike to me."

"That's true, Hiram. A few are brought in because they possess a valuable skill or are predisposed to certain behaviors. Mustafa is in that category. As are you." Louise smiled benevolently.

"From each according to their skills. To each according to their needs," Denise recited.

Louise jumped up and down. "Exactly." Louise pointed a forefinger right at Hiram. "Sounds all very Marxist but—as socialists the world over found out—some of us need a lot more than others. We hope to include you in that category with us, Hiram."

"But, I have no money to join. Why do you want me?" Hiram appeared confused.

"Because of what you can do," Denise said.

"Yes, now more than ever, Hiram." Louise reclaimed the narrative. "We don't want money from you. You will buy your way in with your expertise." Louise walked to the door, beckoning the others to follow. "Good, good, good. A tour is in order. Let's start with the drugs."

Chapter 34

Louise, Dr. Murphy, and Hiram left the main house through the front door. Louise led the way with Dr. Murphy walking close alongside. The dry, bright light cast sharp-edged shadows from the two corrugated-metal, pre-fab buildings in front of them. Louise's long, blond hair fluttered in the breeze and seemed to glow brighter the closer they got to the buildings.

"Hiram." Louise spun halfway around and walked backward, watching him closely. They stopped at the larger building next to an unmarked door, the only opening in the blank wall of pale green metal. "Hiram," Louise repeated. "Hiram, can we trust you with our secrets?"

"Father." Hiram felt a bit woozy. "I would be honored to serve you however I can."

"Good, good, good. Dr. Murphy, would you be so kind as to lead a tour?"

Dr. Murphy grabbed a small, plastic card dangling from a lanyard around her neck. She waved the card down the right side of the door, which responded with a muted click. She leaned into the door, and Hiram felt a slight whoosh of air when the door cracked open. Once they were inside, she closed the door and waved the card again. The door sealed shut, and Hiram's ears popped.

A wall of glass panels, set in highly polished, metal frames, reflected the dim, red light of the exit sign. Dr. Murphy walked over to a six-foot long console with several built-in computer screens and a series of paired gauges. She threw two switches, and, in the darkness beyond the glass wall, long fluorescent tubes flickered to life. Two rows of cylindrical, stainless steel tanks, pipes running from the bottom of one to the top of the next, extended the length of the room. Large pots, trays, and pumps filled a storage alcove at the far end.

Hiram stared into the large room, stunned. "Jesus Christ. It's a brewery."

"Exactly, Hiram." Louise said. "See, Denise. I knew we had a good one here."

"You're financing your operation by brewing beer?"

"No, no, no," Louise laughed. "Hiram, your line of work is terribly illegal, so discretion is essential. That's one of the reasons we knew we could trust you. We too, run a business in which discretion is of the utmost importance." Louise paused.

"But I don't get it. What do you..." Hiram started to ask.

"Dr. Murphy will give you the details." Louise nodded in her direction. "From this point, I'm clueless."

Dr. Murphy stuck her hands into the pockets of her white lab coat and began. "Okay, Hiram, let's go back to biology. You said that lab over there was a brewery." She tilted her head toward the glass. "Technically, that's correct. We're not making beer, but we do use microorganisms to create a product. Hiram, do you know how beer is made?"

"Uh, you put the ingredients into a tank, and a few days later it turns into beer?" Hiram shrugged.

"Conceptually correct. And one of those ingredients is a living creature called yeast. The yeast eats the sugar in the mix, and its waste products are alcohol and carbon dioxide. The alcohol provides the intoxicating effect, and the CO_2 makes the bubbles."

"Waste products?" Hiram's stomach churned noisily.

"Over the millennia," Dr. Murphy continued her lecture, "mankind has learned to adapt microorganisms to the production of alcohol, bread, cheese, even pickles. In fact, prior to canning, pickling provided our sole means of preserving some foods."

"There's yeast waste in pickles?"

"No, no, no." Louise chuckled. "This part confused the hell out of me, too. Yeast is for alcohol and bread. It's bacteria for the rest."

"These things are in our food?"

"That's right, Hiram." She approached the glass and inspected the lab. "Mankind would not have made it this far without the help of these little life forms. Each strain has been designed for a specific purpose."

"Designed?" Hiram asked. "How do you design yeast?"

"Thousands of years ago, one of our ancestors stumbled onto a fermented fruit."

"*Stumbled away* is more like it," Louise interrupted.

"Yes." Dr. Murphy smiled. "The first hangover. Over time, we figured out how to control the fermentation. We learned which fruits and grains worked best and techniques that delivered a consistent product."

"But what's all that got to do with a brewery?" Hiram thought he might puke. He was definitely swearing off cheese. "How's that an illegal operation?" He was completely confused.

Louise interrupted. "It only looks like a brewery, Hiram,

because we use similar techniques and processes. Our output is something different altogether."

Dr. Murphy resumed, "In the last part of the twentieth century a new science called genetic engineering was born. Do you know what a gene is Hiram?"

"Yes," he said as he shook his head side to side indicating no. "I've heard of that."

"Well, traits like the hair or eye color of an animal, the sweetness of a fruit, or the amount of alcohol yeast can tolerate are all defined by long molecules called genes."

"Okay."

"But we have a problem. What happens if the trait you want, say a firefly's glow, is nowhere to be found in the genes for the species you're breeding, like cats?"

"Yeah, right." Hiram shook his head. "You're saying there's a way to make a glow-in-the-dark cat? I'm sorry Dr. Murphy, I may not be smart, but I'm not stupid enough to fall for that."

"Hiram." She patted his arm sympathetically. "It's been done." She picked up a framed photograph from the desk and held it in front of him. "That's Lucifer and Mrs. Twinkle, our pets." The image showed two cats with an eerie light emanating from the fur.

"You're kidding."

"Once we learned how to cut genes out of one species and implant them into another, we were limited only by our imaginations."

Hiram looked through the glass at the facility. "But what does all this have to do with your secrets?"

Louise stood with arms and legs spread wide. "Hiram, the strains of bacteria that we have developed produce the chemical components of raw opium, coca alkaloids, and a nearly perfect copy of the THC molecule."

"THC?"

Louise's arms dropped. "It's the active ingredient of marijuana."

Hiram stood stunned.

Dr. Murphy went over to a small refrigerator and pulled out three bottles of water. She gave one each to Louise and Hiram. She opened hers and took a long drink.

"We met on a plane flight from L.A. to Portland," Louise explained. "The story of our organization piqued Dr. Murphy's curiosity, and she agreed to come for a visit. We discovered a large overlap between her expertise and our goals."

"Father had the resources. And I had the necessary skills to build and equip this lab, and then fine-tune the processes." She took another sip. "It wasn't fast and it wasn't easy."

"Or cheap," Louise added.

"But, in the end, we got there, and the result is right in front of you."

"So you're brewing drugs here? How does it all work?"

"It's a series of steps, Hiram," she explained. "The raw material goes into the first tank."

"What's the raw material?"

"Waste from the agricultural operation. Plant stems, leaves, roots—like what you would add to a compost pile. The bacteria convert this waste into simpler compounds, which then feed a different type of organism further down the line. Our end result is synthetic cooked-flake opium that is easier to refine into heroin than the natural product. We do the same thing to make synthetic coca paste. Our THC product is used directly."

"And, uh…" Hiram stammered.

"The refined product enters our distribution channels when the chemistry is done," Louise added.

"No, no, no, Father. I mean what happens to all the bacteria?"

Dr. Murphy replied, "Some is used to culture the next batch of fermentations. It's preserved in that freezer way in back. The rest is..." She stopped when the door clicked, softly sending a gentle sigh of air out of the room. A person stepped into the doorway.

"Excellent, excellent. Perfect timing." Louise waved the visitor in. "Hiram. Let me introduce you to Hammill."

Chapter 35

The door to the VeggieTech lab closed behind Hammill. After Hiram's eyes readjusted to the interior lighting, he didn't know where to look, what to look at first, or how to look away. Hiram couldn't imagine how Hammill came to look so bad. He stood over six feet tall, but seemed much shorter and boxier, like a stack of cardboard cartons. He also appeared to be naked. Hiram did a double-take and realized that Hammill was not, in fact, naked, just all one color—beige. Maybe not beige so much as khaki, and not the khaki sold at Banana Republic as much as the color of the packaging that Amazon ships their stuff in. Only without the little smile. Hammill was that color, from the khaki ball cap over the sandy-colored hair on his blocky head, to his shirt, pants, socks, and boots. The only way he could be more beige was if he wore vanilla after-shave. Hiram sniffed the air.

Hiram expected the handshake from Hammill's big, blocky, khaki hand to be like one of those hydraulic claws that picks up cars to drop them in a crusher. Instead, Hamill had a gentle, almost childlike handshake. The fourth fingers of both of Hammill's hands had been severed at their bases. A hint of a shattered knuckle remained, covered by pale khaki scars.

When Hiram raised his eyes to Hammill's face, he couldn't help but recoil. Hammill had a mashed rectangle roughly where his nose should have been. A ragged scar began an inch under the left side of his mouth, curved upward, through his left ear, and furrowed his scalp, becoming a trench just before it disappeared under his hair. The injury had sliced his left ear into two pieces, both still firmly attached. The cartilage had tightened as the ear healed, making it appear as if Hammill had an upper and lower ear.

Hiram forced his stare away from the ear and locked onto Hammill's eyes. They were not khaki. The irises were dark gray, but bright, almost impossibly bright. Hammill's face betrayed no emotion, but his eyes sparkled like he was thinking about the punch line to a very funny joke.

"Uh," Hiram stammered. "Pleased to meet you."

Hammill nodded a greeting, but his expression didn't change.

"Unfortunately, Hammill can no longer speak." Dr. Murphy stood close to Hammill and gently rubbed his shoulder. "As you can see, he has suffered greatly. When we first met, I didn't know if he could even be saved. But we were able to nurse him back to health."

At this, a small smile creased Hammill's face, which looked as if it might shatter from the strain.

Louise broke in, "We discovered that Hammill possessed particular skills in industrial food processing. When he learned what our organization was trying to accomplish, he was very excited to become a major contributor."

Hiram regarded Hammill with sympathy. "But how does a food engineer end up injured like that?"

"Yes, yes, yes, a very sad story. Nestlé, Hammill's former

employer, was trying to help rehabilitate a run-down neighborhood in Seattle. They planned to use one of the old fish-processing plants along Seattle's waterfront to experiment with turning kelp into food additives."

"Seaweed?"

"Yes. It's already used in a lot of products. Ice cream, for one. But Hammill had a bigger dream. At the time, the waste got tossed back into the ocean, which Hammill considered an unacceptable misuse of resources. He came up with the idea for a line of kelp-based baby food. The leftover seaweed had all the nutrients a human requires. The flavor and—as they say in the food industry—mouth feel issues presented a challenge though."

"But those are some serious injuries." Hiram nodded at Hammill.

"The residents of the neighborhood—many were illegals—resented being muscled aside by Corporate America."

"But Nestlé's a Swiss company, Father."

Louise made a little noise. "Whatever," Louise huffed, then took a deep breath and relaxed. "The neighborhood's gang-bangers kidnapped Hammill, tortured him for weeks, and then dumped him back at the factory site."

"Seattle? Gang-bangers? Illegal immigrants? That sounds like southern California! I thought Seattle was all software, yuppies, and bad coffee."

"No, Hiram. In Seattle, illegals are everywhere, choking the economy and draining public resources. These illegals are a bigger problem than the ones from Mexico or Central America. They blend in so well that the gangs are practically invisible."

"Russians?"

"Worse." Louise's brow knotted. "Canadians."

"Oh."

"Somehow, Hammill managed to survive. In addition to the physical damage, the torment left him psychologically scarred as well. One day he stumbled into our compound."

"But if he can't talk, how can he run your food operations? He must be able to communicate somehow?"

Hammill looked guilty as he fidgeted with something in his pocket. A faint vibration tickled Hiram's leg through the cloth of his peasant pants. He reached into his pocket and pulled out his Blackberry. The display said: "hi hirm its hml."

Louise, Dr. Murphy, and Hammill all held up their cell phones. "This approach works best, we've found. Just text any of us—any time—and we'll get back to you right away. We took the liberty of programming our numbers into your unit," Louise explained, then gave Hammill a compassionate look. "Unfortunately for Hammill, it's the only way he can communicate."

Louise turned back to Hiram. "Well, Dr. Murphy and I will leave you two alone now. Hammill will familiarize you with his side of the operation, and then, if you'd like, we can all get together for lunch."

The sparkle in Hammill's eyes grew brighter.

Hiram's heart sank at the thought of missing another meal with Aubergine, but he accepted the invitation. "That sounds great, Father."

Dr. Murphy waved her card to open the door. The bright daylight briefly silhouetted her and Louise. For a second, Hiram thought he saw small horns sprouting from their heads.

Hammill nodded to Hiram. His eyes weren't sparkling anymore. Hiram's Blackberry buzzed. He held the phone out and looked at the screen, "lts go," it said.

Hammill plodded for the door that led to the tanks and waved his access card. The door hissed briefly and popped open an inch.

"So all the air flows out of this room?" Hiram asked.

His Blackberry buzzed again, and "tr" appeared on the display.

"T-R?" Hiram asked.

Buzz, "tr thats right lol aim abbrv ezr 2 key."

"Oh." *This is going to be tough.*

Hammill held the door for Hiram and followed him into the room. "Jesus, it's hot in here!" Hiram felt like he had walked into a wall.

Buzz, "4 bgs."

Hiram closed his eyes as he tried to decipher the message. "Oh! For bugs. It's hot for the yeast and bacteria." Hammill nodded with a slight smile on his face, and Hiram felt like he had won a prize.

At the back of the room, Hammill patted a large, stainless steel tank that rested on a frame bolted to the arms of an electric forklift.

Buzz, "tnk old bugs strt 4 nxt stp."

Hammill turned a black key on the forklift, and the pumps started to whine. He squeezed the brake lever to release the lock, but the handle slipped from his pinky-less hand and snapped back open. Hammill shot a frustrated look at Hiram. Using both hands, he released the brake, and the forklift eased forward an inch. Hammill pulled up on the control handle and guided the lift toward a narrow garage door, which automatically slid up. Hammill steered the forklift into the next room with Hiram close behind. After the inner door sealed behind them, the outer one opened, and Hiram's ears popped from the pressure change. The cramped airlock flooded with bright daylight and cool air. The door in the smaller pre-fab building opened, and Hammill drove across a small paved area into the next building.

This space resembled a scaled-down version of the drug

lab, about twenty-five feet long with a single line of stainless steel tanks and machinery spanning the length of the room. A worktable, with a large roll of plastic wrap at the edge, sat at the far end. Every surface gleamed.

Hammill positioned the forklift under a frame hanging from a chain-lift. He secured the tank to the frame with two pins, then lowered the arms, and backed the forklift out of the way, leaving the tank hanging. He lifted the end of what looked like a fire hose out of a bucket of cloudy yellow liquid, let the fluid dribble off for a few seconds, and slipped the hose onto a fitting on the bottom of the suspended tank. He struggled to clamp the two securing levers on the end of the hose, but his damaged hands slipped off. He took a deep breath, set his face with determination, and snapped the levers closed on his second try. With both hands, he twisted a valve, and the contents of the tank flowed into the hose sounding like pudding being sucked through a straw.

Buzz, "cm on." The bacterial waste surged into a large machine emblazoned with a large green *V* logo and a picture of a hot dog.

Hiram held onto a pipe and breathed deeply until his nausea passed. He examined the line of equipment. "But Father said the vegetables were processed into hot dogs. This is the used bacteria."

Hammill pointed to the next piece of equipment. A large pipe from the first machine emptied into a feed hopper. A stainless steel chute filled with rotten vegetables and lawn clippings supplied the hopper from the opposite side. Hiram picked a stick out of the chute and looked at Hammill quizzically.

Buzz, "yum."

A large plastic tub hung above the chute. Hammill pulled a cord, and birds' feet intermingled with shiny, oval slivers splatted onto the compost oozing from the chute into the hopper.

"What's that?" Hiram asked as he tried, unsuccessfully, to look away from the macabre ingredients.

Buzz, "flvr."

Hammill pushed a large, green button, and the machine came to life. Clods of concentrated glop excreted from the pipe above the hopper. The chute vibrated, edging its contents slowly into the mix.

Hiram bent over and puked into a gleaming steel bucket. He stumbled past the second machine, leaned heavily on the table at the far end of the room, and closed his eyes. His head hung forward, and his shoulders heaved as he inhaled and exhaled slowly. When he opened his eyes, he saw wobbly gray tubes spilling out of the machine, jiggling like microbes in a drop of water. He looked to Hammill for an explanation.

Hammill pulled a sheet of plastic off a roll on a packing machine and held it in front of Hiram.

The green *V* logo covered most of the sheet. Hammill pointed to the ingredient list. The third entry said, "hydrolyzed vegetarian protein."

Hiram stood up and stabbed at the wrapper with his finger. "But these are supposed to be vegetarian hot dogs! Those are birds' feet!" He stuck his arm straight out and pointed at the container.

Hammill smiled slightly and started typing. Buzz. Hiram read the display, "brds R vg8ryns."

Chapter 36

After the unsettling tour of the food processing operation, Hiram sat on his bed, his gaze fixed on a crack in one of the terra-cotta tiles. The door to his room opened, and Aubergine breezed in with clean sheets and towels. He barely noticed her.

"Oh, sweetie." She threw the linens on the table and ran across the room. "What's wrong? Are you alright?" She sat down next to him.

"I got the tour."

"Oh, that. You silly guy." She leaned into him and took his hand in hers. "It's really all for a good cause."

I don't believe this. "Aubergine, how can drug manufacturing be all for a good cause? They're killing people."

She poked his arm with her forefinger. "Listen, Mr. Smarty-pants. Right now thousands of peasants in South America work in their fields day and night to grow the plants that drugs are made out of."

Day and night?

"Those evil drug lords down there are killing people, too—poor people who aren't allowed to grow good, healthy crops, like corn for ethanol. With their synthetic drug thing, Father and Dr. Murphy are going to put those nasty drug people out of business—like that." She snapped her fingers. "Besides, all the druggies will keep doing drugs anyway, so nobody extra is going to die."

Druggies? "Aubergine." Hiram stood up and held out his hands to her. "What do you eat here?"

She stood up and faced him. "Only the fresh produce we grow ourselves," she challenged.

"Do you—you know—treat all the veggies before you pick them?"

"Every last one." She wagged her finger at him. "We don't want any of them to suffer."

Oh my God. "Listen, Aubergine." Hiram gently gripped her upper arms. "You've got to trust me on this. Don't eat any more treated produce. The vegetables will, uh, be okay." He searched for the right words. "They know it's their karma to be eaten, and they're okay with that."

"Really?"

"Yeah, really." He checked the time on his Blackberry. "I've got to go. Remember what I said. There's something going on here that's bad for you and the others." He held her close. "I'm going to go find out what it is."

"Hiram!" someone called through the window.

"Time for lunch," Aubergine said, smiling.

The buildings of the VeggieTech compound faded to gray in the last of the twilight. Hiram stood at the window in his room taking in the view. Across the river, a distant finger of lightning momentarily backlit the clouds. *What a day!* A soft knock sounded on his door.

"Yes?" Hiram turned. "Come in." The latch clicked, and the heavy door swung open slowly.

Aubergine took a tentative step into the room and looked around. Her expression softened into a loving smile. "Hiram." She ran across the room and wrapped her arms around him. "I think this was the longest afternoon of my life." She pulled back slightly but held onto his shoulders and looked into his eyes. "I've been thinking about what you said, but I don't know what I should think. These people have been so kind to me. I can't believe they could be as bad as you say. So…" she struggled for a word, "deceptive."

You have no idea. Hiram still reeled from what the leaders had shown him earlier. "Look, they want me in the group," he said. She smiled broadly, but he shook his head. "I'm going to go along with it to see what else I can find out. Please be careful."

With his arms around her waist, he pulled her to him. She reached around and held him tight. "I do love you, Hiram." She snuggled her head against his shoulder. "I don't know how I can feel this way, but I do."

Please don't let it be the drugs. Hiram inhaled her scent and sucked in a wisp of her hair. He choked and hacked it back out. "Sorry." He wiped the sticky strand off his cheek. "I love you, too, Aubergine," he whispered in her ear. *Please don't let it be the drugs.*

Someone coughed, and they broke their embrace. Dr. Murphy stood in the doorway. "Okay, break it up, you lovebirds." Her face could have been carved from granite. "Aubergine, your," she frowned, "animal is running amok again. Please go control it." Hiram caught the implied "or else." Dr. Murphy gave Hiram an emotionless smile. "Hiram, Father is waiting for us. Come with me now."

Hiram followed Dr. Murphy to the dining room. Louise

sat at the head of the table, wearing a navy-blue bathrobe over a peasant shirt. Hammill, who sat to Louise's right with his back to the door, did not turn around but waved a small greeting. He appeared to be focused on the tablecloth in front of him. There was an empty place set to Hammill's right and another to Louise's left. A man Hiram did not recognize sat one seat beyond the empty chair. His clothes, though clean and pressed, looked about three sizes too large. The man's head twitched from left to right, as if having an internal debate over the relative merits of different table cutlery.

"Ah, good, good, good! Dr. Murphy, Hiram—here you are, at last." Louise graced them with a beatific smile. "We can begin." Louise turned toward the kitchen door and called out, "Mustafa! Please join us now!"

Mustafa Farouk pushed a small serving trolley through the swinging door. He placed several serving dishes on the table and slid a fresh salad in front of the fidgety man. Mr. Whoever immediately began shoveling the vegetables into his mouth.

Hiram took the seat next to Hammill, and Dr. Murphy sat next to Louise. Mustafa pulled a chair up to the corner of the table between Louise and Dr. Murphy and sat down.

"Please excuse the rush," Louise said, picking up a bowl and splatting a large pile of unidentifiable mashed vegetable onto the plate. "Mustafa has an engagement downtown. It seems he has become something of a local celebrity." Mustafa smiled. "It also serves us well as an excellent source of information from his...what do you call them? Wait, I have it—groupies." Louise chuckled slightly, and Mustafa blushed.

"Hiram." Louise said and passed the bowl to him. "Our guest tonight is Travis Backster." Louise waved in the general direction of the fidgety man. "Travis is an associate involved with a local competing interest." Travis chuffed a mouthful of chewed salad onto his plate. He quickly scooped it up with his fork and pushed it back in his mouth.

The salad was almost gone, and Travis seemed calmer, but when he looked up at Hiram, his eyes couldn't focus. "Pleased to meet you." Hiram reached his hand out, but Travis, too intent on scarfing down the rest of the salad, didn't notice. Hiram shrugged and addressed Louise. "Competing interest, Father? There's another group like yours here?"

"No, nothing like that. Merely an organization that is at cross-purposes to our own. Let me explain." Louise looked at Travis and back to Hiram. "It all centers around the dam."

Travis stopped eating and gazed blankly at Louise.

"You have a familiarity with what we're about here. You've seen our little operation," Louise said.

Dr. Murphy smiled at her plate.

"You've also heard the philosophical and social ideals to which we aspire."

Hiram nodded. Hammill snorted.

"Well, Hiram, it's all bullshit."

"What do you mean bullshit?" Hiram looked from Louise to Dr. Murphy to Hammill, all peering at him intently. "Everything you've told me over the past, uh, three days?"

"Simply a test, Hiram," Louise went on. "You now know our cover story inside and out. We shared the details of our operation as a sign of our trust. Remember, I also told you that we have need of your skills as well." Louise's eyes bored into him. "Put simply, Hiram, we are at war." Louise stood up, walked over to a small table, and pulled a U.S. Army combat helmet onto his head. Louise tugged a thin cord hanging against the wall, and the drapes separated, revealing a large-scale map of the area. Louise pulled a pen-shaped laser pointer from the pocket of the robe and flashed it across the map. "Our compound is in green. The blue area just south of us is the Wanderfalls recreation area. South of that is the boat ramp and parking area. And, as you can see, south of that is the Wanaduck Dam."

"Okay," Hiram said. "That much is obvious."

"And that..." Louise circled the laser beam around a cross-hatch of streets, "is Wanaduck. It exists only because of the dam. If the dam goes away, so does the town." Louise smiled. "And we'll have all the room we need."

Mustafa stared at the map and quietly said, "Yes!"

"Okay, so you want more room. But the dam *is* there." Hiram looked at Louise, then at Mustafa.

"Not for long," Mustafa said as he stood up.

"Mustafa is the key to the whole plan." Louise squiggled the laser around Mustafa's chest. "He had been trained by Syrian Special Forces in demolition and infiltration. His mission was to smuggle explosives into Israel and destroy large public infrastructure."

"Bridges, highways, things like that," Mustafa said.

"But he was commanded not to distinguish between civilian and military targets. He consulted his religious teachers and learned that, from pure Islamic theology, that was wrong."

"I turned myself in to the Americans in Iraq. They imprisoned me for a few weeks while I was questioned." Mustafa shivered. "But I checked out, and they shipped me to the States. A new name, a new life, and a new start."

"And like everybody else here, Mustafa's path crossed ours, and another piece fell into place." Louise leaned onto the table. "You see, Hiram, VeggieTech is really VeggieTech, Inc. All of this—the compound, the operations, the cover story, and the idiots who believe it—is about the money."

Hiram's face hardened. "Okay...so...what? You're

going to blow up the dam?" Hiram shot an accusatory glare at Louise. "That's ridiculous. With all the security, you wouldn't have a chance."

"Not ridiculous, merely unexpected." Louise chuckled. "Mustafa has developed an explosive delivery system that can be activated at the top of the dam to weaken the structure." A malevolent smile crossed Louise's face. "The pressure behind the dam will begin an irreversible erosion of the structure, which leads to an unavoidable conclusion. Thank you, Mustafa." Louise's face brightened. "I don't want to make you late, so feel free to leave when you must."

"I'll give you more details later, Hiram." Mustafa's black eyes flashed and he left the room.

"Okay." Hiram kept his attention on Louise. "But they can fix the dam."

"Possibly, but it will take decades." Louise nodded to Dr. Murphy.

"Using our gene-splicing techniques, we've created a new species of fresh-water goby." She snickered. "It's found only in the Wanderfalls because that's where we released it. The imbeciles at the Sierra Club will tie the Department of Energy in knots forever."

"Sounds like you've planned for everything." Hiram shook his head in disbelief.

Travis gazed absently at his now-empty plate, distractedly scratching his wrists. His eyelids drooped.

"There's more, Hiram." Louise's piercing blue eyes focused on Hiram. "The competing organization is, in fact, the very Utility that operates the dam. Travis here," Louise nodded at the nearly-catatonic diner, "learned that they have some problems of their own. It seems that they have painted themselves into a financial corner and are planning drastic measures for the dam as well."

"But wouldn't that make your goals the same?" Hiram asked.

"Not at all. They plan to introduce a—how did Travis put it?—structural integrity issue, which would allow them to shut down the dam. Then, using federal money to clear up their financial problems, they would fix the dam, increase its capacity, and make it even more secure. If that happens, Hiram, we are screwed."

Louise nodded at Hammill and turned to face the map. Hammill closed his eyes briefly, pushed his chair back, and walked around the end of the table. Louise stood with his back to the room. "You see, Hiram, we are an organization that is based on trust, and Travis failed that test."

Travis' head lolled, a filament of drool tracing a random pattern on the table as Hammill stepped up behind him.

"If we find we can trust you, you shall do very, very well. If not…" Louise trailed off.

Hammill bent down and wrapped his blocky right arm around Travis' neck and pressed his left arm on the back of Travis' head. Travis twitched like he was trying to wake up.

"Hammill! No!" Hiram jumped up.

"Hiram, sit." Louise commanded.

Hiram sat.

Hammill increased the pressure until Travis' neck made a sound like a chicken being jointed. Hammill relaxed his arms, and the lifeless body collapsed onto the table. Hiram shivered as he felt all hope drain away.

"Here is the answer to your question of why we need your skills, Hiram," Louise said. "Timothy Bentle, the clown, is the muscle behind the Utility. He was snooping around our property the night after you arrived here. He is trying to find—and kill—you. You need to find him and kill him first. With him gone, the Utility loses the one person who is a threat to us."

"Then what?" Hiram couldn't take his gaze off of Travis' bulging eyes.

"The Utility has contracted with a local group to do their work on the dam. They are a multi-legged extension of their leader, Bill Snead," Louise explained. "You take Snead out, and VeggieTech will be the only player left. We can destroy the dam and implement the final stages of our plans." Louise motioned Hiram over to the window. Oil lamps and a cooking fire glowed by the circle of yurts. Hiram heard scuffing behind him. In the reflection in the window, he saw Hammill dragging Travis' body into the kitchen.

"We have made initial contacts with Miguel and Marquesa Rodriguez in Mexico. We hope to become the prime supplier for their distribution system. Once that is in place, we can drop the silly vegetable thing and start producing much larger quantities."

Hiram looked at Louise in disbelief.

"See all those idealistic, young fools living in those squalid teepees." Louise looked out into the night. Dr. Murphy came up from behind and wrapped her arms around Louise's waist.

"Yes?" Hiram stared sadly at the happy people dancing around their fire.

"They all must die."

Chapter 37

Jesse Blake and Durk Duffett stumbled out of the dim interior of the Tuck 'er Inn. Jesse stopped short, squinted, and raised his right hand to block the daylight.

Durk propped the door open with his left hand waiting for Jesse to move. "Jeez, it's bright out here. Maybe we should go back inside."

"No way, Durk. They're gonna start that kerookee shit," Jesse said, glancing back into the bar. "Those little faggots give me the creeps. That ay-rab with the cow eyes…Fuck, I can't even think about it." He shook off the image and stepped out onto the sidewalk.

"Yeah, I guess," Durk said. He held his hand in front of his eyes and weaved down the street. He turned into the alley next to the professional center and dropped his hand. As they meandered down the alleyway, Durk and Jesse bumped into each other every few steps.

"Watch where you're walkin', you di…hic…wad," Jesse warned, his body weaving back and forth in a unsteady relationship with upright. Durk peered intently down the alley. Jesse swiveled his head to see what Durk was looking at.

Halfway down the alley, two kids, about seven or eight, were in a serious tug of war, scuffling and grunting, as they pulled on opposites ends of a cord. Their backpacks lay on the ground where they had thrown them. A yank on one kid's hair prompted a high-pitched tirade. "You pussy!"

"What are they fighting over?" Durk asked, moving closer to get a better look.

"I dunno. It looks like a string."

"Jesse, I think it's a..." Durk stuck his face forward. "Yeah, it is. It's one of those fish doohickeys that Bill wants." They kept walking toward the battle.

Locked in mortal combat of pre-adolescent proportions, the kids didn't notice Jesse and Durk approach. Jesse leaned into the melee and closed his left hand around the cord. He grabbed the one kid's thumb and effortlessly rotated it to the right until the kid's hand opened and let go of the cord. Then, he pushed the kid's ass with his boot to get him completely out of the picture. Jesse started to lose his balance but got his right foot planted back on the ground. He jiggled his knees to make sure he was on solid footing, and turned his attention to the other kid, who had reached down and picked up one of the backpacks.

The kid stood up, and a tiny rage-filled face glared up at Jesse defiantly. Jesse jerked the fish on the end of the cord like bait while he held his other hand against the kid's forehead. The kid took wild swings through the air.

"You fight like a girl," Jesse slurred. The kid's baseball cap fell off, and Jesse came up with a handful of long brown hair. At that moment, the girl twisted her head and bit Jesse's wrist. He screamed and let go of her head.

"I am a girl," she shouted and spun her backpack through a quick three-sixty.

Shooting stars flashed past Jesse's eyes, and his hands

reached down instinctively to cradle his balls. As he toppled over in slow motion, the kid wound up for another blow with the backpack. "Durk!" Jesse squeaked and rolled into fetal position. The pack hit the back of his head, and he focused his inebriated attention on holding onto the flash drive. The girl wound up once more and brought the backpack down on Jesse's face. He let go of his gonads and covered his head. The girl grabbed the flash drive and took off down the alley.

Jesse lay on the ground, breathing raggedly, watching her pull a phone out of her pack as she ran. Durk and the other kid were nowhere in sight. Jesse exhaled in disappointment. *Well, Bill and Father O'Donnell don't have to know.* He pushed himself onto his knees, then carefully climbed into a standing position.

Durk came around the corner back into the alley.

"What the fuck, Durk?" Jesse said. "Where'd you go?"

"I thought you might want this." Durk grinned and held up the flash drive and the girl's backpack. "We got a peanut butter and jelly sandwich too. Ya want some?" Durk held out the sandwich.

"Forget it. C'mon, we have to take this thing to Bill." Jesse shuffled off toward Main Street with Durk carrying the flash drive and backpack.

A police cruiser, its lights flashing, pulled up at the end of the alley and blocked their path. Officer Terry Backster got out of her car and stood with her hand resting on the gun at her hip.

"Did you boys just steal a backpack from two kids?" she asked in a stern voice.

Durk moved the hand holding the backpack behind his butt.

Jesse kicked at the ground and mumbled, "Yes, ma'am. We did."

"Jesse. Durk. First, call me Officer. Second, what the hell are you two thinking? You snatched Sabrina's flash drive at the Wa-Wa—with me sitting right there. Now you took one from a couple of kids?"

Jesse kept his head down, but his right leg jiggled in place. "Well, ma'am…uh, Offisser…me and Durk aren't thinking nothin'."

"Yeah, I can see that."

"Uh, yeah, but Bill and Father O'Donnell, they're looking for a flash drive," Durk interjected. "So, when we saw some, we thought maybe they were the ones they wanted."

Officer Backster held out her hand. "Give me the backpack," she said.

Durk walked over and handed her the backpack.

"And the flash drive."

He reached in his pocket and handed over the flash drive.

"And I want you to go back and close your tab at the Tuck 'er. I got another call said you left without paying. Again."

"Yes, Officer."

"And boys."

"Officer?"

"Get a little more fresh air. I don't want to have to bring you in for public drunkenness."

"Yes, Officer."

Officer Backster walked back around her cruiser, tossed the backpack and flash drive on the passenger seat, got in, and drove off.

Durk took a bite out of the peanut butter and jelly sandwich he held in his left hand.

"C'mon, let's get this over with." Jesse's face screwed up. They walked up River Street and stopped in front of the Tuck 'er Inn. Jesse held out his hand and said, "Gimme a ten."

Durk reached into his pocket and pulled out a wad of

bills. He had nine dollars. Jesse grabbed the money, took a deep breath, and stepped inside. Mustafa wound down on "Why Don't We Live Together," pinned by the amorous gazes of four women at the closest table, their ample thighs spilling off the chairs like spandex-wrapped hams. At the rear of the audience, Simpson burst into premature congratulation. When the door closed, Simpson glanced over and locked eyes with Jesse. He scurried over to him and gave him a quick hug.

"Oh, Jesse," Simpson twittered. "I just knew you couldn't stay away." When Simpson saw the money crumpled in Jesse's hand, he threw his arms around Jesse again and squeezed. "Oh, my. How generous." He pulled back, snatched the bills, rushed over to Mustafa, and tossed the money into an upturned fedora sitting next to the microphone stand. Simpson turned to Jesse and mouthed, "Thank you," then blew him a kiss.

Jesse panicked and bolted through the door. He stopped next to Durk, put his hands on his knees, and waited for his heart to start beating again.

"Wha's wrong, Jesse?" Durk put his hand on Jesse's shoulder.

Jesse jumped back like he'd been stung. "Don't touch me, Durk. Don't ever fucking touch me." His pulse pounded in his temples. "C'mon, let's get the fuck outta here. I'll pay up later."

Chapter 38

The first day of the fishing competition brought measurable progress for the Columbia River cleanup effort. For four hours, Rudy tirelessly reeled in a collection of discarded ice cube bags, a child's stroller, a rainbow assortment of condoms, and one cobalt blue Wonderbra.

Then, Rudy almost dropped the rod in his excitement. "Hey look! It's a fish!"

"Easy, little buddy, easy." A respectable small-mouth bass broke the surface as Juice tried to keep Rudy focused. "Reel it in easy."

"Ted, get the net."

"Yes, sir." Juice grinned, and pulled the net out of the holder.

As the tired bass played out, Rudy wound up the line, snatched the net from Juice's hand, dipped it under the fish, and gently raised his catch out of the water. He quickly lifted the fish out of the net, removed the hook, and laid it out against the ruler molded into the top of the cooler.

"Shit!" Juice patted his friend's back. "Seventeen inches. Doesn't that beat it all?" In the distance a horn sounded, immediately repeated by the other boats in the fleet. Juice punched his horn as well. "Time for weigh-in. Put that guy in the bag."

Rudy opened the top of a clear bag that had "Walt's" and a picture of a bass smoking a cigarette stenciled on the side. He dropped in the fish and stuck a hose into the bag. Juice pushed a button, and the bag filled with water.

"Let's go," Juice said.

Rudy parked himself at the front of the boat and stared intently at the dock the entire way back.

Juice stayed a hundred yards offshore as they passed the ramp. Rudy gave him a questioning look, but Juice held his right hand up in a sign for patience. He did a one-eighty and approached the dock from the south, away from the inebriated and distracted contestants bearing down from the other direction. He eased back on the throttle as they got close. Rudy surprised him by standing up for the final approach and leaping onto the floating wooden platform with the line in his hand. He tied a cleat hitch to moor the boat. *I guess he has been paying attention.*

"Go take your fish up, little buddy. I'll get us ready to go."

Rudy grabbed the bag and ran as fast as he could. By the time he came back empty-handed, Juice's Explorer sat at the boat ramp, the trailer backed into the water. "Two pounds, twelve ounces, Ted. I'm in the lead. Can you believe it?" Rudy pumped his fist then untied the mooring rope. He jumped into the boat for the quick ride to the ramp.

"You are the man, Two Shoes." Juice steered the boat away from the dock and idled up to his waiting trailer. Five minutes later, with the boat secured, they were on the road.

Juice pulled into the parking lot of Whitey's Fishin' Inn. As soon as the Explorer drifted to a stop, Rudy opened the door and slid down to the ground. He turned around and leaned in with his hands on the side of the passenger seat. "I'll see you at the festival, Ted. Thanks for everything!" He closed the door, spun, and skipped away.

"My pleasure," Juice replied to the closed door. He pulled back onto the street. A couple of turns later, he parked his truck and trailer in front of his house. He got out and pushed open his front gate. A nice hot shower called to him.

An hour later, Juice had changed into a fresh white shirt and pressed jeans, his black hair drying into the waves that Dinah used to run her fingers through. For a second, he wondered what she was up to. Then he shook his head. *Not gonna do any good, but damn, I still miss her sometimes.* He walked to the front hall, grabbed his keys, and went out the door. He had a festival to go to.

He walked over to River Street, then turned south. His leg finally felt as good as new. South of the bridge, the street was closed for the opening ceremony, and the area had filled up with festival-goers. The Asparagus Festival was a big deal for Wanaduck. No one in the area would dream of missing the celebration; in a one-game town, this was it. At most of the booths that lined the promenade along the river, vendors set up their wares for the next day's crowds. But it was still early Friday evening, and only two booths were jumping. Veggie-Tech had the first spot south of the bridge, selling sample plates of their vegetarian treats. Across the street, Joe had a booth in front of the Tuck 'er Inn. His beer and burger business was booming.

Rudy waved from the top row of bleachers that had been erected in the Wanaduck Professional Center's parking lot. Members of a local band tuned guitars on the stage across the street as Juice grabbed the railing and climbed up.

"Ted, Ted, they're about to get started. Here." Rudy scooted over on the otherwise empty row. "I saved you a seat."

Ten minutes after six, an ear-splitting screech from the sound system signaled the start of the opening ceremonies. Everyone turned to the stage, their hands over their ears. A short, old man wearing a feathered headdress and a beaded, buckskin vest strolled up to the microphone. Wanaduck's newly-elected mayor, Shecky Schmulker, gently tapped the mike. Muffled thumps pumped out of the speakers. The crowd in the street inched closer to the stage in anticipation. A fishy stink wafted over the bleachers. Juice looked around. Several contestants from the fishing competition still wore their competition clothes, smeared with fish slime and other unidentifiable goo.

Timothy Bentle serpentined through the onlookers. He glanced into the stands. When he saw Juice, he waved and climbed up.

"Hey, Timothy. How'd your first day go?"

"Hello, Ted." Timothy seemed distracted. "Good day. Good day. Not great. You?"

"Good day for my client." He leaned back revealing Rudy. "He really came through." Juice quickly took in Timothy's clothes: an off-white long-sleeved T-shirt, made from some kind of high-tech fabric, perfectly pressed chinos, and dark brown loafers, probably Italian leather. The T-shirt fit him like paint. *Not his Orvis fishing clothes.*

Timothy waved to somebody in the crowd. Juice recognized Simpson, the karaoke M.C. from the Tuck 'er. The guy took the steps two at a time. He gave Timothy a quick hug, then looked at Juice and Rudy.

"Oh! Ted, Rudy, I'd like to introduce you to my friend, Simpson Chanson," Timothy said.

Simpson's lips pursed for a moment. Then, he smiled and said, "A pleasure to meet you, Ted." They shook hands. Very strong grip, very soft skin.

"I'm Rudy!" Rudy waved from Juice's left. "I love your show!"

"Thank you so much," Simpson gushed and sat down.

The mayor took a step back from the microphone and coughed into his hand. "I can't believe that guy got elected mayor," Simpson groused. "No fashion sense at all." He smoothed the lapels on his sport coat.

"Welcome, everyone!" Mayor Schmulker said and waited for the ruckus to die down. "Welcome, everyone, to the Sixth Annual Asparagus Festival!" Polite applause fluttered through the crowd, dying out almost immediately. From somewhere in the crowd, someone coughed, "Asshole!"

"Thanks for that, Mr. Norbert. Well, we have a lot of fun planned for you all this evening!" Mayor Schmulker smiled and extended his arms straight out to both sides. "This entire weekend will be nonstop excitement!"

Someone in the crowd yelled out, "Yeah!" and clapped five times, stopping when no one else joined in.

"Let's get things rolling!" Mayor Schmulker waited for a response. No one reacted, so he continued, "First things first. Today marked the start of the Walt's Master Baiters Bass Fishing Invitational."

The fishermen in the crowd clapped and hooted, "Yeah, Walt!" They looked around and nodded at each other.

"You all know, Walt isn't much for the limelight, so..." The mayor expanded his pause for effect. "I'd like to ask Gary Poppet, the competition's organizer, to join me on stage to announce the first day's leader!"

A guy with craggy good looks and golden-yellow hair jogged through the crowd. Gary smiled and greeted everyone as he rushed past. He bounded up the stairs onto the stage, shook Mayor Schmulker's hand, and waved to the crowd.

Timothy watched nonchalantly. Simpson pinched his partner's leg.

"Hi, everyone!" Gary said as he telescoped the stand holding the microphone. The applause picked up. "We couldn't ask for better weather for the competition and the festival, could we?" A mumbled answer spread through the audience. "I don't want to delay the rest of the fun, so let's get down to business! I'm pleased to announce that the leader after the first day of fishing is..." He stopped and squinted at the sheet of paper in his hand. He leaned into the microphone, nudging Mayor Schmulker out of the way with his right shoulder. "Rudy Touch-House! Rudy, stand up and take a bow!"

The mayor and Gary clapped loudly. People's heads rotated from side to side. People repeated the name to their neighbors and shook their heads.

"Hey, Two Shoes," Juice said. "I think they're talking about you." The bleachers began trembling like a minor earthquake had struck. Rudy, deathly white, sat quivering. Juice chuckled and grabbed Rudy's arm to help him to his feet. "It's okay, little buddy. You're the champ."

Rudy stood up, and the crowd went wild.

"Well, good. Great!" Gary spoke into the mike. "Best of luck for the rest of the competition!" Gary turned his head toward the mayor and nodded.

Mayor Schmulker stepped up to the mike again and brought it back down to his height. "Good work, Rudy! And good luck tomorrow!" He gave three half-hearted claps. "And now, I'd like to ask Dr. Robert Presseley to come up here to announce the Queen of the Asparagus Festival. Dr. Presseley? Where are you?" The mayor made a show of looking all around, while Presseley trudged up the stairs on the left side of the stage.

"Ah, there you are, Doctor!" The mayor faked surprise at

his sudden appearance. Presseley remained expressionless. "Dr. Robert Presseley, folks. C'mon. Let's welcome him!" The mayor backed away from the microphone. No one clapped.

"Thank you," Presseley's words forced themselves out. "I am honored to present the Queen of the Wanaduck Asparagus Festival award, which is given each year to the woman who does the most to convey the spirit of Wanaduck. The citizens of Wanaduck cast votes in a secret ballot to select the Queen." He stared blankly at the crowd. Presseley reached into the inside pocket of his suit jacket and withdrew a small envelope. He tore off the end of the envelope, blew into it, then extracted the paper inside. "June Presseley," he said flatly, and stood motionless while the mayor clapped.

Isolated snickers shot up from several spots in the crowd. "Is that what she conveys?" someone said in a stage whisper.

June Presseley walked to the bottom of the stairs and stopped. She looked up at the mayor and her husband. Robert Presseley didn't move. Spotting the standoff, Mayor Schmulker hurried over to the stairs and went down to meet her. She smiled at him graciously and looped her arm through his elbow. Her emerald-green dress was tight and low cut. With her right hand, she lifted the skirt a few inches, exposing matching shoes.

Simpson went, "Oooh…"

Juice leaned over to Rudy and whispered, "Doesn't quite fit in with the dress code tonight, but it looks good on her."

She crossed the stage with measured steps, her head held high. As the mayor escorted June to center stage, someone stepped up to the back of the platform with a large box. June's lips moved slightly as she passed her husband. Robert Presseley grimaced and stepped to the back of the stage. He gave an impatient come-on motion to the person holding the box. The delivery boy took off the cover, handed the box to Presseley, and left as fast as he could.

Robert Presseley glanced down and did a not-quite-disguised double-take. Even from a distance, Juice could see his face redden as he looked into the box. Presseley tersely announced into the microphone, "Queen of the Wanaduck Asparagus Festival, June Presseley." He held the box out to his wife. "Your reign begins today."

June gave him a cool smile and reached into the box, plucked out the large green bouquet, and cradled it in her left arm. Presseley dropped back to stand next to the mayor, his face darkening. She stepped up to the microphone and tipped the mike to her lips with her right hand. She leaned forward for her acceptance speech, giving the crowd a good look at the arrangement: an oversized, fake stalk of asparagus bedded in a spray of asparagus greenery.

"Hey!" a voice shouted. "Is the Jolly Green Giant lookin' for his junk?"

Juice kept the lid on a smile. Out of the corner of his eye, he saw Simpson lean over and say something to his partner. Timothy looked at him, muttered something, and turned back to the stage with a slight smirk. He was blushing.

"Thank you! Thank you, everyone!" June smiled. "I can't tell you how surprised and honored I am to receive this award for the sixth straight year. I do my best to make Wanaduck a special place!" June took a breath.

Robert Presseley leaned against the mayor. Loud enough for the mike to pick up, he said, "You asshole. Whose idea was it to give her the microphone?" A few snickers and muttered comments bounced through the crowd.

The mayor inhaled and quickly strode forward. "June! Congratulations! Congratulations!" He grasped her right arm lightly and guided her to the stairs. He beckoned to Gary Poppet, who rushed forward to escort her down the steps. Robert Presseley waited a few seconds, then stalked off the stage and disappeared into the crowd.

Mayor Schmulker returned to his place in front of the microphone. Wiping his brow, he forced a nervous smile and soldiered on. "And now, I'm pleased to introduce our homegrown musical stars." A drum roll began. "Please welcome," he said as an out-of-tune guitar plucked out some notes, "Salmon Sammie and the Hand-Tied Flies! C'mon! Give them a big hand, and get ready to par-tay!" The mayor stepped away from the mike and made a beeline for the stairs.

The lead singer moved up to the microphone. Greasy blond hair straggled out from under a faded green fishing hat. Lures, small pieces of driftwood, and a tiny fake fish dangled from the hat band. "Hello, Wanaduck!" he shouted into the mike. "Are you ready to rock?" He pushed the fishing hat back on his head.

The crowd gave a dispirited, "Yeah."

The singer peered out from the stage. "I asked, are you ready to rock?" He pursed his lips, waiting. A couple of drunk fisherman shouted, "Yeah!"

"Okay people, we're gonna start with a number by Pink." The band began hammering on their instruments. "It's 'The One That Got Away'!"

The crowd listened for a few bars, then everybody jumped in, dancing the swim.

Chapter 39

At one o'clock the next afternoon, Timothy followed Robert Presseley up the stairs to the reviewing stand. His boss stopped and shook hands with the few small-town movers and shakers he stepped over on the way to his seat. The front row was reserved for the Utility Board and management team, the town fathers, and the new mayor so they could vote for the winning float in the Asparagus Festival parade. A bright-eyed, brunette cheerleader dressed in the crimson and gray of the Washington State Cougars handed Presseley his voting kit.

"Why thank you, Monica!" Presseley smiled.

"Sure thing, Uncle Robert." She winked at him.

"I trust you and your Uncle Vernon arrived at a successful conclusion?"

"You bet!" Monica pointed to a new, bright-yellow Mustang convertible parked on Broad Street. "Maybe we could go for a drive later?" She gave a little twist, and her cheerleader skirt levitated.

"Another day, perhaps." Presseley shook his head. "I've got some work to do after the parade." He continued across the front row. Timothy trailed one step behind and one row up.

A blue rectangle painted on River Street marked the reviewing area. The judges had an uninterrupted view of the floats from when they left the parking lot of Whitey's Fishin' Inn until they turned the corner onto Broad Street. The backdrop of the Wanaduck Bridge and Columbia River provided excellent photo-copy for tomorrow's newspaper.

Presseley stepped across the legs of the sleeping John Parsons and shot an accusatory look at Timothy. He continued past the seat where Financial Officer Ray Milton should have been and sat next to the newest board member, Vernon Nickers. Presseley had appointed Nickers to the position, vacant since Eddie Snead's death back in February. Ray Milton's replacement had not yet been selected. Timothy wasn't finished combing through the backgrounds of the potential candidates to make sure Presseley had the goods on whomever he chose.

Timothy took a seat one row behind and to Presseley's left. "What's going on with our outside help?" Presseley said while he looked the other way at the approaching cavalcade. "Were you able to locate him?"

"Not a trace, Dr. P." Timothy said. "I searched the Veggie-Tech compound." Presseley held a finger up to his lips, and Timothy lowered his voice further to keep from being overheard. "But he wasn't anywhere—no wreckage, no body, and not at the compound." Presseley shook his head, and Timothy went on. "He seems to have just disappeared."

"Anybody talk to Louise?" Presseley asked.

"The cops did. But Louise," he paused, "gives me the creeps. I had a look around the night after the wreck but couldn't get into most of the buildings."

The blare of a trumpet interrupted the conversation, and they both turned back to the street. The Wanaduck High

School's ten-person marching band strutted into position. They high-stepped in formation behind the Drum Major, then turned to face the stands. The Drum Major blew his whistle twice, pumping time with his baton. On three, the band broke into a brass and drum arrangement of Dave Matthews' song "Tripping Billies." The melody sounded a little weak, but the drummers nailed Matthew's odd, syncopated rhythm perfectly. Behind the band, the school's music director stood swaying with her eyes closed. *So that's who's bringing the pot into town.*

After about a minute, the Drum Major strutted back to the head of the column and blew his whistle twice. The band members pivoted in unison and marched away, still playing.

The group waiting on deck held a blue and green banner that proclaimed: "Wanaduck Tributary of the River Girls" and "Life in the River." The River Girls always tried to present an educational and entertaining float. A new John Deere lawn tractor towed a small trailer holding a large, clear tank filled with water and a number of specimens of river-dwellers. The tractor's irregular starts and stops had splashed a considerable amount of water out of the tank.

Right before the float pulled up in front of the judges, the always-helpful Wanaduck Fire Brigade refilled the tank from a nearby hydrant, the fast influx putting the watery denizens into the spin cycle. Over the past century and a half, the river's inhabitants had adapted to all sorts of pollutants from the pesticides flowing off the farms and orchards to untreated sewage from the cattle and dairy operations. Chlorine was new to them. As the River Girls' float came to a stop, the chemically sterilized city water took its toll, and the float's minute in front of the judges turned tragic as the fish succumbed, twitching and gasping, to the chlorine-laden water. The girls wailed loudly as their floundering display went belly-up. The futile efforts of the River Girls' mothers to comfort their daughters faded out as the tractor towed the float down the street and around the corner.

A diesel engine roared to life at the top of the parade route, capturing the crowd's attention. A bright blue concrete mixer emerged from a black cloud of exhaust pulling a line of floats.

Back in the reviewing area the Pixie Tossers, elementary and pre-school girls twirling batons, launched into their one-minute performance. Their sequined costumes glittered in the afternoon sun, as the youngest marched back and forth holding their batons over their heads. The older girls risked some behind the back passes and airborne tosses. Their grand finale showcased a sixth-grader who whisked through her tricks like a ninja, her final toss going fifty feet into the air. While the stick was still airborne, somebody in the crowd shouted, "Go Sheryl!" Distracted, Sheryl missed her behind-the-back catch. The baton hit the pavement and bounced, spinning up into the bleachers, and square into John Parsons' forehead, which shocked him awake and the crowd into silence. Parsons blinked and looked around like he didn't know how he got there. He picked up the baton and tossed it back to Sheryl who caught it, tossed it once more high into the air, and, this time, successfully snagged it behind her back. The crowd went wild. Parsons waved to the audience.

Presseley tilted back in his chair. Timothy leaned forward to meet him. Presseley growled, "These people are supposed to be dead. I don't care who the fuck gives you the creeps or what the fuck you think. You've got a job to do. I listened to your 'keep ourselves at a distance' bullshit when you hired these clowns." Timothy stiffened. "The first guy was a total fuckup, so you got the new guy. He seemed promising after Ralphie and Ray, and then *POOF!* he disappears off the face of the fucking earth." He paused. "In this town you can't even take a shit without five other people knowing about it. Somebody knows where this guy is."

"Okay, Dr. P." Timothy checked to make sure nobody was listening. "I'll be out near VeggieTech for the tournament. I'll check the shore for a way in that's got some cover. I'll go in tomorrow night and give the place another good search."

"Good, Timothy. Very good. I mean, even if those weirdos catch you, what are they going to do? Chop you up and put you in their hot dogs?" Presseley snorted at his own joke.

Timothy ventured a small chuckle. "I don't think so. I'm not a vegetarian."

Presseley's forehead wrinkled for a second, then he fell back in his chair laughing even harder. Timothy caught him and pushed the chair forward.

"Thanks, Timothy. Not a vegetarian. Oh, that's good."

A loud woof drew their attention back to the parade as the Wanaduck Pooch Rooters marched up with their dogs. Marion Shill led the dog club, apparently unaware that her dog, The Colonel, had thoroughly tangled his leash around the legs of the walker. The rest of the club zigzagged down the street to try and match the snail's pace of the Shill duo. When they stopped in the reviewing area, The Colonel toppled over, gasping for air. A Pixie Tosser rushed in, picked up the wheezing canine, and untangled his tether. The dog quickly revived, and the pack headed off as The Colonel strained to get at a borzoi in heat.

At the sight of Marion Shill, Presseley gripped the railing in front of his chair. "Timothy, Christ, she's barely able to walk in the fucking parade. How difficult can this be?"

Walt Johnson, local fishing legend and the parade's Master of Ceremonies, stepped up to the podium. People downwind scurried away to find different seats. "Ladies and Gentlemen," Walt began nervously, "it is my pleasure to announce that today's leader in the twenty-third annual Master Baiters Invitational, is Frank Hollowell with a catch of…"

Presseley flushed fire-engine red and began to shake. Timothy didn't catch the details of Walt's announcement; Presseley's appearance had him worried.

"And here are the competitors." Walt gestured up the street and stepped away from the microphone.

From the north end of town, a shimmering field of four-wheel-drive pickups rumbled down the street. Each pickup pulled a fishing boat, most finished in glittering, metal-flake gelcoat that matched the custom finish on the tow vehicles. River Street looked like a horizontal fireworks display as the boats and trucks sparkled in the sun. The first convoy represented just under half of the competitors. Arms waved out of truck windows, and, for team entries, some fishermen rode in the boats wearing color-coordinated fishing outfits.

Following the first flotilla, the enormous, blue concrete truck shook the road. Two large bass painted on the side of the barrel spun slowly as the truck ponderously towed a float with a giant papier-mâché bass leaping out of a river constructed from wadded up blue paper. The trailer-mounted fish had a smile on its face and a cigarette hanging from the corner of its thick-lipped mouth. Bill Snead stood braced next to the bass with a bag of candy and a bullhorn, trying to coordinate his massive armada. A frame attached to the bass trailer towed three boats abreast, spanning nearly the width of the street. Each of those trailers pulled six more boats, for an impressive total of twenty-one boats. In each boat, a grinning fisherman tied small pieces of candy to a line and cast them out to children along the route.

"Earl!" The bullhorn roared. "No hooks!"

As the concrete truck pulled in front of the stands, two

large speakers blared the opening bars of "Fishin' is the Train Gonna' Take Me Home" by the local country duo Duck and Run. Three cheerleaders from the Washington State Crimson Girls Dance Squad bounded in front of the truck and thrust their pom-poms and pelvises to the beat.

"Goddammit, Jesse, you little dipshit," Bill's bullhorn blasted from the lead trailer. "Quit tossing condoms at the cheerleaders."

Presseley hung his head.

Behind the last of the Guild boats came the final vehicle—a sparkling, bright-white, Ford Explorer pulling a snow-white, metal-flake Nitro Z-9 bass boat, sporting an eight-foot long "Fresh Squeezed" decal emblazoned down the side. Every surface gleamed in the sun. Ted sat behind the wheel of the Explorer, Rudy sat in the passenger seat with his seatbelt fastened, waving enthusiastically at the crowd. On the boat, June Presseley, this year's Queen of the Asparagus Festival, sat in a throne tied securely to the deck. The brilliant white, all-weather carpeting nicely offset the emerald green of her dress. She waved to the crowd and blew kisses to the men along the route in every direction, except that of her husband.

Presseley stood. "Un-fucking believable." He threw the voting sheet and pencil at Timothy. "Here, take care of this." Then he pointed to his wife as she rode past. "And take care of that, too. No more fucking excuses and no more outside help. You do it." Presseley stormed off.

The hairs on Timothy's neck suddenly stood up. A glint of sun flashed from the open window of the Explorer. Timothy's head snapped around in time to see Ted look away from the stands and face forward, right before the SUV drove into a patch of shade. *What was that about?*

Juice pulled his truck and trailer into the parking lot behind the professional center. He pulled a step stool from the back of the car and set it up behind the boat. The Asparagus Queen sat perfectly still in her emerald-green satin dress, waiting for him to finish. Then she stood up, her phallic bouquet still tucked tightly in her left arm.

Juice reached up with his right hand to take the bouquet and then extended his left hand to June. She grasped his hand with a firm grip and floated down the two steps to the ground.

"Thank you, Ted." She shot him a grim smile. "I appreciate your help." She gazed vacantly at the festival-goers strolling up and down River Street. "I have to get out of this fucking town," she muttered and turned away.

Juice drove back to his house and parked the truck and trailer. He lifted the queen's throne—a Walmart stackable plastic chair and a green blanket—out of the boat and stowed them in the back of his car. The mayor had made it clear he needed them back for next year's parade.

Juice walked back to River Street. The Asparagus Festival wasn't much, but he admired the Wanaduckers for making the most of its meager entertainment. Everyone in town seemed to be there.

Salmon Sammie and the Hand Tied Flies launched into a country-cover of AC/DC's "Big Balls." The dance floor emptied, and the crowd swarmed toward the short string of booths like mosquitos heading for a nudist camp.

Walt Johnson's stand held the prime spot just north of the bridge. Juice strolled over to check the standings in the fishing competition. On the right side of the booth, a large sheet of painted plywood tilted backward at a precarious angle. Plaques from the last five competitions hung from strands of nylon monofilament. Each plaque held the winning fish, stuffed and posed for eternity with the classic over-the-fin, gape-mouthed look that drove fishermen wild, forever biting at the lure that caught it. A small brass plate named the fisherman, the winning weight, the lure, and the date of its purchase at Walt's Master Bait and Tackle.

"Hullo, Ted. Congrats on that client of yours. He using some of my bait?" Walt asked hopefully, an opaque wall of smoke rising like a theater curtain past his face.

"'Course, Walt. What else?" Juice replied. The table on the other side of the booth held boxes of metallic bait, spools of fishing line, and other fishing paraphernalia. The colored lures formed a rainbow exactly like they did at the store. "Nice touch with the colors, Walt."

"Whaddya mean?" Walt asked, perplexed.

"The rainbow. It looks good."

"Oh, my son did that."

"I didn't know you had a son."

"Yeah." Walt bobbed his head in the direction of the booth for Simpson's Flower Shoppe.

"Simpson? You're Simpson's dad?"

"Yup, being straight with ya." Walt's mutant eyebrows twitched.

"I thought Simpson's last name was Chanson?"

"Yup, that's how it's pronounced in French. It's spelled Johnson."

Simpson pranced over with a sparse arrangement of flowers and blade-like leaves sticking out from a flat black board. "Dad, I brought you something to spruce up your booth."

Simpson waggled his fingers at Juice. "Hi, Ted."

Walt accepted the floral offering from his son and hung it in the open space at the center of the trophy wall.

"Oh, Dad!" Simpson gave Walt a quick hug and wiped his sleeve across his eyes.

"Well, Walt. You take care now. I gotta get going," Juice said.

"Sure thing, Ted. Good luck to you." Walt exhaled and disappeared behind a cumulus of cigarette smoke.

"Nice work on the lures," Juice said as he moved on to the next booth with the florist tagging alongside.

"Thanks, Ted. It's been fun helping Dad in the shop." He held up his bandaged fingertips. "But those hooks…" Simpson noticed the heaving crowd of Wanaduck women waiting for the next floral arrangement demonstration. "Well, have to run. My adoring fans call. Ta-ta."

Juice nodded goodbye. He took a few steps, but stopped when he heard raised voices behind fronds of greenery at the back of Simpson's booth. The jungle foliage shook like a troop of monkeys was running through it.

Behind the shaking leaves Timothy stood very still, staring at Presseley's deep red face as his boss shook him by his lapel. Juice couldn't hear what he said, but it looked like Presseley was on a rampage. His elbow knocked one of the palm trees over. Bill Snead caught the trunk and steadied it, then stepped in front of Timothy and said, "But Dr. Presseley—"

Presseley whirled to face Bill and bellowed, "Shut up, you ignorant hick."

Bill pulled back like he'd been slapped.

Presseley looked around at the nearby crowd. He released Timothy's lapel and smoothed the hair at his temple. Then, he turned back to Timothy and spat out, "I mean it!" and stalked away, staring at the ground and muttering to himself.

Bill Snead stormed off in the opposite direction from Presseley without saying a word.

Timothy tugged his jacket down and shot his wrists out to straighten the sleeves, then pushed his way through the palm trees into Simpson's booth.

A martini shaker sat sweating on the back table with an empty martini glass next to it. Timothy picked up the shiny container, took the top off, and stared at it for several seconds. He raised it to his lips and took two large gulps. When he caught Juice staring at him, he raised the metal cup in a toast, and took another large swig. Timothy put the drink back down on the table and dropped into one of the camp chairs alongside it. He stared at his feet with a murderous look on his face.

Juice turned away and went to check out the booths on the other side of the street. In front of the VeggieTech display, crunchy-granola types handed out flyers. They wore T-shirts with the green *V* logo and the slogan "Be a Vegeconservationist" in bright orange letters across the front. One hippie-chick stepped in front of Juice and held out a flyer.

"Will you help us save the fruit and vegetables?" she asked, giving him a surprisingly assertive look.

"Save them from what?" Juice asked, grinning. "From people eating them or from rotting on the ground?"

She flipped her hair behind her shoulder with her left hand and said, "From the oppression and physical trials presented by the dams on the Columbia River, of course."

Juice gave her the once over. She didn't look stupid and she seemed serious. "What's your name?" he asked.

She twitched a little. "Aubergine."

"Sounds fancy."

"It's French for eggplant."

"Well, that's no name for you. You don't look like any

eggplant I've ever seen. 'Course, I mostly see them fried up in parmigiana."

Aubergine's face turned pink. Then, a look of horror came over her when she realized what he said. "Fried eggplant? How awful!" she said heatedly. "We harvest our VeggieTech produce humanely. We treat them with compassion until they leave our facility."

"Is that some kind of a joke?" Juice asked, laughing.

Aubergine shook her left forefinger at Juice. "Our plants are happy, which is why we have so many customers around the country. We ship our vegetables to forty-five states!"

"You don't say." Juice studied the baskets of vegetables on display.

"Would you like a sample of our snacks?" Aubergine grabbed a plate of hot dogs, spring rolls, and sausages, all the same shade of gray. "They're all vegetarian." A large yellow Lab stood up, stretched, and sniffed the plate.

"Oh, no thanks." Juice said quickly. "Just ate."

"They're really good," Aubergine said with disappointment. "Even my dog, Tofu, likes them!" She fed a few to the drooling pooch.

"Maybe another time," he said as he eased away.

The iMUD booth turned out to be everything Juice expected from a local monopoly: slick presentation boards with glossy full-color pictures and diagrams explaining the utility's construction projects and environmental initiatives. Presseley stood at the back of the booth, scowling.

"Mr. Presseley, hello there." Juice held out his hand. "I'm Ted Foteo."

"Doctor," he replied and gave Juice's hand a noncommittal handshake.

"Congratulations on your wife's win."

"Thank you, Ted," Presseley said with barely concealed venom.

Juice tapped a board with a picture of the dam cloaked in scaffolding. "So, problems with the dam?"

Presseley's eyes widened. "What? Oh, no." He plastered on a politician's smile. "Everything's good. That's simply a photo from the initial construction." The smile didn't make it past his lips. "Big safety initiative in the works. Checking our security and disaster-recovery procedures in the face of terrorist threats."

"Terrorists? Really? Out here, huh?"

"A lot of people live along the river. If something were to happen…" Presseley's voice trailed off and he stared across the river.

"How about the oppression and trials that the fruit and vegetables suffer?" Juice hiked his thumb in Aubergine's direction.

Presseley looked over at the VeggieTech booth, his face impassive. "Those conservationists." He stopped. Juice waited. Presseley shrugged. "I'm sorry. I can't help you there. I have no idea what their problem is."

"Well, best of luck with all of this."

"Thank you, Ted," Presseley replied flatly.

At the last booth, in front of the Tuck 'er Inn, Bill Snead and several of his crew stood near the head of the line. A ragged mix of fisherman, locals, and festival visitors queued up behind them, waiting for cheap beer and tasty sandwiches.

Juice had taken a few steps past the table when he overheard Bill say, "Just be ready. He said it's tomorrow." Juice kept walking. As he was about to cross the street, he saw Dickie Gordon sitting at a plastic table nursing a beer.

"Leaving so soon?" Dickie asked with a smirk.

"It's tough to tear myself away, but I have Rudy to think of."

"I wish I had a good excuse. Man, what passes for a good time in these parts."

"Not enough excitement for you? You got Walt and Simpson making up. The Utility's got some really interesting safety work coming up. And VeggieTech wants to get rid of the dams, so they can make sure their vegetables don't suffer. What more do you want?"

"Christ, I have no idea." Dickie scratched his head.

"Then you've got that crowd over there." Juice nodded toward Bill Snead. "Presseley gave Bill and Timothy a lecture that nobody was happy about."

"I know. I've been watching them. But I haven't seen anything I can do anything about. This place..." Dickie stared through the crowd.

"You know, Bill just said something about tomorrow to his guys."

"Last day of the fishing tourney?"

"They didn't look like they were talking fishing."

Dickie shook his head. "No way that bunch would miss out on the tournament."

"My point exactly—when you least expect it." Juice raised his right eyebrow. "Okay, gotta go. Rudy's waiting." He held up his hand in goodbye and walked up the street to meet Rudy at Whitey's.

Chapter 40

A patchy fog blanketed the Columbia River upstream from the Wanaduck Dam. The water's surface rippled with cat's paws stirred up by a gentle breeze. Birds cheeped tentative calls as the light gathered for a new day. Slowly, the shoreline appeared through the mist.

Juice's white boat sparkled as it bobbed near the front of the impatient fleet. Rudy sat near the bow. It was the final day of the contest, and Rudy was locked in a tie for first place.

Timothy's boat floated ten feet behind them with drops of dew glistening on the polished white hull. Timothy and Rudy, apparently competing for the title of Most Color Coordinated, had chosen the same earth-toned outfit for the tournament's last day. Timothy sat erect, idly fingered his fishing pole.

An air-horn blared and, in an instant, the peace evaporated with the simultaneous ignition of fifty-seven outboard engines. Today was the last chance to beat off other contenders and win Walt's Master Baiters Bass Fishing Invitational.

Juice throttled his boat full ahead, aimed the bow at the indentation in the cliff wall that marked his favorite fishing spot, and shot north. "Hit it, Two Shoes," Juice said as he cut the engine and drifted into position about fifty feet offshore.

Rudy picked up his fishing rod with his right hand. Releasing the lure, he snapped his wrist to cast the line. The lure touched down right where he wanted it, inside the boundary of still water. He turned around and gave Juice a smug smile. Juice nodded in acknowledgment, then relaxed in his chair.

Rudy was on a roll. Every twenty minutes or so, the line would go taut, and he would play the fish up to the side of the boat, scoop it up with the net, and gently slide it into the aerated water in the livewell to keep it alive until weigh-in for the total weight prize.

"Two Shoes, I think you got the hang of this," Juice said as Rudy got set to cast again.

Rudy grinned. He cast, and a fish took the lure immediately. The line ratcheted off the spool as the fish ran with it.

"Set the hook, Rudy."

"I got it, Ted!" Rudy shouted as he jerked the rod. The reel screamed a high-pitched *zizz* as the fish took off running again. Rudy pushed his boots against the gunwale and leaned back. He reeled the fish in, let it run, and reeled it in again. Finally, he maneuvered the fish alongside the boat. He dipped the net into the water and lifted the small-mouth bass out, water droplets glistening on its mottled gray sides. The bass looked like it weighed at least six pounds.

"Let's get that fish in the livewell, Rudy." Juice leaned forward. "I think you've got a winner there."

"Do you really think so?" Rudy slipped the fish into the holding tank and admired it. An echoing wave of boat horns swept along the river announcing the close of competition.

"Yeah, Rudy. C'mon, let's go." Juice started the engine and slipped the gearshift into forward.

Rudy closed the lid of the livewell and sat down. Juice

eased the throttle open. The boat lifted up onto plane and sped back.

Juice pulled back the throttle as he approached the dock. He reached over and grabbed a line while Rudy transferred the large fish to a clear, plastic, bag filled with water from the livewell and put the smaller fish into a separate bag.

"Go get those fish weighed." Juice steadied the boat so Rudy could climb onto the dock. "I'll tie up further down and meet you at the booth." Rudy grabbed the bags and scuttled off.

Juice pulled away from the dock right as Timothy arrived, looking smug. "Good day?" Juice asked.

"Very good day," Timothy said as their boats passed one another. "I think I've got a winner."

"Good luck to you."

Juice motored slowly downstream. He nosed up to a small beach away from the crowd and tilted the engine to keep the prop from grounding. He hopped off the bow onto dry ground, pulled the boat up so it wouldn't drift off, and secured the bow line to a piece of driftwood.

As he went to meet Rudy, motion out of the corner of his eye caught his attention. On the dock near Timothy's boat, a red-headed guy standing rooted around in a faded green satchel with papers and wires sticking out at all angles.

That guy looks just like Opie.

Rudy stood at the front of the weigh-in line with Timothy right behind him. Juice reached the booth just as Rudy handed over his entry form. A bored-looking kid, wearing a mottled green vest and a matching baseball cap tipped back at a forty five degree angle, ran the weigh in. His nametag had "Clarence" scrawled erratically across the top. Along the bottom, the tag admitted, "I work for Walt!" in bright red letters. The kid nodded toward the plastic bags. Rudy placed the one holding the smaller fish on the scale. The kid wrote down the total weight. Then, Rudy laid the bag with his monster bass on the scale. The needle spun around, settling at six pounds, five and a half ounces.

"Whoa, that could be a record, Rudy," Juice said and clapped his friend on the back.

"Really? Really?" Rudy bounced on his toes.

Juice turned to Timothy. "What do you think of that, Timothy? Nice, huh?"

Timothy scowled at the scale, his mouth a thin line. He finally looked at Juice. "Yes, very nice," he said without enthusiasm. When Clarence said, "Next," Timothy stepped up to the table and set his bag on the scale.

"Rudy, take the fish over there so they can get 'em back in the river." Juice pointed to the release area near the dock. "Meet me down at the boat."

"Okay, Ted, I will." Rudy nodded his head. "Do you think I won?"

"We'll know soon enough."

Rudy waddled away toward the dock, clutching the bags of fish in front of him. Down by the boats, the red-headed guy pulled out a cell phone and pushed buttons on the keypad. The hair on Juice's neck stood up, and he took off after Rudy. The red-headed guy looked around, perplexed, as if he expected something to happen, then pushed the buttons more emphatically. Juice picked up his pace.

Halfway down the dock, Rudy had returned his fish to the river and started back when a fireball enveloped the back end of Timothy's boat. The force of the blast shot Rudy head over heels off the dock and into a small aluminum craft tied up on the far side. Timothy sprinted past Juice as large chunks of wooden boards and white metal-flake fiberglass rained down over everyone and everything. Timothy skidded to a stop and gaped at the empty hole in the water where his boat used to be. A flying oil filter slammed into Timothy's chest and splattered his olive-green vest with steaming lubricant.

The explosion blew Hiram into the water twenty feet from the dock. The shock of hitting fifty-something degree water snapped him back to consciousness. He kicked once and surfaced in time to see a towering column of gasoline burn itself out. The dock was mayhem. Two boats had been blown away from the floating pier; one landed up on the rocks, and the other crushed a small willow along the shore. Pieces of Timothy's boat still fell from the sky. Timothy stood near the end of the path, staring at where his boat had been.

Hiram stayed low in the water as he swam up to his boat. He grabbed the stained aluminum gunwale and hauled himself in. He pulled the starter cord. Nothing. He pulled again. Still nothing. He remembered the plastic dead-man clip and pulled the coiled, red lanyard out of his pocket. The black safety clip sprung up and snapped him in the forehead. He rubbed his head, clipped the safety on the kill-button, and gave the starter cord a sharp pull. The engine sputtered to life. He squinted back at the shore. Timothy was pointing at him.

Hiram opened the throttle and turned to face the bow. The boat shimmied as his hand jerked in surprise. "Who are you?" he asked the round man in green fishing clothes lying on the floor of the boat.

"Who are you?" the man asked in return.

"I'm Hiram."

"I'm Rudy." Rudy felt his head, then checked his hand. "Where are we going?"

"Outta here. Hang on." Hiram twisted the throttle as far as it would go.

The fifteen-foot jon boat had an old thirty-horsepower outboard for propulsion. It was the only boat VeggieTech had at the compound. Hiram jogged left to clear a shoal, and back to the right to get out of the current. He held the throttle wide open, aimed for the cliffs below the wind turbines, and prayed.

Timothy pointed to the small, gray runabout heading north up the river. "That's your boy, Bill."

Bill Snead peered upriver. "Huh?" He seemed confused. "What? Who? Him?"

"Yeah." Timothy gave Bill a meaningful nod. "That bozo killed your brother."

Bill's shoulders sagged. "Eddie," he sighed once, then launched into action. "Durk!" He pointed to the closest red-neck. "All of you," he yelled. "Listen up, you little dipshits!" As one, the Guild members stopped what they were doing and waited for instructions. "That's the asshole we've been looking for!" The men looked past Bill's extended arm at the frail craft speeding away. "Get him, boys!"

Guild members jumped into fishing boats left and right. Some guys had to leap from boat to boat to get to theirs. Smoke wreathed the dock as engines began sucking gasoline at a rate that would make Arab sheiks smile in their sleep.

Boats crashed into each other. Props snagged on dock lines. Men got tossed into the water or onto their captains as the craft they stood on suddenly dropped into gear.

Two minutes of chaos came to an end. The Guild was in pursuit.

Juice stood near his boat with his binoculars to his eyes. The aluminum boat grew smaller as it retreated upriver. Ten of the Guild boats finally cleared the dock area and shot off across the water at sixty-five miles per hour. The jon boat's small engine wasn't a match for the high-powered craft in pursuit. Within twenty seconds, Juice couldn't see the chase boats through the clouds of spray coming off their wakes. But they were catching up on the runabout holding Rudy and the guy who had been punching the cell phone buttons.

Juice winced. *This is gonna hurt.* As one, the Guild boats stopped as they slammed full throttle onto the shoal. Most of the motors ripped off on impact. Captains and passengers flew through the air and skipped over the rocky bar like so many spinning stones. *I guess two hundred and seventy-five horsepower doesn't make up for not knowing where you're going.*

A shout off to his right grabbed Juice's attention. He refocused his binoculars on the dock as Bill Snead stumbled onto the deck of his boat, yelling at the boat's on the shoal. Bill's boat caromed off two others and swerved to clear some debris before he rocketed away followed by four other boats.

Juice went back to searching for the jon boat and found it two miles upriver, pulled up on shore at the base of the rock cliffs. *Where the fuck is Rudy?*

Juice let the binoculars drop to his chest, pulled his phone out of his pocket, and dialed Dickie.

"Chief Gordon," Dickie answered.

"Dickie. Juice." He realized what he had said and snapped his head around. No one within earshot. "Someone blew up the dock! Where are you?"

"I heard. I'm on my way," Dickie replied. The feeble siren on Dickie's car whined through the phone.

"No, don't come here!" Juice shouted into the phone. "Go to VeggieTech."

"What?"

"Rudy got knocked into a boat. I think the guy who blew up the dock kidnapped him."

"What?" Dickie's voice garbled through the handset. "Rudy blew up a boat?"

Juice spoke loudly and slowly. "Rudy was in a boat that's sitting at the base of the rocks near the wind turbines. Dickie? Dickie?" His phone beeped. He pulled it away from his ear and glared at the screen. The signal was gone. He shoved the phone back in his pocket and took off for the parking lot.

Timothy stared at the oil slick that marked his boat's last location. Juice stopped, grabbed Timothy by his fishing vest, and shook him. "What the fuck is going on?"

"I think somebody just tried to kill me."

"That guy? That took off in the boat?" Juice pointed up the river.

"Yes, his name is Hiram."

Hiram dragged a wheezing Rudy up the last few steps onto the slope beneath the wind turbines.

"Come on!" he said between ragged breaths. "We've got to get to those buildings!" He pulled Rudy along toward the main house at VeggieTech. As they got closer, Louise, Dr. Murphy, and Hammill came out of the front door. Hiram pushed Rudy flat against the foundation wall. "Shh!"

They stood there for several seconds trying to catch their breath without making any noise. Then, Hiram motioned to Rudy to follow him. When they reached a door, Hiram opened it. "Get in there and stay put." He pushed Rudy inside and closed the door behind him.

Chapter 41

A thick frosting of sparkly fiberglass and splintered wood covered the water near shore. Juice stood on the beach watching the cluster-fuck out on the shoal. Bill and the four other Guild boats idled up to the shallows, where fifteen guys now stood in a tight group, fighting with one another to be the first ones rescued.

"Three per boat, you idiots!" Bill shouted through his bullhorn. The guys on the shoal froze as if the challenge of counting to three shut down all other activities. Bill's voice blared, "Let's move it, you dipshits! We gotta get going." Feedback from the bullhorn screeched out over the water.

When Bill and his boys were finally on their way back, Juice turned away from the river, charged up the hill toward his truck, and hit the unlock button on his ignition key from about a hundred feet away. He opened the passenger door, pulled his Glock from under the seat, and popped the clip to make sure it was full. Juice slammed the clip home and chambered a round. He slipped the gun under his belt, covered it with his shirt and closed the Explorer's door. He glanced once at the greasy handprint he left on the paint. *That can wait.*

Juice angled down to the shore as the remaining Guild boats floated into shallow water. Everyone jumped out and pulled their boats a few feet up the beach, tying off to anything nearby. Durk was wrapping a rope around the bow seat support post on Juice's boat, the other end tied off on one of the engineless hulks that had grounded on the shoal.

"Hey, don't tie that there," Juice yelled as he ran up to Durk.

"Fuck you, asshole." Durk flipped him the bird. "We're in a hurry."

Juice lunged the last four feet and grabbed Durk's shirt, lifting him upright. Durk's eyes crossed, focusing on the gun barrel pointing at his nose. Juice didn't blink. Durk did.

"Untie the fucking boat."

As one, every Guild member untied whatever line he held, and boats began drifting aimlessly.

Thirty feet down the beach, Bill Snead yelled into a cell phone. "No, Jesse, you goddamn dipshit, move now. We'll be at the windmills. Come in at Wanderfalls and follow the old road." He glanced over his shoulder and noticed the unrestrained flotilla. "Goddammit!" Bill yelled and snapped his phone shut. "Leave the boats! Let's get out of here." The Guild members waded ashore and followed Bill to the parking lot like baby ducklings.

The entire crew amassed at the front of Bill's truck, river water pooling around them in the parking lot. Bill raised his bullhorn to his mouth. "Okay, here's what we're going to do," Bill spoke slowly like he was lecturing kids. "We're heading up to pay those veggie-terrorists a little visit. Let's lock and load!"

Juice untied his bow line from the grounded log and tossed it onto the deck. He lifted the front of the boat, shoved it off the beach, and quickly jumped aboard. He lowered the motor and turned the key. Checking for mooring lines hanging from the Guild boats, he carefully maneuvered through the abandoned fleet into clear water and accelerated.

Dickie revved his underpowered Ford down the access road to the parking lot, the siren cutting in and out as the car skittered around the turn. He nearly sideswiped Timothy's misshapen frog-car heading the other way. "Watch it asshole," Dickie muttered as he swerved to avoid a collision. Dickie stomped on the brakes, and the car skidded to a stop five feet away from the anglers in the weigh-in line. They all rotated their shoulders away from the car, protecting their precious catches.

Dickie pushed the passenger door open and crawled out. He cut to the front of the line. "Where's Ted?" he asked the kid behind the counter.

"Who?" Clarence asked with a clueless look.

Dickie turned to the waiting fishermen. "Any of you see Ted? Where is he?"

"He was here with his client a while ago," one guy offered.

"Where is he now?"

Everyone in line shrugged.

Dickie turned away from the weigh-in staion as Bill Snead's GMC pickup led four other Guild trucks out of the parking lot. Bill spun his tires through the left turn onto the highway heading north, a bright yellow ATV rocking against its tie-downs in the back. Three trucks followed him, and one turned back toward town.

Empty Guild trailers sat scattered throughout the parking lot. Guild boats floated free, drifting away from shore. Dickie flipped open his cell and speed-dialed the station.

"Wanaduck Police," Terry Baxter's cheery voice answered.

"Yeah, Terry," Dickie said in greeting.

"What's up, Chief?"

"I'm at the river access. Snead and a bunch of his guys took off a couple of minutes ago heading north, and one truck went south."

"Chief, those guys have been up to all sorts of stuff the last few weeks."

"I want you to meet me at VeggieTech. I think something's going down."

"Okay, I'm on my way," Terry replied and hung up.

Dickie closed his phone and holstered it on his left hip. He headed for what remained of the dock and approached a fisherman standing at its charred, splintered end. "Hey, Frank, you see Ted?"

Frank stood forlornly next to a half-sunk fishing boat.

"Frank! Do you know where Ted is?" Dickie tried again.

Frank pointed out over the water. "I saw his boat go by a little while ago, heading up river."

"Thanks." Dickie turned and ran for his car.

"Somebody blew up my boat," Frank called out to Dickie's back.

"Come by the station later," Dickie yelled over his shoulder. He got to his car and jumped in. The car lurched up to the weigh-in line. The fishermen stepped back. Dickie threw the car in reverse, backed away, and took off.

Hiram stood under the wind generators with Louise, Dr. Murphy and Hammill watching the white boat approach. Louise looked like the misbegotten progeny of a Viking princess and a Mexican bandito out of the movie *Ride, Vaquero!* Long, blond hair flowed from beneath a light-weight combat helmet with an integrated radio and night-vision scope. Louise wore the usual peasant shirt and pants, but the *zapatas* had been replaced by a pair of highly-polished combat boots, dyed the same bright green as the *V* in the VeggieTech logo. Two bandoliers filled with bullets crossed the front of Louise's shirt. Louise held a small Heckler and Koch MG4 machine gun with an ammo belt already locked in.

Louise aimed a pair of binoculars down at the water. "It seems Mr. Bentle is gathering his troops," Louise said. "All of you come with me. We must be ready to greet them."

"Wait…" Hiram began, but Louise was already walking down the hill toward the lab. Hiram shrugged and followed.
"Wait…" Hiram began, but Louise was already walking down the hill toward the lab. Hiram shrugged and followed.
He nervously scratched at his shirt where the tape holding the thick file he had stolen chafed his skin. He thought he might be allergic to the adhesive. Hiram found the papers while snooping around the packing house two days ago. It was a stack of names and addresses, but he thought it might be the key to what was going on.

As they approached the house, Mustafa staggered out of the brilliantly painted school bus holding a bundle of wires.

"Are we ready?" Louise asked. Mustafa gave a quick nod. "Mustafa, timing will be everything." Louise paused and glanced at Hammill, who smiled slightly. "Remember, you'll have fifteen seconds. Do you have the keys?"

Mustafa had a dreamy look in his eyes. "Yes, Father." He slurred his words.

"Good, good, good. Now go hide near the bus and be ready to go." Louise pulled a small flask from a pocket. "Drink this when you're set." Mustafa took the bottle and weaved out of sight behind the main house.

"What was that?" Hiram pointed at Louise's now-empty pocket.

"Starbucks double-shot Mocha Machiatto Iced Coffee," Louise said. "We're going to need the little towel-head awake."

"But he'll only have fifteen seconds," Hiram protested. "How do you expect him to clear the dam that quickly?"

"I don't. Besides, Hammill reset the detonator for four seconds. Mustafa won't see it coming, and we'll have one less loose end."

Hiram opened his mouth to say something but thought better of it.

Hammill stood next to the building, punching the keys of his Blackberry. The rolling door to the lab opened, and the foursome entered the airlock. Hammill keyed some more and the inner door opened. He vanished into the lab.

A dull buzzing sound grew into the whine of several small engines.

"Ah." Louise gazed up the hill. "I see our visitors have arrived."

Juice idled his boat up to the base of the cliff and jumped off onto the rocks along the narrow shore. He tied the line around a small boulder at the base of the steps hewn into the three-hundred-foot high cliff face. Juice's leg twinged when he looked up the cliff. He began climbing.

Ten minutes later, at the top of the stairs, sweat poured off him. He stopped to catch his breath, but his leg didn't hurt at all. To his right, a group of ATVs raced up the hill through the scattered trees, their small engines revving wildly. Behind them, a big diesel engine growled, and black smoke belched upward. He snatched the gun out of his belt and ducked behind a rock.

Bill Snead came over the top of the hill. A hunting rifle stuck out of a gun boot on the side of his ATV. He roared across the open area and skidded to a stop in the middle of the three wind turbines. He pulled the rifle out of the scabbard and sighted down the hill.

At the outer door, Hiram checked back the way they had come. A bullet smacked into the metal a foot above his head. He leaped into the airlock and ducked inside. Hammill maneuvered a forklift from the lab to the inner door of the airlock, lowered the forks to the ground, and squeezed himself through the nearly-blocked doorway. Hammill took six long boxes off the pallet on the forklift and stacked them to one side.

"Quickly now, Hammill," Louise urged. "We haven't much time."

Hiram went the opposite way to get into the lab and leaned against the wall. He heard a whizzing sound followed by a muffled explosion.

Hammill stood next to the six forest-green fiberglass cases. The top case sat open and empty, the lid labeled "9K115-2 Metis-M." Hammill held a still-smoking launch tube with a length of fine wire trailing from the end.

"Where did you get those?" Hiram asked Hammill, who shrugged and nodded his head in Louise's direction.

"eBay."

"eBay?"

Louise nodded his head indifferently.

A shot ricocheted off the floor. Hiram peeked out the door. "That looked like it came from the greenhouses." The only thing on the low hill was a small bush. "There's a pickup truck blocking the lane," Hiram announced to no one in particular.

Louise nodded. "Hammill, please remove the threat in the drive. I'll cover you." Louise dashed past the opening and extended the bi-pod barrel support of the little machine gun. "Whenever you're ready, Hammill." Louise aimed out at the hill as several shots hit the floor nearby.

Hammill struggled with the catches on another case. Without his pinkie fingers, he couldn't flip and twist the metal tabs to release the clips . He worked his way down the box, opening each of the latches one at a time. He flipped the lid and reached in to grab the tube. It slipped from his grasp and clattered onto the floor in front of the door. Hammill mouthed, "Sorry." He stretched out on the floor and reached over to pull the weapon back to him. Several shots smacked into the concrete near the launcher.

"Quickly, Hammill, quickly." Louise steadily gazed down the sight.

Hammill stood up and popped off the tube's end protectors. He clipped on the sight, face shield, and firing handle, then swung the tube to his shoulder, and nodded.

Hiram jumped two feet into the air as three ear-splitting burps erupted from Louise's machine gun.

Hammill stepped into the open doorway and took aim. He flipped a lever on the control handle, and three green lights lit up in the heads-up display of the face shield. A fourth green light flashed twice, then went steady. Hammill pulled the trigger, and the rocket whooshed out of the tube.

A massive explosion lifted the pickup in the driveway off the ground and tumbled it through the air. Hiram's ears popped from the compression wave. The truck landed upside down fifteen feet to the side of the lane. "Holy shit!" he whispered.

More bullets slammed into the metal siding. "Up the ridge this time," Louise shouted and retreated back into the building.

Hammill unloaded another launcher and fired the rocket. The recoil proved too much for his tired hands, and the tip of the tube rocked upward. The missile passed harmlessly over the spinning blades of the southernmost wind turbine, its control wire dragging behind.

Chapter 42

When the door closed behind Rudy, all light in the room cut off. Already disoriented, he tried to find the door. He held his hands out in front of him and shuffled forward slowly until his hands met the wall. He sidestepped to the right. When he came to a corner, he reversed direction. His fingers found the doorframe, and he slowly slid his hand across the door, moving it up and down, groping for the handle. He grabbed the lever, twisted it, and pulled. *Locked.*

Rudy turned his back to the door. He thought he heard something scurry across the room, and his heart jumped into his throat. "Who's there?" He waited for an answer. None came. Another scuffing sound, followed by a smothered groan. "Who's there?" Rudy repeated. He was answered by more scratching and mumbling.

"Hang on," Rudy said as he felt his way along the wall again. "I'm coming." He reached the corner, turned, and followed the wall to another corner. He turned again and took a step. His foot connected with something on the ground, and he heard a smothered "Unnh!" at his feet.

"Wait a second." Rudy carefully lowered himself to one

knee and groped around. *A leg!* He moved his hands up the body, feeling for ropes but finding, instead—breasts. His hands jerked away like he had touched a live wire. More carefully, he retraced the woman's outline until he reached her head and found a gag over her mouth. He untied it, and the woman took a deep breath.

"Are you okay?"

"Hands off the merchandise, buster."

"Sorry," Rudy stammered. "Why are you tied up?"

"Where are the others?" she asked, ignoring his question. The room filled with scraping sounds and muffled calls for help. "Quick, untie my hands, then go help them."

Rudy reached around the woman's back to undo the rope. He was close to her, so close he could feel the heat of her body. The strong scent of patchouli wafting off her skin sent his head spinning. He quickly untied the knots and pushed himself away.

"Ouch. Careful there, bub."

"Sorry."

"Get the others."

Rudy fumbled along the ground until he came to another body. He moved his hands up its outline and found a binding around its head. He untied the gag and heard another whoosh of fresh air sucked into oxygen-starved lungs.

"Thanks," a man's voice croaked. "Who are you?"

"I'm Rudy."

"Karat."

Carrot?

"Where's Stu and Mustafa?" Karat asked. No one answered. "Rudy, how did you get in here?"

"Hiram pushed me in here." The sound of a desperate struggle erupted from further down the wall.

"Aubergine!" said the woman who Rudy had untied. "Hang on."

Rudy felt a hand against his back. The woman's heady aroma enveloped him as she passed. He untied Karat's hands and feet.

Rudy groped the ground as he moved past Karat. He came to another body. It didn't move. "Someone's hurt." He untied the strip of cloth in the man's mouth. The body slumped over. Rudy felt Karat next to him.

"It's Stu." Karat's voice got quiet. "I think he's dead."

The woman said, "Just a second, Aubergine." Someone sobbed and the woman murmured, "There, there. It's going to be alright."

"Oh, Marissa," another woman's voice spoke in the dark. "Is Hiram okay?"

"Hiram's fine," Rudy answered. "The dock blew up, and I ended up in a boat. Hiram was driving. He said something about people in danger. Something about having to save his little eggplant. He said they were all drugged. I don't know. It didn't make much sense."

"Oh, Hiram," Aubergine sighed.

"Come on. We've got to get out of here."

"What about Stu?"

Rudy felt a sticky spot on the floor, checked for a pulse, and felt nothing. The body was too cool. "Stu didn't make it." One of the women started to cry. Rudy shook off his fear. "We've got to get out of here before they come back."

"Where's the door?"

"It's locked. I tried."

"Maybe there's another one."

"Start looking."

The three others shuffled around the room. Rudy stood up, put his hands out in front of him, and stepped forward.

After two paces he collided with someone. "Sorry."

"It's okay," Karat said. "The door's not back there."

Rudy turned ninety degrees. He took a step and landed on a foot.

"Ouch!" Aubergine yanked her foot out from under his. "Don't worry, Karat. Hiram will save us."

"It's Rudy."

"You, too."

Once again, Rudy turned and inched forward. The room grew warmer. *She* was nearby. Slowly, he took another step. Then another. Her breath tickled his face. Their outstretched arms had missed each other, and their bodies touched.

"Thanks for saving us," she said. Her arms closed around him.

"But...but..." His mind couldn't find traction with his heart skipping wildly. "I didn't do anything."

"Yes, you did." She embraced him and squeezed. "If you hadn't shown up, we'd all be..."

The building rocked. She and Rudy bumped together and fell to the ground. Rudy landed first.

"Look—light!" Aubergine sat upright on the concrete floor. The doorframe had shifted on its mounts, and a bright rectangle outlined the door.

Karat jumped to his feet. "Let's go."

Rudy looked up into the eyes of the woman on top of him. She took his breath away. "It's you! I saw you in the video!" he squeaked. "I can't breathe."

She hopped easily to her feet and helped Rudy to his. She smiled at him. "Thanks," she said again. "Really."

Karat kept tugging on the door. "I think we can pull it open. Everybody help."

The four of them pulled and pushed on the handle and hinges, but the doorframe wouldn't budge. Another explosion buffeted the building, and the door shuddered. They pulled again, and metal screeched against concrete. With another yank the door fell away from the wall. A few screws clinked to the floor. They pushed the door to the side and gazed out onto Armageddon.

Juice had been watching the action from behind a rock, waiting for an opportunity to present itself, when his cellphone rang. A moment later, Bill Snead stepped around the rock and leveled his deer rifle at Juice.

"What the fuck are you doing here?" Bill asked.

Juice's answer was drowned out as a rocket shot out of the pre-fab building and exploded, sending the pickup truck in the lane flying through the air. Bill turned and ran back to his ATV, shouting at his troops. Juice stooped back behind the rock.

The sound of grinding gears rattled through the trees. A plume of black smoke erupted as the blue concrete truck roared onto the slope. Liquid sloshed from the overfilled mixer and spilled down the swaying chute. Bill snatched up the bullhorn. "Goddammit Jesse, you little dipshit! Get that truck up here!" The lumbering vehicle turned and ground its way up the hill to the cluster of ATVs. "Not here! Behind us!" Bill shouted through his bullhorn, but Jesse ignored him, brought the truck to a halt next to Bill's ATV, and jumped down to the ground. The reek of gasoline was overpowering. "Damn it, Jesse," Bill screamed. "You're gonna get us all killed." He pointed down the hill to the large building. "They're firing missiles and tracer loads. Get that truck behind the hill. Now!" Jesse climbed onto the step to the cab. Bill pointed the bullhorn over at the woods. "You eight. Get into that house!"

"Uh, Bill." Jesse spoke softly.

"Later, Jesse." Bill watched his foot soldiers advance through the low vegetation.

Down the hill from Juice's position, four people came out of the lower level of the house, one dressed in muted earth tones. *Rudy!* The group from the house ran up the hill to the greenhouses. A lone figure clothed in tattered strings of fabric stood up, raised a rifle, and fired once. One of the runners fell to the ground, clutching his thigh.

"Uh, Bill." Jesse said a little louder.

"Not now, Jesse!"

"Bill!" Jesse shouted. "I locked myself out of the damn truck!"

"Jesus Christ, you little dipshit." A puff of smoke bloomed from the doorway of one of the buildings. "Incoming!" Bill screamed.

Everybody flattened themselves on the ground. The rocket flew out over a wind generator and disappeared over the cliff.

Hiram bolted from the pre-fab building and dashed up the hill toward the people near the greenhouses. Bill clambered onto his ATV and started it up.

"Bill, what should I do?" Jesse sounded panicked.

"Break the goddamned window, Jesse. Just get that truck out of here." Bill cranked the throttle and sped off down the ridge, heading for Hiram.

Juice ran up behind a Guild member sitting on another ATV. Juice smashed his Glock against Durk's temple and pulled his limp body off of the four-wheeler. He got on, and took off after Bill. A detonation rocked him from behind. He glanced back over his shoulder. One of the windmills was a flaming wreck. A blade from the wind generator sliced through the air over his head.

⊕ ⊕ ⊕

"Tofu! Tofu! Come here!" Aubergine called. Hiram peeked out the door and watched the group head toward the greenhouses with Karat in the lead. The bush on the hill shook violently, then stood up, strips of camouflage cloth fluttering in the breeze. It raised a rifle and fired a single shot. Karat dropped, grabbing his thigh. The bush reached up and pulled the hood off its ghillie suit.

"Timothy Bentle. The sniper is Timothy Bentle!" Hiram shouted to Louise.

"Denise," Louise pointed out the door. "Please remove that nuisance from the property. I'll cover you."

Dr. Murphy grabbed a Mac-10 machine pistol from the open trunk on the pallet, made sure it was loaded, and dashed out the door. Louise stepped into the opening and fired bursts in both directions.

"You idiot," Hiram screamed. "You're going to kill somebody."

"That's the idea, Hiram." Louise pointed the gun at him. "Perhaps you would consider helping with that effort and go save your precious Aubergine."

Hiram reached into the trunk and pulled out a small-caliber pistol.

"Poor choice of gun, Hiram," Louise scoffed.

"It's all you have left."

Hiram glanced outside, then bolted through the doorway and around the packing plant. As he cleared the far end of the small building, he came up short. A rocket swung beneath the southernmost wind generator dangling from its control wire. As the blades spun, the hub of the generator wound up the control wire, raising the missile like it was reeling in a fish. The rocket reached the hub and blew up. One turbine blade flew out over the river, and another crashed in pieces at the base of the tower. The third arced like a scythe across the compound, flying over the onrushing four-wheelers.

"Denise!" Louise shouted from behind Hiram. She turned at the sound of Louise's voice, and the whirling blade sliced her in half.

Hiram jumped over Dr. Murphy's bisected body, pushed through the people huddled together, and aimed his pistol at Timothy. "Drop the rifle!" he shouted. Timothy spun in Hiram's direction and fired a shot. It went wide.

Before Hiram could get off a shot, the first ATV skidded to a stop next to Rudy and Aubergine. Bill Snead snatched his rifle out of the boot, leveled it at Hiram, and said coldly, "Drop the gun. You killed my brother."

"I didn't kill anybody." Hiram dropped his puny pistol.

Bill worked the bolt, chambered a round, and aimed at Hiram's chest. "Bullshit."

A gunshot cracked. Bill's rifle spun out of his hands and landed in the dirt.

"Juice!" Rudy shouted.

Juice advanced up the hill, his Glock in a two-handed grip, aiming at Timothy's head. "Put down the rifle now," Juice said flatly. "Do not do anything stupid."

Timothy knelt slowly and lowered the rifle to the ground. He kept his left hand in the air, and his eyes fixed on Juice. He pushed the rifle an arm's length away and pulled his hand back to his leg with his fingers open.

"Freeze, Bentle." Dickie Gordon and Officer Backster approached with their service weapons drawn.

Timothy's head hung in defeat. Dickie and Juice kept their

guns trained on him as Officer Backster pulled his Walther PPK from an ankle holster. She fingered the safety on, stuck the gun in her belt, and pulled out her handcuffs. Timothy eyed the restraints. A small smile crossed his face.

"You asshole!" Bill glanced from the sniper rifle to the Walther to Timothy's face. His shoulders sagged. "You're the one who shot Eddie?"

A dull *fwoop* sounded from the bottom of the hill. "A mortar!" Hiram shouted.

A trail of smoke arched up into the air toward the ridge. The round landed behind the concrete truck, and the gasoline-soaked ground ignited. The truck began rolling down the hill with fingers of fire trailing behind. Jesse jumped down from the cab of the truck.

"Goddammit, Jesse, you little dipshit." Bill Snead struggled onto his ATV and shot off after the truck that was bearing down on the buildings. His four-wheeler slid sideways when it hit the gasoline-slick dirt in front of the advancing flames. Bill swerved as he caught up with the truck. A burst of machine gun fire from the pre-fab building blew out the truck's right rear tires. It yawed right, its inertia tilting it over further and further. The dump-chute swung wildly, spraying gasoline through the air, against the buildings, and onto Bill. He pulled a hard left away from the truck and accelerated up the ridge, smoke trailing from his flaming ATV. He fell off his four-wheeler at the top of the hill. The remaining Guild members gathered around him, and beat him with their jackets to put out the blaze.

The inferno spread out behind the truck, following the trail of spilled fuel onto the gas-soaked buildings. A finger of flame jumped onto the dump chute and slowly made its way closer to the barrel. The truck ripped the smaller pre-fab building from its footings with the shriek of tearing metal, slid into the open door of the larger building, and stopped. For a second, there was nothing but yellow fire, black smoke, and the roar of burning gasoline.

"The lab! Everybody get down!" Hiram yelled. He grabbed Dickie and Terry, threw them onto the ground, and dove on top of them. Juice pulled Aubergine down next to Karat and tried to shield them. Rudy grabbed Melissa's hand and pulled her into the small ditch where Timothy had been standing.

A blast of heat washed over them.

It took a couple of minutes for the inferno to subside. When everyone stood up, both pre-fab buildings were completely gone, and fire licked up one side of the main house. The VeggieTech logo lay in pieces on the ground. Behind them, the greenhouses had been leveled by the force of the blast. A crumpled ghillie suit sat on the ground looking like a deflated sheep dog. Timothy had just disappeared.

The growl of a diesel engine came from behind the burning house. Machine gun fire burst from the driver's window of a green and orange Bluebird school bus as it drove up the lane. The group dropped back to the ground.

"Hiram," Louise shouted from the bus. "Come!" Another burst of gunfire followed.

"Shit," Hiram crawled over to Dickie. "Look, I've got to go." Hiram watched the school bus slowly accelerate. "If I don't, another innocent person is going to get killed."

"Hiram, come!"

"Then get out of here," Dickie said.

Hiram picked up his gun and took off running. He caught up with the bus and vanished through the passenger door. A final volley of gunfire spit out of the window as the bus lumbered away.

Officer Backster applied pressure to a cut on Aubergine's forehead. Dickie got to his feet, pulled out his cell phone, and dialed 9-1-1 for Karat.

Juice surveyed the destroyed compound and let out a long whistle. "Now that's something you don't see every day."

Rudy helped Melissa to her feet. "Hi, I'm Rudy."

"Hi," she said, dusting grass off the front of Rudy's fishing vest. "I'm Marissa. M-E-L-I-S-S-A."

"Of course." Rudy flicked a bug from her shoulder. "How else would you spell it?"

Chapter 43

From the cover of the ditch, Timothy watched the concrete mixer explode. He quickly shed his shredded lettuce disguise, flattened himself against the ground behind a low earthen berm, and crawled toward his car through a carpet of glass fragments, mangled pieces of plastic tubs, shreds of vegetation, and, what he hoped was, the nutrient-rich hydroponic glop for the plants. It smelled like an outhouse. When he had put some distance between himself and the others, he jumped to his feet and ran the rest of the way to his car. The new coating of natural vegetable material had given his earth-tone fishing outfit a thin crust of actual earth, but Timothy focused on the sparkly reflection from thousands of tiny glass shards embedded in the goo. He looked like an Earth Day disco-ball and felt like an excellent target.

When Timothy reached his tiny 2CV, he tore off his clothes and left them on the ground, instantly regretting this morning's choice of bright red briefs. A shout resounded across the compound followed by machine gun fire. A garishly painted school bus cleared the main house and accelerated up the lane straight at him. Louise fired a belt-fed gun out the driver's side window.

Timothy hopped into the car and turned the key. Nothing—not even a click. He turned it again—still nothing. He disengaged the parking brake, got out of the car, and pushed. The tiny car slowly built up speed as it rolled down the slight incline to the main road. When he almost couldn't keep up with it, he jumped in, depressed the clutch, and threw the gearshift lever into second. Timothy glanced in his rearview mirror and flinched when he saw nothing but the reflection of a chrome grill, a small bird in the center. He popped the clutch. The car bucked once, and the engine caught. He pressed the accelerator to the floor, and the bus receded behind him.

He didn't slow down when he reached the highway, just jerked the wheel to the right. All four wheels drifted out into the far lane. He upshifted when the speedometer hit fifteen kilometers-per-hour, gunned it again, and, at thirty KPH, raced back to town. Timothy checked his nearly-new *Octopussy* collector's edition Seiko watch. "Fuck. I'm late."

Timothy flipped open his cell phone and speed dialed his boss.

"Yes?" Robert Presseley answered.

"Our team dropped the ball." Timothy spoke in code in case anyone was listening on Presseley's end. "It was a major loss in the final seconds of the game." He paused. "The blue team showed up late and is still on the field, but unexpected players showed up for the game."

"Explain," Presseley said flatly. "And cut the bullshit. There's nobody else here."

"Louise's wackos had some serious weaponry. Snead went nuts, and his idiots got their asses kicked," Timothy continued. "The cops showed up, and I had to clear out. Our plans for the dam are cooked."

"When can you report fully?"

"I'm heading down to Grant County right now to take care of a job for Commissioner Caley," Timothy explained. "That should be two or three hours. How about seven this evening?"

"Fine." The call dropped.

"Come, Hiram!" Louise barked from the bus, holding the Heckler and Koch past Mustafa's head and firing short bursts out the driver's window.

Hiram struggled to his feet. "Coming, Father." He gripped his arms against his chest as he ran to catch the bus.

Louise squeezed off another volley to cover Hiram. "Go, go, go!" Louise yelled.

Hiram darted in front of the bus' bumper and spun. He launched himself through the door and landed at Louise's feet. He gasped in pain as the file inside his shirt bit into his ribs.

Mustafa crammed the gearshift into second and gunned the big diesel. The bus shuddered violently, and the front end screamed as the transmission took the load. Smoke from the toasted clutch made Hiram nauseous. He sat up and spat out the door to clear the bile from his throat.

Louise stood over Hiram. Louise did not look happy.

"Up," was all Louise said.

Hiram stood up and grabbed the overhead bar.

"Hiram." Louise's face sagged. "I'm sure you know how disappointed I am in you. Give me your gun, please."

Lying was out of the question, so Hiram worked his hand into his jacket and pulled out the Puma twenty-two he had taken from the lab. Hiram winced as the barrel scraped against his bruised ribs. He grabbed the gun with his other hand and held the weapon out.

"Thank you, Hiram." Louise took the gun and turned away. "Please remain here."

Hiram turned to look out the front of the bus and saw the shotgun intended for their protection. He checked the load. *Empty.* He looked in the box of shells on the dash. *Empty.* He leaned the gun back against the dash. *I'm fucked.* He turned to face the back of the bus, which was packed with twenty-two shiny stainless steel barrels, each holding two-hundred kilos of potent explosives.

Mustafa had tried to explain the process to him a week ago. The barrels were shaped charges, each capable of reducing twenty feet or so of reinforced concrete to rubble. When the charge detonated, a white-hot beam of metal moved downward at ten miles per second, cutting through everything in its path.

Louise scrambled over the barrels, then turned and smiled at Hiram.

Oh, shit! I'm going to die with Mustafa. Hiram had never seen anything as frightening as this cargo. *At least it'll be quick.* Louise finished inspecting the charges, checked some kind of electrical device, and began the cumbersome climb back to the front of the bus.

The dam's access road appeared through the trees. In another quarter-mile they would crest the ridge. It would be all downhill from there. "This is wrong," Hiram said.

"What?" Mustafa glanced over at him.

"You shouldn't have to die to do this. There's got to be another way."

"I won't die. I have fifteen seconds to get clear."

Hiram leaned in and whispered, "Fifteen seconds might be enough if you were a track star. But you're not." Hiram squeezed Mustafa's shoulder. "And Hammill reset the delay to four seconds. You'll be vapor."

Mustafa's face went gray. He nodded and gripped the wheel even harder.

The bus crested the hill just as Louise returned to the front. The overloaded vehicle accelerated down the slope approaching the security gate at the east end of the dam.

Louise backed Hiram down onto the steps. "Thank you for everything, Hiram." Louise pulled out the Puma and shot Hiram in the chest.

Hiram didn't have time to react. His world collapsed. The combination of the force of the bullet and the inertia from going around a bend in the road threw him from the bus into the dusty weeds by the side of the road.

Louise jumped as Mustafa screamed.

"Shut up, you little camel-jockey!" Louise yelled at him.

Mustafa's hands gripped the wheel, fighting to keep the overloaded bus on the narrow road. He kept his eyes on the road as the speed piled on quickly.

Louise leaned over Mustafa's shoulder and shouted, "I'm going to jump out at the first tower. Remember, you hit the second tower head on, then get out and run like hell."

"But I'll die."

"No, you have fifteen seconds," Louise lied. "If it gets close, jump into the lake. You'll be perfectly safe there." Louise smiled.

"This is wrong," Mustafa whispered and glanced at the gun aimed at his head. "I'm going to die." Mustafa braced against the steering wheel. When the bus slammed through the security gate, the sudden deceleration threw Louise forward into the heavy Lexan windshield, then back, stunned, into the first row of barrels.

Louise watched everything happen in what seemed like slow-motion. Mustafa let go of the wheel and jumped from the bus, tumbling to a stop, sitting upright on the concrete roadway. The bus slewed right, rammed the concrete abutment on the upstream side of the dam, and scraped along the safety barrier. The rolling bomb slowed, but the big diesel did not give up.

A sucking sound, like a Shop-Vac emptying a bathtub filled with Jell-O, came from the weeds by the side of the road. Hiram rolled onto his back and ripped open the zipper on his coat. He felt his chest where pain radiated like heat from the desert sun. His hand came back clean and dry, holding only the splayed shape of the twenty-two caliber bullet that had barely penetrated the thick file of papers he had taped to his chest. Other than a hole through the center of the first inch, the package was safe.

He grabbed a sapling and dragged himself vertical. Turning back toward the dam, Hiram saw Mustafa at the near end of the dam struggling to get up.

"Run, Mustafa," Hiram croaked in a voice that sounded like he was breathing leaves. He tried to yell, and failed, again. Mustafa finally stood up and staggered back to the crushed security gate. Hiram willed him on.

The faint, persistent, sound of metal on concrete dragged

Hiram's attention away from Mustafa. In the middle of the dam, the bus scraped along like a slow-motion train wreck. The security gate had wedged under the bus' front end.

Hiram could just make out Louise sitting in the driver's seat, wrestling with the wheel, but the bus was not responding. Louise jumped from the seat, crawled across the barrels to the rear of the bus, then back to the front. The bus kept going.

The front end of the bus hit something in the roadway and bounced, knocking the gate free. The vehicle veered suddenly to the left and crossed the surface of the dam. It slammed through the concrete guardrail. The front end dropped, the rear end tipped up vertically, and the bus plunged into space. The bus' tires contacted the sloping concrete face, tires squealing like a plane touching down. A small human shape fell in front of the bus, flailing like it was trying to swim away. *Louise!*

A blinding flash.

Sound and shock waves staggered Hiram where he stood. He blinked to clear the spots before his eyes. The bus and Louise had just disappeared.

A blackened crater about thirty feet deep, bordered by concrete rubble and mangled reinforcing rods, marked the bus' last position. A concentric shock ring spread across the face of the dam, finally reaching the bedrock at the edges. Like a ripple in a pond reflecting off a stone wall, the wave moved back into the center. It amplified, cracking the face of the dam. When it reached the crater, the wave focused at the exact point of the explosion. A single block of debris popped out of the face of the dam, flew through the air, and splashed into the seething torrent of the Columbia River.

A low, almost sub-audible, grumbling vibrated the soles of Hiram's feet. A fissure in the blasted concrete snaked away in fits and starts, up and to the left, creeping like a crack across a car's windshield. A second large crevasse popped open and expanded from the point of the explosion up and to the right. Hiram stood silent as a giant *V* slowly etched itself across the face of the dam.

From the dam towers, the emergency sirens started to wail.

Chapter 44

From where Bill stood, "HITMAN3" stuck out like a bas relief on Father O'Donnell's back.

"I guess the Lord was trying to send me a message," the priest said.

The Wanaduck surgeon had not found a safe way to remove the Indiana license plate embedded between O'Donnell's spine and the skin of his back.

Father O'Donnell couldn't seem to find a comfortable position. "It stings a bit, Bill."

"I know how you feel." Bill struggled to his feet, the lower part of his good leg wrapped in gauze. "When that truck tipped over, I guess I got some gas on my jeans." He shook a small prescription bottle. "Don't think it'll bother me much once these kick in.

When Bill passed Father O'Donnell's status to the rest of the Guild, they searched for a way to accept the bad news. As one, they found it. *Let's get drunk!* For the kind of drunk they had in mind, the Gorge Princess was just the ticket.

"Listen up, you dipshits." Bill's bullhorn was deafening

inside the hospital's garage. He held up a tattered brochure. "I booked the whole fucking boat. You get cheap food and an all-you-can-drink bar for twenty bucks. Listen to this." He read from the flyer, "Seven days a week the Gorge Princess whisks select groups of sightseers on scenic tours of the majestic Columbia River between the Wanapum and Wanaduck Dams. See the *towering* basalt cliffs, the *distant* glacier-covered Cascades, and the *breathtaking* spawning salmon! Whether you're a visitor or a local, the Gorge Princess has something to offer you and your group."

"Like free drinks!" Jesse shouted.

"Would you shut up and listen." Bill faced Jesse down with the bullhorn, then continued reading the sales pitch. "Originally commissioned in 1897 as a pleasure vessel for local land baron and developer, Walter Wanshucht, the Gorge Princess acquired a new lease on life as a floating bordello and bar during Prohibition, and later served as entertainment for leave-taking World War II soldiers stationed nearby. Now, fully restored to her original splendor, she guarantees to be the highlight of your Columbia River visit." The room filled with feedback and Bill released the button on the bullhorn. "You know what that means?" he shouted.

Silence.

"It used to be a whorehouse."

The garage rang with cheers and applause. Everyone raced to their vehicles. Bill hobbled over to Jesse's Chevy pickup and dropped his jeans. The mud-flap girl's silhouette in Teletubby-purple decorated his bright yellow boxers. He leaned back against the seat, unstrapped his prosthetic limb, pulled out the sawed-off Browning, and chambered a round. He slid another shell into the magazine and put everything back together. Bill hiked his jeans back up and pushed against his left foot to get up into the truck. His burned leg protested, and he struggled against the pain to slide into the passenger side of the cab.

"Why the *fuck* didn't you get a goddamned real truck?" Bill grimaced through the sparkles of agony the Vicodin hadn't dulled.

"Jeezus, I'm sorry, Bill," Jesse began, but Bill immediately cut him off.

"Just shut the holy-fucking-Mother-of-God up would you?"

Five guys jumped in the truck bed, and the vehicle sagged under the weight. Bill winced with the motion. "Hit it, Jesse. The Princess is waiting."

The passenger-side mirror reflected the other two trucks loaded and following behind. They passed the "You're Leaving Wanaduck, Why?" sign at seventy-five miles per hour with Jesse in the lead.

"Ellis, this is better than we could have possibly hoped," Presseley said.

Ellis Spelt caught a disconcerting gleam in Presseley's eyes as he studied the shattered dam. A backhoe belched a toxic cloud of diesel exhaust as the driver downshifted. A man emerged from the smog, coughing. He put a cigarette to his lips and took a long draw. He coughed again.

"Jimmy! What's she look like? How soon can you start lowering the pool?"

The head of maintenance for the dam shook his head. "Not good, Dr. Presseley." He pointed at the bottom of the dam. Only a trickle ran from each of the three large outflow pipes. "Turbine room's flooded. All three generators shifted when the bomb went off. The blades stopped, and flow basically shut off."

"What about the bypass?" Presseley asked.

Jimmy D. shot a glance at Ellis. "Yeah, we're working on that. The valves are stuck. If we had divers, we could get to the plates but..." The ground shuddered. Water started spraying from the shattered *V* along the face of the dam. "Shit!" Jimmy D. sprinted away down the access road.

"Yes, Ellis," Presseley said, rubbing his hands together. "Much better than we could have hoped."

The ground trembled again. A single loud snap echoed up and down the river. The V-shaped concrete wedge lurched about six feet out from the face of the structure. The disintegration of the dam sounded like the finale at a fireworks display accompanied by the screaming squeal of metal. Sparks flew as wires pulled out of the towers. Ellis watched in horror as the giant concrete triangle hesitated for a second, then toppled into the river. The lake behind the dam poured through the gap and rushed downstream as a fifty-foot tall wave. The emergency sirens renewed their ear-splitting warning.

Chapter 45

Timmy the Clown packed up his supplies and stepped out of the cabin of the Gorge Princess wearing his clown costume. The yacht's crew was exchanging the "Happy Birfday Benjamin Caley and Partie!" sign with one that read, "Welcome Aboard Dail Earnart Memoral Lettery Gild" when the Guild's convoy unloaded at the end of the dock. A loud debate commenced over the spelling of "Gild."

The members of the Guild stopped arguing and glared at Timothy for a few seconds. Suddenly, they rushed the gangway and, in their stampede, knocked Bill Snead down. Fighting to fit onto the three-foot-wide boarding ramp, two members fell into the water and sank under the weight of the weapons they still carried.

Timothy calmly pulled out his Heckler and Koch USP Compact, flicked the safety off, and shot the leading attacker in the chest. The Guild kept coming, so Timothy emptied the remaining thirteen cartridges into the onrushing crowd.

Timothy fled back into the cabin, ripped off his wig, and kicked off his clown shoes. He tossed his bag onto the counter, reached into the side pocket, and pulled out a loaded clip.

He tossed it against the wall. *The spare for the Walther.* Rummaging through the bag, he came up with a single nine-millimeter parabellum cartridge, covered with clown paint and god-knows-what-else. *Not good.* He wiped it clean, loaded it into the gun, and turned to face the door.

Timothy changed his mind. He opened the porthole on the side opposite the dock, checked the deck, and clambered through. He climbed up one deck and stood outside the wheelhouse door.

"Jesse, get this boat moving," Bill Snead barked from the dock.

Timothy crept to the front of the wheelhouse and looked along the deck. At the wheelhouse door, Jesse chambered a shell into his shotgun, braced himself against the rail, and kicked in the door with his boot. The metal door was much stronger than the old wooden frame that held it. The hinges and bolt pulled from the rotten wood like they had been screwed into tapioca. The heavy door sailed through the air and out the open door on the opposite side. Jesse fell forward, tripped on the sill, and landed flat on his face.

The startled captain looked at Jesse, eyed the shotgun, and bolted out of the wheelhouse. He jumped over the railing into the water and swam away. Timothy considered taking Jesse down but didn't like his chances against the pump-action shotgun.

Jesse looked like he had no idea how to get the boat moving. He grabbed two metal levers, one topped with a red ball and the other with black, and pushed them all the way forward. As the massive prop bit into the river, the boat shuddered and began inching forward. Jesse grabbed the wheel, turned it hard to the right, and began singing. "I'm drivin' a boat. I'm drivin' a boat. I'm drivin' a boat. I'm drivin' a boat." Timothy made his way aft as the yacht surged forward.

A line trailed along the side of the yacht, the slack going out of it. "Shit. Cut that line, Durk," Bill shouted from the main deck just beneath Timothy. Bill spun on his artificial leg and hobbled for the bow. Timothy followed one deck above.

The bow line went taut and started stretching. The bow of the boat skewed to the left. The rope held against the pull of the engine. The boat's timbers didn't. Splinters flew as the heavy deck cleat ripped free from its mount and shot aft. The bow cleat buried itself in the wall of the main cabin right under the wheelhouse, ripping rearward, and severing the rotten planks of the superstructure. As the boat heaved forward, the rope clothes-lined six Guild members and swept them over the stern.

With the back of the boat mostly cleared, Timothy jumped down to the main deck. To his left, two guys scrambled to their feet. He sprinted to the bow, stopped, and turned to face them. More angry rednecks approached from the port side. The red dots from nine laser sights danced on his chest. He was trapped.

"Let me the fuck through, you assholes," Bill growled. The Guild members to starboard parted, and the clump, clump, clump of Bill Snead's new walk came through the crowd. "You little fuck. You killed my fucking brother. You killed my fucking friends. And you almost burned my foot off."

"Yeah, Billy, I did. But your friends were all dirt-bags, and your brother was an asshole who wore stripes with checks. I didn't roast your foot, but don't worry about it." Timothy half-smiled. "You already walked funny anyway."

"Fuck you." Bill tossed aside his crutch and raised his U.S. Army issue Colt forty-five automatic. The boat rocked. Bill's weight shifted onto his shattered left foot just as he pulled the trigger, and the shot missed.

Timothy took his one and only shot. It went through the

plastic of the Bill's prosthetic leg and hit the concealed shotgun. The round in the chamber went off. That shell took off the bottom of Bill's leg, tore through the rotten planks of the yacht's deck, and blasted a three-foot wide chasm through the water-logged hull. The force of the shell lifted Bill three feet into the air and triggered two more blasts, which sent Bill pin-wheeling asymmetrically into the lake. Half of the Guild members stared at the water flooding into the boat, and the other half watched the diminishing circle of bubbles that marked Bill's splash down. The boat began slowly sinking.

Timothy took advantage of the distraction and dove head first into the water. He struggled to swim deeper against the buoyancy of the air trapped in his clown pants as the *fwip* sound of bullets slicing through water came from all around him. He was almost out of breath by the time the sinking yacht thudded away and the sound of bullets abated. Timothy ripped off his clown pants and surfaced, gasping for air.

The engine on the aged yacht stuttered, then stopped. In the ensuing silence, Jesse's song floated across the water. "I'm drivin' a boat. I'm drivin' a boat. I'm drivin' a boat. I'm drivin' a boat," sung in harmony with the distant sirens.

From upriver a large, round wave approached. Timothy floated up the gentle seven-foot roller and slid down the other side. The wave caught the Gorge Princess and dipped its bow underwater. Like a scaled-down Titanic, the stern rose vertically into the air, and the yacht plunged downward. The Gorge Princess sank in seconds, and, as one, the Dale Earnhardt Memorial Literary Guild vanished into the depths.

Timothy watched until the bubbles from the drowned vessel stopped. He gave a kick and swam toward shore.

Chapter 46

Juice turned away from the grill when he heard footsteps approaching. Rudy and Melissa walked hand-in-hand down the sidewalk. Rudy opened the gate and held it as Melissa stepped through. He followed and carefully latched it behind him.

"Marissa!" Juice saluted them with a can of lighter fluid. "Rudy! It's about fucking time."

Melissa gave Juice a hug, then stepped back and poked him in the chest. "Listen, buster." She kept poking. "You don't even have the fire going yet. Besides," she added with a sly smile, "we were busy."

Rudy's face flushed pink.

"Rudy, you dog!" Dickie shouted from the porch. Sabrina punched him in the arm. "Ow!"

"Two Shoes, I'm glad to see you were paying attention during all those fishing lessons," Juice teased. "You caught a good one there."

Rudy turned a deeper shade of red and stared at his shoes. Melissa circled his waist with her arms and kissed him on the cheek.

"Now that you two are here, we can get this party going." Juice turned back to the grill and lit the edge of a charcoal briquette. A small, blue flame took hold. He turned to his audience and winked at them, took three steps away from the grill, and waited. Everybody stared at him. Suddenly, an eight-foot high column of fire flared from the Weber. The inferno died away after a few seconds.

Hiram laughed hysterically. "Boy Scout water," he gasped. "I love it!"

"Yeah." Juice wiped some soot from his face. "Gasoline in the middle and one piece with a little lighter fluid on it."

"Like a fuse."

"Right." Juice winked at Melissa. "Okay, Marissa. Your fire's ready."

She scrunched her face at him, went over to Aubergine, and gave her a hug. "How are you doing, sweetie?"

"I'm good. Hiram and I—"

The loud blat of a sports car downshifting interrupted her answer. A bright-yellow Porsche Carrera convertible screamed up Back Street with two six-foot-long cloth streamers billowing behind the cockpit. The driver downshifted again, turned sharply, and came to an abrupt stop in front of Juice's house. The flowing scarves collapsed.

Juice's eyebrows lifted when he saw who was in the car. *Now that's something you don't see every day.* All conversation stopped as the other guests checked out the new arrivals.

June Presseley waited in the driver's seat. Simpson got out of the passenger side, pranced around the Porsche, and opened the driver's door. June smiled at him, took his hand, and allowed him to extract her from the driver's seat. She smoothed her short skirt while Simpson held the gate open for her. She walked up to Juice, flashed him a quick smile, and kissed him on the cheek.

Simpson followed her wiping his nose with a lace-edged handkerchief. He pushed June aside, threw his arms around Juice, and launched into loud weeping.

"Whoa." Juice pushed him away, but kept a grip on his shoulders. "What's going on?"

"Oh, Ted," Simpson blubbered, "there's nothing. Nothing!" He blew his nose, and a dog across the street barked. "He hasn't called. There's been no word at all. He—" Simpson stared at his feet. "He must be dead."

"Nah, you just keep the faith, big guy," Juice tried to sound sincere. "Every cop in the country is looking for him right now. He'll turn up."

Simpson took a moment to digest the information. "Waaaa…" Another dog joined the chorus. Simpson minced back to the car and threw himself in. He sat with his face in his hands, shoulders shuddering.

"How you doing?" Juice asked.

"Not good." June shook her head, then looked him in the eyes. "But I will be soon. Robert took a plea bargain."

"I heard."

"Ellis cracked when they questioned him. Spelt it all out for them—dates, times, who and where. Hard numbers. Robert knew he didn't have a chance once they found the rest of the video and matched everything up. He's going to be doing five-to-ten down at Sheridan, Oregon. Ellis got a year's house arrest for being cooperative."

"Yeah, in Seattle so the Marshals can keep an eye on him." He thought about Sabrina and Amy. "Gonna be tough on his kid."

"She'll be okay. They have Dickie." June faced Juice again. "Anyway," she continued, "my divorce went through. It was the last thing I had to take care of. Now I'm free." The corners of her mouth twitched, almost a smile. "Juice, I've never been free before."

Juice jerked back and stared at her. "What did you just call me?"

"Small town, Juice. Lots of gossip." She gave him a quick wink. "Well, I'm off to see what I see."

"Where are you heading?"

"Down the Coast. California, maybe. Simpson thinks Timothy may have gone to Vegas to hide out," she glanced over her shoulder to make sure Simpson wasn't listening, "if he isn't dead." She gave him a hug. "You take care of yourself. Thanks for being different." She released him and hurried back to the car. The Carrera pulled away with a roar. By the time they turned the corner, the scarves flew free.

Juice let out a long, low whistle.

"You got that right," Dickie said from the porch. "But I think that could have been your last chance."

"Sabrina," Juice picked up a spatula and pointed it at her. "Slap him for me."

Sabrina gave Dickie a gentle slap, then kissed his cheek.

"I still can't believe this," Dickie chuckled. "If you would have told me in January that Chief of Police Richard Gordon would be celebrating the Fourth of July with two hit men and a forensic accountant, I'd have said you were nuts."

"And the three most beautiful women around," Rudy added.

"The only three women around," Dickie shot back. This time Sabrina slapped him for real.

"But Hiram doesn't count." Rudy offered.

"As a beautiful woman?" Dickie asked.

"No, as a hit man." Rudy shook his head sternly. "The prosecutors called him a hero."

"Okay, I stand corrected." Dickie leaned across and patted Hiram's leg. "Rudy's right. That package of files you smuggled out of the VeggieTech compound told the whole story." He shook his head. "Who would have thought that those hippies out there had a bioengineering operation going on?"

"Yeah, right under the watchful eyes of local law enforcement," Aubergine gave it back to him. "Besides, it wasn't the hippies. It was the wackos running the place."

"Touché. But that list of names Hiram got has already shut down ten cocaine traffickers, and now we've got the first hard evidence of how the Rodriguez gang moves heroin from Mexico to the West Coast."

"Anyway…" Aubergine said, shaking her finger at Dickie. "Now Hiram's something better than a hit man or a hero. He's a farmer."

Everybody laughed.

"Aubergine was sharp enough to get her partnership papers recorded at the court house." Hiram took Aubergine's hand and beamed at her. "When the other partners died, the land ownership transferred to Aubergine as the only surviving owner."

"What about everybody else?" Juice asked, looking at Melissa.

"Louise, that scum-sucking bastard, kept the rest of the partnership papers," Melissa sputtered. "He locked them in his safe, and when his house burned down, they went up in smoke. He got what he deserved." Melissa looked like she might burst with anger.

"That's all in the past, honey." Rudy rubbed her hand. "Aubergine had new agreements drawn up. Your dreams are still alive."

"But Stu's not." The group grew quiet.

"What's that?" Juice broke the uncomfortable silence and pointed his spatula at Melissa's hand. She raised her left hand and waggled her fingers to show off a sparkling diamond.

"We're getting married," Rudy said proudly.

"You not only caught her, Two Shoes, you reeled her in!" Juice shouted as he took the steps to the front porch two at a time. He shook his friend's hand. Aubergine and Sabrina mobbed Melissa and took turns admiring her ring.

"When's the big day?" Dickie asked.

"August first!" Rudy and Melissa said in unison. Everyone clapped and hooted.

Sabrina held her left hand up, palm out, and stared at her ring finger.

"Don't get any ideas, darlin'," he teased. His comment earned him another smack.

"And we're going on a cruise to the Caribbean for our honeymoon." Rudy leaned over, drew Melissa close to him, and planted a passionate kiss on her lips.

The group cheered them on.

"Okay, all this excitement is getting me hungry." Juice slipped his "Kiss the Cook" apron over his head and walked back to the grill in the front yard. "Who wants a veggie burger?"

Nobody responded, so Juice tossed seven all-beef burgers on the grill. "Medium?" he asked. Five hands went up. He pointed at Aubergine.

"I'll have mine rare."

Everyone turned to her. Her eyes shifted from one to the next. "Well, it isn't a hot dog!"

Everybody hooted. The party was back in full swing.

Juice's cell phone rang. He reached under his apron and

pulled out the phone. He pressed the hands-free button and answered, "Fresh Squeezed Fishing Expeditions, happy Fourth of July."

"Hello, Juice." A rough voice came out of the tinny speaker, drowned out by an outburst of laughter from the gang on the porch.

"Hey, you guys," Juice shouted to the crowd, "keep it down. This is just business." He turned back toward the grill. "Who's this?"

"It's Mikey, Juice. Your brother, Mikey."

Acknowledgements

We owe a boatload of thanks to Sarah Whelan, our editor, for her hard work, patience, and tolerance for endless questions. (Is the punctuation correct?) Thanks also to Donna Murillo for the great job on our mascot, the cigarette-smoking, smiling fish. Andrew Hill provided invaluable help on the graphic design of the cover.

Never-ending gratitude goes to everyone who read the manuscript and shared their thoughts and advice: JimmyJo Allen, Mike Befeler, Darla Bartos, Debra Borys, Thaddeus Gunn, Chuck Heuertz, Lori Lacefield, Robert Lint, Jedeanne MacDonald, Rahul Pratap Maddimsetty, Purple Mark, Becky Martinez, Norman Smith, Jayant Swamy, Debra Synovec, and John Turley.

For putting up with his endless complaining, James thanks Ishya Silpikul and Ann Frederick.

Bonnie thanks the Rocky Mountain Fiction Writers and Mystery Writers of America groups for their support, education, and, most of all, for welcoming her into the tribe without making too much of a fuss. She also wants to recognize Jim Bunch from the Grant County Public Utility District for telling her to write a novel because that's where the big money is. Please prove him right.

About the Authors

Bonnie Biafore is a project manager and author of 23, er, make that 24 books, numerous training courses, and hundreds of articles on personal finance, project management, technology, and now, stupid criminals. She lived in mid-Washington State while managing a software project for a local utility that coordinates power generation along the Columbia River. (Remember, any resemblance to actual events, organizations, persons, et cetera, is entirely coincidental.) She lives on a mountaintop in Colorado. Find out more at http://www.bonniebiafore.com.

James Ewing writes a weekly blog (http://blog.jamesewing.com) loosely based on the proposition that life is really much more absurd than we know. Several of his humorous articles based on his seven-year sailing adventure have been published in Latitudes & Attitudes magazine. He currently lives in western Washington State, isolated on an island, because it's really better for everyone that way.

CPSIA information can be obtained at www.ICGtesting.com
Printed in the USA
BVOW010807010812

296699BV00001B/2/P

9 780985 819507